The Puck

Arrangement

ALSO BY TRINITY LEMM

The Forever Series:

Forever Burn
Forever Frozen
Forever & Ever

Standalones:

Home

Poetry:

Fingerprints

Playlist

"Meet Me Halfway" | Black Eyed Peas

"Broken" | Seether & Amy Lee

"Lips of an Angel" | Hinder

"Ghost" | Justin Bieber

"Video Games" | Lana Del Rey

"With or Without You" | U2

"Thinkin Bout You" | Frank Ocean

"Late Night Talking" | Harry Styles

"Say Yes to Heaven" | Lana Del Rey

"Not Over You" | Gavin DeGraw

"Say It Ain't So" | Weezer

"Inside Out" | Eve 6

"pov" | Ariana Grande

"Dirty Thoughts" | Chloe Adams

"I'm Good (Blue)" | David Guetta, Bebe Rexha

"Seven Nation Army" | The White Stripes

"Hanging By a Moment" | Lifehouse

"Put Your Records On" | Ritt Momney

"Use Somebody" | Kings of Leon

"Just Can't Get Enough" | Black Eyed Peas

"Habits of My Heart" | Jaymes Young

Cedar U Team Roster

#1 | Lane Avery

#4 | Keith Sunset

#5 | Sawyer Peterson

#7 | Matt Gallagher

#10 | Mason Makela

#11 | Brayden Thompson

#14 | Cody Holtz

#18 | Nicholas Crew

#20 | Nathan Bailey

#21 | Joseph Costa

#25 | Jett Jameson

#27 | Robert Shesky

#30 | TJ Douglas

#32 | Brody Moore

#39 | Ross Hughes

#42 | Jonah Morgan

#44 | Griffin Edwards

#50 | Riley Davis

#54 | Bryson Miller

#60 | Derek Wrigh

Trigger warnings:

This book contains content about topics such as car accidents, the death of a family member, adoption, and the mentioning of verbal abuse.

To all the girls who wish they were stuck living with two hot hockey players.

You're not the only one.

Chapter One

Bridget

"**P**erfect, there's no one in here!" Kota shouted in relief as I followed her into the girl's bathroom.

"That's a first," I said. Stallions was the most popular bar in town, especially on Saturday nights. It was a rare sight for there to not be a ridiculously long line down the hallway for the girl's bathroom. There had been times where Kota and I even had to sneak into the guy's bathroom just to pee. Not my proudest moment, but any toilet was better than pissing on the floor. But fortunately for us tonight, most people were still home for the summer, granted the fall semester didn't start for two more weeks.

Kota waddled in her heels into a stall and shut the door as I stepped into the stall next to her.

"It feels weird not being in the same stall as you," she said.

"I know. I can't remember the last time we didn't have to cram into one."

Within a minute, we were both washing our hands. I peered over at her in the mirror, noticing that devious little smirk she always got when she had something mischievous on her mind.

"What?" I asked, lifting a brow as I smirked myself.

She shrugged with one shoulder. "Just counting down the days."

"One more week."

"One more week," she repeated, grabbing a paper towel to dry her hands, "and then we'll never have to speak to our least favorite people ever again."

Our current roommates, Claudia and Carolina, were a nightmare in human form.

When I first came to Cedar University, I didn't know anyone. All my friends from high school attended Minnesota State or UofM Duluth. I was the only outsider that decided to go to Cedar. I had my own reasons for making the decision though.

Regardless, the university gave me a random roommate freshman year in the dorms.

I thanked my lucky stars every day that Kota was the one I got stuck with.

Dakota Darling was one of the fiercest women on the planet. With her half-Filipino roots and being raised by a single mom, she was beautiful, bold, and bitchy when necessary. But God, I loved her.

We lived in the dorms together again sophomore year, and when junior year rolled around, we decided to get an apartment. Since four-bedroom apartments were cheaper, we figured we'd find roommates. *Big mistake.*

Just a hint of advice— *never* search for roommates on a Facebook group chat.

Claudia and Carolina seemed normal at first, and we even hung out with them a few times before signing our lease just to make sure they weren't weird, but they still ended up being fucking weird.

Claudia hung her underwear up to air dry because she thought it "preserved them better," which I wasn't even sure what the hell that meant. All I knew was that I was not a fan of her g-strings hanging all over the place. Not to mention that we were pretty sure she was into some dark magic stuff, leaving Kota convinced she was sacrificing small animals in our house.

Carolina was just as bad. She'd use everyone's things without asking, regardless of how unsanitary. Hairbrush? Makeup? Clothes? Didn't matter. She'd take it all. I wouldn't have been surprised if she took one of Claudia's drying g-strings and wore it out one night. She'd even take everyone's food too. We caught her munching on Kota's chips one night when she thought Kota wasn't home. Kota didn't take that well. She was very protective of her snacks.

Now our lease was finally ending, and we were one week away from moving into our own apartment. Even though rent for a two-bedroom was a bit more expensive than our current rent, we knew it would be worth every dime.

Kota stood in front of the mirror, reapplying her lip gloss. "Goddamn, my lips are so dry."

"Well, that's what happens when you use lip gloss in place of chapstick."

She playfully rolled her eyes, tucking the tube of lip gloss back into her purse. "Alright. It's time."

"For?"

She gave another one of her infamous smirks. "To add to my collection."

I sighed, glancing in the mirror at the wall behind us. They always had small liquor posters in the bathrooms, and every time we went to a bar, Kota took one. At this point, her room was covered in liquor ads from Budlight to Pink Whitney.

Kota pranced over to the door and peeked outside. "We're in the clear. Now's the time to take action."

I watched in amusement as she lifted onto her tippy toes, trying to reach the sign that had a sexy blonde model holding up a Modelo on the beach. She grabbed at it repeatedly, muttering expletives under her breath with each miss.

"B, help me!" she insisted.

I smiled at her, standing in place. "You're a criminal."

She stood on her flat feet and turned towards me, letting out a huff. "Yeah. And you're my accomplice," she said. "Now help me out."

"Fine," I gave in, "but you're buying my next drink."

"Deal."

I wasn't that much taller than Kota. I had a good two or so inches on her, sitting at five-foot six. My awkwardly long arms though were a God send in situations like this.

I grabbed the poster in less than five seconds, handing it over to Kota immediately as if it were a murder weapon I was trying to get rid of.

She gave a content grin as she rolled it up and stuck it in her purse. "Good teamwork."

We exited the bathroom, heading towards the bar. Even though the school year hadn't started, it was still pretty packed.

We weaved in and out of people, but just when we were a few feet shy of the bar, Kota let out a small squeal. "Wait, there's Bobby!" she said, pointing across the room at the guy she'd been seeing for the past month.

"Oh, so now you're gonna ditch me?" I teased.

"Ditch is a strong word," she said. "I'm just gonna go say hi."

"You mean you're gonna go make sure he's coming home with you?"

She let out a laugh. "Exactly. I'll be back in just a few minutes, B. I promise." She dug around in her purse, pulling out a ten-dollar bill. "Here's your crime money. Go crazy."

I giggled, gladly taking it from her. She let out a deep breath, regaining her composure before strutting in Bobby's direction.

There were a lot of people surrounding the bar, waiting to be served, but it seemed like half the space was taken up by a group of large, beefy men. There was cockiness oozing through the air around them, so much of it that I could've sworn I was about to choke on it.

I pushed my strawberry blonde hair over my shoulder as I tried squeezing in closer to the bar. I caught a glimpse of one of the guy's faces, immediately recognizing him.

Lane Avery. Hot-shot hockey player.

Not a fan.

Our hockey team was incredible, I'd give them that. I loved going to the games, especially since we were named as having the best student section in college hockey, which made the games fun and rowdy. But when it came to the actual people beneath the jerseys? No thanks.

In my opinion, they were all egotistical assholes. I had a few of them in my psychology class last year, and I was fairly certain they only passed because they would shamelessly flirt with our TA. Other than that, they'd just sit in the back of the lecture hall and fuck around for the whole class.

One time, one of them asked me if I wanted to come over and "study," which in my mind meant *Let's hookup and then you give me the answers to your homework.*

I was pretty sure his name was TJ, but I wasn't certain. I tried not to pay much attention to them. I only knew some of their names because their faces were everywhere. All over the school and all over social media. It was impossible not to recognize some of them.

I inched closer to the bar, and before I knew it, I was wedged between two hockey players. They seemed oblivious to my presence though. I wasn't sure if it was because they were a solid six plus inches taller than me and didn't notice I was there or if they just simply didn't care. Either way, I was getting bumped back and forth between them like a ping pong ball.

This was a bad idea, I thought.

I tried to carefully push my way out of the group, but it didn't seem to be working. Suddenly, a large shoulder knocked into me, and I took a step backwards, just in time for cold liquid to be spilled all over the front of my body.

I gasped, eyeing the ground as beer dripped off me, making a small puddle on the floor. My head slowly lifted, and there I was, standing face to face with Lane Avery.

His mouth was slightly parted, eyes wide in shock as he held his now empty beer. "Oh shit," he muttered.

"Oh shit?" I brought my brows in. "What a sincere apology from someone who just spilled their drink all over me!"

"I..." he panicked, opening and shutting his mouth with words that weren't coming as his eyes trailed me up and down.

With liquid trickling down my body, I let out a frustrated screech, turning on my heels and shoving my way out of the group much less politely than before.

I stomped my angry ass over to Kota, blowing a heavy breath out my nose. Bobby had an arm around her waist, and they were both enveloped in laughter, but their conversation slowly came to a halt as their attention shifted onto me.

Kota's smile dropped. "What the hell happened to you?"

My entire body felt sticky. I spoke through clenched teeth, my clothes gluing to my skin more and more by the second. "A hockey player spilled on me."

Kota's brows shot up. "Did he at least apologize?"

"Not really."

Her eyes blazed over like hot coals. "Oh, those boys are going to get it."

She was off before anyone could stop her, flouncing back towards the bar. Because I knew how drastic Kota's devotion to destruction was, I immediately switched from angry to concerned, following briskly behind her.

"Kota," I warned, but it was no use. Once she was on a mission to do something, there was no stopping her. She'd burn down this whole building before anyone had the chance to convince her not to.

The second we were standing in front of the hockey boys, Kota's mouth was open. "Hey!" she shouted. "Which one of you spilled all over my friend?"

As if her anger were tangible and smacked each one of them in the face, they all turned to look at her at the same time.

Kota's finger immediately went up, pointing at a blonde who had his drink halfway to his mouth. "Was it you?"

He lowered his cup, a sheepish look overcoming his face even though he wasn't the guilty one. "No."

"Kota," I murmured, touching her forearm.

She lightly shook it off, throwing her finger up at the next guy. "You?"

This one held both hands up. "I didn't do anything."

"It was me," a husky voice called. Lane raised a hand as he stepped forward, head down.

Kota crossed her arms. "So, you poured your drink all over her and didn't apologize? What the hell!"

I shifted around, uncomfortable by both my wet clothes and the situation. *"Kota,"* I warned.

She finally turned to look at me. "What?"

I leaned towards her. "It's fine."

"It is not *fine*," she hushed me before taking a step closer to Lane. "Well?"

He blew out a stressed breath, his gaze shifting over to me. "I'm sorry."

16

Another guy with shaggy brown hair came forward. He stood directly beside Lane with an amused smirk on his face. "Alright," he said, defensively raising his hands in front of him, "calm down. It was an accident."

At this point, everyone was watching, and I was hating every damn second of it. I didn't like having eyes on me, period. It was bad enough that I was walking around in a wet tank top and jeans, and now we were in the midst of a commotion with the group of people that everybody in the room knew.

Kota jutted her chin out at the newcomer. "Haven't you ever heard that you should never tell a woman to calm down?"

His smirk grew lightly, seemingly trying to pull it down. "There's a lot of fury in that tiny body."

Her eyes narrowed, hand resting on her hip. "You haven't seen the half of it."

He gave a slow nod, that pompous smirk still resting comfortably on his face. "Alright, let's see it."

"Do *not* encourage her," I said, grabbing her wrist and yanking her away from the group.

"B!" she chided as I dragged her away.

"Kota, really, it's fine. I'm fine. I don't need you to get into a bar fight with a group of hockey players on my behalf."

She groaned, sounding disappointed, as if she *wanted* to get into a fight with them. I was more than thankful for how loyal of a friend Kota was. She'd kill for me. Most people who said that were exaggerating, but I wasn't. She was feisty and protective and although I loved that side of her, I sometimes wished she toned it down a bit.

When we got back to the table that Bobby was sitting at, Kota halted, her mouth falling open to find that the table was now empty. "Did he fucking leave?" she fumed.

"Why don't you call him?"

She angrily snatched her phone out of her purse, dialing Bobby's number and holding the phone up to her ear. She rocked side to side as it rang, and after a few moments, she dropped it. "No answer."

I sighed, pulling my shirt away from my chest to give my skin the ability to breathe. "Let's just go home."

She nodded in frustration. "I'll get us an Uber."

17

That was the other bad part about our current apartment— it was so damn far from everything. It was a ten-minute drive from both campus and the bars, which may not have sounded like much, but when we needed to walk home for some reason, the walk was a solid forty-five minutes. Our new apartment was going to be in the brand-new building that was directly across the street from Stallions, which was going to be much more convenient.

"The WIFI is sucking," Kota said, tapping at her phone.

"Let's go wait outside," I gladly recommended, glancing around at the wandering eyes that were peering over at us, probably whispering about the dispute.

"Alright," Kota agreed, following me out.

Since it was still August, it was a little below seventy-degrees out, which normally I'd say was the perfect temperature, but since my clothes were wet, it felt much colder.

We'd been standing outside the bar for a few minutes, waiting for an available Uber when the door opened.

Right when I caught sight of Lane and his friend that Kota wanted to fist fight, my stomach plummeted. I kept my gaze on the ground, arms crossed over my chest as I casually rocked on my heels.

The light from the nearby lamppost lit up Mr. Shaggy Hair's smirk. "Look. It's Little Miss Fury."

Kota shot him a glare so fierce that it probably should've left him dead on the ground.

"Shut up, Crew," Lane said, leaning against the building.

Crew snickered lightly. He stood between Lane and Kota, back resting against the brick building, eyeing Kota as she stared down at her phone. "What are you guys doing out here?" he asked.

She glanced up at him. "Waiting for an Uber," she retorted. "What are you doing out here?"

He gestured to the building. "Waiting for our buddies."

"Good for you," she murmured. There was a beat of silence before she looked up at me, all anger wiped from her face. "It's not working."

18

I groaned. "It's always hard getting an Uber on Saturdays. We might have to wait a bit."

Crew straightened. "Do you want us to walk you guys home?"

I quietly shook my head at the ground, giving a small shiver as a breeze went by.

Kota crossed her arms at Crew, her eyes narrowing. "Is that code for something?"

His frown lengthened and he leaned forward in the slightest, annoyed. "Yeah, it's code for *Do you want us to walk you home?*"

"No thanks," she replied. "It's fine. We'll wait for an Uber."

"Fine. Didn't want to anyway," Crew muttered under his breath, giving a small eye roll.

Just as Kota and Crew started bickering, there was a light tap on my shoulder.

I turned, my breath hitching in the slightest as I took in Lane's face under the light.

I wasn't going to lie. He was a handsome dude. His brown hair was shorter but slightly quaffed in the front. The light was hitting his face just enough to notice how deep his blue eyes were, and my gaze dropped to his broad shoulders and built chest. There was a tightening feeling in my stomach at the sight, but I ignored it.

"Hey," he said.

"Hi," I forced out.

He briefly glanced over my clothes. "I'm sorry again."

I shook my head, the tiniest grin touching my lips. "Don't you mean *Oh, shit?*"

He let out a chuckle. "No," he responded. "I mean, I'm sorry."

I shrugged. "It's fine."

A charming yet impish grin lingered on his face. He shoved his hands into his pockets. "I get the feeling you don't like me."

"Well, you did spill your drink all over me."

"Yes," he acknowledged, swaying side to side, "but it seems like a bit more than that."

19

My brows came in for a moment. "What do you mean?"

Now that I'd gotten a good look at his face and really saw how attractive he was up close, I was trying not to stare. My eyes were wandering around, refusing to stay on him for longer than five seconds at a time.

"Seems like you already didn't like me before that," he said, his head tipping towards his shoulder. "It's just a vibe I get."

"Well, I'm not a big fan of your species," I admitted. Once again, I wasn't looking at him, but I could feel his eyes on me, and I couldn't decide if I liked the feeling or not.

"My species?" he chuckled. "Human?"

"No," I said, finally getting the nerve to look back at him. "Hockey player."

His eyes clouded over with intrigue, studying me intently. "And why is that?"

I stood my ground, a sense of bravery coming over me, refusing to look away from him anymore. "Because ninety percent of hockey players are assholes."

Apparently, Crew overheard, because he was quick to jump into the conversation. "Hey," his brows came in and he placed a hand over his chest, "my ego is hurt."

Kota's dark eyes landed on him. "It *would* be."

Lane rolled his eyes as the two began bickering *again*. He turned his attention back onto me. "What about the other ten percent?"

I placed my hands on my hips, staring upwards, pretending to be in thought. "You're right. It's probably a hundred percent."

Lane smiled, dropping his head. "I still haven't gotten your name."

"Bridget."

"I'm Lane," he said with a single nod.

"I know." His eyes lit up a little, just enough to notice. I tipped my head. "Don't act surprised."

"Why not?"

I stared at him blankly, unsure of how to respond. Just as I opened my mouth to spit some nonsense out, Kota grabbed my hand.

"Uber's here. Let's go."

I gave Lane one last look, knowing this was probably the first and last time I'd ever speak to him. "Kay," I nodded, letting Kota drag me along without looking back.

Chapter Two

Lane

Other than my bed and a few miscellaneous things that hadn't found a box yet, my room was empty. After living here for an entire year, it was strange to see the bare walls, the vacant closet, and the way the room felt smaller without all my belongings in it.

I pulled packing tape over another box, taping it shut.

Only three more boxes to go.

TJ appeared in the doorway, a long frown on his face. "I can't believe you guys are moving out."

"I know," I said, avoiding his gaze as I pulled another box towards me.

Crew and I had lived in the hockey house for the past year and that sure as hell was enough. Don't get me wrong, we loved our teammates more than anything. But goddamn, they sometimes sucked to live with. I'd never seen the house clean, ever. It was a complete dump and I hated living in the filth. There were always girls in and out, which I wouldn't have minded if the girls weren't nosy and lingered all over the house. Not to mention that the guys were loud as hell, blasting music in the middle of the night whenever we had time off hockey.

I knew there would be things I'd miss, like always having someone to hang out with or mess with but getting an apartment with Crew would be the best thing for me.

Nicholas Crew had been my best friend for four years now. We played on the same team when we were in the National Junior Hockey League before committing to Cedar University to play hockey here. He was the closest thing I had to a brother now.

"Well since it's your last night," TJ said with disappointment laced into his voice before a small grin spread across his lips, "let's get rowdy."

I glanced at him with a menacing smirk. "That's a given."

I finished up the box I was packing as TJ shook his head with a laugh, walking off. He reappeared sixty seconds later.

"Heads up," he called.

I looked up with just enough reaction time to catch the beer he'd tossed at me. "You fucker," I laughed, popping the can open.

He held up his beer and I mirrored him. "To our last night as roommates," he said.

"But not our last as teammates."

"Hell yeah," he grinned as we both brought the cans up to our mouths.

***

A few hours later, Crew had a fat ass smile on his face as he sat there on the recliner in the corner, a beer in one hand and his other hand glued to the brunette's waist that was sitting on his lap.

Meanwhile, I had a dirty blonde clawing at my chest as I sat on the couch adjacent from Crew. Whereas Crew was enthusiastic about the girls lined up for him, I was practically the opposite.

I occasionally hooked up with girls, but honestly, I wasn't the biggest fan of hookups. They made me feel kind of grimy, used. I mean, a man needed to get laid every once in a while, but a different girl every night wasn't really how I rolled.

It was how Crew rolled though.

"So," the blonde said, lifting a flirtatious brow as she leaned in closer, "you're captain this year?"

I let out a huff under my breath, looking away from her simply so that I could roll my eyes without doing it right in her face.

Half the girls that wanted to hook up were only doing it to add a notch on their bedpost that they thought was worth more than the others for some reason.

"Yeah," I responded indifferently.

"Oh nice," she murmured. "That must be a lot of work, right?"

Goddamn, I wanted to roll my eyes again.

It was all the same shit.

No one ever asked me questions about myself outside of hockey. It was like that was my only personality trait. As if I didn't have other interests or hobbies or a past.

Granted, I could go without questions about my past, but it would've been nice if someone had at least *acted* like they were interested in anything about me other than my penis or my damn hockey stick.

"Right," I muttered, taking a sip of beer. I wasn't sure if the blonde replied. Honestly, I kind of zoned out as my eyes scanned around the room, trying to take in our final hang out with the guys as roommates.

TJ and Jett were playing Xbox on the couch across from me. Cody had taken some girl upstairs ten plus minutes ago and was probably fingers deep in her by now, or more. And Matt was lying on the other side of the couch that I was on, his arm hanging over it, clutching onto his beer even though he was passed out.

I'd be lying if I said I wouldn't miss nights like this. *Minus the random girl beside me, of course.*

The good thing about our new apartment was that it was only two blocks away from here, which meant that Crew and I could come hang out whenever we wanted.

My thoughts were interrupted when the blonde gripped my hand.

"Lane?" she said.

"Yeah?" I spoke, not bothering to ask what her name was.

24

"Do you wanna go upstairs?"

I took the last swig of beer before tossing it in the trash can in the corner. "I'm actually gonna head to bed."

Crew's head popped up. I swore that guy had the superpower of insane hearing capabilities.

"What? You're going to bed?" he chided.

"I'm tired, bro," I stood.

"Boo!" TJ and Jett yelled, eyes glued to the TV.

"Don't be a pussy!" Crew said, crushing his empty beer can and throwing it in my direction.

I let out a meager chuckle. "Shut up, dickhead. You should go to bed too. We've gotta get up early tomorrow."

He dropped his head back with a groan.

The brunette on his lap whispered something to him that sounded along the lines of "that sound was hot."

Gross. And that was my cue.

"Alright, night," I said, giving TJ and Jett a thump on the back of their heads as I walked by.

"Hey!"

"Fuck you, Lane! We're in the middle of a game!"

I turned around briefly with the slightest of smirks on my face, taking one last look at the room.

The blonde was sitting there pouting. The brunette was dangerously close to Crew's lips. The guys still hadn't pulled their eyes away from the TV. And Matt was still sound asleep.

Yeah. I was going to miss this just a bit.

Chapter Three

Lane

"Get the fuck up," I said, pulling Crew's covers back.

He groaned once more in protest, his eyes remaining shut as he grabbed the covers and draped them back over himself.

"Crew," I warned.

"Bro, it's our one day off. Just let me fucking sleep," he grumbled.

I sighed in annoyance, running a hand through my hair. "It's already nine and we agreed to start moving our shit by ten."

"Fifteen more minutes," he complained.

"You fucking suck," I said, turning on my heels.

"Fuck you," he murmured, half asleep.

I went back to loading boxes into my car. Both Crew and I had SUVs, which made moving not God-awful, but we were probably still going to have to take two trips each. We wouldn't even be able to fit our mattresses in either of our cars. Thankfully, Cody said we could borrow his truck to help move the big stuff.

After fifteen minutes of tossing boxes into my car, I trudged back into Crew's room.

"Crew," I said, "time's up. Get your ass up."

There was no response besides the lightest of snores.

I groaned, striding into the kitchen and filling a cup with cold water. A mischievous smirk settled on my face as I pranced right up to Crew's bed. I lined up the shot and all at once, dumped the cup on his head.

He sprang right up. "The fuck!"

"Oh good, you're up."

He let out a heavy breath, droplets of water falling off him as he shook his head like a wet dog. "That was uncalled for."

"I believe it was very called for."

He shot me a look so irate that if we weren't best friends, I probably would've thought he was about to throw a punch.

My eyes wandered over to the other side of his bed, and I brought my brows in when I realized for the first time since being in here at all this morning that it was empty.

"Your bed's empty."

"I know," he said.

"What happened to the girl from last night? You get any?"

A crooked smile popped up on his face. "Messed around a little, but she left before any of the good stuff happened."

"Why's that?"

His eyes suddenly narrowed. "Because you cock-blocked me."

"What the hell did I do?"

"If you kept her friend occupied, then she wouldn't have left so early."

I rolled my eyes. "Sorry, I wasn't into it. Sue me."

"Maybe I will."

"Yeah?" I said through a laugh.

"Yeah," he said, finally tossing the covers off him and swinging his legs over the side of the bed, "for interference of justice."

"It's called *obstruction* of justice, you dumbass, and that's not even close to what it means."

"Fuck off. Stop trying to act smart," he mocked.

I chuckled, checking the time on my watch. "Forty minutes."

"Until?"

"Until we leave. So get your ass moving."

***

Crew and I stopped at the leasing office on the way to pick up our new apartment keys.

Luckily, our new apartment was on the second floor, which was perfect because I definitely didn't want to lug all our stuff up four flights of stairs. The apartment complex had an elevator, but since so many people were moving in today, it was being used every second.

Crew and I grabbed one hefty box each, not wanting to grab too much on our first trip up before we even knew where the actual apartment was.

"What's the number again?" Crew asked, following me down the hall.

"Two-twelve."

He nodded once. "It's on the left up there."

I set my box down as we approached the door and began digging in my pocket for the key.

"Uh oh," Crew said.

"What?"

"I don't think our new neighbors are gonna like us very much."

I faltered, glancing up at him as I took the key out. "Why? What do you mean?"

His eyes were fixated down the hall. "Because they already don't like us."

"Huh?"

"Hey, dickwads!" a voice yelled. "Why the hell are you trying to get into our apartment?"

I turned, my brows shooting up to find the two girls from the bar last week striding our way. I remembered the strawberry blonde's name was Bridget, but the closest thing I had to a name for her feisty friend was Little Miss Fury.

And furious, she was, coming at us with a crease in her forehead and a stormy gleam in her eye.

28

My gaze trailed over to Bridget as they reached us. She was much softer, a little more on the shy side but could get fierce if she needed.

Like when I spilled my drink on her.

I'd never seen her before last week, but I'd be lying if I said she hadn't found her way into my mind at least once every day since then.

I wasn't sure if it was how beautiful she was, if it was my remaining guilt for spilling on her, or if it was simply how refreshing it had been to have a playful conversation with a girl that wasn't trying to hook up. Regardless of whatever it was, I was a little disoriented seeing her right now after assuming I'd never run into her again.

"*Your* apartment?" Crew challenged.

"Yeah," Bridget's friend nodded. "*Our* apartment."

Bridget's voice was much more delicate than her friend's. "We've already brought some boxes in there."

My mouth formed a hard line in confusion. "Okay..." I stuttered. "Maybe they just gave us the wrong apartment number."

Bridget gave a tiny shrug. "Maybe."

"Just try the key," Crew said.

With an irked glance at Crew, I stepped forward and tried shoving the key into the lock, prepared to turn around and head back down to the leasing office for the right apartment number, but when the door opened with no problem, all four of us stared at it for a moment.

"Um," Little Miss Fury lifted a brow, "why the fuck did they give you keys to our apartment?"

"Because it's our apartment," Crew argued as I stepped inside.

"No, it's not," she muttered back as I pushed my box inside, everyone following me in.

I glimpsed around. The girls weren't lying. There were already a few boxes sitting near the door.

"Have you guys walked around yet?" I asked over my shoulder.

"No," Bridget said. "We just brought a few boxes in so far."

I took it upon myself to take a quick walk-through of the apartment. The kitchen was right when you walked in with the living room on the far side of the room. There were two short hallways, one to the left and one to the right. I took a glance down both. When I walked back out to where everyone was, the girls were putting their boxes down as Crew stood there, still holding his.

He noticed the dazed look on my face. "What?"

"This is a four-bedroom," I said.

Little Miss Fury raised a brow. "Excusez-moi?"

Bridget casually placed her hands on her hips, shaking her head. "That can't be right."

Everyone dispersed to see for themselves.

"You guys are sure they gave you keys to this place?" I shouted.

Bridget reappeared from down the left hallway. "How else would we have gotten in before?"

Good point.

When we were all standing in the living room again, Bridget spoke. "We're just gonna have to go down to the office and see what's going on."

Crew sighed. "Alright, let's go now then. Cause I'd rather not bring all my shit in here and then have to move it somewhere else."

Little Miss Fury gave a joking smile, turning to Crew. "Wow! Your first good idea!"

He narrowed his eyes at her before leading the way out.

Chapter Four

Bridget

The woman at the front desk seemed flustered with four people firing question after question at her.

"Okay, okay," she said, holding her hands up. "One thing at a time, please. First, what are all of your names?"

"Lane Avery."

"Nicholas Crew."

"Bridget Bell."

"Dakota Darling."

"Okay," the woman said, "thank you. Just give me one moment please to look all of you up."

I tapped my foot on the ground, glancing at her name tag. *Camila.*

"Okay, I see," Camila said. "You guys are in apartment two-twelve."

"No," Kota said, motioning to herself and me, "*we* are. *They* were given keys to our apartment."

The woman glanced over the four of us as if we were insane. "Yes. It's a four-bedroom."

"But we're supposed to have a two-bedroom," I said.

"Same with us," Crew added.

Camila's face sank. "Oh... oh, I see." She tapped her long, pink fingernails nervously on her desk. "Didn't you all see the revision of your lease that was sent out in February?"

Kota rested her arm on the front of the desk. "What damn revision?"

"You all should've gotten an email before you signed, explaining that we messed up the numbers on available two-bedrooms and that your lease was changed to a four-bedroom..."

"I didn't get an email," I said.

Her eyes shifted between each of us. "None of you got the email?"

The boys shrugged.

Kota shook her head.

"Well, did any of you carefully read over the lease before you signed it?" Camila asked.

My sheepish gaze diverted away from her. I would've read through the lease if it hadn't been forty damn pages long. I swore they did that on purpose, just to make people not want to read it.

I looked over at everyone else, whose expressions matched mine.

Camila slowly shook her head. "I'm sorry... I mean, I can see what I can do, but at this point, all the two-bedroom apartments are gone."

Kota's eyes grew as she lifted a sluggish finger at the boys. "So, you're saying we're stuck with them?"

Camila's mouth fell into a deeper frown. "I'm afraid so."

I stayed silent, taking a heavy breath. Keeping my chin down, I peeked over at Lane. His head was tilted at just the right angle to see his sharp knife of a jawline. He had one hand planted on the edge of the desk, leaning faintly into it. His aura screamed exasperation and I couldn't help but wish I could read his mind before chiding myself for the thought.

Stop looking at him. Who cares what he's thinking right now?

There was a horrifying knot of anxiety in my gut. We barely knew these guys. We met them once. And now the four of us were being thrown in an apartment together? Pretty much against our will?

Not to mention these were probably the worst guys that we could've gotten stuck with. I think it was fair to say our first time meeting hadn't been pleasant for anyone.

"Oh no," Kota shook her head. "No, no, no, no. I *cannot* live with them. Especially this one," she pointed at Crew.

He gave her a wicked side eye. "The feeling's mutual."

Lane tapped his fingers on the desk a few times before stepping back altogether. "Alright, I guess let's go back up and figure this out." He gave a subtle nod to Camila. "Thanks for your help."

She winced. "Sorry I couldn't help more."

"It's not your fault," I assured her.

The four of us retreated up to apartment two-twelve, and the second the door closed behind us, complete silence filled the room. We looked at each other in both anger and wonder, unsure of who was going to be the one to diffuse the bomb that was sitting between us.

But of course, it was Lane.

"So..." he started slowly, "what do you guys think we should do?"

"I'll tell you what *I'm* gonna do," Crew said, snatching his keys off the kitchen island. "I'm gonna ride my ass over to my dad's house and make him read this dumb lease."

Lane lifted a brow. "You sure that's a good idea?"

"No," Crew admitted. "He's gonna be pissed at me for not reading the full lease in the first place, but it's the only idea I've got."

"You're from here?" I asked.

Crew nodded. "Yeah, I'm from the next town over."

"His dad's a contract lawyer," Lane explained.

"Good," Kota spoke, lightly crossing her arms. "Maybe he can find a way to get us out of this mess."

Crew sighed, "Yeah, we'll see." He looked at Lane and cocked his head towards the door. "Come with."

Lane followed him, peering over his shoulder from the doorway. "We'll be back in an hour or two."

"Alright," I said, tucking my hands into my pockets.

"Don't feel obligated to," Kota murmured.

The second the door closed, Kota tipped her head back and let out a wail.

I brought my hands up, gesturing towards her. "What?"

Her head snapped neutral to look at me. "How are you so calm right now?"

The truth was that I wasn't. Inside, I was freaking out probably worse than Kota; I just wasn't showing it yet.

"I—I'm not," I shook my head. "I guess I'm just in shock a little bit."

She stepped towards me, planting her hands on my shoulders, a few tiny tears trickling down her cheeks. "Well, let it sink in, B. We're most likely stuck living with *boys*. Mean, annoying, stupid hockey boys, above all."

I stared at her silently.

"Do you know what this means?" She let out a frantic huff as she began pacing back and forth, talking with her hands. "Dirty socks and hockey equipment everywhere!" She stopped mid-step, gasping. "And oh my God... They're going to eat all my food!"

"I'm sure they—"

"Think about it, B! Do you know how much hockey players eat? It's like Thanksgiving every day for them!"

I cringed.

The racing anxiety in me hadn't eased, but I was making a conscious effort to try to stay calm. If I let myself go on a spiral of thoughts about how terrible it was going to be, I'd drive myself to insanity before any of us were even moved in.

"On the bright side," I said with a horrible lack of confidence, "at least their rooms will be down the opposite hall from us. They'll have their own bathroom too."

She completely ignored everything I said. "You know you're not gonna be able to walk around in just a t-shirt and your underwear anymore, right?"

My mouth parted slightly. *I didn't think about that.*

"Or leave the community period calendar in the common areas?"

Mouth dropped open wider.

"It's probably going to be like living with Claudia and Carolina all over again, but *worse*."

"Oh my God," I finally cried. "This is going to be awful!"

She gave a strong nod. "Fucking awful."

"What are we gonna do, though? Even if we found another apartment, which is highly unlikely at this point, we'd probably still have to pay for this one. I can't afford two apartments!"

"You're right, you're right," she said, back to pacing. "Maybe we can scare them into moving out."

"How?"

Her head popped up. "Let's put the period calendar up."

Last year, we had a community period calendar hung up in the corner of the living room, where everyone would write their projected ovulation and period days. It was our own civil way of telling everyone, *Hey, fuck off on these days* or *Sorry if I'm a bitch right now.*

"Okay," I slowly nodded, biting my lip in thought. "We'd have to find which box it's in."

"Well, let's go!" she frantically said, motioning towards the door and dashing for it.

I jogged after her. "But," I said, stopping in my tracks and clutching onto her wrist, "if we can't get them to move out... then what?"

"Then we make sure we've got a long list of dos and don'ts. Cause I sure as hell am not dealing with their shit."

"Agreed," I swallowed nervously.

Chapter Five

Lane

"**O**h my fuck. This is a fucking disaster," Crew said for what I'd sworn was the hundredth time.

I sighed as we walked down the hall to the apartment. "Say that one more time," I warned through clenched teeth.

"This is a fucking disaster."

I stopped in my tracks, causing Crew to bump into me. "I was being sarcastic."

"I wasn't," he shrugged bitterly. "This. Is a fucking. Disaster."

I let out a huff, shaking my head as I walked the remainder of the way to the apartment.

Don't get me wrong, I wasn't thrilled about this living arrangement, but I wasn't going to cry about it like Crew. If there was nothing we could do about it, then there was no point in sulking.

"Let's just go back to the house," Crew said.

I groaned once more. "Bro, how many times do I need to remind you? Jonah and Keith are moving in there *tomorrow*. We can't go back."

"Fuck Jonah and Keith. They're practically still freshman."

"Do I need to remind you that we're only juniors?"

"Technically yeah, but we're about to be twenty-two."

"And they're about to turn twenty-one."

"Whatever," he whined.

When we walked into the apartment, the girls were unloading a few boxes in the kitchen. Their heads snapped over to us.

"So?" Bridget asked. "What did he say?"

"Well first," Crew started, striding past me. He stepped around the kitchen island. "He began by giving me a long spiel about how stupid I am for not reading the lease in the first place."

Bridget's eyes roamed over to me, her brow lifting lightly. "Don't look at me," I said. "I wasn't safe from the scolding either."

"Yep," Crew nodded. "He gave Lane an even worse speech about how he's supposed to be the responsible one and he didn't read the lease either, yada, yada, yada..."

"Just get to the freaking point," Kota snapped.

Crew raised a frustrated brow, his spine stiffening. "You want the freaking point? Here it is— we're stuck living together."

Bridget's shoulders slumped. "There's really no way out of our lease?"

I shook my head. "Not unless someone breaks it."

Bridget and Kota traded glances.

"What the hell is this?" Crew blurted out, pointing at something hung up on the living room wall that he'd wandered over to.

Both girls began fighting a laugh.

"It's um," Bridget said, tipping her head as a light blush overcame her face. "It's a period calendar."

Crew's eyes landed on me, both outraged and mortified. "Absolutely not."

I scanned over everyone in the room, unsure if I was going to laugh or cry. "Um," I managed to get out.

"What's the matter?" Kota teased. "Do you have a problem with women's menstrual cycles?"

Crew shivered.

Now, I was laughing.

He turned to me. "How the fuck do you think this is funny?"

"It's not. Your reaction is what's funny."

"This doesn't gross you out? We are men! We can't live with menstrual cycles on our damn walls!"

"Calm down," I laughed.

Kota raised a brow. "Seems like there's only one man in this room," she taunted as she put plates in one of the cupboards, "and it's *not* the one crying over a period calendar."

Crew squinted at her with animosity. "I'm a man."

"Yeah, a large man child," Bridget chuckled, earning a high-five from Kota.

"Lane," Crew grumbled, "we can't live here. They're being mean already."

I gave a small sigh. "Suck it up, bro. We don't have a choice."

After the laughing subsided, there was a short moment of silence.

"Well," Bridget said, "why don't we start moving our stuff in and then we can all sit down and have a chat?"

"Okay," I agreed.

"Yeah, alright," Crew muttered reluctantly.

"On the bright side," Kota smirked as we headed for the door, "at least we've got two strong little boys to help us carry the heavy stuff."

"I'm a man!" Crew blared.

"Yeah, well, agree to disagree," Kota said.

I sighed to myself. This was going to be a long year.

Chapter Six

Bridget

After grabbing the period calendar, Kota and I had gone back down to the leasing office to try to figure something else out. After talking to nearly every person that worked there, they all told us the same thing— unless we were okay with being financially penalized or potentially subleasing our apartment, there was nothing they could do.

The rest of the time the guys were gone was spent calling other apartment complexes and seeing if two bedrooms were available, hoping to sublease our current apartment.

But we couldn't find any available two-bedrooms left in the area.

In other words, we were shit out of luck.

We all spent the next two hours moving stuff into the apartment. Lane forced Crew to help him bring some of our heavy stuff in, which was nice of them to do. They did make us move our period calendar into our bathroom, though.

Now that the situation had fully sunk in, there were a million and one thoughts running through my mind.

What if the boys were rude and loud and messy twenty-four seven? Lane had been pretty decent so far, but I still didn't know him well enough to get a good read on him. On the other hand, Crew seemed like more of the sporadic, wild one. He was like Kota in male form. But even if we ended up getting along with them, what the hell was I supposed to tell my parents? How was I supposed to explain to them that I was living with two boys? Let alone boys that I barely knew.

This year was supposed to be Kota's and my year. Our best year yet, just the two of us doing our thing. *Hot girl senior year*, as Kota had been calling it.

And now, hot girl senior year had taken one, berserk U-turn.

"Wait, wait, wait," one of the boys called out, "turn to the left."

They were carrying in my wooden dresser, stepping carefully through the doorway with it. My eyes immediately landed on Lane's arms, his muscles bulging out of his navy t-shirt. Even with the noticeable strain in his muscles, it looked like he was lifting the dresser with far too much ease, like he had the superpower of strength. To my surprise, my heart quickened against my chest, and I found myself unable to look away until there was a light smack against my arm.

"Hey," I scolded quietly, rubbing the spot as I turned to Kota.

"I saw that."

"Saw what?"

"You're drooling."

"I am not," I whispered.

"Mhmm," she murmured.

I opened my mouth to respond, but snapped it shut when Lane's voice echoed through the apartment. "Where do you want it, chief?"

"Oh," I muttered in a rush, jogging after them and into my new room. "If you guys could just put it in that corner," I pointed to the empty spot underneath my Lana Del Rey poster, "that'd be awesome."

I watched, particularly watched Lane, as they set it down in the instructed corner.

"Thank you, guys," I said.

"No problem," Lane answered, standing upright.

The second our eyes met, there was a light, tingling sensation in my stomach, one that couldn't be mistaken for anything besides butterflies.

We just stood there for a moment, eyeing each other. And once again, my heartbeat picked up.

"Can we take a break now?" Crew fussed, causing my gaze to snap over to him. "I'm exhausted."

"Y—yeah," I said. "Let's all take a break."

"We can go have our meeting or whatever you wanna call it," Lane offered with a charming smirk.

I took a deep breath as I nodded, heading back into the living room. Since most of the stuff at our old apartment belonged to Kota and me, our new living room was almost entirely furnished.

I sat next to Kota on the couch. Crew grabbed a stool from the kitchen island, Lane following his lead.

"We should get a second couch," Crew suggested as he turned the stool around and took a seat, resting his arms on the backrest.

"You could just sit on here with us, you know," Kota said. "We don't have cooties."

"Debatable," he replied, causing her to roll her eyes.

I ignored them, getting straight to the point. "Look, if we're stuck living together, then all we can do is try to get along and lay down some basic ground rules."

"Such as?" Lane asked.

Kota and I exchanged a look, silently reiterating what we discussed while the boys were out of the room earlier.

I listed them off one by one. "Stay out of each other's way." *For everyone's sanity.* "Clean up after yourself." *For my sanity.* "Don't eat each other's food." *For Kota's sanity.*

"Fair enough," Lane agreed.

"No hooking up with each other," Crew added.

Kota scoffed. "Yeah, as if that was gonna happen anyway."

Lane let out a small huff. "You two are gonna have to try to get along."

Crew pointed a finger at Kota. "She always starts it."

"Do not!" she argued.

This living arrangement was going to be awkward and uncomfortable enough; we didn't need two arguing children added into the mix. For how smart Kota was, I wished she'd realize that her and Crew weren't going to make it any easier on themselves if they kept this up.

"Geez," I said, "I feel like we're your freaking parents. Both of you, shut up!"

Crew and Kota's mouths snapped shut, but I didn't miss the way Lane's eyes were on me as the corners of his mouth tugged upwards.

"Alright, fine. We'll try to get along," Crew stood. "Are we done now?"

I shrugged with one shoulder. "I guess so."

"Cool," he grumbled, putting his stool back. He shot Lane a desperate look. "I'm going to the house for a while."

Kota grabbed my hand, tugging me off the couch. "Yeah, let's get outta here for a bit, B. I'm already overwhelmed by all the testosterone."

Chapter Seven

Bridget

I woke up well before my alarm went off due to my desert of a mouth.

I reached towards my nightstand, but when I felt nothing on it, I sighed. I usually slept with a full glass of water beside me. I must've forgotten to fill one up last night.

Groaning, I angrily tossed my comforter off and plodded out of bed. A fat yawn engulfed me as I trudged down the hall and into the kitchen half asleep, heading straight to the cupboard I unpacked the glasses into yesterday.

"Hey."

I screamed, jumping backwards. My hand hovered over my chest as I caught my breath.

"Good morning to you too," Lane said, amused.

"Sorry," I let out, shaking my head. "I forgot."

He leaned against the kitchen counter, eyes peeking up at me from over a cup of coffee. "Forgot you're stuck living with two dudes?"

I nodded. "Yeah."

He wasn't wearing a shirt, and it was taking every ounce of self-control not to stare at his bare chest.

Although I was looking away, it was impossible not to notice when his eyes practically smoldered as they started at my face and slowly trailed down my entire body. Within seconds, my insides were twisted tight. I pretended not to be affected, but I was pretty sure I gave myself away by shifting my weight side to side so uneasily. His lips curled upwards in the slightest.

"What's the smirk for?" I asked.

Lane lowered his cup with a light shrug. His voice was smooth and enticing as he spoke. "Just thinking that living here may not be so bad after all." My heartrate doubled as his eyes found their way back to my legs, and—

My legs.

My head dropped down, eyes wide. "Oh my God, I need to put pants on." I ran straight to my room, tugging on the first pair of pajama pants I found, which were covered in pugs wearing Santa hats.

When I walked back into the kitchen, I kept my head tilted down, letting out a long sigh.

Lane's smile grew at the sight of my pants. "What's the big, disappointed sigh for?"

"Just sucks that I won't be able to walk around without clothes like I used to." I finally grabbed a glass and used the Brita in the fridge to fill it.

He chuckled, and it sounded so seductive even though I knew he didn't mean for it to be that way. "You can if you want," he said, taking another sip of coffee. "Wouldn't bother me."

I let out a flustered breath. "I'm sure it wouldn't." I did the lightest double take to the deep ridges on his stomach, and as my eyes landed there again, it was as if they were stuck there.

I gulped lightly, trying to silence the butterflies within me with a quick chug of water.

His grin set my entire body on fire. "You know it's not polite to stare."

My eyes jumped away, falling to the countertop. "Yeah, because I'm sure it makes you *so* uncomfortable."

"Maybe it does," he said as his alluring smirk grew. After all, you are my roommate."

With that, he strolled out of the kitchen.

I let out a breath so heavy that it sounded like I just ran two marathons in a row.

Get a grip, Bridget. He's your roommate.

Chapter Eight

Lane

$\mathbf{S}$_weat._ So much fucking sweat under my gear. The only thing getting me through practice was the thought of hopping in the shower as soon as possible, going to class, and then heading home.

Home. AKA the apartment that Crew and I were now sharing with two girls that hated our guts.

Except I wasn't entirely sure that Bridget hated me. I couldn't quite tell. This morning when I ran into her in the kitchen before practice, she seemed a bit playful with me. And I could've sworn I caught her blushing.

On the other hand, Kota definitely hated us. Why did I not want Bridget to feel that way though?

Even though our living arrangement was brand new, and I'd only been around Bridget a handful of times, there was this sort of excitement that washed over me every time she was in the room.

I skated to the bench, heading straight for my water. Since we lost a handful of seniors from last year, coach had been on our asses about getting into shape before the season started. We gained a lot of talented freshmen, and we had one hell of a starting lineup, nicknamed the _"Assassin Line"_ by some sports reporters, but we still needed to put a lot of work in if we were going to make it to the Frozen Four.

We hadn't even had our first game of the season yet, but as captain, I was already feeling the pressure.

Everyone looked up to me, which meant I had to be at my best both on and off the ice. Eleven times out of ten, I put in more effort than my body could handle, pushing myself beyond my own limits.

Hockey had always been a key part of my life, and I wanted that passion to pay off this year.

After practice, I showered in the locker room and grabbed a bite to eat at the student center before going straight to class. I usually tried to go to the library at some point early in the week to try to get all my homework done. It was a habit I had, but I considered it a good one. During the season when we had games on the weekends, it was nice not having to worry about my schoolwork.

Today though, I was feeling lazy. Instead of heading to the library after class, I decided to go back to the apartment.

I let out the smallest sigh when I stuck the key in the lock and opened the door. I paused in the doorway, the lightest smirk dancing across my face at the sight of Bridget sitting cross-legged on the couch, her nose deep in a book.

She had her sun-kissed hair in a loose braid, rocking a tight tank top with grey sweats and fuzzy socks.

"Hey," I said.

Her head lifted. "Hey."

I slowly trekked over. "No class today?"

"I, uh, only had one class today," she said before her gaze dropped back to her book.

I nodded, then motioned to the opposite end of the couch. "Do you mind if I join you?"

She raised a brow, her honey brown eyes peering over at me as one side of her mouth tugged upwards in the slightest. "Go ahead. You do live here."

"Yes, I do," I responded, taking a seat as I dropped my backpack at my feet.

There were a few strums of silence between us as I dug out my homework.

"What were you doing up so early?"

I froze for the briefest moment, taken off guard at her interest in starting a conversation. After all, I still wasn't sure if she hated me or not.

"We had practice at seven-thirty," I explained. "Why were you up so early?"

She shrugged. "Just needed water. I went back to bed for a little bit before class."

I nodded lightly, forcing my attention back to my homework.

There was something about her that was intriguing. I wasn't sure if it was the way she had this strange ability to switch back and forth between fiery and soft so easily, or if it was the overwhelming sense of innocence that radiated off her. Either way, I kept finding myself hoping that she didn't see me as her mortal enemy.

I stayed quiet, not wanting to bother her as I tried to focus on my homework, but it was becoming harder to.

I was getting that feeling again— a small wave of excitement crashing through me.

What the fuck is happening to me? I thought.

"What about Crew?" she suddenly asked.

I blinked at her, confused. "What about him?"

"He wasn't awake when I saw you this morning and it was almost seven at that point."

"Yeah," I said, "I usually wake him up a half hour before our practices start."

Her brows came in and she snorted. "You wake him up? What are you, his mother?"

"Practically," I chuckled. Just then, a yawning Crew strolled down the hall as he threw on a t-shirt. "Speak of the devil."

He gave a nod of acknowledgment in our direction.

"Did you just wake up?" I asked in disapproval.

He shrugged nonchalantly, slipping his shoes on. "I took a nap."

"Where are you going?"

"Ashley's."

I gave a blank stare, my voice a little harder than intended. "Who's Ashley?"

Crew shrugged again. "I dunno. Some chick." He spoke over his shoulder as he walked out, "See ya."

The second the door closed, Bridget let out a whoop of laughter, slamming her book shut. "I take it Crew's a bit of a man whore?"

I sighed jokingly. "A bit."

Her voice dropped, turning serious, shy even. "And what about you?"

I took in her earnest expression, trying to decipher the curiosity on her face. "I'd like to say no."

Bridget cocked a brow again. "You'd like to?"

I was a bit more zoned in on her than I would've liked to admit, but for whatever the reason was, I refused to show it. "You know... for someone who hates hockey players so much, you seem real interested in hearing about this one."

She brought her knees into her chest. "If I'm gonna be stuck living with you, then I'd like to know who I'm living with."

"Fair enough," I agreed. "You got any other questions for me then?"

She grinned, picking her book back up. "Nope."

Back to silence.

After finishing two short questions on my homework, I wasn't sure why I decided to speak again.

"Is Kota here?"

"No."

"Ah," I joked, nodding, "so that's why it's so quiet."

"Hey!" Bridget laughed, taking a small, decorative pillow and hurdling it towards me. "Be nice."

Our laughter mixed, filling every crevice of the apartment. When it subsided, my tongue lightly brushed over my top lip. "But for real," I said, "it's only you and me here?"

She smirked, a fascinating combination of both fire and grace. With maybe even a bit of bravery thrown in there too. "Are you trying to make a move?"

My grin was dangerously big, but I suppressed it as I leaned towards her slightly. "If I was trying to make a move, you'd know." I collapsed back into the couch. "Plus, *you're* the one that was walking around without pants this morning."

"This conversation sounds awfully flirtatious from your side. Pretty sure that's against the rules we put into place yesterday."

Technically, the rules said we couldn't hookup. Didn't say anything about flirting. *Was* she flirting with me though? The conversation did sound flirtatious but was it one-sided?

I took my bottom lip between my teeth, my head dropping.

"Don't you have some hockey groupies to go make out with or something?" she said.

I chuckled. "Do I give off the impression that that's what I do in my free time?"

"Of course. You play hockey."

I tipped my head towards my shoulder, eyeing her. "Hockey players aren't that bad."

She closed her book once again. "Thought we've been over this."

"Alright, correction. Not *all* hockey players are that bad."

"Again, thought we've been over this," she repeated.

"You're kinda stubborn," I said through a smile. I watched as her lip barely curled upwards, so lightly that if I hadn't been staring at her mouth, I wouldn't have caught it.

"Sometimes," Bridget murmured, eyes down. *Back to being shy, I see.* Her head shot back up as she spoke, her words sounding almost like a dare. "Mostly only with dudes that spill their drinks on me."

Annndddd there was the feistiness again.

"I said I was sorry!" I laughed as I brought my hands up and dropped them into my lap. "You gonna hold it over my head forever?"

She shrugged with one shoulder. "Probably."

I hopped off the couch and into the kitchen, grabbing an ice-cold beer. I popped the can open and held it towards Bridget.

"Here," I said.

Her eyes jumped between the can and me. "What?"

"Pour it on me."

"What? No!"

"Yes," I urged. "And then we'll be even."

She scoffed. "It's gonna get all over the floor."

"Then let's go on the balcony."

"Lane..."

"C'mon," I insisted.

She sighed, tossing her book aside. "Alright."

I handed her the beer as we walked onto the balcony. We stood there, facing each other. My eyes on Bridget. Her eyes on the beer.

"You're sure?" she asked skeptically.

"One-hundred percent."

A mischievous grin settled on her face as she stepped onto her tip toes and dumped the beer over my head.

"Not my head!" I screeched. "I didn't spill mine on yours! What the hell, Bridget?"

She shoved the empty beer can at me, giggling. "Well, you can't just go around breaking rules, Lane."

"I haven't!"

She glanced at me over her shoulder. "No more flirting."

Leaving it at that, she trotted back inside.

Goddammit.

Now I was soaked in beer and somehow a little turned on at the same time?

She's right, Lane. Cut the fucking flirting. She's your roommate.

Chapter Nine

Lane

The past few days had been a little strange. Hockey was going fine. School was going pretty well. It was the atmosphere in the apartment that was throwing me off.

Bridget and I had hardly been in the same room since I let her pour beer all over me the other day.

I wasn't sure if it was just a coincidence or if she was avoiding me on purpose. I was starting to really regret the flirting. Maybe it made her feel awkward. After all, we were *roommates.* Roommates by force, not by choice. And considering she blatantly told me to stop the flirting made me assume she hated it, or even worse, hated *me.*

The bathroom unleashed a cloud of steam as I stepped out of it with a towel tied around my waist. I got dressed in my room, then headed into the kitchen to make something to eat.

Crew was sunk back into the couch, watching TV while piling popcorn into his mouth. Bridget was sitting against the armrest on the other side of the couch, as far away from Crew as possible. Once again, she was reading a book. The same one she was reading a few days ago when I interrupted her.

When Bridget's honey brown eyes caught sight of me, she seemed to tense up. Her gaze danced between the book and me for a moment, her chest expanding quicker than it was prior.

"Hey," I casually said.

She swallowed, looking down. "Hey," she let out quietly.

Starting to take stuff out of the fridge to make a sandwich, I watched Bridget out of the corner of my eye and saw that she was seemingly doing the same.

I bit down on my bottom lip, breathing heavily out my nose. I wasn't sure what was going through my mind that convinced me it was a good idea to try to speak to her.

"How was your day?" I blurted out, grabbing two pieces of bread.

Her head swung over to look at me. She hesitated. "It was good," she said, closing her book. She stood, nervously running a hand over her forehead. "I'm... gonna go take a nap," she let out, retreating to her room without another word.

I frustratingly dropped the bread onto my plate. "Goddammit," I muttered to myself, shaking my head. Bridget was the one girl I felt compelled to be around, yet it seemed like she wanted nothing to do with me.

I planted my hands on the kitchen island, waiting a moment until I was sure Bridget was in her room.

"Crew," I said.

No response.

"Crew," I let out louder.

Still no response.

I sighed, shaking my head as I marched into the living room. Grabbing a small handful of popcorn, I tossed it at him. "Hey, shithead."

"Yo, what the hell?" he finally answered.

"I called your name twice and you didn't answer."

"Sorry, bro. I'm watching a movie," he said with a full mouth, motioning to the TV as he began plucking the popcorn off his lap.

I took a glimpse, lifting a brow. "*Titanic*? Really?"

"Fuck off," he spurred. "It's a cinematic masterpiece."

"Yeah, alright," I said, plopping down beside him. I let out another sigh, stressfully running my hands over my thighs. "I have a question."

"What?"

"Do you think Bridget is avoiding me?"

He eyed me like I just spoke gibberish. "Why do you care?"

I avoided his sharp gaze, giving a small shrug to pretend like it wasn't that big of a deal. "I don't know, I mean... she's our roommate."

He lifted a suspicious brow. "What about Kota?"

"What about her?"

"You don't care if she's avoiding you."

"That's because I know she's not," I said.

Crew studied me harder before letting out a humorless laugh. "Don't tell me..." He leaned forward, a misleading grin on his face as my silence told him everything. "You've got a thing for Bridget."

"No, I don't."

He swiped his hand through the air. "Oh, don't give me that shit. You couldn't lie to me if your life depended on it."

I let out a huff, dropping my head into my hands for a moment before finally growing the balls to look back at him. "Do you think she's avoiding me?" I asked again.

"The problem isn't that she's avoiding you," he said, tossing popcorn into his mouth as if the conversation were as entertaining as *Titanic*. "The problem is that you're crushing on her."

"I'm not crushing on her," I said.

Crew shook his head. "You're gonna have to get over it, bro. It's not gonna happen. She's our roommate. It's against the rules, remember?"

I tipped my head back in annoyance. All I wanted was for him to answer my goddamn question. "Yes, I remember," I spoke through gritted teeth. My voice came out sharply as I asked a third time, "Do you think she's avoiding me?"

He shrugged, still eyeing me like I was an idiot. "I dunno. I haven't been paying attention."

"Of course not," I stood.

54

Crew spoke again as I was halfway back to the kitchen. "Lane?"

"Yeah?" I looked over my shoulder.

"Do you wanna watch *Titanic* with me?"

I shot him a look of irritation. "I hate you sometimes."

Chapter Ten

Bridget

The past week had been fairly quiet in the apartment, at least for me. Which was probably because I'd been doing my best to avoid Lane at all costs.

That man should've come with a warning label. Being around him was getting harder. The more I was around him, the more he was slowly breaking down my wall, because he was too likeable. His energy was exhilarating. Not to mention he was irresistibly gorgeous. In other words, everything I knew so far about him led to one conclusion— he was dangerous.

If I was going to be stuck living with him for the next year, the best thing I could do for myself would be to keep my distance.

On the other hand, Crew and Kota were not getting along in the slightest, which wasn't really a shock to anyone. At this point, they were ignoring each other to the extreme. Any time one of them walked into the room, the other walked right out. I would say they were being overdramatic, but I guess I wasn't really one to talk, considering I was sort of doing the same thing, just more discreetly.

Since I had a better idea of Lane's schedule now, I was able to kind of map out my own.

Kota and I worked our asses off every summer, working forty to fifty hour weeks just so that we didn't have to work during the school year. It was three months of hell in exchange for nine months of financial stability and more free time.

Since I didn't have any other responsibilities to get done, I headed to the library after class to work on the literature essay I had to do. In the essay, we needed to analyze Daisy Buchanan from *The Great Gatsby*. In other words, I was basically writing two-thousand words about why she was a selfish bitch.

Whatever, though. I'd always thought the book was great and I'd be lying if I said I also didn't enjoy watching the movie because *hellooo?* Leo DiCaprio!

I was sitting at a table alone in the corner of the library on the second floor, about five-hundred words into my essay when a figure appeared across from me.

"Hey, roomie," Lane said, taking a seat. "Funny seeing you here."

There was a small burn forming within my lungs, similar to the tiny flicker of a flame as it lit up a pile of dry leaves.

"Hey," I said, surprised. "What are you doing here?"

He slid his backpack off and onto the floor. "I gotta do some homework."

"Do you usually come here?"

"Yeah," he said. "I'm most productive here. Last year, it was impossible to focus at the house. The guys were always so damn loud, so I used to come here to get shit done."

I nodded slowly, my eyes dropping to my computer. I'd been doing my best to steer clear of Lane, but apparently, I couldn't get away from him.

"If I didn't know any better, I'd say you were avoiding me," he said with a sly grin.

I am.

"What makes you say that?"

He wiped the grin off his face, his sapphire blue eyes turning solemn as he gave the lightest shrug known to man. "We haven't spoken much."

"Didn't know we had to."

"I mean, I'd prefer if we were friends."

My gaze jumped up to him, tummy dipping as we eyed each other. He sat there quietly, waiting for me to answer. I couldn't tell if my cheeks were flushing or not. All I could do was pray that they weren't.

"Stop being so nice," I shot at him.

He laughed, "Why?"

"Because it makes it harder to hate you," I blurted out.

A few heads had turned in our direction, and I wasn't sure if it was because of the conversation or if we were just simply being too loud.

Ignoring people's stares, he folded his arms across the table, his impish grin returning. "So, you don't hate me?"

Gosh. It was so unfair that someone so charming could also be the biggest pain in the ass.

I was trying to hate him. Trying a little harder than necessary. Trying as if my life depended on it, because I knew damn well that my heart did.

I got attached too easily. I got hurt too easily. Part of me knew it probably had to do with me being adopted and never knowing my biological parents, along with being screwed over by my fair share of guys. I had insecurity and abandonment issues that followed me throughout my life, and they definitely weren't going to disappear anytime soon.

He was still looking at me, staring as if I were an experiment he was studying.

"Hate is a strong word," I finally said.

"So, you dislike me?"

"I mean, you're not my favorite," I admitted.

"Why?"

"Why aren't you my favorite?"

"No," he corrected, "why do you dislike me?"

Sometimes I put on a front, pretending like I had more confidence than I actually did. But other times, the barricade was lowered.

And right now, it was lowering against my will.

"I need to get this essay done," I murmured, turning my attention back to my computer.

"Alright..." he said, placing a textbook on the table. "But just so you know, we're gonna end up being good friends."

"We'll see."

Chapter Eleven

Lane

"**W**e really should invite them," I said.

"Hmm, how about no?" Crew replied sharply, seated on his bed.

"Crew," I scolded.

"I already vetoed the idea," he said.

"And I already vetoed your veto."

He sighed, still fighting me on it.

Since our season hadn't actually begun yet and it was a Saturday, there was a party tonight at the hockey house.

"Look," he started, "we all know you've got a little crush on Bridget, but—"

"No, I don't," I snapped, a little too eager to deny it.

"Um," his brows drew in, "yeah, sure. Anyway—"

"If I've got a crush on Bridget, then you've got one on Kota."

His laughter echoed throughout the room. "Yeah, the fuck right. I'd rather get gasoline injected into my veins."

I raised a brow, giving him a harsh glare.

He brought his hands up defensively. "Yeah, she's hot, but she's a bitch."

"Maybe you're a bitch sometimes."

"Watch it, bro."

"What's the problem with just inviting them? You're probably not gonna see them all night anyway. I'm sure you'll find some girl to spend the night with and you'll be hanging out with her."

He huffed, ruffling his hair. "Why do you wanna invite them? I don't get it."

Because I want Bridget to like me.

"Because we need to get along," I insisted. "And that starts with all of us calling a truce and being decent to each other."

He stressfully ran his hands over his face. "Fine."

I quietly sighed a breath of relief. "Alright, let's go." I cocked my head towards his bedroom door.

"What, now?"

"I mean, I'm pretty sure they're just sitting in the living room right now."

There were daggers in his eyes as he looked at me. He finally stood. "I hate you for this."

"Don't be so damn dramatic," I said, leading the way out.

The girls were sitting in the living room like expected, their eyes glued to an episode of *The Bachelor*.

"Is he fucking serious?" Kota shouted, lunging forward.

Bridget shook her head at the TV. "He just made a big fucking mistake."

"Hey," I interrupted.

Their heads reluctantly turned towards me, both looking irritated. Kota picked up the remote and hit the pause button. They eyed us silently, wondering why in the hell we just interfered with their beloved show.

"What are you guys doing tonight?" I asked.

"We don't know yet," Bridget responded. "Maybe going to the bar."

I peered over at Crew, waiting for him to say something, but it seemed like he was planning on having me do all the talking, which I guess was fair. After all, it was my idea to invite them anyway.

Regardless, I still nudged him.

Crew groaned. "There's a, um..." He moved his hands around as he paused.

"Are you having trouble speaking?" Kota mocked.

Crew's eyes narrowed. "No."

"Then spit it out, buddy," she spurred.

His jaw tightened, and I sighed as I took the lead again. "There's a party tonight at the hockey house. Do you guys wanna come?"

The girls looked at each other in bewilderment.

Bridget scoffed, eyeing us in doubt. "You guys are inviting us out with you?"

"Yes," I said.

All eyes landed on Crew, and I nudged him again.

"Sure," he rumbled through gritted teeth.

Kota's devilish smirk lit up the room. "Hmm... I'm a little intrigued. Maybe we should go, B."

To my surprise *and* my delight, Bridget's eyes were on me. "Alright," she said, "let's do it."

***

Crew was huffing and puffing, impatiently shifting his weight around. "Can they hurry the fuck up?"

"It's only nine. Calm down."

"Well, everyone's there already."

"You know that's not true," I said.

He ignored me, tapping his foot on the floor. "The house is probably filling up right now." I rolled my eyes. "Probably with some hot girls that are dying to see me."

I laughed. "You're way too full of yourself, man."

"Confidence is key," he nodded with a devious smile.

"Yeah, well, you've probably got the key to the wrong lock."

"Nah," he waved me off.

Laughing echoed down the girl's hall, getting louder by the second as they headed towards us.

The moment they appeared, my eyes were locked on Bridget. Her hair was curled in perfect ringlets, and she was wearing a skin-tight brown shirt that was tucked into her jeans.

I nearly whistled, but restrained myself, struggling to take my eyes off her as arousal shot through my body.

She slung her purse over her shoulder. "Ready?"

"We've been ready," Crew muttered at the same time I said, "Yeah."

"Bet," Kota said, her hips swaying lightly as she strode past us. "Let's see what this whole hockey buzz is about."

Chapter Twelve

Bridget

"So, are you gonna spill your drink on me tonight?"
I joked, walking beside Lane up the front steps of the hockey
house.

He gave a crooked grin. "Gonna try my best not to."

"Good to hear."

I'd never been to the hockey house, which wasn't a
surprise to anyone. Why would I go somewhere that was filled
with people I didn't bother to know?

The house looked small from the outside, but was
surprisingly spacious on the inside, having a ground level, an
upstairs, and even a basement, which was apparently where
they threw their parties at.

There was a good amount of people there, but luckily,
the house wasn't packed shoulder to shoulder. It seemed like
the party was invite-only, which was another reason why Kota
and I hadn't been there before.

We'd never been *invited*. Until now.

I was a little shocked earlier when the boys invited us
in the first place. It wasn't hard to figure out that it was all
Lane's idea, and that Crew was kind of forced into it.
Nonetheless, I couldn't figure out why Lane had been recently

going out of his way so much to be nice. I knew he wanted to be friends, and of course I wanted that too, but Lane was the kind of guy that seemed too easy to fall for, which meant I was better off running the other way.

Within five minutes of being inside, the boys had wandered off after catching sight of their hockey buddies.

"Should we go check out downstairs?" Kota asked.

"Sure."

She grabbed my hand and led the way, walking confidently with her chin tipped upwards past the various groups of girls that were glaring at us like we were trespassing on their property.

The basement had strobe lights going off, music blasting, bodies swaying. Kota let out a dark chuckle as she tugged me over to an empty spot near the far side of the room.

"Did you see all those girls looking at us?" she snickered. "They looked so pissed."

"They probably think we're here to steal their man-boys."

"*Hah!* Man-boys!" she laughed.

"Body of man. Brain of boy."

"Do you think their brains ever reach man status?"

"Rarely," I said.

"Bobby is one of the rare ones."

"What's Bobby up to tonight?" I wondered.

"I think he's at Stallions, but I'm not completely sure. Should I text him and ask him to come here?"

I shrugged. "Why not?"

She snagged her phone out of her back pocket and began tapping away. "Ugh. There's no damn service down here."

"It's probably better upstairs."

"Yeah, let's go try it out. And where the fuck are the drinks in this damn house?"

"We'll have to look."

Kota decided to call Bobby instead, standing by the front door since that was apparently where "the best service ever" was.

Meanwhile, I spotted Lane in the living room talking to what I could assume was one of his teammates. I headed over. "Hey."

His tense shoulders melted a little. "Hey."

I opened my mouth to speak, but his teammate beat me to it. "Hey," he nodded at me.

It wasn't until I looked right at him that I realized it was TJ.

"Hi," I said stiffly.

"I know you," TJ said.

Lane grew wary, his eyes narrowing in the slightest.

"Uh," I played dumb, "you do?"

"Yeah," TJ said, "we had a class together last semester."

"Oh! Right."

For whatever reason, Lane seemed to relax a little. I turned towards him, a little hesitantly. "Um, is there anything to drink?"

"Yeah," he nodded. "You want a beer?"

I scrunched my face in mild disgust. "Is that the only option?"

Lane chuckled lightly. "I can find something else for you." He looked at TJ. "Where's Jett?"

"Last time I saw him, he was in the kitchen," TJ said.

Lane gave him a friendly tap on the shoulder. "Thanks, man. I'll see you in a bit."

TJ nodded, diverting his attention to a tall brunette across the room that was practically undressing him with her eyes. He took it as an invitation, smirking as he wandered over.

Lane guided me towards the kitchen, his hand trailing along my lower back. I breathed in sparks and blew them back out, using all my focus to pretend like his hand was quite literally *anything* other than his hand.

He led us over to a small group of people. "Jett," he nodded.

Jett was a few inches shorter than Lane with ironically, jet-black hair and the most piercing blue eyes I'd ever seen in my life. They looked like straight ice cubes.

"Captain!" Jett exclaimed, bringing Lane in for a quick hug.

Lane smiled as he pulled away. "I need a favor."

"What's up?"

"You got any vodka and lemonade?"

Jett eyed his captain with a bit of suspicion. "Ah, no."

"Oh, don't give me that shit," Lane cocked his head.

Jett let out a single chuckle, arms raised. "What do you mean!"

"I know you've got some."

"Is it for you?" Jett asked.

"No," Lane said.

Jett's eyes slid over to me, a sinful smile touching his lips. "I see."

"Oh, shut up. She's my roommate," Lane said.

Jett's face lit up. "So, she's off limits for you, but not for me?"

I stood quietly, a sheepish look on my face.

Lane stiffened. "She's off limits for you."

"Is she off limits for me?" TJ asked, appearing in the doorway.

"Yes," Lane hissed. "She's off limits for *all* of you."

TJ brought his hands up defensively, his beer in one hand. "Alright, captain. Whatever you say."

"What if she's into it?" Jett pushed.

"What if she's not?" Lane shot back.

Finally, I spoke. "You all know I'm right here, right?"

All three of the boys eyed me in amazement as if they had expected for me to keep my mouth shut the whole time. I pointed at Jett. "I'm not into it. And you," I pointed at TJ, "weren't you just with some brunette in the living room?"

"Snap!" Jett laughed.

TJ smiled. "So?"

"So, where'd she go?" I questioned.

"She went to the bathroom," he said, sipping on his beer. He took in my judgmental expression. "What was I supposed to do? Sit outside the door and wait for her? She didn't even bother to invite me in!"

"You guys are all ridiculous." My eyes landed on TJ. "And kind of gross."

Lane's blue irises were on me, an admiring grin plastered on his face.

I placed my hands on my hips. "And what are *you* smiling at?"

He brought his hands up, chuckling. "Nothing, nothing!"

"Damn. Crew was right. She is kinda bitchy," Jett said with amusement.

"Nah," Lane shook his head. "He was talking about Kota. She's the nice one," he gestured to me.

"The *nice* one?" TJ shrieked. "She just chewed me out for being a dude!"

"Yeah, and rejected me," Jett added.

I raised a joking brow. "You guys gonna cry about it?"

"Maybe," Jett smirked.

"*I* probably will," TJ said.

I let out a small huff. "You got the vodka and lemonade or not?" I asked with a smile.

"Yeah," Jett finally admitted with a chuckle. He cocked his head towards the stairs. "Follow me."

Both Lane and I started following, and Jett halted, lightly bringing a hand up to Lane's chest. "Just her."

"What?" Lane jeered. "Hell no."

Jett's eyes wandered over to me as he raised a brow.

"Lane, it's fine," I said.

Lane's eyes were hardened as he studied me for a moment. "He's probably gonna try to make a move on you."

Why do you care?

Jett rolled his eyes. "Oh, c'mon, dude. She already said she wasn't into it. I'm not that much of a scumbag."

"Then why can't I come?" Lane asked.

"Lane, really, it's fine. I can handle it," I said.

He studied me harder, then let out a defeated sigh. "Alright."

We left Lane standing there, and I'd be lying if I said I wasn't the tiniest bit intimidated knowing I was walking upstairs with a hockey player whose intentions I wasn't entirely sure of.

But when we reached Jett's room, he belted out a laugh.

"What's so funny?" I wondered aloud.

I stood in the doorway as he shook his head, heading over to his mini fridge and pulling out lemonade, followed by a bottle of vodka.

"I've just gotta ask," he said, grabbing a plastic cup. "Is there anything going on between you and Lane?"

I shifted around before leaning against the doorframe. "No," I shook my head. "No, of course not. Why?"

Jett poured vodka into the cup. "He just seemed a little on the protective side down there."

I stayed quiet, unsure of what he was inferring.

His eyes glanced up at me. "I hope you know I was joking downstairs, by the way."

I crossed my arms, giving a light snort. "Sure, you were."

"I was. Promise," he insisted. "I like to bust Lane's balls a bit. He's usually so cool and composed. Sometimes it's fun to piss him off."

For some reason, I took it as an insult. I could feel my face fall in the slightest, and apparently, he caught it, because he was quick to correct himself.

"Don't get me wrong. You're a really pretty girl. But for me, off limits means off limits," he assured me. "TJ is a whole other story though."

I nodded along quietly.

"What's your name again?"

"Bridget."

"Bridget," he repeated. "I'm Jett."

"I figured that one out," I said with a friendly smile. But my smile fell flat, heart picking up as I forced myself to ask my next question. "So... you think he was being protective?"

"Oh definitely," he said, brows drawing inwards as he handed the cup over to me. "Either he's got a thing for you, or he views you as a sister."

My face inevitably scrunched in disgust. *His sister?*

"Is that why you asked me to come up here alone? So that you could ask about Lane?"

"Pretty much," he admitted, grabbing himself a beer. "I couldn't ask Lane. He'd lie right through his teeth."

I gave a small nod, letting out a shy laugh. "Are you ready to go back down?"

"Yep," he said. "But if you really wanna find out what he thinks about you, tell him we just fooled around pretty hard."

"Funny," I smiled, rolling my eyes as I turned over my shoulder and headed for the stairs, Jett on my heels.

To my surprise, Lane was still standing where we left him. Some girl was talking to him, and he seemed oddly disinterested, cracking a fake smile that he didn't even bother to let reach his eyes.

Right as he spotted us, he quickly ended the conversation, excusing himself and stepping over to us.

"You okay?" he immediately asked me.

"I'm fine," I said.

"She's more than fine," Jett declared. "Said it was the best orgasm of her life."

I shot Jett a look before slowly turning to take in Lane's expression.

His mouth was parted in exasperation, eyes filled with furor. "What?"

Jett's amused grin grew further, glancing at me as if he was trying to say *Told you so.*

"He's just joking," I said.

Lane looked at me for a moment, taking in my honest expression. His eyes pierced into Jett. "Dick," he muttered, lightly shoving him with one hand.

"Alright, alright," Jett said through a laugh. "Calm down."

Lane huffed, softly placing his hand on my back again and leading me into the next room over.

I brought my brows in, my feet digging into the ground as I halted, causing Lane to follow suit. "Are you alright?" I asked.

He eyed me almost nervously. "I'm fine."

"Okay..." I mumbled, cautiously bringing my drink up to my mouth. I wanted to push him a little more, to really see what he was thinking about. But I was also too scared to ask.

Lane took it as an opportunity to change the subject. "Vodka lemonade?"

"Yeah."

He shook his head towards the floor, letting out a charming chuckle.

"What?"

"I'm not laughing at you. I'm laughing at Jett."

"Why?"

"You wanna know the real reason why he always has vodka and lemonade on hand?"

I eyed him curiously. "Sure."

"Because once girls know he's got it, they all swarm around him."

"Oh my God. Of course," I laughed. "Does it work?"

"Like a charm."

"Wow. That's sad."

He gave a joking shrug. "Kind of genius if you ask me."

"He's an innovator."

"He is," he said, running a hand over the light stubble on his chin as he snickered. "Also, where's Kota?" his brows came in.

My eyes widened. "Oh my gosh, I left her alone for so long! I'm the worst friend!" I screeched, sprinting towards the front door.

When I reached the spot I'd left her in, Kota was still standing there, but thankfully, Bobby was by her side. I sighed a breath of relief.

"Who's that?" Lane asked, appearing beside me once again.

"Bobby."

"I didn't know Kota had a boyfriend."

"She doesn't," I said. "They're a thing though."

Lane nodded, eyeing Bobby as if he didn't approve.

"Lane! Lane!" a frantic voice shouted. A hockey player I hadn't been introduced to yet appeared in front of us, his face full of panic as he stood there, somewhat out of breath.

"Sup, Cody?" Lane asked.

"It's Matt."

Lane's spine straightened like a growing tree. His mind seemingly headed to the worst places. "What? What happened?"

"He's got his hand stuck in a Pringles can again."

My brows came in as I held back a laugh. What a huge emergency. A complete catastrophe for the hockey team.

Lane grunted in frustration, tipping his head back. *"Again?"*

Cody cringed. "Yeah..."

"Goddammit, he's a fucking idiot."

"It's really stuck in there, man. Maybe worse than last time."

Lane sighed, then chugged the rest of his beer, crushed the can in his hand, and tossed it in the garbage can in the corner of the room. He shook his head, "Alright, go see which one of the guys has some lube. We're gonna have to lube him up and pull him out."

"Ew," I thought out loud, but neither of the boys seemed to catch it. They were too caught up in their "team emergency."

"I've got some," Cody said.

"I figured," Lane replied. "Go get it." Cody began speeding in the direction he came, causing Lane to yell after him. "Where's Matt?"

"Hiding in his bathroom because he's embarrassed!"

"He should be!"

I brought the back of my hand up to my mouth to try to hide my entertained smirk. *Talk about a party foul.*

Lane's voice softened as he turned to me. "I'm gonna... go take care of this real quick."

"Okay," I giggled.

"I'm sorry. I'll see you later."

"Don't apologize," I said. "I get it. When captain duty calls."

72

"Yeah," he exhaled. "Something like that."

"Good luck!" I called after him as he rushed off.

Within seconds of Lane being gone, a guy appeared next to me.

"Hi," he said, a friendly smile plastered on his face.

He was fairly shorter than most of the other guys in the house and not anywhere near as built. He didn't give off the same confident and carefree vibe as everyone else, which all led me to believe he wasn't a hockey player.

"Hi," I responded shyly.

He shifted his weight lightly. "Do you have a boyfriend?"

I frowned. "You're asking me if I have a boyfriend before you even ask for my name?"

He chuckled. "I'm sorry, you're right. I'm Mitch," he said, holding his hand out.

I stared at it for a moment before giving it a cautious shake. "Bridget."

"I only asked because I saw you talking to Lane Avery, so I wasn't sure if I should come over or not."

Definitely not a hockey player. No one would call their teammate by their first and last name like that.

"Oh, yeah," I said casually, glancing down the hall that Lane had disappeared down. I didn't want to flat out say he was my roommate, because talking to a girl that was living with another guy would potentially scare any guy away, especially when the roommate was Lane Fucking Avery. "He's just a friend."

"Gotcha," he nodded.

I wasn't quite sure what he wanted. I was assuming he was hitting on me, granted he'd just asked if I had a boyfriend, but did I want him to hit on me? He was cute for sure, but he wasn't giving me those same lovely, yet unpleasant butterflies that Lane gave me.

Then again, Lane was off-limits.

Maybe I should be entertaining this.

"Where are you from?" I asked, starting up a conversation.

"I'm from Denver actually," he said. "How about you?"

"I'm from a small town called Sumner. It's about three hours north."

"What are you studying?"

"English literature," I said. "You?"

"Sales and marketing."

"Oh nice. What year are you?"

"Senior."

"Same," I smiled.

Mitch smiled back, and for the first time since he walked up to me, there was the tiniest flicker of a spark that ignited in my core.

"So," he spoke, still smiling, "I know we just met like five minutes ago, but would it be out of line if I asked for your number?"

My smile grew a little. "Not at all."

"Great," he replied, taking his phone out of his pocket and handing it over.

I typed in my number, slightly struggling since I was still holding my drink. I double checked to make sure I typed it in correctly and gave it back.

"Cool," he smirked, glancing at his phone before sliding it into his pocket.

"Cool," I repeated.

"Well, I'm gonna go find my friend that I came with, but I'll text you?" he said, sounding hopeful.

"Sounds good," I beamed, swaying lightly as he walked off.

"Omigod!" Kota shrieked in a tone so high pitched that it reminded me of nails on a chalkboard. I cringed. "Who was that guy?"

"His name's Mitch. I just met him."

"He was so cute! Did you get his number?"

"He asked for mine," I said with the faintest blush.

She grabbed my hand excitedly. "Maybe coming here *was* a good idea!" she squealed with a wicked smile.

74

Inevitably, Lane's face flashed through my mind and my stomach dropped in the slightest, but I forced my grin not to drop with it. "Maybe."

Chapter Thirteen

Lane

For the first time tonight, I ran into Crew while I was walking through the upstairs hall.

"Where the hell have you been?" I spewed. "We just had to tug Matt's hand out of a Pringles can again."

He snorted. "Why am I not surprised?"

I narrowed my eyes at him in annoyance. He was supposed to be my right-hand man, yet he was nowhere to be found when I was wrists deep in lube, pulling our teammate's hand out of a goddamn Pringles can. "Again, where the hell were you?"

"You want my honest answer or my PG one?"

I rolled my eyes, scoffing lightly. "I'm sure you're gonna give me your honest answer anyway."

He gave a cheeky grin, his eyes creasing in the corners from so much delight. "You're right," he said, resting his arms on the banister atop the stairs. I didn't think it was possible for his grin to grow wider, but somehow, it did. "First, I was getting blown in the bathroom." Suddenly, his grin shrunk. "I don't know if you wanna hear the next part."

I eyed him in disgust. "Does it have to do with your balls?"

"No, it has to do with Bridget."

Disgust gone. Instantly replaced by uneasiness. "What about her?"

He casually leaned further over the banister. "She was talking up a storm with some guy downstairs."

"Who? Is he on the team?"

"Nah," he shook his head. "I don't know he is. She seemed pretty smiley though if you ask me."

I clenched my teeth together, jaw grinding. There was a clawing, desperate feeling brewing in the center of my stomach that I needed to go find this dude and see who the hell he was.

I wasn't sure why I was feeling so... protective? Possessive? I couldn't even tell at this point.

"Sorry, man," Crew said softly. "I know that's probably not something you wanted to hear."

I swallowed my bitterness. "It's fine," I muttered. "We're just friends anyway.

Chapter Fourteen

Bridget

I was on my way to class Monday when my phone buzzed in my pocket. I didn't bother to check it since I was in a rush.

My essay on *The Great Gatsby* was due today and I didn't know until last night that our professor wanted us to print it out and turn in a hard copy. Most of my other professors wanted us to turn stuff in online. So, after having a small heart attack about not having a printer at the apartment, I rushed onto campus this morning to print my paper at the computer lab.

Now I was practically running to class.

Luckily, I made it on time, diving into my seat right as our professor started collecting our essays.

Once I was relaxed and could actually breathe, I slid my phone out of my pocket to see a text from a random number.

Hey, it's Mitch from the other night. (:

I lightly bit down on my finger as I stared at the message, fighting a small smile. It had been two days since the hockey party and although I didn't expect for Mitch to text me that same night, I was a little surprised when he didn't text at all yesterday. I thought about it a few times yesterday until I realized I needed to print my essay, then I forgot about it altogether and was panicking all night instead.

Me: Hey!

Mitch: How are you?

Me: I'm good. How about you?

Mitch: I'm good! Are you busy tonight?

My smile was growing. I could only hope no one in class was looking at me while I was grinning at my phone like a dork. I placed my elbow on the table and tried to nonchalantly cover my mouth with my hand just to hide it.

Everything the professor was saying was going in through one ear and straight out the other. My brain was in all sorts of other places rather than in class.

Me: Don't think so

Mitch: Would you want to go out tonight?

That was what did it. My smile was way too wide for a casual texting conversation.

I wasn't sure if it was because of Mitch specifically or if it was because I hadn't been asked out on an actual date in well over a year. Most of the guys that had tried talking to me since then were only looking to hookup, and they made their intentions clear from the get-go.

I wasn't really one to do hookups. In reality, I'd only ever slept with two people before and I was dating them at the time.

The first one was back in high school. We were together for about a year until he dumped me shortly before we were supposed to head off to college. Granted, we were going to different schools that were an hour away from each other, but *c'mon.* An hour wasn't that bad. It was hardly long distance in my opinion. And then of course the second he got to college, he got a new girlfriend there. It didn't surprise me much, but I'd be lying if I said I hadn't been heartbroken about it.

My second boyfriend was during freshman year of college. Kota and I took a trip to Darby College, a small school close to her hometown, to visit one of her friends from high school. We went out one night and that's where I met Ethan. We hit it off and started dating shortly after, but it didn't get past the six-month mark before I found out he'd been cheating on me with numerous different girls. But what was even worse about Ethan was his ugly side. He had a temper and a huge ego, picking fights with people whenever he saw the opportunity. The last time we spoke, he had some pretty nasty things to say to me even though he was the one in the wrong.

Overall, I'd never had a solid, healthy relationship before.

The common denominator in both failed relationships consisted of two things. One: me. Two: hockey players.

Hence why I wasn't very fond of hockey players, and unfortunately for me, Minnesota was one of the biggest hockey states in the country.

Me: Sure, I'd love to

Mitch: Awesome. Pick you up at 7?

Me: See you then(:

I finally put my phone down and tried to pay attention to class, but every few minutes, my mind kept wandering right back to the same exact thought.

Holy shit, I have a date tonight.

Chapter Fifteen

Lane

I'd just gotten back from the gym and decided to make a protein shake. I tossed all the ingredients into the blender and just before I pressed the start button, I heard Bridget's small voice from behind me.

"Hey."

I turned, feeling myself brighten. "Hey."

"So..." she said nervously with her hands innocently laced together, "since Kota isn't here right now, can I ask for your opinion?"

"Sure," I smiled lightly. "On what?"

She had the cutest, timid grin on her face as she held up a finger, signaling for me to wait before running to her room.

I rested my back against the counter, gripping onto it as I waited for her to return.

After a minute, she reappeared with her hands behind her back.

"Okay!" she squealed. "Option A." She brought a small black romper out from behind her back, and I stiffened in the slightest as I envisioned her in it.

It'd probably push her cleavage up. Probably curve perfectly around her little waist. Probably illuminate her beautiful strawberry locks.

The image was driving me crazy.

I bit the inside of my cheek, shifting around to try to hide the semi that was starting to grow in my pants.

"Or... Option B!" she said, pulling out a tight, white long sleeve shirt with a v-cut in the front. "This would go with jeans obviously."

My eyes bounced between both outfits and her. "What's the occasion?"

The corners of her lips tugged upwards. "I have a date."

Semi gone.

"Oh." I took in a sharp breath, trying to hide the disappointment on my face. "With who?"

"His name's Mitch. I met him at the party the other night."

Why was I regretting bringing them now?

I immediately felt like a jerk for even thinking it, but I couldn't help it.

"That's great," I said as convincingly as I could manage.

"Thanks!" She wiggled both outfits around. "So, which one?"

There was something inside me that was crumbling a little bit. I still hadn't admitted aloud that I felt something towards Bridget, but I knew I secretly did.

I could feel it every time she came around. I wasn't sure what it was about her that made me want her. Maybe it was the way she was immune to hockey players or the way she was sweet but didn't deal with bullshit at the same time.

She was so much more real than the other girls I'd talked to before. It seemed like she was in her own world, worrying about her own responsibilities instead of being interested in my hockey career or wondering how to end up in my bed.

But now I was going to have to sit around all night, impatiently waiting for her to come home from going on a date with another guy.

"The black," I said honestly, my voice falling. "The black will look great on you."

Bridget's smile slowly faded, and she eyed me with a sort of longing in her eyes, drawing in a deep breath. Her head fell for a second, her hair creating a curtain between us.

Slowly, her eyes found their way back to me. "Thanks."

"You're welcome."

She motioned towards the hall. "I should probably go get ready."

I gave her a tight-lipped smile. "Alright."

"See you later?"

I nodded once. "I'll be here."

She chuckled lightly, sounding as sweet as sugar. "Not like you have a choice."

"Exactly," I grinned, but this time, it was sincere.

I watched as she pranced off down the hall. Letting out a defeated sigh, I turned back towards the blender and started it.

Chapter Sixteen

Bridget

I was thankful I went with Lane's advice and wore the black romper. The other outfit would've made me stand out terribly at the nice Italian restaurant we were at.

"You look really pretty, by the way," Mitch said, the dim light illuminating his dark features.

"Thank you," I blushed.

"Did I already say that?"

"You did."

"Sorry," he grinned with embarrassment, "I'm forgetful sometimes."

"It's okay." I hid my smile through a sip of wine, sitting back awkwardly in my seat.

I wasn't good at this. I forgot what first dates were like. I had a long list of casual questions in the back of my head that I'd thought of earlier in case the conversation seemed to dry out, but now that Mitch was actually in front of me, my mind was completely blank.

"So, tell me more about you," he requested. "Do you have any hobbies or interests? Do any sports growing up?"

I was glad he couldn't see me fidgeting with the cloth napkin on my lap. "I, uh, tried a little bit of everything growing up. Horseback riding, swimming, ballet... but nothing really stuck. I'm an avid reader now though. How about you?"

"I pretty much grew up on a snowboard."

"No hockey?"

"Nah. It's fun to watch but I never really got into it myself," he answered.

Green flag.

I nodded along. "You said you're from Denver?"

"Yep!" he smiled proudly.

"Why'd you come to Cedar then?" I asked.

Other than wanting to avoid any awkward silence, I truly was interested in hearing about him. He had this friendly, inviting aura that none of my exes had. It was invigorating.

Mitch shrugged casually. "My older brother came here, so I kinda followed in his footsteps. You?"

Pass. I wish I hadn't asked in the first place.

"Just felt right," I said, leaving it at that.

"I know what you mean. My older brother definitely influenced my decision process, but I fell in love with the campus."

"Me too," I nodded.

"Oh! I've been meaning to ask you since I picked you up." He folded his hands on the table, leaning forward. "You live in the new apartments. How are they? Are they nice?"

I couldn't help but give a small cringe. "Yeah."

Mitch chuckled. "You don't sound too convincing."

I jumped to assure him, nervously smoothing out my hair. "Yeah, no! They are nice, for sure. My best friend and I are just... not the most fond of our other roommates." Immediately, a flash of regret ripped through me, feeling like I was disrespecting Lane when he'd been so sweet recently. "I mean," I hesitated, "they're alright, but..."

"Are they messy or something?"

"Well, it's a funny story actually."

"Let's hear it," he smiled.

Hesitation coated me again. There was a very good chance that telling him this story and admitting who my roommates were would make him run the opposite way. But

85

then again, any guy I was going to see over the next year of my lease was going to have to be okay with my living arrangement.

Nerves skated up my spine, and I found myself gripping onto the napkin like it was somehow supposed to calm me. "So, on move-in day, we went to move into our two-bedroom, and quickly realized that the leasing office fucked up and accidentally gave us a four-bedroom instead."

Eyes widening, he laughed once without humor. "Seriously? That's a pretty big fuckup on their part."

"I know... Except it was also kind of our faults because they had sent out a revised lease and none of us read through it to catch the change."

"Damn," he said in awe. "So, is there a specific reason you don't like the girls or?"

I bit the inside of my cheek. "They're actually not... girls."

Mitch let out a small gasp. "You got stuck living with two guys?"

"Yeah," I stiffly nodded.

"Wow. Who are they?"

Oh God. I was kind of hoping I could avoid name dropping but I didn't want to lie to his face, especially on our first date.

"Um," I stuttered, sipping my wine. "Lane Avery and Nicholas Crew."

His drink froze halfway to his mouth, and he stared at me for a moment like he was waiting for me to tell him I was joking.

"Everything okay?" I slowly let out.

He brought his drink home, slightly choking on it. "Yeah! Yeah, sorry, I just wasn't expecting you to say that."

I pretended to be oblivious, asking a question I already knew the answer to. Quite honestly, I was trying to get a better read of what he thought about them. "You know who they are?"

"Of course," he said. "Everyone knows who they are. Especially Lane. That kid is fucking incredible."

My stomach dipped like it would on a rollercoaster. Hearing his name, I missed Lane a little bit; I wondered what he was up to right now.

"Yeah," I agreed. "He's really good."

"Better than really good," Mitch nodded. "He's the best in the NCAA."

"So..." I stumbled again, "it doesn't weird you out at all? Like you're cool with it?"

His delicate chuckle helped me relax. He gave a small smile, eyes twinkling. "I mean, I'll admit, it is a little intimidating knowing they're your roommates, but if nothing's going on between you and them, then I don't really see a reason for me to not be cool with it."

Finally, I was able to let go of the napkin, resting my hands carefully on the table. "Okay good!"

The only thing was that I wasn't sure if I could promise there was nothing going on.

But with or without Mitch, I was damn set on pretending there wasn't.

Chapter Seventeen

Lane

Ten-thirty rolled around. Both Kota and Crew had turned in early, which I was assuming was because they refused to be in the living room at the same time, so they both retreated to their own bedrooms.

Now, it was just me. Sitting on the couch. Impatiently and dolefully waiting for Bridget to return.

I had some random movie on that I wasn't paying attention to. My mind was on a long loop of thoughts.

I couldn't get over this annoying jealousy that was gnawing at me. She seemed so excited earlier before she left, which made me feel kind of guilty for hoping she had a terrible time with the guy. I was also a little worried for her at the same time. She only met the guy once prior to tonight. What if he ended up being a creep? What if he ended up putting her in an uncomfortable situation and she needed an out? What if she tried calling for help?

I had my ringer on just in case.

More than anything though, I was confused. I obviously cared about her, so being protective of her was one thing. I would've felt concerned all the same if it had been Kota going on a date with someone she barely knew. But I couldn't pinpoint why I couldn't rid my jealousy. I was trying to brush it all off, to become indifferent and careless about the situation, but it seemed impossible to.

In an attempt to get my mind off it, I grabbed my phone and shot my mom a text, knowing she'd probably be awake right now due to her messy sleep schedule.

She was a secretary at a hospital and worked nightshifts, so whenever she wasn't working, she was often up pretty late.

Me: Are you coming to my game next week?

Mom: Not sure yet. I'll let you know.

With a shake of my head, I tossed my phone aside. I wasn't sure why I bothered asking in the first place, knowing the chances of her coming were slim to none.

When the apartment door finally opened, I nearly sprang off the couch, but managed to stay seated.

"Hey," I immediately said, noting the blank expression on Bridget's face, not giving any hint as to how it went.

"Hey," she said softly, kicking off her shoes and striding over.

I gulped as she walked towards me, attempting to keep my eyes on her face, but failing miserably. She looked just like I expected. Her boobs were pushed upwards, her romper skin-tight against them. The sway of her hips was easy to spot underneath the fabric and her hair sat in those perfect strawberry ringlets that I adored.

She sat beside me on the couch, and I kept my eyes forward, biting down on my lower lip. I let a moment pass before I spoke.

"How'd it go?" I asked, focusing a bit too hard on keeping my voice steady.

"Pretty good, actually," she said. I could spot her small smile out of the corner of my eye, and I could only hope she didn't catch my displeasure.

"That's good." I hated everything about this. I hated seeing her come home from a date with another guy. I hated seeing her dolled up like that, hoping to impress somebody else. I hated that the date went well. I felt a little guilty for not being supportive, but I couldn't help myself.

I fucking hated this.

She nodded shyly. "Do you have practice in the morning?"

"Sadly, yes."

She scrunched her face. "Doesn't sound fun."

I gave a faint smile. "Not at all." There was a cloud of awkwardness hanging in the air, the conversation feeling horribly dryer than the Sahara.

Bridget stood. "Well, I've got class in the morning, so I'm gonna head to bed. You should too."

"I will soon," I assured her.

Just before she strode down the hall, she stopped, placing her small hand on the wall as she turned back towards me. "Goodnight, Lane."

I took a deep breath, ignoring the fire that was sitting in my lungs. "Goodnight."

Chapter Eighteen

Lane

It was already Friday, which meant we only had four more practices until our first game of the season.

Crew and I were suiting up for practice in the locker room, and I could see him glance back and forth between his skate and me a couple times.

"Alright," he finally said, seated on the bench next to me. "What's the matter?"

I shrugged, avoiding eye contact with him as I tied my skate. "Nothing."

He narrowed his eyes in the slightest, tipping his head. "Don't fucking lie," he said. "You seem all glum."

Again, I avoided his gaze, but this time, I remained quiet with it.

"Is it Bridget?"

"I'm fine," I said sharply.

"Fine, my ass," he called out. I began tying my other skate, earning a sigh from Crew. His voice mellowed. "Look, I know this week has been hard for you watching her go out with whatever the fuck his name is, but either way, she's off-limits, remember?"

Seeing Bridget go out with Mitch not just once, but almost every night this week was making my jealousy slowly build up like a volcano that was on its way to an eruption.

"Yeah, yeah, I know," I responded with a bitter edge. "The rules."

"Exactly. So, I'll tell ya what," Crew replied, giving me a casual tap on the shoulder. "We're gonna go out tonight and we're gonna find you a girl."

I clenched my teeth together. "I don't want another girl," I grumbled, giving him a harsh side-eye.

His face twisted into a bewildered expression. "Damn, bro. You're down bad."

I rolled my eyes. "I told you, I'm fine."

"Fine, my *ass*," he repeated, growing agitated. "I'm not letting you mope around all night, waiting for her to come home again."

I let out a huff. "You're making me sound like a loser."

"Then quit acting like one," he demanded, standing. "It won't do you any good to stay home tonight. Let's just go out with the guys and blow off some steam."

I eyed him in thought; I hated knowing he was right. Since when the hell was Crew right about anything?

"Fine," I agreed.

"Good," he said with a light, satisfied grin. "Now wipe that sad ass look off your face and get your goddamn head in the game, captain."

***

We didn't even talk to the girls before leaving, so we had no idea what they were up to tonight. Crew practically dragged me out of the house before I had the chance to speak to either of them.

I guess it was for the best though.

The whole team didn't come out tonight, but we still had our closest friends out with us, which was pretty much all our old roommates. It didn't take much convincing to get them out.

We were hanging out by the dartboard and billiards tables in the far corner of the bar.

"What about that one?" Crew said with a nod, lightly licking his lips.

I glanced at the blonde he was referring to. She was pretty, but either way, I still turned to Crew with "No."

"Alright. What about her friend?"

"No."

"Goddammit, Lane," he said in frustration, throwing his hands up. "I've picked out almost every girl in this bar and you've said no to every single one."

I took a strained breath, my eyes on the door. "There's one you missed," I let out.

I could recognize Bridget's strawberry locks from here as she walked in, her hand glued to a guy's that I could only assume was Mitch.

He wasn't very tall, probably five-nine or five-ten, medium built. My jaw shifted, studying him as if I could shoot laser beams out my eyes and burn him.

"Uh oh," Crew muttered beside me.

The moment my stare shifted from Mitch to Bridget, the hardness in my gaze softened, annoyance replaced with a small dose of heartache.

Damn. I *was* down bad.

"Do you wanna go to a different bar?" Crew asked quietly.

"Nah," I said with a sigh. "I'm a big boy. I can handle it."

"Alright..." he said doubtfully. I didn't blame him though. I wouldn't believe me either; I wasn't convincing in the slightest. He gave me a nudge, prompting me to snap out of it. "Hey, just try to pretend they aren't here."

I nodded once, grabbing my beer off the table and gulping down half of it. We started to play a two-on-two game of pool. Cody and Crew versus Jett and me.

Jett and I were kicking ass when a familiar voice rang in my ears, causing me to freeze mid-shot.

"Hey, guys!" Bridget exclaimed. "I didn't know you were coming here tonight."

I finished the shot, completely missing from being so damn distracted. My head dropped, slightly relieved when Crew jumped to the rescue, responding so that I didn't have to.

"Didn't know you were coming here either," he accused her jokingly.

Gripping my pool stick like it was my lifeline, I stood off to the side as Cody took his shot. My eyes were wandering around aimlessly, doing everything possible not to make eye contact with Bridget.

"Whatever," Bridget responded lightheartedly.

"Here, you go," a guy said, causing me to snap my head over to take a peek.

Mitch had apparently just walked up and was handing Bridget a drink.

Crew and I exchanged glances. He seemingly winced for me.

I mouthed, "I'm fine."

"Silly me," Bridget said. "I forgot you guys haven't been introduced yet." She stood a bit too close to Mitch for my liking as she motioned to him with her free hand. "This is Mitch. Mitch, this is Crew and Lane."

Mitch nodded to us in acknowledgement with a stupid, friendly grin that I wanted to smack off. "Nice to meet you, guys."

"Nice to meet you," Crew muttered indifferently.

"Yeah," I said.

"Obviously, you guys are on the hockey team, right?" Mitch asked.

"Yep," Crew answered, turning his back on Mitch to take the next shot.

Mitch's eyes carried over to me. "First game next week?"

I followed Crew's lead. "Yep," I said, diverting my attention to the pool table.

"Who are you playing against?"

I let out a small groan, thankful that it was drowned out by the noise of the bar. I wasn't sure if it was the vibe that we didn't like Mitch or if it was the hockey talk that caused Jett to hop in on the conversation.

"North Dakota," he said dryly.

Mitch nodded casually. "They're supposed to be pretty good this year, right?"

Shut up and fuck off, I wanted to say.

He wasn't wrong though. North Dakota was always good, but they were said to be *really* good this year. Either way, it was that *he* was the one saying it that was bothering me.

"Yeah," Crew said, shooting Mitch a mean grin, "but we're better."

"I'm sure you guys will be fine," Bridget said, clueless to our disdain towards her new boy toy.

Immediately, some of my irritation drained away from the sound of her voice. And then I was distressed just knowing she had the ability to do that to me.

"Oh, don't you worry, Bridget," Jett said. "We'll be more than fine."

Bridget gave a friendly grin, casually stirring her straw in her drink. "I'm sure," she replied, taking a sip.

"Babe," Mitch said, "how's your drink?"

What did he just call her?

So, they went out for one week and were suddenly on a nickname basis?

I froze with my pool stick in one hand and my other hand gripping the edge of the table so hard that if it were a throat, preferably Mitch's, he'd probably be dead by now.

"Oh, it's good!" Bridget said. "I don't usually drink tequila, but I actually like this a lot. What is it again?"

"Tequila pineapple."

"Oh, yes, that explains it. I love pineapple." She smiled at him as she took another sip, this one a bit longer.

I watched her lips as they circled around the straw, sucking, and sucking, and sucking, until...

"The hell are you doing?" Crew yelled at me in a whisper.

I shook my head, snapping out of it. "Sorry."

He leaned in. "I can't help you if you're not willing to help yourself." He raised his brows at me and subtly tipped his head to the side a few times.

My line of sight followed to a girl a couple of tables over, her eyes on me. When I caught her, she quickly looked away, but I still caught the hot pink that swirled around in her cheeks.

I eyed her curiously for a minute, waiting to see if she looked back at me.

Some of her light brown hair was pulled back in a half-up, half-down hairstyle. Every time she laughed at something her friend said, one small dimple popped up. She was sort of reminding me of Bridget. They didn't look anything alike, but they had this same innocent vibe that radiated off them. I was pretty sure that was why I was still entertaining the thought.

But when I heard Mitch's bothersome voice again, my head inevitably turned that way.

"Do you wanna dance?" he asked Bridget, one hand on her waist.

"Sure!"

I watched in disgust as he swept her onto the dance floor, and the disgust only grew when she turned her backside towards him and started swaying her hips.

My hands tightened around the pool stick again and an overwhelming amount of envy clogged my throat.

Crew eyed me with both worry and curiosity. I knew exactly what was going through his mind, and for the first time tonight, I listened.

"Fucking take this," I said, shoving my pool stick at him and stomping past him.

"Atta boy!" he shouted after me as I made my way directly over to the cute girl at the table.

Chapter Nineteen

Bridget

The three tequila pineapples I had last night were fake friends. Two-faced bitches that liked me in the moment and decided to screw me over the next morning with a horrible hangover.

I was sitting on the couch, chugging Pedialyte with some old, low-budget sci-fi movie on that sucked pretty bad, but I didn't have enough energy to simply reach over and grab the remote to change it.

When I heard a door open from down the boy's hall, I didn't think anything of it until a girl's voice followed.

My brows came in for a moment, then when I realized it was probably just one of Crew's nightly conquests, I disregarded it once more.

Until the mystery girl appeared, followed by a shirtless Lane.

My mouth dropped wide open, and I snapped it shut, not wanting either of them to catch my expression.

The girl was quite pretty, walking by with her brown hair in a messy bun and a shy smile on her face. By the jeans and black top she had on, I assumed it was what she was wearing from the previous night. And considering I'd never seen her before and Lane hadn't mentioned any girls he was talking to, I could also assume he only met her last night.

I watched silently as Lane led her over to the door, and to my surprise, a small twinge of pain came over my chest.

I looked away, unsure of what the pain meant. After all, I liked Mitch a lot. I hadn't known him long, but we'd been spending a good amount of time together over the past week and I was enjoying every second of it. I wanted to continue hanging out with him and see where things went.

But why did the thought of Lane's hands on this girl drive me mad?

I mean, let's be real, if she spent the night, there was a pretty big chance they slept together.

Just that thought caused another pang within the walls of my chest.

I took a deep breath, finding it difficult to, as if there was a boulder sitting on top of me.

Lane and the girl murmured something to each other that I couldn't quite make out before he gave her a hug and she went on her way.

He closed the door behind her, and when he turned, he caught my gaze, holding it for a painful moment.

My mouth opened, about to attempt to take away the awkwardness in the air with small talk, but before I had the chance to get a word out, he hung his head and walked back into his room without saying a word.

Great. Was *he* avoiding *me* now?

I thought we got over this whole avoidance thing, but maybe all we did was switch roles.

***

I didn't see Lane again for another two hours. At this point, Kota was awake and had joined me on the couch. I filled her in on this morning, minus the way I was feeling about it, and she ate up the story like she was munching on scones at a tea party.

Lane was in the kitchen now, quietly making a protein shake.

Kota was watching him curiously, seemingly studying his every move. She turned to me. "You know," she whispered, "for someone who just got laid last night, he seems kinda sad."

I bobbed my head side to side, watching the way he was moving at a sloth's pace with tired eyes and a light frown.

"A little," I whispered back.

"Hey," Kota called out to Lane.

He didn't look at us as he dumped protein powder into his shake. "Hey."

She didn't hesitate as she spoke. "Heard you got laid last night."

I hit her on the shoulder. "Kota," I scolded quietly.

His voice didn't have the same friendly ring to it as it usually did. He sounded almost monotone, still unwilling to look at us. "Where'd you hear that?"

Kota glanced at me briefly, and I usually didn't support when she told little white lies, but I was thankful for this one.

"Crew," she said.

That immediately caught Lane's attention. His head raised just enough to look at us, his eyes full of skepticism. "Crew?"

"Yep," Kota nodded.

He dropped the scooper of the protein powder back in its container and pushed it away. "You're telling me that you and Crew had a conversation?"

I'd admit that Kota was usually a pretty good liar, but apparently the idea of having a conversation with Crew was so disturbing that she blew it.

"Yes..." she slowly let out, trying to keep her face from twisting into a look of revulsion.

Lane pressed his hands into the counter. "I don't buy it," he said. His eyes shifted over to me, and the second we made eye contact, his expression melted and there was a light crease that formed in his forehead.

His razor-sharp jaw shifted beneath his skin, and I sat there, watching him watching me.

"So, is it true?" Kota asked, oblivious to our unsaid tension.

Finally, he looked away, his eyes dropping down to his shake. The next words out of his mouth were like the lash of a whip.

"Yeah," he muttered, "it's true."

There was a sort of stinging in my throat, the same type you'd get when you woke up with a sore throat. I was tempted to get up and walk out of the room, but at the same time, it felt like I was glued to the couch.

"Then why do you seem so damn pouty?" Kota accused.

His brows slanted inwards. "I'm not pouty."

Kota gave him a cordial grin. "Dude, you're pouty."

"No, I'm not."

"Well, you're not smiley," she shot at him.

He sighed.

"Was it bad?"

"No," he said through his teeth. "Not at all."

Another fucking blow.

Why the hell was this conversation bothering me so much?

Lane's eyes were on me again, as if he was trying to read my expression. I was doing my best to keep the pain from showing on my face, but I wasn't sure how good of a job I was doing.

"Then what's the problem?" Kota said.

"Nothing," he responded as he finished making his shake. "I've gotta go to the gym. I'll see you guys later." He forced the conversation to come to an end as he grabbed his keys off the key holder we had on the wall by the front door. "Can you guys tell Crew to meet me there when he wakes up?"

We didn't even have the chance to respond before he was out the door.

"That was weird," Kota said.

"Very."

"I wonder what's up with him."

"Yeah."

Her head swung over to me. "Why do *you* seem all gloomy now?"

"I'm fine," I lied, forcing a small smile. "Just hungover, remember?"

"Oh yeah," she brushed it off.

A yawning Crew slumped down the hall. Kota kept her eyes on the TV, animosity immediately oozing off her just from his presence.

"Hey," I said casually.

"Hey," he said, grabbing a glass of water from the kitchen.

"Lane wants you to meet him at the gym."

"Yeah," he said, "he'll have to wait a bit. I need to piss and get dressed." He wandered off, sipping on his water all the way to the bathroom and closing the door behind him.

Within less than a minute, a high-pitched scream echoed throughout the apartment.

Kota and I looked at each other with wide eyes. Crew came running out of the bathroom, his face a bit pale and his eyes as wide as ours.

He spoke almost breathlessly. "What... the fuck... is in our bathroom?"

Kota and I exchanged another clueless glance. "What are you talking about?" I asked.

He looked as if he'd seen a ghost, struggling to get the words out. "There's a, uh... *thing* in the trash."

I raised a brow, jutting my chin out. "A what?"

"A girl thing," he said with disgust.

"Oh, Jesus," Kota rolled her eyes. "A tampon. Say the word, Crew. *Tampon*."

I could tell he was trying his best to scowl at her, but it looked like he might have been holding back tears. I twisted to look at Kota.

"What?" she shot at me. "I had to change it this morning while you were in the shower, and you wouldn't let me in."

I recoiled shyly into the couch. "I was shaving my legs."

Kota shrugged, turning back towards Crew. "So, I went into your guy's bathroom to change it. Big deal."

"Big deal?" Crew heaved. "Why didn't you flush it down the toilet?"

"You're not supposed to," Kota and I said in unison.

"Excuse me, what?" he said through a layer of repulsion.

"Yeah, it could clog the pipes," I explained.

He buried his head into his hands.

"Oh my gosh," Kota said, "don't cry about it. It was wrapped in toilet paper anyway. You couldn't even see it. The most you probably saw was the damn wrapper of the new one."

Crew looked at her with a blank expression, mouth propped open. He gagged through the words. "You wrapped your used tampon in toilet paper and threw it into our trash can?"

Kota's voice didn't waver in the slightest. "Yes." He put his hands behind his head, blowing out a long, stressed breath. "You live in an apartment with two girls," Kota said. "It's bound to happen."

"Well, it can happen in your bathroom. Not ours."

"You're a child," she spat at him.

"Shut up," he retaliated, letting out a huff as he turned on his heels and stomped away. He was back minutes later wearing a muscle tee and gym shorts, still huffing and puffing as he trampled out of the apartment.

Kota's gaze scanned the room and landed on me, and I instantly recognized that devious gleam in her eye. She gave a malicious grin.

I sighed. "What?"

"I just got an awesome idea."

"Oh God," I tipped my head back. "No."

"You haven't even heard it yet!"

"I don't need to hear it to know that it's probably not a good idea."

"C'mon," she pleaded, desperately grabbing my hand. "I just need your help."

"Ugh," I groaned. "What is it?"

And once again, that evil little smirk of hers grew.

Chapter Twenty

Bridget

"**B**," Kota said, voice sharp, "I'm telling you, this guy looks exactly like a golden retriever."

I sat on one of the kitchen stools as she made herself a sandwich. Brow lifting, I raised a hand and aimlessly dropped it on the kitchen island. "I don't know what you mean."

Her head shot over to look at me as if I were an idiot. "You know, the dog?"

"I know what a freaking golden retriever is," I said through a laugh. "But how does he look like one?"

She'd been giving me a long rant about her microbiology class for twenty-plus minutes now, going on and on about how much she hated her professor and how she was just assigned a project where her partner was an awkward, golden retriever-looking kid who was absolutely clueless.

"Do I need to spell it out for you?"

"Yes," I admitted.

She took a bite of her sandwich, washing it down with some juice. "Picture this," she said. "Long, shaggy blonde hair. Big brown eyes. Energetic as hell and follows you around like a lost puppy."

"Hah!" I let out. "Maybe he'll ask you out."

Her eyes darted up to me, wide and fearful. "He better not."

"How do you think Bobby would feel if you dumped him for a golden retriever?" I joked.

Her voice turned almost hostile. "Who knows? He still hasn't even asked me to be his fucking girlfriend."

I scoffed, shaking my head. "Still? It's been what—two months? What's he waiting for?"

She shrugged, speaking between bites. "No idea, but I'm starting to get frustrated."

"You should."

"Hey," a voice called, causing my heartbeat to triple.

I'd recognize that voice from anywhere.

Kota's sandwich stopped halfway to her mouth, and I froze before practically oozing into liquid on the floor at the sight of Lane and Crew appearing from down the hall, wearing crisp suits.

Lane was in a cobalt blue suit that miraculously matched his eyes and brown dress shoes, his hair slicked back, clean and enticing.

Crew was equally attractive at the moment, dressed in a black suit and dark purple tie. His hair was also gelled, pushing the front of his curls back. A dimple appeared as he gave an award-winning smirk, pleased by our reactions. "Well, don't drool over us," he said, fixing the cuff of his suit.

Kota's voice came out flustered, sounding like she was choking on air. "We're not drooling."

"Yeah, okay," Crew said.

Meanwhile, I was pretty sure I was drooling.

Lane was always handsome, even in the wee hours of the morning, but right now, he looked like a shiny little present that I wanted to unwrap.

I sat there, lust clouding my eyes as I imagined what was underneath the wrapping paper.

When Lane's beautiful blue irises glanced over at me, I knew he'd caught me staring, but I couldn't manage to look away. As if he could read my mind, a seductive grin popped up on his face, satisfied.

Things between us had still been kind of weird over the past few days. I wasn't entirely sure if he was avoiding me or not. He'd been awfully quiet and always seemed to find an excuse to leave the room if it was just the two of us. The only time he seemed to act fairly normal was if other people were in the room. But if he was avoiding me... why?

Nonetheless, that suit was getting to me. I wasn't ever immune to his boyish good looks or sapphire blue eyes, and I *especially* wasn't immune to it all while he was wearing a goddamn suit.

Stop staring. You like Mitch, I reminded myself.

"Are you guys coming to our game?" Crew asked.

Kota scoffed, but it seemed like she was doing everything in her power not to look at them, fumbling her hands around. "Why would we do that? We spend enough fucking time under the same roof as you two."

I smiled, turning to the boys. "We'll be there."

"Cool," Lane said.

"See ya," Crew said as the boys grabbed their hockey bags and headed out the door.

Kota let out a noise that sounded like a cross between a sadistic growl and a gratified moan. "Goddamn!" she shouted, hopping around as if the floor was made up of hot lava.

"What?"

"They look sexy as hell," she said. "Even Crew."

My brows skyrocketed to my hairline, mouth falling open.

"*Never* repeat that."

I raised my right hand. "You have my word."

Her mouth formed an O as she blew out a breath.

I changed the subject, attempting to get Lane out of my head. "Is Bobby going to the game?"

"Nah, he said he already has plans. Mitch?"

I shook my head. "No. He has his mom's birthday dinner."

"Lame," she said.

"I know. I'll probably see him tomorrow though."

She nodded, then the conversation took a turn, and she began telling me about all the terrible pranks she was planning to pull on Crew next.

The other day was bad enough. I was ashamed to say I had participated in Kota's evil plot, helping her hang dozens of tampons from Crew's bedroom ceiling. They were clean, of course, but he still wasn't a fan of the prank.

After an hour of me trying to talk her out of her future pranks and getting nowhere, we finally agreed that it was time to get ready for the game.

Our school colors were black and silver, so I threw on a black Stallions long-sleeve and some leggings, grabbing a small jacket since the arena was cold.

When I met Kota back out in the kitchen, she was wearing the same clothes as before, eyeing me with a suspicious look and her hands on her hips.

"Take that off," she ordered.

"Why?" I asked, looking down at my outfit.

"We're wearing something a little more... hockey-esque."

My brows furrowed. "What are you talking about?"

She kept her wicked smile plastered on as she walked backwards. She made it all the way to the laundry closet and in one swift movement, she shoved the doors open, revealing the boy's clean, black jerseys that they wore during away games.

I let out a single, humorless laugh. "Absolutely not."

"Oh, c'mon!" she urged. "Why not?"

"So many reasons," I shook my head.

"Name one."

"I could probably name five right off the top of my head."

She motioned for me to continue.

I sighed, using my fingers to count off each reason. "One, what if we ruin them or get them dirty or something? Two, they're going to be so ridiculously long on us that we'll be swimming in them and probably look stupid. Three, the boys are going to kill us. Four, people are going to give us weird ass looks. And five, the boys are going to kill us."

Kota didn't hesitate at all, her confidence not wavering in the slightest. "First, we won't get them dirty. They're black. Second, they'll probably look cute, like an oversized sweater type of vibe. Third, fuck the boys, no they won't. Fourth, I hope people do. And fifth, I'll kill them first."

I ran my hands over my face. "This is an awful idea. You do know you're the worst influence probably ever, right?"

"Don't act like you don't wanna know what it looks like on you."

Well, she got me there.

Kota's lips pulled into a playful smile, knowing she had me.

"Goddammit, Kota, fine."

"Yes!"

"But," I said, holding a finger up.

"But?"

"I'm wearing Lane's."

Her face scrunched together with the realization that that meant she'd have to wear Crew's. But within a few seconds, her expression switched to a sinful grin. "Actually, that's fine by me. Because I know damn well that it'll piss Crew off. And that's my favorite pastime."

Chapter Twenty-One

Lane

Finally. Gameday.

The energy and adrenaline in the locker-room were at an all-time high as everyone geared up.

Crew was grumbling some nonsense to himself next to me.

"What?" I asked sharply.

"Just pissed off still."

I sighed, "Crew, it was days ago. Get over it."

He was still bitching about the prank the girls pulled on him. Personally, I thought he was overreacting, but this was Crew we were talking about, so I guess the reaction was accurate.

"No," he said. "I hope you know it's going to fuel my rage on the ice."

"That's a good thing."

He shot me a look. "I also hope you know I meant it when I declared war."

I rolled my eyes. "You seemed fine towards them before we left the apartment."

"That's because I'm trying to catch Kota off guard," he said. "I can't let her know that I'm plotting."

"Well, count me out of your dumb war."

"What!" he shouted. "You're supposed to back me up!"

"I will not be participating in your prank wars."

Crew looked at me as if I'd just committed treason. "Are you kidding me? It's going to be two-on-one then!"

I stiffened, grabbing my hockey stick. "It is *not* two-on-one. Bridget said she didn't wanna be involved either, so you better leave her out of it."

The disdain on his face deepened. "Fine, I won't touch your precious little Bridget."

I shook my head, pretending like his words didn't bother me. "Oh, shut up."

I gave a final glance at my phone, checking my messages. I'd texted my mom last night to ask if she'd be coming today, and I was still waiting for her response. I knew my dad would be here, as always, but my mom's attendance was a wild card.

Mom: Sorry, I won't make it. Have a good game

Throwing my phone into my bag, I lightly shook my head. I wasn't sure why I'd expected her to come, knowing she hated coming to my games and pretty much loathed doing anything that supported me in any type of way.

For the past seven years, I'd been her least favorite person on the planet, and I knew it.

"Boys!" Coach called. The room grew quiet immediately, everyone turning. "Almost time to warm-up. Every single one of you needs to get your fucking head in the game. I shouldn't hear another damn conversation about anything besides this game."

"Yes, Coach," everyone agreed in unison.

"When you get back in here from warm-up, I want you to make sure you stay warm. We'll regather and your captain will say some words before we hit the ice for puck drop," Coach said, his eyes on me.

I nodded, swallowing the lump in my throat.

There was a lot of anticipation leading up to this game, along with a lot of hard work, sweat, and blood.

But especially the sweat.

We'd been getting worked like dogs since August, and that didn't even count the hours we were individually putting in on the off-season.

I was proud of my team already for their work ethic; I just hoped it all paid off tonight. This game was going to set the tone for the rest of the season, so getting the win was important.

When Coach gave us the signal, we headed out of the locker room, through the tunnel, and onto the ice.

The air was always electric during a home game, and the first of the season was no exception. The student section made up an entire side of the arena, and although it wasn't entirely full yet, it was on its way to getting there.

The ice felt good beneath me as we went through our warm-up routine, taking shots at Cody, who was our starting goalie.

I couldn't help but wonder if the girls were here. My adrenaline heightened at the thought of Bridget watching the game, watching *me*.

The image of her reaction when we walked into the kitchen lingered in my head. The way her eyes glazed over with lust. The way her throat dipped as she gulped. The way she seemed to tense up, focusing a little too hard on breathing.

I'd never be able to forget that image. And quite honestly, I wouldn't want to.

Maybe I should walk around the apartment in a suit more often, just for the hell of it.

After taking shots at Cody, I skated off to the side to get some stretching in, which may or may not have been an excuse to check the student section for the girls.

It didn't take long to find them. They were sitting in the front row, right behind the glass. But it wasn't their convenient location that caught my eye. It was what they were wearing.

I did a double take, seeing the numbers *1* and *18*.

Were those...?

110

I could hear Kota yelling through the glass. "Hi, Lane!"

I let out a chuckle in disbelief. When my eyes landed on Bridget, a rush of air left my mouth. She was wearing my jersey, my number and last name sprawled across the back for everyone to see.

I liked how it looked on her. Long, oversized. The darkness of the jersey was making her hair color stand out, and underneath the fluorescent lights, she was glowing.

I could tell by her apologetic smile that none of this was her idea, but even if it was, she wouldn't need to apologize.

I wasn't mad that she was wearing it.

I sort of just wished she was wearing it for another reason.

Crew skated up, not stopping until he bumped into me. I gave him a light push back, but he ignored it.

He didn't bother looking at me as he spoke. "Are those our fucking jerseys?"

"Looks like it."

His jaw came unhinged, so much so that it was noticeable underneath his helmet. I could see his cheeks flush with anger as he went right up to the glass. He lifted a fist and banged against it. "Take my fucking jersey off, Kota!"

Kota held a malevolently pleased gleam in her eye. She blew a bubble of pink bubblegum, holding it there while she brought up not one, but two middle fingers. If that didn't make the most perfect sticker in the world, I wasn't sure what would.

I started cracking up, earning a sharp glare from Crew. His eyes were blazing. He was already a bit fired up in the locker room. Now he was practically engulfed in flames.

"This isn't funny! She's gonna get her germs all over it!" he shouted.

I glanced across the rink at North Dakota warming up, and I leaned in close to Crew. "Look, we can deal with this later. Right now, we have a game to play."

His fiery eyes glanced at our opponents for a second. Reluctantly, he nodded before skating off.

I gave one last look at the girls, my eyes staying on Bridget for a moment too long as my lips lifted into a light grin. I took a mental snapshot of her, smitten by the view.

And all at once, I let out a deep breath, skating away.

Chapter Twenty-Two

Bridget

The start of the hockey games were always the best part.

Right before our players came out, they killed the lights, the only source of light being the kick-ass hockey reel they threw together to pump up the student section— and pumped us up, it did.

Everyone was extra loud and rowdy for the first home game of the season.

Kota and I got here early to make sure we got good seats, so we were happy to be right against the glass.

The tunnel was directly across from us, and right as the hockey reel ended, strobe lights lit up the tunnel, accompanied by a cloud of fog.

A little dramatic for an entrance if you asked me, but I'd be lying if I said I didn't like it.

The boys took the ice one by one, skating in a huge circle around the home side, filing into a long line in front of the goal.

The announcer blared over the speakers, and that was everyone's cue. Every person in the student section turned away from the rink, a sheer sign of disrespect as they began announcing the opposing team's starting lineup.

Year after year, the NCAA awarded our school with having the best student section in the country. But not just for outperforming every other school with attendance. We screamed some pretty rude and obscene things, which usually did the trick to get inside the opponent's heads.

I rocked on my heels as the announcer began speaking. "At left wing, number seventeen, Mac Eisher."

The entire student section responded as one. "Who cares? You suck, bitch!"

"At center, number forty-nine, Hugh Bardot."

"Who cares? You suck, bitch!"

"At right wing, number eleven, Wilson Taylor."

"Who cares? You suck, bitch!"

They went through the whole lineup, and we responded ruthlessly after each one. As usual, they saved the coaches for last, and just like with their players, we gave them an equal amount of disrespect.

"They suck too!" we finished, turning back around with hoots and hollers.

The boys were still standing in line, most of them shifting their weight with anticipation.

"And now," the announcer said, "it's time to meet your Cedar University Stallions!"

Everyone exploded in cheers, including Kota and me. But a small surge of butterflies flew around in my belly, waiting for Lane's name to be called.

Left defenseman. Number seven. Matt Gallagher.

Right defenseman. Number thirty. TJ Douglas.

Left wing. Number twenty-five. Jett Jameson.

Right wing. Number eighteen. Nicholas Crew.

Goalie. Number fourteen. Cody Holtz.

Center. *And captain.* Number one. Lane Avery.

All the players got situated, retreating to their starting positions. And the moment the puck dropped, both teams were playing for blood.

The puck was moving at an impossible speed around the ice, propelling back and forth between teams for the first few minutes of the game.

It was hard taking my eyes off Lane, and every time his line went to the bench, I found myself disappointed.

But when they were on the ice, which was most of the time, I was in awe. Every move they made was done with so much purpose and precision that it looked like the game was staged.

With a failed shot on goal from North Dakota, the puck was swooped away by Crew, breaking out of the cluster of bodies and hurdling towards North Dakota's net, where a defenseman was ready and waiting.

With zero fucks given, Crew's shoulder noticeably stiffened before ramming into the guy, sending him flat on his back.

At first, I was waiting for a whistle to be blown, for the refs to throw Crew into the penalty box, but apparently the hit was clean.

With two green jerseys on his ass, Crew carefully sent the puck far across the rink to Lane, who snatched it so quickly that I was struggling to keep up.

As if he was the only one on the ice, he effortlessly skated behind the net, sneaking the puck into the goal as he rounded the other side.

The buzzer sounded, and every Stallions fan shot to their feet.

"With your first Stallion goal of the season," the announcer exclaimed, "Lane Avery with an assist from Nicholas Crew!"

"Wow!" I cheered. "Those are our roommates!"

"Sadly," Kota smirked.

"Oh, c'mon. It's kinda cool."

She made a face. "Kinda. But I'd never tell them that."

I rolled my eyes before grabbing her by the sleeve of Crew's jersey. "Oh! Number four!"

I read the back of his jersey as the new North Dakota player took the ice. *Martin. Number four.*

Poor guy. He had no idea what he was in for.

"It's only a matter of time now," Kota said.

And that "matter of time" happened to be thirty seconds.

"Four's a bitch! Four's a bitch! Four's a bitch!"

There was no reasoning behind the chant, other than simply harassing our opponents. The chant was probably half my age, but everyone loved it, and it was bound to last far beyond our years. It was nothing personal; the guy hadn't done anything to be singled out other than choose the wrong number.

Within another five minutes of playing time, there was another goal scored by TJ. Either North Dakota wasn't as good as people thought they'd be, or the boys were just better.

Either way, I was enjoying the game. Maybe even a little too much.

Chapter Twenty-Three

Lane

I'd been awake since six am, staring at my ceiling. I'd probably gotten a solid two and a half hours of sleep. I hadn't really been expecting to sleep well though. I never did on the night prior to today.

After last night's win, I went straight home, locked myself in my bedroom, and hadn't come out since.

Luckily, it was a Sunday, which meant I could lay in bed all day without worrying about any responsibilities other than grieving and wallowing in my guilt.

My phone buzzed beside me, and I closed my eyes for a moment, dreading looking at the screen. I blew out a painful breath, feeling like fire was leaving my lungs as I reached over and grabbed my phone, giving it a single glance.

Dad: Happy birthday, son! Love you

Mom: Happy birthday

I could feel her hatred through the text as if it were seeping out of the phone like battery acid.

The realization never got any easier.

My mother hated me.

She wasn't the only one though. I also hated myself most of the time. On this day especially though.

I dropped my phone, squeezing my eyes shut as I rolled onto my side.

But I immediately regretted it.

The first thing my eyes landed on was the framed photo of my brother and me that I always kept on my nightstand. There was never a time where it didn't hurt to look at it, but the pain was amplified today.

We would've been twenty-two.

He would've been twenty-two.

But he would forever be fifteen because of me.

My throat tightened and a breath got caught in my chest. It felt like I was choking.

I wished I was.

Chapter Twenty-Four

Bridget

Kota and I were making breakfast for ourselves, and Crew was sprawled out on the couch, watching a hockey game from the previous night.

I glanced at the clock. It was already close to eleven.

"Hey," I said to Crew from the kitchen, "where's Lane at? He's usually up by now and I haven't seen him since last night."

"Yeah, um," he spoke quietly, "you probably won't be seeing him today."

Kota and I traded curious, yet worried glances. "Why?" I asked.

He took a deep breath, his mouth falling into a long frown. "Well..."

My heart started beating a little harder, a small jackhammer against my chest. Was everything okay? Did something happen?

"Crew?" I pushed.

Crew stood, roaming into the kitchen. He leaned over the island, his voice dropping to a whisper. "Don't make a big deal about it or say anything, okay? Trust me."

Kota spoke warily. "Is he alright?"

Crew glanced down the hall, giving a slight gulp. "It's his birthday—"

"It's his *birthday*?" I practically shouted.

Crew was quick to hush me. "Shh!" he hissed. "Keep it down."

"Why?" Kota challenged.

His mouth alternated between a tight line and a frown, contemplating what more to say. "Just trust me."

"Why would we trust *you*?" Kota spat.

Crew rolled his eyes, turning his attention to me. "Trust me. Just let him be today."

"But if it's his birthday, we should do something nice for him," I said.

"Oh!" Kota squealed. "Let's bake him a cake."

"That's a horrible idea," Crew said, his jaw twitching. "That's the complete opposite of what I just told you to do, and he doesn't like cake anyway."

Kota made a face. "Who doesn't like cake?"

Crew tipped his head, his eyes closing with annoyance. "Just fucking listen to me. I've known him for years. He wants to be left alone."

"But why?" I wondered. "Why doesn't he like his birthday?"

Crew sighed, his stone-like stance softening. "He just doesn't, okay? Trust me," he repeated before pushing himself away from the island and into his bedroom.

Kota and I stood in silence. I bit my lip, letting a deep exhale out my nose as I flipped my French toast over.

Curiosity was gnawing at me, but empathy was gnawing harder. I wasn't sure why Lane didn't like his birthday, but the thought of him spending the day upset and secluded made me a little sad.

"Alright," Kota muttered across the kitchen.

"Alright what?"

"We're baking him a freaking cake."

***

120

Two hours later, the kitchen was covered in flour and sugar. The mess didn't stop there though. Kota and I were also covered. We looked like we'd just raided a crime lab and came out of it coated in cocaine.

The good news was that the cake was done and looked nice. Well, for the most part at least. We tried writing on it in frosting, but Kota messed up the spacing of the letters and ran out of room halfway through it, so instead of saying *Happy birthday,* it just said *Happy birth.*

"Looks good," I said, nodding.

Kota raised a brow. "Don't lie to me."

I winced lightly. "Hey, it's the thought that counts. Plus, as long as it tastes good, then who cares?"

"You're right," she picked it up. "Ready?"

I nodded, following behind her.

Crew was still in his room, so we tried to stay quiet, tiptoeing down the hall.

Apparently, we weren't quiet enough though.

His bedroom door swung open. "What the hell are you guys doing?" I swore that kid had magic hearing. Kota and I sank back a little, sheepish looks overcoming our faces. Crew's eyes drifted down to the cake in Kota's hands. "Jesus," he said, shaking his head.

Kota's spine straightened as she regained her confidence. "We're giving him his cake," she said, stepping forward.

Crew leapt in front of her, bringing a hand up. "No," he whispered, then sighed. "Let me."

We stood back as Crew took the few remaining steps to Lane's door. He tapped the door with the back of his hand. "Hey, man. You wanna open up?"

There was a beat of silence before Lane responded loudly. "You should know better than to knock on my door today."

Crew turned back towards us with a single brow raised, his facial expression screaming *I told you so.*

Shyly, I brought my hand up. "Can I?"

He gave a light scoff. "Be my guest," he shrugged. "But if he won't open it for me, I doubt he'll open it for you."

I wasn't sure what gave me the confidence to step forward. Nervousness ricocheted around the inside of my stomach.

I brought my hand up, knocking so lightly that it sounded like a feather against the door. "Lane? It's Bridget."

Silence. Followed by rustling. Followed by the door slowly opening.

Lane's head was facing the floor. He slowly looked up at me with haunted eyes.

My mouth lightly parted as I gasped under my breath. I could feel the melancholy wafting from him like he just showered in it.

"Hi," I forced out.

His voice came out scratchy. "Hi."

"What the fuck?" Crew called out from behind me. "So, you open the door for her but not for me?"

Lane's eyes stayed glue to me as he raised a middle finger towards Crew.

Kota hopped forward with no hesitation. "We made you a cake!"

"Oh," Lane said.

"I told you he doesn't like cake," Crew butted in again.

I looked up at Lane from under my lashes with shy eyes. The corners of his mouth twitched in the slightest. "I'll try it," he said.

"Yay!" Kota squealed, pushing it towards him.

His brows came in. "Happy birth?"

"It's the thought that counts," she sighed.

***

Lane didn't like the cake.

After five minutes of watching him try to force feed it to himself just to make Kota and me happy, we finally told him to stop.

Now the four of us were standing around in the kitchen, hanging out.

122

"You know," Lane said, "today hasn't been that bad so far."

"And why is that?" I asked.

He nodded towards Crew and Kota. "Because those two have gone a full hour in the same room without trying to kill each other."

Crew and Kota's heads snapped towards each other, both sets of eyes narrowing.

"I can stir up something good if you want," Kota said.

"No thanks," Lane and I said in unison before giving each other matching smiles.

As Kota took her Oreos out of the cabinet, Crew let out a suspicious giggle, looking like he knew something we didn't. His laughter grew a little louder.

"Shut up," Kota spat at him. "I hate when you make noise."

Crew shrugged quietly, his questionable smirk still resting on his face. He watched with enjoyment as Kota stuck an Oreo in her mouth, chewed on it for a second, then gagged and swung around, spitting it into the sink.

"Why the fuck do these taste like ass!" she screeched.

Crew's voice was steadier than ever as he responded. "Maybe because I replaced the filling with toothpaste."

Kota spun around with malice. There was still chocolate in her teeth as she spoke with a tight jaw, breathing heavily. "You what?"

He shrugged again, nonchalantly. "I told you I was gonna get you back."

"Apparently, I spoke too soon," Lane said.

I let a sigh escape. "One of them is probably going to end up dead by the time we move outta here."

Lane leaned towards me, keeping his eyes on our wacko roommates. "I've got money on Crew."

"To die or to survive?"

He scoffed as if the answer was obvious. "To die, duh."

"I'm not taking that bet," I said, glancing at him. His blue eyes were already on me, and the longer I looked at them, the more they seemed to deepen. Lust and desperation formed a

123

lethal mix in my bloodstream, and the only thing that forced my mind out of the trance was the ire in Kota's voice.

I could see her chest expanding with deep, ragged breaths. "You have no idea what you just started."

Crew leaned over the kitchen island with a grin. "Oh, but I do."

She shook her head at him. "I'm going to make your life a living hell."

"Good luck," he challenged. "This is war."

Both of them glanced over at us at the same time and I held my hands up. "Don't look at us."

"Yeah," Lane added, "we both already said before we don't wanna be involved."

Crew's jaw tightened as he eyed his best friend with betrayal. "Fine," he said firmly. "One-on-one then."

Kota's infamous smirk of sin appeared. "Fine."

"Can you at least pretend not to hate each other for the rest of the day?" Lane asked.

"That's nearly an impossible task," Kota murmured, tossing the rest of her Oreos in the trash.

Crew painted on a phony smile. "I'll try my absolute best, just for you, buddy. Because I care," he said, twisting towards Kota. "Unlike *some* people."

"Hey!" she barked, her brows nearly touching. "I care! I'm the one that baked him a cake!"

"Um," I butted in, "I also helped." Like normal, the two started going at it, completely ignoring Lane and me. We gave matching sighs, turning towards each other.

"Well," he said, "I tried."

I giggled. "It's the thought that counts," I repeated for probably the tenth time today.

"Speaking of which," he said, shifting slightly towards me, "thank you for the cake."

"You're welcome. I'm sorry you didn't like it."

He shook his head, grinning. "I just don't like cake in general."

I raised a skeptical brow. "Any cake?"

"Any cake."

"Cupcakes?"

"Eh," he said. "They're alright."

"Well, what's the difference between cake and cupcakes?"

He shrugged. "They taste different."

"No, they don't."

"Uh, yeah they do."

"How?"

"I dunno. They just do."

I opened my mouth to respond with a snide comment, but I blew out a tense breath instead. "We're turning into them."

Lane and I gave a glance at Crew and Kota, still arguing, per usual.

"Yeah?" Crew spewed. "Why don't you take that smartass mouth of yours and run all the way back to Boobie with it?"

Kota smacked a hand down on the counter. "His name is *Bobby*."

"Same thing!"

Lane let out a laugh. "Geez."

I shook my head with a smile. At this point, Lane and I had learned that once the arguing started, there wasn't much either of us could do to stop it. I wasn't going to lie, though. Sometimes, they were entertaining to watch. It was like watching a live episode of *The Bachelor*.

"Anyway," I turned back towards Lane, "what are you up to for the rest of the day?"

"Um," he shifted on his stool, his words halting. It was as if he'd forgotten it was his birthday and I'd just reminded him. I still wasn't sure why he hated today so much, but as much as I wanted to know, I wasn't going to pry. If he wanted to tell me, he would on his own terms. "I don't really have anything planned," he finally finished. "How 'bout you?"

"I'm supposed to see Mitch later."

He gave a tense nod. I stared at him, noticing the way he'd gone from okay to upset to sullen all in the matter of a few minutes.

I wasn't sure why, but I didn't like seeing him that way. I wanted the optimistic, happy-go-lucky Lane back. The vibes between us had been so strange over the past few weeks and it finally felt like we'd been making some progress today.

Originally, I planned on staying as far away from Lane as possible. But since I was seeing someone else now, I didn't have to worry about falling for him, right? I was safe from any possible heartbreak coming from him, so there was no need to run from our friendship any longer... Right?

I found myself responding without a second thought. "I can reschedule with him."

I pretended not to notice the spark that raced up my spine when he gave a small smile. It felt like he was pulling me into his orbit, and I couldn't resist gravity.

Let's face it though. With or without gravity, I was screwed.

Chapter Twenty-Five

Bridget

The dishes were piling up, and although I was pretty sure most of them were Crew's, I was running out of patience to wait for him to do them.

He left twenty minutes ago to head to some girl's house that he met the other night, which meant he'd probably be gone awhile.

I took the chore upon myself to do; I would've made Kota help me had she not done the dishes yesterday.

Some sports channel was on the TV, untouched after Crew's departure. Since my back was to the living room, I wasn't sure what Kota was doing that distracted her enough not to change it, but I was about to ask her to turn it off and play some music instead when the sound of Lane's name carried into the kitchen.

Briskly, I shut the water off, grabbing a rag to dry my hands. "Turn that up."

Kota tossed her phone aside, raising the TV's volume before leaning forward with sudden interest.

Two sports reporters were discussing the current status of NCAA men's hockey, and apparently, the current topic was Lane.

"Lane Avery has lit the NCAA on fire since the moment he stepped foot at Cedar. Last season, he led the nation in points, racking up fifty-five points throughout the season, and by the looks of it, Hank, I have no doubt he'll meet that again or surpass it."

Highlights of Lane from his most previous game came on the screen, one after another as the reporters continued their conversation.

"I agree, Rick. I think he's one of the most solid players we've seen in the history of college hockey. Not only does he put up incredible numbers, but he's so consistent in his game, so precise, and so..."

Kota and I started shouting over the TV. "Lane! Lane! Lane, come here!"

Heavy footsteps shook the floorboards, and Lane appeared in a sweat, a hockey stick in hand. His muscles were taut, ready for action. I hadn't expected him to run out with no shirt on and gym shorts that hung dangerously low on his hips; I nearly choked on air, my eyes settling on the V that met his waistline. I'd forgotten how impeccable the ridges spread across his stomach were, and I found myself lost in a fantasy of what they felt like. *Or tasted like.* He was so flawless that it would probably make the hottest male model on Earth jealous.

"What? What?" he spun, eyes darting around the apartment.

Kota blinked at him with a stout frown. "What the hell are you doing?"

"I thought you guys were in trouble."

"So, you grabbed a hockey stick?"

He looked at her with a face that said *Yeah, what of it?*

"And go put clothes on," Kota judged. "No one wants to see that."

I wanna see it.

Lane's sigh had a raspy ring to it. "What's wrong?"

"Nothing's wrong, Lane," I said. "Look! You're on TV!"

"It would be an absolute loss for the hockey world if we did not see Lane Avery in an NHL jersey at the end of his career," one of the reporters said.

128

"I'm surprised he's not in an NHL jersey already."

"I think a lot of people have had that same thought, Rick."

"He didn't enter the draft when he was age-eligible, and unfortunately, no one knows why."

"It's a—"

"Alright," Lane jumped forward, snagging the remote with a tight grip. "That's enough of that," he said, turning it off.

"Lane!" we whined.

"Why'd you turn it off?" I asked.

"Yeah," Kota pouted, "we wanted to listen to them talk about how cool you are."

"I'm not cool," he uttered under his breath.

Repositioning herself on the couch, Kota's expression softened. "Lane! You are cool. You need to hype yourself up more."

His gaze circled over to me, and as a pompous smirk flickered on his face, I realized why.

I hadn't stopped staring at him.

With smoldering eyes, his gaze scanned me over, the same way he had when we first moved in. I guess I hadn't realized until now that I missed the feeling.

"I'll be in my room," he announced.

I watched him swivel around, and I cursed every step he made that took him farther and farther away.

When I forced myself to go back to cleaning, not only was I still daydreaming about Lane's intrusive gaze, but I was also stuck on the question— If Lane was good enough for the NHL already, why wasn't he there?

Chapter Twenty-Six

Bridget

Cedar was never my first choice.

If I was being honest, Minnesota Duluth was my first choice. They had a great English Literature program and all my friends from high school were going there.

But there was one factor and one factor only that made me decide to go to Cedar.

My mom.

Not my adoptive mom, but my biological mom.

I'd never met her before, but I wanted to. Ever since my senior year of high school, I'd been doing my best to find her. It probably would've been a faster process had I hired an investigator, but I didn't have the money for that, and I also didn't want my parents knowing.

I loved my parents a lot. They were wonderful parents and gave me everything I needed growing up. But I wanted to know where and who I came from. I wanted to know why I was given up, and why my birth parents never tried finding me, or if they *had* tried finding me, but just never succeeded.

For nearly four years, my parents tried to have a child. They visited specialist after specialist, and nothing ever worked for them. That's when they decided to adopt. I was only a few months old when they adopted me, and I became their world.

But six years later, my mother remarkably conceived, and my sister Bianca was born.

I knew my parents loved me, but Bianca was their miracle baby, and regardless of what they said, I knew they loved her more.

Either way, I was afraid my mother's feelings would be hurt if she knew how badly I wanted to find my birth mom.

I sat in a café, staring at my computer and sipping on my coffee. I could feel how close I was to finding her.

Growing up, all I knew was that I was born on April fifth at Jefferson Memorial Hospital, which was thirty minutes away from Cedar's main campus.

After years of insane internet sleuthing and going through as many public records as possible, I'd narrowed my search down to a few different names of potential women that could've been my mother.

But I'd been at a standstill for months now.

I'd already tried numerous different reunion websites and although they helped a lot of people find their families, none of them had worked for me.

Kota sat across from me, scribbling down in her notebook. She sighed, "I need a goddamn break."

I didn't respond, eyes locked in on my computer screen.

"Are you doing homework or sleuthing?"

"Sleuthing," I answered.

"Find anything new?"

"Nope," I muttered with disappointment. "Not in months." I rested my elbows on the table, dropping my head into my hands.

"Don't give up, B," she said. "You're so close."

"I *am* so close. And that's what's so frustrating."

She tipped her head, eyeing me with sympathy. "You know," she said, tapping her pink fingernails on the table, "why don't you just take one of those DNA test things?"

My head shot up at her. "What?"

"Yeah, like one of those DNA tests you can order? I did it once when I was younger just to see what ethnicities I got from my dad's side and a bunch of relatives came up as matches."

I stared at her with a blank expression, completely baffled with both her and myself.

"How the hell did I never think of that?" I asked.

She shrugged. "I dunno."

"Why didn't you give me this idea years ago!" I shrieked, typing angrily into my search bar.

"I don't know. I just thought of it now."

"Well, you may be a genius," I said.

"*May* be?" she shot back. "I am."

"Mhmm," I hummed, looking over the search results. "Goddamn, these are kinda expensive."

She winced lightly. "I know. It's like a hundred bucks just for them to look at your spit."

I blew out a strained breath. "Oh well," I muttered, hitting the order button and putting in my card information.

After a few minutes of silence, I looked up at Kota with worried eyes, my words coming out slightly louder than a whisper. "What if she doesn't want to know me, though?"

Kota had always had a tough exterior. But if you knew her as well as I knew her, you'd know that her tough exterior was just that— *an exterior.*

She only let that wall down for very few people in the world, and luckily, as her best friend, I was one of them.

Kota let out a small sigh, gripping my hand across the table. "We don't know the circumstances of anything just yet. So, don't make yourself sick worrying about it." I gave a small nod as she pulled away. "And plus," she added, her steel armor returning, "if that's the case, then she's a bitch anyway."

I snorted, shaking my head.

She shrugged, "I said what I said."

Slowly, I shut my computer. "Do you wanna have a movie night tonight?"

"Sure," she said. "What movie?"

I gave a sly grin, and the second Kota caught it, hers appeared, matching mine as she read my mind with ease.

"Oh, definitely," she agreed.

Chapter Twenty-Seven

Lane

After one of the roughest practices of our lives, Crew and I walked down the hall to our apartment in utter silence. We had no energy to even speak.

We had an away game next week against our rivals, St. Cloud State, and Coach Palmer was not taking it easy on us in the slightest.

Our practices were typically only in the mornings, but since Coach was so fired up about this upcoming game, he demanded we fit in two practices today since we didn't have practice over the weekend.

My body felt like a brick, heavy and fucking lifeless. I was pretty sure I had at least one gnarly bruise on each portion of my body. Not to mention how sore I already was, which meant I would feel even worse in the morning.

"That was brutal," Crew murmured as my heavy hand took it's time opening the apartment door.

"Tell me about it."

Crew and I stood still in the doorway, taking in the scene before us.

Bridget was standing on the couch, holding her hands up beside her head as if she was about to swing a bat. Kota was running around the room like a lunatic, moving her arms in front of her like a robot.

"What the fuck is going on here?" Crew exclaimed.

"It's *Twilight* night!" Bridget shouted, her eyes stuck on the TV.

Kota responded as she zipped past us. "We're reenacting the baseball scene!"

Crew covered his eyes. "What the fuck."

"First *The Bachelor* and now *Twilight*?" I raised a brow.

"This place is the fucking worst," Crew muttered, pouring a glass of water. "I'll be in my room. No one talk to me."

Bridget finally plopped down on the couch, making a face. "Damn. He seems grouchier than normal."

"Rough practice," I said, dragging myself into the living room.

"Ah," she nodded.

"You guys going out tonight?" Kota asked, catching her breath.

I shook my head. "Absolutely not."

"Too tired?" Bridget's sweet voice asked.

"Yes," I replied, collapsing onto the couch and immediately closing my eyes as if it were an instinct. I kept my eyes shut as I spoke, not having the energy to open them in the slightest. "Are you guys going out?"

I could hear Bridget respond. "Nah."

"Maybe we should, B!" Kota said. "We haven't had a girl's night out since... well, since we met our dingbat roommates."

"Hey," I chided softly.

They both ignored me. "I guess I'd be down to go out," Bridget said.

"Yay!" Kota squealed, making my head pound from the noise. "This means no inviting the boys."

"Damn," I muttered. "No invite for us?"

Even though my eyes were closed, I could tell Kota was rolling hers just by the tone of her voice. "Not you. I meant Mitch and Bobby."

I could make out the slight trace of disappointment in Bridget's voice as she responded, and even though I was practically half-asleep at this point, *her* disappointment caused *me* to be disappointed. Because I hated knowing that she wanted him there. "Fine," Bridget said.

"And it's pitcher night at Campus Tavern!" Kota announced. "We can start off there and then walk over to Stallions after."

That caused me to spring up, eyes shooting open. "Hell no," I said.

Bridget seemed taken aback, her mouth slightly parted open. "What?"

"You guys are not walking by yourselves."

Kota shrugged. "It's only a few blocks."

"I don't care," I shot at her. "I'm not letting you guys walk." I sank back into the couch, my eyes inevitably on Bridget. "Call me when you're ready to switch bars and I'll come pick you up and take you."

The girls traded glances. I watched Bridget tug on the ends of her hair for a moment before ultimately nodding.

***

I wanted to sleep more than anything. My body hurt. My eyes were struggling to stay open. My brain was seemingly turned off at the moment.

But I couldn't sleep yet. Not until I knew the girls were fine.

So, the next best thing? Force Crew to stay awake with me.

I bribed him with a case of beer and his favorite movie— *The Terminator.*

It was a good thing we'd gotten another couch because we wouldn't have fit on the same one, considering we were each sprawled out with ice packs all over our bodies.

136

In reality, it was only eleven o'clock, but it felt like one in the morning. I could only hope the girls weren't going to be out late.

Meanwhile, Crew's phone was blowing up, buzzing on the coffee table every twenty seconds.

"Are you gonna get that?" I finally mumbled.

"Nope."

"Who is it?"

"Probably Sandra."

"Who?"

All I got back was a meaningless shrug.

Of course. I wasn't even sure why I still asked at this point.

"You gonna invite her over?" I asked.

"Definitely not," he said. "I don't have the energy to fuck."

I let out a snort. When my own phone lit up beside me, I reached for it so fast that I winced, my body refusing to move that quickly.

Kota: We're ready to switch

I squeezed my eyes shut as I carefully pushed myself up. My phone buzzed once again.

Bridget: Are you sure you want to drive us? Really, we can walk

I let out a small chuckle at how sweet and shy Bridget came off even over text. It was almost comical how different her and Kota were in every type of way.

"You wanna come with me?" I asked Crew, slowly standing as I tried to hold back another wince.

"Where?"

"I gotta pick the girls up and take them to Stallions."

He let out a single, dull laugh, looking at me with disbelief. "You want me to be in a small, confined space with Kota for *fun*?"

I gave a light roll of my eyes. "Really?"

"Alright, let me rephrase that," he offered, sluggishly pushing himself onto his elbows. "You want me to be in a small, confined space with Kota by *choice*?"

I sneered at him in silence, causing him to respond to his own question.

"Well, the answer is no. I do not want to come with," he said, lying back down. "We'll hang when you get back from your ride with the she-devil."

I sighed, shaking my head as I slipped my shoes on. "A child," I muttered to myself as I made my way out the door.

I wasn't going to lie; I wasn't thrilled about driving them. But it had less to do with them and more to do with myself.

I didn't like driving if other people were in the car. There was a huge weight of responsibility that came with it, and I really only did it if it was necessary.

And tonight, there wasn't a choice. I refused to let the girls walk at night by themselves.

I buckled my seatbelt, trying to rid my aching anxiety, and with a shaky breath, I started the car.

Chapter Twenty-Eight

Bridget

I was convinced those pitchers were at least fifty-percent vodka.

Kota and I were feeling adventurous tonight, so we each got our own. Usually, we shared one, so we were both pretty drunk by the time Lane got there.

I hopped in the passenger seat. "Hi, Lane."

"Hey," he said with a light grin. "Drunk?"

"Very," I admitted.

"Extremely!" Kota exclaimed from the back seat.

"Thanks for driving us," I said.

Kota leaned forward between our seats. "Yeah, thanks, Lane!

"No problem," he murmured. His grin disappeared, a sense of discomfort replacing it as he sucked in a ragged breath. "Seatbelts?"

Kota sat back in her seat and we both put ours on.

I kept my head forward but shifted my eyes over to look at Lane every few seconds. He seemed tense. His body was currently resembling a stone, his knuckles whitening against the steering wheel from gripping it so tightly.

My brows came in. The liquor must've wiped any sort of conscience I had because before I knew it, I was reaching towards him, resting a hand on his wrist.

"Are you okay?"

His tone was soft, but he kept his eyes on the road, strikingly focused. "I'm alright."

"You don't seem alright," I whispered.

"I'm alright," he repeated.

The moment I took my hand away, there was a heavy feeling in my gut, as if I missed the absence of his skin even though I didn't have the right to feel that way.

The drive lasted less than five minutes, and I felt a dose of disappointment when Lane pulled into the parking lot. Luckily though, he seemed to relax a little once we were parked.

"Thanks again," I spoke quietly, undoing my seatbelt.

Lane finally turned to look at me, the first time he had since before his foot touched the gas. "You're welcome."

"Are you gonna go to bed when you get back?" I asked, grabbing my purse off the passenger floor.

He bobbed his head side to side. "I'll probably wait until you guys get home."

I tipped my head at him, raising a drunken brow. "Lane. You're exhausted. Just go to bed."

"No," he refused.

"Why?"

His mouth twitched as he tried holding back what he was going to say. I eyed him with enough curiosity to kill a cat, pressuring him to give in.

He glanced out his window for a brief moment before responding, as if he didn't want to be looking directly at me while he spoke. "I need to make sure you guys get home safely."

My heart began beating in a sharp rhythm, threatening to burst through my ribcage. Typically, my shyness would take over and I'd stay silent, but apparently that pitcher was filled to the brim with both vodka and a confidence serum.

"Lane," I said quietly with a small smile, "we're right across the street."

140

Lane studied me with those pretty eyes of his, their color getting washed out from the darkness. He took his bottom lip between his teeth. "I know."

"You don't have to stay up."

This time, his gaze stayed on me, his voice adamant. "Yes, I do."

I gave a small sigh. "Alright... Well, I'm sure we won't be out too late."

As he nodded, I turned around in the front seat to look at Kota, who was tapping away on her phone.

I shot her a look. "Are you texting Bobby?"

She slowly glanced up at me with shameful eyes. "No."

"You fucking liar," I accused.

She sighed, giving a light shrug. "Technically, I didn't hit send yet."

"Delete the message. This is a no boys night, you cheater."

"Fine," she agreed with an eye roll, hitting the back button and aggressively shoving her phone in her pocket.

"Bye, Lane," I said with a friendly grin as I hopped out of his car. "Thanks again."

"No problem," he said with a small, forced smile. "It's what friends do."

***

After two drinks, we were done. Completely gone for.

I hadn't been this drunk in quite some time. Luckily, I didn't have class until three tomorrow. *Un*luckily for me, there was a ninety-percent chance I'd have a hangover, so go me.

Kota and I stumbled out of Stallions, laughing at quite literally nothing. We interlocked elbows, shuffling through the parking lot.

"B," she suddenly said through a smile, halting.

"Yeah?"

There was nothing but sincerity and hope dripping from her voice. "Promise me we'll always be besties."

"Promise," I smiled, offering my pinky finger. She hooked hers around it, and we each kissed the pads of our thumbs before connecting them.

When there was a small rustling noise coming from behind the dumpster, my head shot over. I immediately gripped the pepper spray that was on my key chain as Kota stiffened, her drunken eyes struggling to focus on our surroundings.

We stood there in silence for a moment, frozen. As a figure appeared, slowly stepping towards us, I raised my pepper spray, but I instantly dropped my hand at the sight of a tiny, furry face.

"A kitten!" Kota and I screeched.

A woman was cradling a tiny grey kitten in her arms, walking towards us.

"Ain't she adorable?" the woman said.

It probably wasn't smart of us to walk towards a random lady that had just appeared from behind a dumpster, but c'mon. Two drunk girls and a kitten? All our better judgment was currently gone.

I glanced over the woman as we reached her. Her blonde hair was cut short in a pixie cut, revealing her not-so-done-well neck tattoo of a bunch of random swirl patterns.

"Can we pet her?" Kota asked hopefully.

"Sure, go right ahead," the woman said.

Kota and I had giant smiles plastered on as we ran our hands over the kitten.

"What's your name?" I asked.

"Her name is Louboutin," she said.

"Louboutin!" Kota shrieked. "Oh my God. That's so cute."

"It is cute," I confirmed. "I meant your name though," I asked the woman.

"Oh," she said. "Well, my friends call me Britney Bitch."

Kota and I froze, trading a quick glance as we held back laughter.

"Okay," Kota said through a small giggle.

"Where'd you get her?" I wondered.

"I found her 'bout a week ago underneath a car. Poor little kitty was terrified."

"Awe," I frowned. My hand stopped on her neck, lightly pinching the shoelace that was tied around it. "Um, what's this?"

"She kept trying to run away, so I put a leash on her," Britney Bitch responded.

Kota blinked at her mindlessly, her mouth agape. My expression matched hers for a moment until I finally managed to brush it off.

"Quite honestly, there were a few more kittens that I found with her, and I can't take care of all of them," Britney Bitch said.

Kota looked up at her with wide, sanguine eyes. "Are you saying—"

"Kota," I cut her off, holding up my small hand in her direction before turning back to Britney Bitch. If this conversation was going where I assumed it was going, we needed a bit more information. "What does she usually eat?"

Britney Bitch shrugged. "She'll eat whatever. Dry food, wet food. She likes it all."

"Does she have her shots yet?" I asked.

"Yep, she's got 'em all."

"Is she fixed?"

"She's not fixed yet," she answered. "I believe she's still a bit too young."

Kota eagerly jumped back into the conversation. "Are you saying we could have her?"

Britney Bitch tipped her head side to side, swaying lightly. "You can have her for thirty bucks."

I took another long look at the kitten's tiny face. She was innocently glancing around, her "leash" hanging off her neck. I pushed my mouth into a hard line as I looked at Kota, who already had her eyes on me. We both gave a small sigh at the same time.

"Yeah, alright," Kota said, swinging her purse off her shoulder.

I did the same, and within another minute, we each had fifteen dollars extended towards Britney Bitch.

She held Louboutin under one arm as she shoved the money in her pocket, then handed her over to me. She squirmed, attempting to hop out of my arms and run, but I brought her to my chest, giving her a sense of safety, and finally, she relaxed, nuzzling against me.

My smile threatened to break my face in half. "Thanks."

"Yep, yeah, no problem," Britney Bitch said, slowly retreating backwards. "I gotta go now. You girls have a good night."

"You too..." Kota said warily.

We waited for Britney Bitch to disappear before we strode towards our building.

There was a small circle of guilt that was growing in my stomach. I scrunched my face together. "Do you think we should've asked the boys first?"

Kota waved a hand through the air, shaking her head. "Fuck the boys."

"What if they're allergic or something?"

"Good, I hope Crew is."

I rolled my eyes as we crossed the street, batting Kota's hand away each time she tried to steal the kitty from me.

She let out a frustrated groan. "Fine, but I get to hold her when we get inside."

"Fine."

Kota's eyes trailed up to me as she took her apartment key out, the corners of our mouths turning upwards at the same time, and within another moment, we were both hysterically laughing, the same way we had been before Britney Bitch emerged from the shadows.

Louboutin started shaking lightly in my arms, so I cradled her a little tighter, softly running a hand over her head. "It's okay," I said gently.

When we walked in, the boys were lying on the couches, looking half-dead. Their heads slowly raised in our direction. There was a comforted gleam in Lane's eye from seeing us.

144

But the comfort disappeared when Crew shot up, wincing as he did. "What the hell is that?" he spewed.

Kota bellowed out laughter.

"Is that a cat?" Lane asked.

"Yeah," I quietly admitted with a light burn in my cheeks. "Are you allergic?" I blurted out.

"No," he responded, the corner of his mouth curling upwards. I sighed a breath of relief, glancing down at the kitten.

Kota looked at Crew. "Are *you* allergic?"

"No," he said.

"Damn," she cursed under her breath as the boys wandered over, practically limping. "You guys look like shit."

"Thanks," Lane mumbled.

"So do you," Crew spat, "but at least I have an excuse."

"That was mean," Lane chided him.

Crew's mouth formed an O as his brows came in, hands raising in confusion. "Oh, so it's fine when she says it but I'm a dick if I say it back?"

"Exactly," Kota said, taking Louboutin from me.

Crew let out a huff, dodging Kota's glares as he pet the kitten in her arms. "What the hell is this?" he asked, pointing to the shoelace.

"Oh yeah," I said, "we should cut this off."

Kota nodded, sliding open our kitchen drawer and grabbing scissors. She carefully snipped the shoelace and tossed it into the trash.

"So, where did you guys get this cat?" Lane finally asked.

"Britney Bitch," Kota answered.

"Excuse me?" Lane raised a brow.

"Some woman in the Stallions parking lot," I explained.

Crew leaned against the kitchen island. "Let me get this straight. Some random lady in the parking lot offered you two a cat and you thought nothing of it?"

"Oh, well she was definitely on drugs," I said.

"One-hundred percent on drugs," Kota agreed.

"Wow, even better. So, some *druggie* offered you a cat and you just took it without a doubt?" Crew asked.

"Well, we paid her thirty bucks," I said, causing Lane to let out a laugh.

"Jesus," Crew mumbled, shaking his head with his eyes closed. "Of course, you did."

Kota's voice raised in the slightest. "We had to! You saw that freaking shoelace tied around her neck. We couldn't leave her with that psycho."

"Agreed," I said.

Kota set Louboutin down on the floor and the four of us watched her warily step around, beginning to explore the apartment.

I kept my eyes on her as I spoke to Kota. "Also, I think we should change her name."

Kota gave a nod. "What to?"

"She already had a name?" Lane asked.

"Louboutin," we responded in unison.

"That's a dumb name," Crew said.

"Oh, I got it!" I exclaimed with a finger in the air, turning towards Kota. "Kim K!"

Kota's smile grew wide, and she smacked a hand down on the kitchen island. "Yes! I love it!"

Lane scratched the back of his neck. "I know you guys are real excited right now and what not, but what about food and a litter box and stuff? Are you guys just gonna go get some in the morning?"

Kota and I looked at each other in realization. We definitely hadn't thought this through.

Before I could say anything, Kota was jumping in front of Lane with her hands intertwined in front of her. "Lane, will you take us? Please, please, *please*?"

His eyes widened and he took a small step backwards. "What, like right now?"

Kota nodded rapidly while I shook my head. "Kota," I scolded, "he's already done enough for us tonight. Leave him alone."

Lane was looking at me with that same flicker of longing in his eye that I'd seen dozens of times before. He let out a lengthy exhale. "Do you want me to take you?"

I gave a light shake of my head, along with a tiny shrug. "It's up to you."

He quickly rubbed his eyes. "Alright," he said. "Walmart, it is."

Chapter Twenty-Nine

Lane

I didn't usually take mid-day naps, but after being worked like a dog by coach over this St. Cloud game, a nap was seemingly in store.

I had to say though, my nap was fucking incredible.

With a yawn, I wandered down the hall, brows drawing in at the sound of a guy's voice.

Mitch and Bridget were smushed against each other on the couch, petting Kim K.

Oh, fuck no. Not in my house.

Why did they have to be so close? The rest of the couch was entirely open. It made me wonder how much closer they'd been behind closed doors, and I immediately regretted the thought, feeling bile rise in my throat.

"Hey, Lane," Mitch acknowledged.

"Hey." I cleared my throat, hands resting on my hips, keeping my distance from them. "You guys hanging out here awhile?"

Please say no. Please say no. Please say no.

"Yeah, probably," Bridget said. "We were gonna go see a movie, but it doesn't start until eight."

Eight?! That was in two hours. No way in hell was I sitting here watching this for that long. I couldn't even go to my room and relax because I'd just be laying there knowing this was going on.

I had Crew's voice in my head, nagging me.

Put yourself out of your misery.

You just need to find a new girl.

She's off limits anyway.

Giving them a nod, I retreated to my room and gave into the pain, texting Ava, the cute girl I took home from Stallions a few weeks ago and asking her to come over.

Within two minutes, she responded that she was on her way.

Chapter Thirty

Lane

Ever since I started hanging out with Ava more often, being around Bridget was a lot less painful.

Bridget and I had been spending a decent amount of time together over the past few days, and I was finally feeling like we were forming a good friendship. Was I still attracted to her? Yes. Did I enjoy her company maybe a little too much? Probably. But it was a start.

We decided to head to the library together to get some homework done. It was nice to have someone to go with. There had been a few times last year that I forced some of the guys to go with me, and they either distracted me the whole time or asked to leave after thirty minutes.

If I was being honest though, Bridget might have been just as distracting.

She didn't mean to be, which only made it worse. It was just hard not to look at her when she was sitting directly across from me. Every little movement she made caught my attention, causing my heart to slightly speed.

Her strawberry locks framed her face perfectly as she scribbled onto a pile of notecards, hyper-focused. I watched with an amused smirk as she plucked each notecard off the pile one-by-one, glancing at each one before stacking them into a new pile.

She seemingly gave a small nod to herself before looking up at me. I snapped my head down to my notebook, gulping as I hoped she hadn't caught me watching her.

"Lane?"

"Yeah?" I spoke towards the table.

"Can you quiz me?" she asked softly, holding out her notecards.

"Sure," I grinned, taking them. "Do you have an exam or something coming up?"

"Yep. Psychology."

"You're in psych? I thought you were an English lit major?"

"I am," she nodded, "with a psych minor."

"Oh," I nodded. I glanced down at the first card. "Ready?"

"Yep!"

One-by-one, I read off the questions on the flashcards, and one-by-one, Bridget got every answer correct. I didn't even know what half of the words meant that I was reading. She was so fucking smart, it was insane. But it was also so, *so attractive.*

She got through them within minutes, and I sat there, eyeing her with both admiration and awe. "Wow, look at you. A little genius."

There was a light shade of pink that sat heavy on her cheeks as she gave a shy smile, and damn if that sight didn't cause my heart to ignite like a marshmallow that you put too close to the fire.

"You're gonna do great," I said.

Bridget dodged my gaze. "Are you almost done with your stuff?"

"Yeah, we can head back soon. It's not due until next week. I just wanted to get a head start on it."

Since I hated driving people anywhere with a burning passion, I had requested that Bridget drove, and she was happy to comply with no questions asked.

Before this week, we'd been dancing around each other while living under the same roof, each keeping a safe distance for whatever the reason was. Now I felt like I was learning more about her with each day that passed, and with every new thing I learned, the more interesting she came to be in my eyes. Like how she was a psychology minor on top of being an English lit major. Or how I'd been assuming this entire time that her favorite movie was *Twilight*, when really it was *Rocky* because she used to watch it with her family a lot when she was younger. Or how she only liked ketchup with her French fries and nothing else. It was the little things about her that were so enjoyable.

I glanced over at her as I sat in the passenger seat, noticing the crinkle in the corners of her eyes from the charming grin she had. "What're you all smiley about?" I asked, inevitably smiling myself.

"I'm excited to see Kim K," she admitted.

My laughter echoed throughout the car. "Of course," I shook my head. "I still can't believe we have a cat at the apartment now."

"I still can't believe we haven't checked the lease yet to see if we can even *have* a cat."

I laughed again. "What are you gonna do if we can't?"

Her mouth formed a hard line and she glanced back and forth between the road and me, shaking her head. "We'll keep her anyway."

I let out a playful gasp. "Bridget Bell breaking the rules? I've never heard of such a thing."

"Hey! I can break the rules."

My brows shot up, nearly meeting my hairline. "Kota can break the rules."

"Yeah, but I can break them too sometimes."

I leaned against the door, slightly turning my body so that I could face her as much as my seatbelt would allow. "Tell me about a time that you broke the rules."

Bridget smiled, taking a deep breath. "I don't have to tell you anything."

My head tipped back, enveloped in laughter. "It's because there's nothing to tell."

She smacked her hand on top of the steering wheel, intending to look tough and serious, but looking closer to a cute puppy that thought it was a grown Pitbull. "I can break the rules!"

I spoke as we approached a red light. "Then do something bad right now."

She held her foot on the brake as she turned to look at me, arms crossed. With each second that ticked by of us looking at each other in silence, her breathing became deeper, more obvious. Her eyes were clouded over with some sort of yearning that I couldn't quite figure out. And as her line of sight dropped ever-so-slightly from my eyes to my lips, hers parted.

"I could," she murmured.

Something deep was pulsing within me, something bad, something sinful. If I didn't know any better, I'd say she was thinking about kissing me.

Lord knows I was thinking about kissing her.

I let out a troubled breath. "The light's green," I muttered.

She shifted around, her attention turning back towards the road and stepping on the gas. After a minute, she gave a content smirk, shaking off whatever the hell just happened between us. "Look, I'm speeding."

I leaned over to get a glimpse at the speedometer. "You're only going five over."

Her smile dropped and she held up a middle finger as I let out a hoot.

Both of our brows knitted together when we walked into the apartment, catching sight of Crew staring at Kim K with a puzzled face.

"Why are you making that face?" Bridget asked. "Did she do something funny?" I slipped my shoes off, watching Bridget wander over with her ever-lasting smile. She took a seat on the floor next to Kim K. "Did you do more backflips?" she asked, petting her.

On our late-night Walmart run the other day, the girls got her a bunch of toys, one of which included a stick with a tiny bell and string attached to the end. Kim K went crazy for it, doing a long array of backflips just to try to catch it.

"No..." Crew responded warily.

"Then what?" I asked.

His chest expanded with a long inhale, brows nearly touching as he pointed to the cat. "Um... Well Kim K was lying down on her back, and I noticed, um..." He scratched the back of his neck, pausing. "Well, I mean, I'm not an expert on cat anatomy or anything, but... her private parts didn't look right to me."

Bridget's eyes shifted back and forth between us, confused. "What are you talking about?"

Crew looked to me for help, and I rubbed my chin, covering my mouth.

"It looked sort of like..." Crew trailed off, waving his hands in a circular motion to try to get her to catch on.

"Like what?" Bridget snapped.

Crew finally spit it out. "Like a ballsack."

Bridget's mouth popped wide open, and I stifled a laugh.

"Excuse me, what?" she said.

He put his hands up. "Look for yourself."

She let out a groan, grabbing Kim K and carefully flipping her onto her back. I stood above her to get a closer look, and the second I caught a glimpse at Kim K's privates, I burst out laughing.

Bridget's shoulders sagged. "I can't believe this." Her eyes were sullen as she looked up at me, as if she just found out her whole life was a lie. "Kim K is a Rob K."

Crew placed his hand on Bridget's shoulder. "I'm sorry for your loss."

She sighed with her chin tucked into her chest. "We're gonna have to do something scary and slightly dangerous now."

Crew moved his hand off her shoulder as if it were a flame, his brows coming together once again. "You're gonna cut his balls off?!"

"What the fuck? No!" Bridget said, taken aback. She sighed again, her mouth pulling over to the side in disappointment. "We're gonna have to tell Kota."

Chapter Thirty-One

Lane

Kota wasn't very pleased about Rob K being a Rob K. But after a day or two, she accepted it.

I was honestly growing attached to Rob K myself. I'd never been a big cat person; I usually preferred dogs, but after countless times of Rob K snuggling up with me on the couch and entertaining me with backflips, he'd become my friend. Not to mention he was pretty fucking cute.

I originally had plans with Ava tonight, but I ended up cancelling on her.

I told her I had too much homework to get done before our game this weekend, and even though I did have a little bit of homework, it felt like I was trying to convince myself that that was the only reason.

But like most decisions I'd made over the past two months, I was pretty sure it had to do more with Bridget.

She was reading on the couch when I got home earlier, and somehow, I ended up sitting next to her. Now, the thought of moving from this very spot was brutal.

Bridget tossed her book beside her, curling up into a little ball with her eyes closed and her face scrunched together as if she were in pain.

"You okay?" I asked softly, poking at her side.

She gave a lethargic nod. "Just got a massive migraine."

I frowned. "Do you want some Tylenol or something?"

"Yes please."

I got up without a second thought, grabbing her a glass of water and two Tylenol. "Here," I whispered, causing her eyes to slowly peel open.

She sat up, downing the Tylenol before lying back down. She sighed, "I hate this."

"I know," I said, rubbing her back. "Migraines suck."

"Yeah," she agreed, "especially because all I wanna do is read and relax."

"Do you want me to read to you?"

Her eyes suddenly popped open, her voice turning almost frantic as she began pushing herself up. "No, that's okay."

"No, really, it's fine," I said, gently pushing her shoulder to guide her back down to the couch. "Just lay down."

"Lane—"

"Bridget," I cut her off with a light smile as I reached for her book, "just let me."

She covered her face with her hand as I opened the book. The moment my eyes met the page, they practically popped out of their sockets.

"Um," I let out through a laugh, "Bridget?"

"Yeah?" she said in a shy, embarrassed voice.

"Are you reading smut?" I laughed.

She sighed, eyes closed. "Just put the book down, Lane."

"No, no, it's fine. I told you I'd read to you," I insisted. I cleared my throat, blowing out a breath as I sunk back into the couch and started reading. "His tongue left a trail on my inner thigh, setting my skin on fire. I could feel the pulse in my lower core, my pussy begging to be filled with him. Hands digging into my flesh, he branded me with his fingerprints, and in one swift movement, his hands were wrapped around my ankles, and I was being pulled to the edge of the bed."

156

I paused, fidgeting in my seat. I was so glad her eyes were closed and that she couldn't see the rock that was currently growing in my pants.

"'Are you gonna be a good girl for me?' he growled. 'Yes, baby,' I hummed, more than prepared to do whatever was asked of me. I jolted as his thumb brushed over my clit, but as good as it felt, it still wasn't enough. I needed him inside me."

Jesus.

Why was I envisioning this being Bridget and me?

It was becoming a bit painful to read. The temptation to launch this book across the room and grab her right now to reenact this scene was building.

"I was about to beg. It was—"

"Lane?" Bridget quietly interrupted.

"Yes?"

"Please stop."

Thank God.

"Okay," I murmured, setting the book aside. "I'm gonna, ah, go shower."

In other words, *I'm gonna go jack off because my dick hurts from being so fucking hard right now.*

"Alright."

"I hope your headache goes away," I stood.

Her eyes started to carefully pry themselves open, and I ran, praying she hadn't caught sight of the bulge in my pants.

Chapter Thirty-Two

Bridget

After throwing on my oversized Lana Del Rey shirt and some sweatpants, I rung my hair out with a towel before hanging it back up in the bathroom. My hair was still a little damp, but I preferred to air dry it anyway.

Rob K ran between my legs at full speed as I stepped out of the bathroom. A sigh fell from my mouth. *Crew probably gave him more catnip.*

The potent aroma of garlic filled the air, and I roamed into the kitchen, following it with curiosity.

"What're you cooking?" I asked. Lane jumped slightly, turning over his shoulder to spot me with a smile. "Did I scare you?"

"Yeah," he laughed, "I didn't think you were home. I'm cooking fettucine alfredo."

I hummed. "Yum."

"Do you want some?"

I sat down on one of the bar stools at the island, watching him run back and forth from the stovetop and the fridge. "I mean, I don't wanna eat your food," I replied.

He swiped a hand through the air. "That's Kota's rule, not mine."

I let out a giggle. "Alright, I guess I'll take some."

"Good," Lane smiled, stirring the alfredo sauce. "Now you can finally see what a magnificent chef I am."

"Oh, really?"

"Really," he said. "It's one of my many hidden talents."

"What's another hidden talent of yours then?"

He stood there in thought for a moment. "I can say the ABC's backwards."

"No fuckin' way," I challenged.

He cocked a brow and in one large breath, sang the ABC's from back to front.

My mouth parted, lips curling upwards. "I'm impressed."

"Told ya," he smirked. "Do you have any hidden talents?"

My eyes fell to the countertop as I shook my head, but my smirk seemingly gave me away.

"Oh c'mon," he pushed. "There's gotta be something."

"Well," I said shyly, "I guess there is one thing... I can't do it for you though."

"Why not?"

"Because it's not lady-like."

His smile grew along with his interest. "Well, now you gotta tell me."

I sighed. "I can burp while counting to ten."

He let out a laugh in disbelief. "As in you can say the numbers while burping?"

"Correct."

"Let me hear it."

"No!" I drew my brows in. "I told you I can't do it for you."

Lane playfully rolled his eyes as he turned the stove off. "What happened to the Bridget that breaks the rules? Plus, who gives a fuck about what's deemed as lady-like?"

I tapped my fingertips along the corner of the island. "Well either way, I have to drink like half a can of soda in order to do it and I don't have any soda, so..." I trailed off.

"I've got some in the fridge," he shrugged.

"I'm not burping to ten in front of a boy."

He lightly bit his lip, leaning into the island across from me. "Please? I actually wanna hear this really bad."

I let out a light groan. "Why?"

Lane shrugged lightly. "I like knowing things about you."

"I mean, you can know this about me without hearing me do it," I argued.

He shook his head. "No, cause how do I know if it's really true?"

I rolled my eyes. "You think I'm making it up?"

His pearly whites sparkled underneath the kitchen light as he smiled. "I have my suspicions." He pushed himself away from the island, grabbing two plates from the cupboard and tossing fettucine on them. He held one out to me. "Consider it a trade." As I reached for the plate without saying anything, he pulled it back, raising a brow. "You get to eat my food and I get to hear you burp numbers," he said.

"Hey! I thought you were sharing out of the kindness of your heart."

His eyes were so full of amusement at this point that they were lit up like a carnival. "Maybe I changed my mind."

I let out a low grunt. "Fine! Grab me a freaking soda." I didn't think it was possible for his grin to grow wider, but it managed to as he plucked a can of soda from the fridge and slid it across the island to me. "You know you're the worst, right?"

Lane tipped his head, his playful yet smug grin still lingering. "Am I?"

The can made a popping sound as I cracked it open. "I'm doing this one time and one time only and then we are never speaking about it ever again, okay?" He smirked at me in silence, causing my gaze to turn harsher. *"Okay?"* I repeated.

"Okay," he finally agreed with a single nod.

I exhaled deeply out my nose, sitting up straighter as I brought the can to my mouth. I chugged for a solid five seconds.

Silence overcame us for a moment as I sat there, avoiding Lane's stare.

"Well?" he said.

"Don't rush me," I snapped. "It's settling."

I focused hard and before I knew it, I was burping to ten, refusing to look at Lane the entire time.

But the second I finished, I couldn't help but look at him. Because he was *laughing hysterically.*

The type of laughing where you had to bend over.

I let out a small sigh. "Can we forget about it now?"

Lane's laughter was echoing throughout the kitchen. I was surprised it hadn't woken Crew up from his nap.

He spoke between spurts of laughter with the air he could manage to breathe. "I cannot... believe... I just heard that."

I was trying my best to scowl at him, but the harder he laughed, the harder it became. His voice just had this sort of musical sound to it, the type that could sing screaming babies to sleep. It was such a lovely and addictive sound that it had the ability to suck all negativity out of a room.

"Lane," I chided with a tiny snicker.

He shook his head, holding one hand out towards me while the other stayed planted on his stomach. "I'm sorry, I'm sorry."

"We're pretending it never happened," I pointed a finger at him.

"Okay," he nodded, finally starting to compose himself a little. "Right."

I fought a grin as I picked up my fork. The moment the food hit my mouth, my eyes widened. "Lane," I spoke between bites, "this is actually really good."

He shrugged with one shoulder. "Told you, I'm a little chef."

"Where'd you learn to cook?"

"I used to cook a lot with my mom before..." he trailed off, looking down.

"Before what?"

"Nothing," he murmured, straightening. "Um, you got a package today, by the way."

"I did?"

"Yeah," he nodded, pointing a sluggish finger towards the front door.

My gaze followed, landing on a small box sitting on the floor. I hopped off my stool and rushed for it.

My DNA test.

I could feel the nerves physically swirl around in my gut, threatening to force the pasta back up. Luckily, Lane's voice snapped my mind out of the horrible rabbit hole it was about to fall down.

"What'd you order?"

I wasn't sure if I should tell him or not. I trusted him, of course, and I didn't think there'd be any sort of judgement coming from him if I did tell him, but at the same time, I didn't really feel like explaining my whole life story. It would only make me more anxious, and I currently had enough anxiety to last a lifetime.

"A shirt," I blurted out.

"A shirt? In that tiny box?" he questioned with a laugh.

My gaze dodged him, staring at the box. "It's a... small shirt."

When my eyes slowly pulled upwards to meet his, I could tell by the look on his face that he didn't believe me. I didn't really blame him though. We all knew I was a terrible liar.

But to my surprise, he didn't push for an answer. All he did was nod. "Okay," he said.

"Okay," I repeated with a friendly, thankful smile. Jogging into my bedroom, I tossed the box on my bed before making my way back out to the kitchen and sitting down.

I started eating again, being sure to eat slowly so that my already upset stomach wasn't overwhelmed.

It was quiet for a few minutes until the tiniest giggle escaped from Lane's lips.

"What?" I asked.

He dropped his fork, his smile brighter than diamonds. "Can you burp-count again please?"

Chapter Thirty-Three

Bridget

"That waiter was weird," Mitch said, one hand on the wheel and the other sitting casually on my thigh as he drove.

"Extremely," I chuckled.

"Why was he using so many fake accents?"

"You think it was fake?"

"Well, considering he kept switching from a British accent and an Australian one, I'd say it was fake." Our laughter mixed throughout the car before falling into silence. "Did you wanna come over for a little?"

"Sure," I said.

We drove the remaining few blocks to his apartment while silence sat between us along the way. I wasn't sure what it was, but there was something off about him tonight, as if his mind was elsewhere.

There had been a few times during dinner where he seemed to zone out almost, and obviously, I couldn't read his mind.

Sometimes when I was with Mitch, I thought about Lane.

Thought about how easy it was with him. How even in moments of silence, I was comfortable. How no conversation was forced or overthought.

It was strange how I always felt like I had a better idea of what was going on in my roommate's mind than I did the guy I'd been seeing for a month.

Mitch only had one roommate that was rarely ever there, and tonight was no exception. The apartment was empty, per usual.

"Wanna turn a movie on?" he asked, tossing his jacket aside.

"Sure," I said, grabbing the remote and clicking the power button. "What do you wanna watch?"

He sat beside me, scooting closer until our thighs touched. "I don't care. You can pick."

I clicked on the first good movie I saw— *Rocky*.

My mind immediately landed on Lane, because I was thinking about how he kept saying he wanted to have a *Rocky* movie marathon.

I wasn't opposed, of course, considering it was one of my favorite movies ever.

But after the first ten minutes of the movie, I was still thinking about it, and a small surge of guilt washed over me from dwelling on it for so long.

Was it wrong to be thinking about a guy while another had his arm draped around me?

I did my best to shake off the thoughts, reminding myself of where I was and who I was with. I managed to let the thoughts drift away, but when Mitch slowly reached up, turning my head towards his to connect our lips, my mind began swimming once again.

But I wasn't sure if it was a good type of swimming or a bad type of swimming.

There was the type that occurred when a kiss was so powerful that it sent your head spinning.

But there was also the type that sent your head spinning when a kiss didn't feel quite right.

And right now, it almost felt like a mixture of both.

164

I'd never experienced an all-mighty kiss before in real life. The closest I'd ever gotten to it was from reading it in books.

I let myself take in the feeling of Mitch's lips on mine, but as his hand slowly trailed down the side of my body, stopping just shy of my crotch, I instinctively pulled away.

There was a trace of disappointment clouding over his eyes as he stared at me. "Is everything okay?"

"Y—yeah," I stuttered, slowly shifting away from him.

He brought his hands back, letting me create a foot of space between us.

"What's wrong?" he asked.

With thoughts still roaming a thousand miles per hour, it was hard for me to piece together a coherent thought.

Mitch and I had kissed an abundance of times by now and had gotten a little handsy at times, but that's as far as we'd gone. I was worried he was becoming impatient with me, but at the same time, I was becoming a bit impatient with him.

He was making initiatives that were clear he wanted to have sex, but I was waiting to be a couple before we crossed that line.

"I just..." I struggled, shaking my head lightly, "I don't really sleep with someone unless I'm dating them."

He gave a small nod. "Okay," he said. "No problem. I understand."

My brows lifted in the slightest.

I understand?

Why had I sort of been expecting him to pop the question right now? In reality, I could've done it myself. I wasn't a strict believer in men always having to make the first move, but at the same time, I pretty much just told him what I wanted and that was how he responded?

I wanted to push the topic, to get a better understanding of what was currently going through his head, but instead, all I did was whisper, "Okay."

He gave a light shrug. "It's alright. I totally get it," he said, wrapping his arm around me once again.

But this time, it felt even more wrong than it did before.

Chapter Thirty-Four

Bridget

My anxiety hadn't been so high in probably years. I sat on the edge of my bed, staring at the text that Mitch sent me ten minutes ago that I had yet to respond to.

Mitch: Hey, come over? I wanna talk

My lungs struggled, my fingers shaking as I finally answered.

Me: Okay... what about?

Mitch: Us

I figured that had to be the topic, but for some reason, I'd been hoping it wasn't.

There were only two possibilities in my mind. Either he was going to tell me he wanted to be a couple, or he was going to end things.

The worst part was that I didn't feel prepared for either outcome.

***

I couldn't see a damn thing.

My tears had completely drowned out my vision.

At least I made it out of his apartment before the tsunami hit.

I walked briskly to my car and managed to drive down the street before pulling over and letting out a weak whimper. Because there was no way in hell that I was going to sit outside of Mitch's apartment like that.

Before heading over to Mitch's, I had a feeling of what he was going to say. But no amount of preparation was ever enough to hear that someone no longer wanted to pursue things with you.

Even though I'd been having doubts about Mitch, I still had feelings for him. And with that, came a whole surge of painful thoughts.

Why didn't he want me?

Why do things like this always happen to me?

Maybe if I'd just had sex with him, he wouldn't have changed his mind.

My grip on the steering wheel tightened as I bent over it, sobbing.

It seemed like Cupid was never in my corner. All I wanted was the type of love that I read about in books, yet all I ever got was heartache.

I loved love, but it seemed like love hated me.

I ripped my purse open and dug my phone out, pulling up Kota's contact. My shaking finger hovered over the call button as I stared at it.

Before I knew it, I was exiting out of Kota's contact and calling Lane instead.

Chapter Thirty-Five

Lane

Ava and I were hanging out at her place, in the middle of a tennis match on Wii Sports when my phone rang.

Quite honestly, I would've just ignored it had I not seen Bridget's name on the screen.

I paused the game. "One second," I said to Ava and brought the phone up to my ear. "Hello?" There was no response besides a light cry. My brows knitted together, and I stepped a few feet away from Ava. "Bridget? Are you okay?"

"No," she whispered through a sniffle.

A rush of urgency went through me, and my mind immediately began racing. "What's wrong? What happened?"

"Mitch dumped me," she let out. "I'm so sad, Lane."

Even though I couldn't see her, I could *hear* how distraught she was. And just that in itself was enough to make a small shard of my heart break off.

Yet at the same time, my grip on the phone tightened, jaw shifting. Because I wanted to hit this kid for hurting her.

"I'm so sorry, Bridget," I said softly. "Where are you right now?"

I was surprised I could even make out her reply through her sobs. "Parked on the side of the road."

"Do you need me to come home?"

"I don't think I can even drive myself home. I can hardly see."

"Okay, don't worry, alright? Just stay there. I'm on my way."

"Okay," she whimpered quietly before hanging up.

I turned to Ava, my chest heavy. "I'm sorry," I said, handing over the Wii remote. "Roommate emergency."

With a hardening gleam in her eye, she gave a stiff nod, her stance becoming rigid. "I get it."

I quickly gathered up my things and gave her a kiss on the cheek before rushing out the door.

Since we were all roommates, we'd decided it would be smart to share our locations with each other on our phones. Everyone had gladly exchanged locations, besides Crew and Kota, of course.

I followed Bridget's location to a side street that wasn't too far from our own apartment. When I pulled up behind her, I swung my door open and raced up to hers, opening it without a second thought.

Her small arms reached for me, and I bundled her up, running my hand along the back of her head. She was still sobbing, her face red and her eyes blotchy.

It was as if every tear of hers was like a bullet hurdling towards my heart.

She shook against me, and I squeezed her tighter. "It's okay," I murmured, resting my cheek on top of her head.

"Can we go home?" she muttered against my chest.

"Yeah," I said gently. "Do you want me to drive us, and we can come back later for your car?"

She nodded, and I grabbed her hand, trying my absolute best not to look directly at her face because the sight was wrecking me.

I led her to the passenger side and opened the door for her, helping her climb in.

A dose of anxiety trickled in as I jogged around to the driver's side. I stiffened for a moment as I started the car back up.

Goddammit, I fucking hated driving people anywhere.

But right now, it needed to be done.

I carefully took Bridget's keys out of her hand and held her car fob up, hitting the lock button.

Other than her small, continued sniffles, it was quiet as I drove, and thankfully, we arrived home within three minutes, which eased my crippling anxiety.

The second we got through the apartment door, Bridget let out another small sob as she stood in the front walkway of the apartment, stopping there as if she were immobile.

I wasn't sure if anyone else was home, but I didn't bother checking as I scooped her up bridal style and carried her into her bedroom, setting her gently on the bed.

I fidgeted around awkwardly, shifting my weight. "I'll um... let you have some space," I said, taking a step back.

Bridget's head snapped up as if in panic. "No!" she shook her head, a hand extended towards me. "No," she repeated quieter. "Please stay."

She sure as hell didn't need to ask me twice.

I climbed on the bed with her, and before I even had the chance to reach towards her, she was reaching for me. I wrapped my arms around her once again. "What did he do?" I asked in a whisper.

"He dumped me."

"I know," I said, "but did he say why?"

"Not really. I have a pretty damn good idea though."

"Which would be?"

"Well, the other night we were watching a movie and we started kissing and whatever and I could tell he wanted to... you know..." she trailed off, waving her hand around.

The image of Bridget kissing him inevitably went through my head and I cringed, my jaw tightening for a brief moment before I ultimately let out a small gasp. "He dumped you right after you had sex with him?"

"No," she cried. "He dumped me because I didn't."

Relief overcame me, before it quickly switched to guilt for feeling that way. But why was I relieved to know that he never got to know her like that?

Because you're jealous, I thought to myself.

170

I quickly spoke before I could start an internal argument with myself. "Then fuck him," I said. This kid was beyond lucky that I didn't know where he lived. I wasn't usually a violent guy outside of the rink, but murderous visions were flashing through my mind like a slideshow.

"I just want to be dating someone if I'm going to have sex with them."

I gently twisted her so that she could see how serious I was. "Bridget," I said firmly, "you do not need to explain yourself to me or anybody else, okay?" I shrugged, "If you didn't want to have sex with him, then you didn't want to, and there's no problem with that."

She wiped away a tear. "I know, but—"

"No," I cut her off, shaking my head. "No buts. If he was a decent guy, then he'd understand and respect it. And it's shitty that you're feeling like you're being penalized for respecting yourself."

"That's not just it though, Lane," she sadly said, struggling to look up at me.

I placed my pointer finger under her chin and lifted it. "You can tell me," I assured her.

She didn't turn her head away, but she did close her eyes. "I just feel so unwanted. I've felt that way my entire life."

I had to snap my mouth shut and bite the inside of my cheek to prevent myself from confessing that *I* wanted her.

"Why do you feel that way?" I got out.

She spoke quietly, barely louder than a soft breath. "I was adopted when I was a baby."

I frowned. How come I didn't know this? Bridget talked so highly of her parents and her sister, not to mention that she talked about them fairly often, so I guess there was no reason for me to suspect anything.

"I've never met my birth parents, but I've always wanted to," she explained, "especially my mom. I've been looking for her for years now. She's the reason I came to Cedar."

I rubbed her back, nodding to encourage her to keep talking if she wanted. To my surprise, she did.

"I lied to you a few days ago," she said. "That package I got... I didn't order a shirt. It was a DNA test." I stayed quiet, unsure if she was done speaking or not. The last thing I wanted to do was interrupt her. "I'm hoping it'll lead me to my mom."

I took a deep breath, exhaling through my nose. I gave her a light squeeze, keeping my voice gentle but firm. "Bridget, I hope you know you're more than enough. Have you ever wondered if maybe the universe is kicking these people out of your life because they're just simply not good enough for you?"

"I don't know," she whispered.

There was a lull of silence that lasted for what seemed like a long time when it was probably just a minute or two.

I couldn't help but feel this overwhelming urge to make her feel less alone. She just gave me such a huge part of her. I felt like I needed to give her part of me.

"I had a brother," I blurted out. Her head briskly popped up, but she didn't say a word. I had the tiniest trace of a smile on my lips as I talked about him. "His name was Liam; we were fraternal twins. He was my absolute best friend in the entire world. We did everything together. Played hockey together. Hung out with the same group of friends. Pretty much we were attached at the hip."

When I paused for a moment too long, Bridget's small hand found mine and squeezed, giving me the courage to continue. But my smile was far from gone.

I choked through my explanation. "When we were fifteen, we were taking driver's ed together. We were on a drive with our instructor. I was driving. Liam was in the backseat. I was in the right lane and stopped at a red light. The instructor told me to turn right, so I did, but... I didn't look first." I paused, sucking in a sharp, stinging breath. "A truck hit the back corner of the car, and... Liam didn't make it."

I didn't realize there was a single tear falling from the corner of my eye until Bridget swiped it away. "My dad didn't blame me or anything. He didn't think it was my fault. Or at least if he did, he never admitted it. But my mom... she blamed me. It put a huge wedge between my parents and led to their divorce. To this day, I'm pretty sure she still hates me. And I'm

172

convinced she wishes it was me instead of him." My voice dropped to a whisper. "Hell, I wish that."

"I'm so sorry," Bridget expressed, sympathy and sorrow coating her voice. "That's horrible."

I nodded silently, resting my cheek on top of her head again.

"That's why you hate your birthday."

"Yeah," I admitted. "So, I know what it feels like to feel unwanted."

I looked down at her, surprised to see that her eyes were already on me. Her gaze was trapping me like a Venus fly trap. Her lips were close... so, so close, testing every ounce of self-control I had.

It was quiet besides our heavy breathing, both of us unsure of where the moment was leading us. And now she was inching closer and closer, until...

"B!" Kota screeched, busting through the door.

Bridget pulled back, recollecting herself as she looked up at Kota.

"I got your text!" Kota shrieked, kneeling in front of her and reaching for her hand. "Are you alright?"

Bridget glanced over at me; the smallest hint of a smile, barely traceable, touched her lips. "Yeah," she said, turning to Kota. "Lane helped a lot."

Kota grinned, giving me a light smack on the shoulder. "Good job, Laney Lane. What a guy!"

I gave a small laugh, leaning back into my hands. "It's what I do."

As Bridget explained what happened to Kota, I sat there quietly, zoning out.

Because all I could think of was the inevitable question— *If Kota hadn't just burst in, would Bridget have kissed me?*

Chapter Thirty-Six

Lane

I hadn't seen Ava since last week, and I felt like shit about it.

She'd asked me to hang out a few times ever since I left her apartment to go rescue Bridget, but I came up with an excuse every time.

I liked Ava. Truly, I did. She was beautiful and fun and kind, but for some reason, my heart wasn't in it. And I knew that I needed to tell her that. It wasn't fair of me to string her along. She didn't deserve that at all.

I kept telling myself that I was going to tell her how I really felt and essentially break things off with her, but I was dreading it.

I was thinking about it in the shower, rehearsing what I was going to say.

I was trying to convince myself that this had nothing to do with Bridget and that this was just simply how I felt, and although there was definitely some truth to that, I couldn't confidently say that Bridget wasn't involved in the decision.

Ever since Mitch ended things with her last week, she'd been... almost clingy?

Kota was still seeing Bobby, and although she'd been seeing him less in order to hang out with Bridget and comfort her as much as possible, Bridget was surprisingly hanging out with me more often.

I ran a hand through my wet hair, tipping my head back into the hot water as my eyes shut. Inevitably, Bridget's face sat behind my lids, and I couldn't help but think about our almost-kiss.

She had been so close that I could feel her sweet breath fanning across my lips. I wanted to kiss her so damn bad, and I'd been silently cursing Kota ever since for ruining the moment.

I kept daydreaming about what kissing her would be like. How soft her lips probably were. How her small hands would find their way through my hair. How she'd *taste.*

Right now was no exception. I was daydreaming again, and before I knew it, my hand was wrapped around my dick, and I stood there under the water, practically panting as I stroked it to the thought of her.

I let out a sigh, thankful that the sound was drowned out by the loud stream of water. My pace quickened, the minutes ticking by as I got closer and closer to finishing.

Until the bathroom door burst open.

"Lane!"

My eyes widened to a record width as I dropped my cock. "What the f— Bridget?!" I screeched, immediately embarrassed. I grabbed the shower curtain, using it to cover my body as I peeked my head out. Heat crept into my cheeks, and I could only pray she wasn't able to read my mind and know all the dirty things I was just thinking of doing to her.

"I'm a little busy," I insisted frantically.

There was a small crease in her forehead, a shadow of horror covering her. "It's important."

"What's wrong?"

She hesitated, shifting her weight. "There's a spider."

My mouth pulled into a goofy smile. "That's the big emergency?"

"Yes," she answered dreadfully. "It's dark and plump and hairy and—"

"Bridget," I interrupted, "just kill it."

"But I..."

"Just grab a shoe and smash it."

She innocently twirled a small strand of hair, her chin dipping. "I can't."

"Why?"

"Because I'll feel bad," she admitted quietly, barely audible over the running water. I eyed her silently with my mouth propped open, completely engulfed in awe. "It's mean," she added.

She was the only person on the planet that would consider killing a spider to be a sin.

I was trying so hard not to laugh at her, but the longer she stood there, staring at me with puppy dog eyes, the harder it was becoming.

I managed to choke back a chuckle, but my enchanted smirk lingered. "How would you like me to help you?"

Ringing her hands together, she asked, "Can you take it outside?"

I emphasized each word like I was speaking a foreign language. "Take it outside?"

She gave a rapid nod.

"Alright," I sighed, giving in. "Well... can I at least finish my shower?"

"Are you almost done?"

This girl. Here I was, butt ass naked standing four feet away from her with only a shower curtain covering my bare body, and there she was, seemingly unfazed.

"Uh, yeah," I said. *Well, I* was *before you barged in.*

"Okay," she nodded, staying put.

My eyes darted around the room in uncertainty. "Um, Bridget?"

"Mhm?"

"Are you just planning on standing there?"

"Well, I don't want to be out there with the spider."

I kept my eyes on her, managing not to ask her to join me for the remainder of my shower, but just the thought in itself was enough to make my dick begin hardening again.

As I shifted around uncomfortably, the curtain seemed to draw back a bit, exposing my shoulder and part of my chest.

Her honey eyes darkened as they dropped to my bare skin, her lungs expanding deeply.

I fought back a cheeky grin as she snapped her head away from me.

"On second thought," she huffed, "I'll wait outside."

I slid the curtain shut as she slipped into the hallway, then finished myself off as quickly as possible so that I could go save the princess from a spider.

Chapter Thirty-Seven

Bridget

Lane, otherwise known as my knight in shining armor, successfully used a piece of paper and a jar to take Mr. Spider outside safely.

Afterwards, we ran to the store to pick up some cat litter and get some things for dinner.

We'd been cooking a lot together over the past week and just spending more time together in general.

Although I'd had real feelings for Mitch, he'd also been my distraction to keep me away from Lane. But now that Mitch was gone, I didn't have it in me to run from Lane anymore, especially not with how kindly he'd been treating me. Not to mention how exhausting it was constantly having to hide in my own apartment.

Currently, we had all the ingredients for chicken parmesan scattered across the kitchen counter. Lane had already pounded the chicken while I preheated the oven.

"What's next, chef?" I asked.

He lightly smirked, glancing at the recipe on his phone. "Keep calling me that."

"Pass."

Melodic laughter spilled out of his mouth as he glanced up at me. "Why not?"

"Is that your thing?" I leaned against the counter with my arms crossed. His laughter was damn near infectious, and it was taking an awful amount of concentration just to keep mine at bay.

He matched my stance, arms crossed, smirk dancing across his face. "Is what my thing?"

"Getting called strange, dominant nicknames in bed," I joked.

Lane's head tipped back this time as he laughed, a deep, husky sound rolling off his tongue. I swore I could feel the effects of the sound all over my body; my toes were curling in my socks, thighs lightly tingling, muscles tightening.

"You think that's my kink?"

"Maybe," I said, squeezing my thighs together.

His tongue jutted out, lightly sliding over his bottom lip and damn if that didn't send me closer to losing my shit. "Well, it's not."

I needed this conversation to come to a close, because all it was doing now was making me envision Lane in bed and seeing him in the shower earlier wasn't erased from my memory either.

"Just read the recipe," I insisted through a shaky breath.

Lane turned away from me with a huge smile on his face, reading off his phone. It seemed a bit self-destructive, but I took the opportunity to drag my eyes across every inch of him.

His black long sleeve was rolled up to his elbows, exposing the few veins that faintly popped out of his forearms. His grey sweatpants were snug in all the right places, notably his ass.

And when he spoke, the gruff timbre of his voice made my heart do a dolphin-flip before struggling to get back to a normal rhythm.

"The seasonings are next."

"Okay," I uttered, turning back to the counter. I started seasoning the chicken, and my hand stopped mid-shake when I felt a swarm of heat coming from behind me.

My breath hitched, and suddenly, it was difficult to focus on anything other than Lane standing off to the side of me, the front of his hip dangerously close to my ass.

As my jittery hand placed the saltshaker back on the counter, a giant hand planted itself on the countertop beside me, so close that I could feel the skin of his forearm brushing against my side.

One more hand on the other side and he'd have me caged in.

I inhaled a strained breath, trying to focus on cooking, but with each second that passed, it became harder and harder to. My brain was fogging up like a mirror, struggling to keep myself from wandering to sinful thoughts or to keep my heart from accelerating to a pace that would kill me.

"Bridget?" Lane said, his chest skimming against my upper back as he spoke.

"Yeah?" I swallowed.

He leaned in, his mouth inches from my ear. "Don't forget the pepper."

I was thanking the sweet, dear Lord up above that Lane didn't have a view of my face at the moment, because I was more than one-hundred percent sure that it was as red as a cherry tomato.

"Lane," I stammered.

"Yeah?"

"It's on the island."

My eyes closed, lungs blowing out a breath of fire as Lane stepped away from me and grabbed the pepper.

Chapter Thirty-Eight

Lane

Was it bad that I was thinking about telling Bridget how I felt about her while I was technically still talking to someone else?

Yes.

Was it bad that I wanted to ask her to join me in the shower earlier or that I had thoughts of bending her over the kitchen island when we were making dinner?

Yes.

Would I technically be breaking a house rule if I let those things happen?

Yes.

But goddamn, it was getting harder.

The first step in any of this though was to break things off with Ava, which I was planning on doing tonight. I'd already texted her asking if I could come over later and she said yes so now I was just waiting for her to get home.

"Why are you so antsy?" Bridget asked beside me, her lips pulling into a playful smile.

I hadn't realized I was bobbing my knee up and down, moving around restlessly against the couch. I pushed my hand down on top of my leg, forcing it to still.

"I, uh, I'm seeing Ava in a bit," I said, studying her reaction.

Her shoulders seemed to sink, lips dropping into a small frown. "Oh."

"I promise I'm not ditching you."

"Kinda sounds like it," she muttered, lying her head against the couch.

The disappointment in her voice was a small blow to the heart, and I found myself letting out a strained breath from the impact. "Well," I started, "I'm actually... going to end things with her."

Bridget's head shot up almost eagerly, her frown flipping for just a moment before she caught herself and forced it back down. "Oh," she spoke, "why?"

I eyed her, taking too long to respond. This was definitely not the time to tell her how I felt, but was there ever really going to be a right time?

She blinked at me, those beautiful brown and innocent eyes waiting for me to answer.

I twisted more to face her, and as she just barely shifted closer to me, I could feel my heart lodging in my throat.

I could handle a two-hundred-pound man coming at me with a hockey stick and ramming me into the boards, but I couldn't tell a girl how I felt? How pathetic.

I'm just going to spit it out.

"Well, honestly—" but that was all I got out before Kota barged through the apartment door.

***

Two times.

Two freaking times that Kota interrupted.

Granted, both times were unintentional, but still.

On one hand, I was kind of relieved she interrupted this time, because I wasn't sure if I was ready to have that conversation with Bridget.

After all, she only ended things with Mitch two weeks ago and I was currently on my way to end things with Ava now, but I wasn't sure how Bridget felt.

My gut was telling me she felt the same way about me that I felt about her, but I still had some doubts, insecurities that were peeking through.

But for now, I needed to push Bridget to the back of my mind and give Ava all my attention.

I wasn't deliberately trying to jump right into the conversation, but the moment I sat down on Ava's bed, my rigid body language seemed to give me away, because she got straight to the point.

"What's wrong?" she asked.

I'd never had an actual girlfriend before in my life, not that Ava was my girlfriend but this sure as hell felt like I was about to break up with her.

After Liam died, I wasn't in the headspace to pay attention to girls. All my time and energy were put into hockey, because that was one of the only things I still enjoyed doing and one of the only things that made me feel closer to my brother even though he was gone.

So, I'd never done this whole breakup thing before, and I felt like after all the rehearsing I did in the shower, everything I'd planned on saying was just out the door and wiped from my memory.

"Okay, um," I said, awkwardly shifting.

Her face fell, blinking back tears.

Jesus, no. Please do not cry.

She sat there, looking small, studying her lap. "I'm kind of assuming where this is going. Are you... ending things?"

I kept my head down, physically unable to look at her. I just nodded. "I'm sorry."

"Is there a specific reason? Did I do something wrong?"

The crack in her voice made me wince, but I immediately spoke. "Absolutely not," I shook my head. "You didn't do a single thing wrong."

183

Her eyes were glossy, her lip giving a slight tremble. "Then what is it?"

I guess I hadn't realized she liked me so much. I didn't want to lie to her, but I also felt like the full truth would make her feel worse.

"I just... don't think pursuing things would be right for either of us. Hockey is getting more intense as the season goes on and," I paused, shaking my head, "I have a team to lead. I can't give you the time or attention you deserve."

She gave a small nod, but when her head finally raised, a cloud of surprise lingered over me. Because she didn't look sad anymore. She looked almost... skeptical? Pissed?

"Are you sure?"

Nothing that I said was a lie. It may not have been the number one reason why I was cutting things off, but I didn't think there ever really was a time where I envisioned Ava becoming my girlfriend.

"Yeah?" I shrugged.

The sharpness in her voice softened but barely. "Be honest with me," she insisted. "Does this have anything to do with your roommate?"

"My roommate?"

"Bridget."

Well, shit.

Pinpricks of chagrin zipped up my spine. I told myself I wouldn't lie to her, but I'd never been so tempted to lie in my life.

"Um," I stuttered, glancing off, "why do you think that?"

Her dark eyes were on fire at this point, and I wasn't sure if me dodging a direct answer to the question was an answer in itself.

"You've just been spending a lot of time with her lately. And it seems like whenever she's in trouble, you're the first one jumping to help."

I shrugged again, because really, that was all I could do. "We're good friends."

Ava gave a tight-lipped nod. "Right."

I knew I could never win an award for world's best fibber, but geez, was I really that bad of a liar?

It didn't look like there was a single part of her that believed a word I was saying. Technically, nothing that came out of my mouth was even a lie. I meant the whole part about hockey. I meant what I said about Bridget and I being good friends.

What I obviously failed to mention was that my feelings for Bridget were growing by the day, but was dancing around the truth the same as telling a lie?

"I know we were never actually dating and that we've just been a thing or hanging out or whatever you wanna call it, but... it almost kind of feels like being cheated on," she explained.

Oh geez.

"No, no, no," I softly said. "It's not like that."

Except it is.

Goddamn, this whole conversation just took a turn for the worst.

We'd already been driving on a bendy road up a mountain and now we just tumbled over the edge.

I didn't want to make her feel like she'd been cheated on. That was the very last thing I'd ever want her to think or feel. But if that was truly how she felt, then her feelings were valid. I guess this was just my fault for letting it all go on this long.

I felt like a dick.

"I'm really sorry you feel that way," I said gently, covering her small hand. The fire in her eyes was gone now, completely put out by the few tears that were falling down her soft skin. "Ava," I winced, reaching forward and wiping the drops off her face, "please don't cry."

"I'm sorry."

"Don't be sorry," I shook my head.

"We're still gonna be friends though, right?"

"Of course."

Her lips pulled into a strained smile. "Okay." I gave her hand a light squeeze, but she recoiled almost immediately. "Um, I think I just need some... alone time."

185

I released a heavy breath. "Okay," I stood. "Text me if you need anything, okay?"

She didn't bother looking at me as she nodded, but luckily, it seemed like the tears had stopped.

Either way, the second I was out of her room, my steps became brisker, and I was almost ashamed to say I was relieved that was over with.

Maybe it was a good thing I'd never had a girlfriend before. Breakups sucked.

Chapter Thirty-Nine

Bridget

I wanted to know what Lane was going to say.

It felt like reading a mystery book and spending the entire thing trying to figure out what the hell was going on, and just as you were about to get the answers you were looking for, the rest of the pages were missing.

After Kota busted into the apartment, heading straight into Crew's room and reappearing with a pair of his boxers, along with a box of hot pink fabric dye, we knew nothing good was about to happen.

These prank wars were getting out of hand. It was to the point where Crew had been staying at the hockey house for the past few days because he feared how Kota would retaliate after he covered her entire room with tin foil a week ago.

Lane and I were close to intervening just for the sake of breaking it up.

But since the thought of Crew wearing hot pink boxers was apparently hilarious to Lane, he decided to let this one slide.

On the other hand, I didn't have it in me to stop Kota because I was too busy fantasizing over what Lane was going to tell me. And considering he went straight to his room after getting home from Ava's, I assumed I wasn't going to get the answers I wanted.

It had already been days, and it felt like at this point, if I were to ask Lane about it, it would almost be a little random and awkward. If it was truly something that mattered, something that he really wanted me to know, he would've brought it up again since then.

So now, I was pretty much trying to forget about it, and it wasn't that hard to distract myself at the moment because I'd been staring at this dumb DNA test for the past hour.

It was almost paradoxical how I'd been waiting my whole life to take it, yet I'd been putting it off ever since getting the package.

I slowly opened the box, taking out the contents for what seemed like the hundredth time.

I laid all the pieces out in a straight line on my bed. There weren't many, but my eyes jumped between them repeatedly. I blew a breath out, my mouth forming an *O*.

Following the instructions, I spit into the small plastic tube. It took a few minutes, along with numerous breaks since my mouth was getting so damn dry.

But finally, I finished and packaged it up, again making sure that I was following the directions word for word.

And just like that, I had my future sitting in my hands.

Tomorrow, I'd mail it back and wait two more months to hopefully get some sort of answers for myself.

Chapter Forty

Lane

I was used to getting asked questions about the possibility of me going pro.

Crew had been on my ass about it for years, along with his dad. My teammates made comments pretty often; strangers even had the nerve to bring it up. And ever since Bridget and Kota saw that segment about me on the sports channel, they'd been asking too.

But reality was— I hadn't brought myself to accept that opportunity.

At the end of high school, I had the chance. I had the numbers; I could've gone straight to the draft, straight to the NHL, but I just couldn't do it.

It wasn't that I didn't want to play at a professional level. Truthfully, I'd thought about playing in the NHL since I was a kid, but guilt was one hell of a beast.

It just didn't seem right to live out my brother's dream when he didn't get the chance to.

Growing up, every move that Liam made revolved around hockey. It was all he wanted to do in life, and he sure as shit would've made it if I hadn't taken it away from him.

At eighteen, in my gut, not going to the draft felt like the right thing to do. But even so, I hadn't been ready to give up hockey, which was why I went to juniors.

But now, with Crew heading off to play for the Blackhawks after this year and the end of my college hockey career in sight, it felt like I needed to make a choice.

If I wanted to stay at Cedar, I had one more year. But if I decided not to go pro at the end of all this, would playing one more year, especially without Crew, be worth it?

There was only one person that I felt would give me the right answer.

I threw a grey sweatshirt and black joggers on since it was a bit chilly today. Hopping in the car, I stopped at the store to grab some flowers like I usually did.

After a half hour drive, slabs of grey stone sticking out of the ground came into view beyond the black fence, and the entrance of the cemetery came up quickly.

The cemetery was huge with over five hundred graves resting on the land. When I was younger and came to visit by myself, I used to get lost, and it would take me fifteen minutes to even find the right section I was looking for.

But now, I knew the place like the back of my hand, following the trail to the correct section and parking on the side.

As I walked up to the tombstone I'd come to see, a hollow feeling in my gut took over, the same one that swarmed me every time I came here.

With flowers in hand, I stood a mere two feet away, reading the words that were etched into the stone before sinking to my knees.

Liam Michael Avery
Beloved Son & Brother

I dropped the flowers and buried my head into my hands, guilt contaminating me like a virus.

Part of me hated coming here because of this feeling. It always brought back so much pain, so many horrible memories.

190

I wished I could forget it all, but I would never be able to erase the image of Liam getting buried. It had been like looking at myself in a casket. When he died, part of me died with him.

But there was a small part of me that somehow found comfort here, having a place to feel closer to my brother.

With aching lungs, I sat back, positioning the flowers in front of the stone.

"Hey, bro," I murmured. With a sigh, my eyes flitted around.

The cemetery was empty today, eerily quiet like you'd see in the movies. Orange and brown leaves were scattered throughout the grass, and I made a mental note to myself to come back in a few weeks to replace the flowers once they were surely dead.

The weather was getting colder as the days went by, and another wave of guilt hit me like a tidal wave because I hadn't taken enough advantage of the nice weather in the recent months to come and visit.

I thought about what things would be like if the roles were reversed. Surely, Liam would be in the NHL right now, and I'd be the one six feet under, which was how it should've been. He'd probably be busy on the road for months on end, playing the sport we both loved, but regardless, I knew he would've found a way to visit me as much as possible.

I, on the other hand, had only been here a handful of times since moving into our apartment, which was pathetic of me, considering I only lived thirty minutes away.

I shook off my poor thoughts, reminding myself that I came here to spend time with my brother, not to bask in my own grief.

Typically, I treated my visits like a visit I'd have with anyone else in my life, as if I were grabbing lunch with someone I hadn't seen in a while. Only in this case, the conversation was one-sided.

"Remember last time how I was telling you I had a thing for my roommate?" I sighed, "I think we're finally friends now, so that's good, at least. But now, she's hopped on the bandwagon of encouraging me to go pro. I just... I—I don't know what to do. I feel like I know what you'd tell me if you were here, but," I dropped my head, "it just doesn't feel right."

I sat there quietly, as if waiting for him to speak back to me. I wished more than anything to hear his voice, to get a response.

But the only sound was the light rustling of the leaves as the wind came and went.

"Liam," my voice fell, "what do I do?"

The closest thing I got to a reply was the flickering of a memory running through my mind, becoming more and more distinct with each passing second, as if Liam planted it into my head like a seed that was bound to sprout.

"Lane," a voice quietly buzzed in my ear, turning to a strained whisper. "Lane!"

"Hmm?" I hummed.

"Get up. Let's go."

Slowly, my eyes peeled open, seeing my brother seated on the edge of my bed. "Where are we going?"

His bright smile broke through the darkness of my room. He chuckled softly. "You know where." I watched with heavy eyes as Liam stood and wandered over to my closet, quietly digging through it until he found what he was looking for. Turning, he shoved my hockey stick in my direction.

I smiled. "Again? That'll be the third time this week."

Liam strode back over to me. "Oh, c'mon, Lane. Don't make me go alone."

"You wouldn't," I said. "You'd be too bored."

"True," he agreed, "which is why I won't take no for an answer."

With a sigh, I pushed myself up in bed, my hand gingerly rubbing over my eyes.

Our old house used to be smaller, meaning Liam and I used to share a room. But when we turned thirteen a few months ago, our parents figured it was time to give us our own space, and ever since we moved into our new house last month, Liam had been making his way into my room a few nights a week, wanting to sneak out and go skating at the frozen pond in our new neighborhood.

I wasn't sure if he'd been having trouble sleeping or if he just felt the need to do something hockey-related quite literally twenty-four hours a day.

"What time is it?" I asked, putting appropriate clothes on.

"Two."

My brows shot up. "Have you been up this whole time?"

"Don't be crazy," he smirked. "I had an alarm set."

"Of course, you did," I chuckled quietly.

We were lucky that our parent's room was on the other side of the house, which made it much easier to sneak out the back patio door each night. But still, we made sure to be as quiet as possible, knowing how unhappy our parents would be if they caught us sneaking out on a school night.

I pointed at Liam accusingly. "One hour."

He brought his hands up. "One hour," he agreed.

Once we were both dressed and each had a stick and puck in hand, we made our way out the back, taking the trail through the woods that led from our backyard to the pond.

A net had been left there in preparation of all our late-night hockey sessions. It was our old, tattered net, the one that neither of us cared much about, in case something happened to it when we left it there.

We took turns shooting, practicing our slapshots. We played a quick round of one on one, where unfortunately, I lost five-to-four to Liam, but that was nothing new. He'd always been a bit better than me.

When we got back to messing around, I watched Liam skate in a circle around me, switching from forwards to backwards as he stick handled the puck the entire way. He spoke aloud, pretending to be an announcer at a game.

"Avery picks it up; he's got the breakaway, flying past the defenseman with a huge lead." Before I could blink, the puck was in the goal. "He shoots and sinks it into the net. He SCORES!" Liam made his way around the pond with his hands up as if he'd just shot a winning goal and was making a victory

lap around the rink. *"And the crowd goes wild! Liam Avery with the goal!"*

He made his way to me with a massive smile plastered on his face, as if nothing in the world could tamper it. With a tap on my shoulder, he said, *"We're gonna be in the NHL someday, you know that?"*

"You will be," I shrugged lightly. *"I don't know about me."*

Liam tipped his head, and contrary to my belief, his smile had managed to disappear. *"Lane,"* he chided.

"I'm not as good as you."

There was a sharpness in his voice, a bit of anger, even. *"You are as good as me. If not, you're better."*

"Ah, I don't know," I mumbled.

"I'm gonna get there. It's my dream," he declared, then tapped me again, causing me to look up at him. *"Promise me,"* he said. *"Promise me that if you have the chance to go to the NHL, you'll take it."*

I didn't do anything besides stand there, staring silently at him.

"Lane," he pushed.

"Alright," I reluctantly agreed. *"I promise."*

Chapter Forty-One

Lane

I think hell had officially frozen over.

I had no idea what happened between Kota and Crew since his birthday a few days ago, but whatever it was seemed to be monumental because they'd been acting somewhat decent to each other since then.

When Bridget and I got back from the library, Crew was cooking himself dinner while Kota was napping on the couch. We didn't think anything of it until Kota woke up and surprisingly stayed in place instead of dashing to her room.

Now, we'd all been in the common areas together for nearly an hour and the two still hadn't tried strangling each other yet. Granted, they hadn't actually spoken either, but being in the same room for this long after their whole prank wars fiasco was kind of impressive.

Bridget and I were of course cooking dinner together, taking turns glancing into the living room, where Crew and Kota were sitting on opposite couches quietly with a movie on.

"How long do you think they'll go?" Bridget whispered.

I leaned towards her. "I'd say no longer than another hour."

She gave a light tsk, shaking her head in disagreement. "No way. They've been doing so well. I'd say they might even be able to go the rest of the night."

A rowdy chuckle poured out before I quickly snapped my hand over my mouth to silence it. Bridget's eyes widened, her small hand playfully smacking my arm.

Our eyes lingered over to the living room at the same time, hoping neither of our roommates were suspiciously peeking over. Luckily, they weren't.

I could hear Bridget sigh a breath of relief, slowly turning back to me. "Would you like to make a bet?"

I leaned back against the counter, arms crossed with a sprightly grin. "What are you proposing?"

"I'd say the two can go the rest of the night with no big arguments."

"Okay," I nodded along, "and if they can't?"

She shrugged. "Then you win."

I straightened, my teeth digging into my bottom lip so hard that I was surprised it didn't start spurting blood. "And what do I get if I win?"

I could see her visibly gulp, attempting to blink away whatever thoughts she was currently having. "What do you want?"

"Well, what can I have?" I blurted out.

Bridget shrugged again, this one much more subtle as she shoved her hands into the back pockets of her jeans.

"Alright," I nodded, "well, either way, I accept your bet."

She gave the angelic grin of a saint before it quickly turned dark and mischievous. "Hey, guys!" she shouted towards the living room.

Both Crew and Kota turned to face us, staring silently.

"Let's go out tonight," Bridget proposed.

Kota's mouth pulled to the side in displeasure. "The four of us?"

Crew's expression matched hers. "Like... all together?"

"Yeah!" Bridget smiled. "We haven't done anything for Crew's birthday yet as roommates and it was days ago."

"Uh," Crew sat back, "I don't think I need any more birthday celebrations."

Bridget tilted her head, her eyes innocently scanning over the room. "Oh c'mon."

Everyone stared at her quietly for a moment, taking in her sweet expression. She was hands-down the hardest person in the apartment to say no to.

If only they knew what her intentions were tonight.

A sigh came from Crew as he stood. "Yeah, alright."

Kota shortly followed his lead. "Sure, I guess."

"Yay!"

I shot Bridget an assuring smile, but all I could think about was causing some chaos so I could win this bet.

***

Well, it was easy for Crew and Kota to continue being in the same room when there was loud music playing and a good, twenty feet between them.

The girls were on the dance floor, dancing to some Rihanna song, backed up against each other while they screamed the words.

Crew stood beside me, shaking his head as he brought his beer bottle up to his mouth. "It's a shame, really."

"What is?"

His eyes smoldered. "That Kota looks like that, yet she's such a bitch."

I rolled my eyes. "Knew you had a crush on her."

He twisted towards me, eyes wide. "Not a crush."

"What's the difference?"

"A crush involves liking someone. I don't need to like her in order for my body to react to her ass moving back and forth."

"Fair enough," I muttered.

I watched Crew ogle the girls like a creep for another minute before I sucked in a sharp breath. I was excited to have this conversation with Crew, but I was also a little nervous. I'd made up my decision and I had a good feeling he'd be happy about it, considering how much him and his dad had been dropping hints for years.

But at the end of the day, this decision had less to do with him, or even myself.

I was doing this for Liam. No one else.

"I wanna talk to you about something," I blurted out.

Crew tipped his head at me, jumping to conclusions. "What'd you do?"

"Why are you assuming I did something?"

"Because why else would you start a conversation like that?"

I eyed him like he was giving me a headache. "I didn't do anything."

"Then what?" he shrugged.

"I've..." I stuttered, wondering why in the hell this was so difficult to tell him. "I've been thinking."

"Oh no," he shifted, worry creasing his features. "Don't tell me you're gonna confess your love for Bridget."

My brows pulled in so far that they almost touched. "What? No!"

"Don't act like the guess was that out of pocket," he spoke. All I did was shake my head. No wonder why it was so hard to tell him. He wouldn't let me get more than two words out without interrupting and skewing to another topic. "Well, I'm just glad you're at least no longer denying it."

"Will you just shut up and listen?" I shot at him. His mouth snapped shut, eyeing me like a kid that just got in trouble. "I've been thinking a lot about hockey and everything we talked about with your dad on your birthday and... I think I'm gonna go pro."

Crew stared at me like he'd just won the lottery and wasn't sure if it was real or not. The corners of his mouth lifted in the slightest, but not completely, afraid I was messing with him. "Are you serious?"

"Yeah," I nodded.

His mouth flipped the rest of the way, eyes brightening in a way I'd never seen before. "That's fucking awesome, Lane! I'm stoked!"

Before I could react, Crew was jumping into me, his arms wrapping around me and squeezing like a boa constrictor.

"Geez," I let out, inevitably smiling. When he finally pulled away, my brows furrowed. "Are you fucking crying?"

Looking away, he placed a hand on his hip, the other hand shielding his face with his beer. "No."

"Please tell me you're not fucking crying right now."

"I'm not crying right now."

"Move your arm."

"No."

"Oh my God," I judged quietly.

"They're happy tears," he replied.

"Well, I figured that, dumbass."

His arm fell, revealing slightly glossy eyes. "Hey! Don't call me a dumbass."

"You gonna cry about it?" I teased with a light grin.

Chapter Forty-Two

Bridget

I was winning the bet so far, but considering Lane and I hadn't determined what the outcome of the bet would be, I had no idea what I was currently winning. All I needed to do was keep Kota and Crew separated for another hour or two.

I'd admit, the only good thing that came out of my fling with Mitch was being introduced to tequila pineapples.

I'd already had two, but the bartenders made them so strong that it might as well have been four.

Usually, I hated drawing attention to myself, especially in public places, but apparently, I was tipsy enough that flinging my body around like an idiot alongside Kota wasn't crossing the line.

The boys were standing on the edge of the dance floor, and although Crew's mouth had been moving for two minutes straight, Lane's gaze hadn't left our direction.

With another song change, Kota and I turned to each other in delight. The intro to "Buy U a Drank" by T-Pain filled the bar; it was a song we used to blast freshman year in our dorm room before getting noise complaints from our neighbors.

Hips swaying as we screamed every word, Kota and I ran the dance floor, our drinks slightly spilling over every time we bounced too wildly. I chugged the rest of mine and set the empty cup on a nearby table.

I grabbed Kota's hand, pulling her towards me. "How are you feeling after last week?"

Her and Bobby recently ended things and considering how wary Kota was about showing her real emotions, I couldn't tell if she was actually okay or not.

But she gave me a massive smile, pumping her free fist in the air. "I'm great, B!"

"You're sure?"

"Hell yeah!"

I smiled. "Okay then."

When I peeked at the boys again, nothing had changed besides the look in Lane's eye.

His irises had become hazy, two deep sapphires boring into me.

The space between us dwindled as I danced towards him, pulling him onto the dance floor with more confidence than I'd ever had in my life.

"Bridget," he laughed, "I don't know how to dance."

"Just jump around, Lane!"

"I'm going to look stupid."

Kota wiggled her shoulders around. "You're going to look more stupid if you just stand there!"

"Yeah!" I agreed.

Lane didn't seem pleased. He looked like he'd been enjoying himself much more watching on the outside.

I rolled my eyes, shoulders slumping with disapproval. I clutched his hand again, nearly dropping it by instinct as an electrocuting spark shot all over my body, searing my skin and charring my bones.

My grip loosened as I caught my breath, and I wondered if the blaze had been one-sided, or he'd felt it too.

"Here," I choked out, extending our arms as I took a step back, waiting for him to pick up what I was putting down.

A small smile broke through his lips; he was getting the hang of it. Swinging around like we were ballroom dancing, things around us seemed to still.

Aside from the initial zap of electricity, his touch was easing me, and when one hand gripped my waist, the other leading me into a dip, I forgot every thought.

Up was down and left was right and not only was I seemingly dreaming but judging by the dozens of emotions and *hormones* jumping through my body, I was also in big trouble.

The second I straightened, Lane's hand snaked around me and flattened on my stomach, nearly big enough to take up the entire thing as he pulled me against him, my ass smushed against his front.

My heart tripped, stumbling over itself and almost breaking an ankle.

Was I supposed to be dancing right now? Was this Lane trying to make a move?

I stood frozen for a moment, paralyzed, but when I realized Lane had only been pulling me out of the way to allow a large, sweaty guy to pass through, flakes of disappointment fell off me like autumn leaves.

"Mr. Avery? Mr. Avery!"

I stepped away from Lane, trying to regain my composure and force my soul back into my body.

George was a bigger guy, African American with the brightest and friendliest smile I'd ever seen in my life. Everybody knew who he was; he was essentially a campus icon for his outgoing personality and exotic persona.

"Hey, George," Lane greeted him with a striking smile. "How many times have I told you to just call me Lane?"

"Sorry, Mr. Avery, I always forget."

"Lane," he corrected him again.

"Oh right. Lane," George nodded. "Can you do a quick interview?"

George had a sports blog and social media account dedicated to his love for sports, especially hockey. He was a huge fan of all the boys and even led the student section during games.

He could often be found interviewing athletes wherever he went, a phone camera in one hand and a microphone that didn't actually work in the other.

"Uh, sure, George," Lane said, guiding me back to Kota before disappearing.

I wasn't sure if she'd been watching Lane and I together, but if she happened to see visible sparks flying, she didn't admit it.

"We gotta get off the dance floor," she said.

"What? Why?"

"I have something to do."

With no further explanation, she dragged me behind her, and right as I realized what *or who* her target was, I dug my heels into the floor, a weak attempt to stop her.

"Kota!"

Animosity and fear swirled in Crew's brown eyes as Kota beelined for him, ripping the microphone away from his mouth. "I would like everybody to know that Nicholas Crew sucks eggs," she said into it.

His jaw clenched, snagging the microphone back. "Why do you have to ruin everything?"

"Because we haven't argued in days, and it makes me uncomfortable being nice to you for too long."

"Oh, so you're *trying* to start a fight?"

Lane comfortably crossed his arms, the cockiest grin I'd ever seen lighting up his face.

I stepped beside him as Crew and Kota did their thing. "Don't even start."

His chin tipped upwards, showing off that razor-sharp jawline of his. "I haven't said anything."

"I know, but you're about to." I snuck a peek at my phone. *Twelve-oh-seven.* "Lane."

"Yes?" he beamed.

"It's past midnight."

"So?"

"So, technically the night is over."

He didn't even blink as he swung to look at me. "Don't try to do that."

"Do what?" I smiled.

"Put a rule in place that wasn't originally there."

"I didn't invent time," I disputed.

"No, no, no," he smirked, pointing an accusing finger. "You lost fair and square."

I sighed, resting my hands on my hips. "What do you want?"

Cockiness drifting to interest, the jovial glimmer in his ocean eyes melted to something a bit more serious. My mind spun, and in the moment, I'd do absolutely anything just to know what was going through his head.

Indecisiveness slashed across his face. Clearing his throat, he gave a light shake of his head. "Nothing," he faltered.

"What?"

"Nothing. I don't want anything."

"But—"

"Mr. Avery?"

Lane looked up at George, and although it wasn't as golden as it was before, his amiable grin came back. "Lane."

"Yes, Lane," George smiled. He held the microphone up.

Lane nodded. "Yeah, let's finish up. Sorry about that George," he said, leaving my side.

Chapter Forty-Three

Bridget

Thanksgiving was one of my favorite holidays, right behind Christmas. I just loved that there was an entire holiday dedicated to family and eating.

My childhood home was decorated with fall leaves, turkeys, and other Thanksgiving-themed décor.

I took my designated spot at the table, the same one I'd sat at during every meal growing up. Impatiently, I waited for my parents and Bianca to take their seats so that I could start eating.

I purposely skipped lunch today to save extra room for dinner, and the turkey, mashed potatoes, and stuffing filling my plate were calling my name. _Especially_ the mashed potatoes.

Eagerly, my foot tapped the floor, and as Bianca shuffled over, I wished I had magic powers so I could make her hurry up.

My parents took their seats last, and we said grace before digging in.

I wasn't proud to admit that I was eating like a cavewoman, but personally, I called that the spirit of Thanksgiving.

I glanced around the table at my family as I chewed. Like hundreds of other times in my life, I didn't quite feel like I belonged.

My father had dark hair that was slowly disappearing, and obviously, since he wasn't my biological father, I looked nothing like him. My mother was a beautiful African American woman with dark hair that sat right at her shoulders. She was always smiling, always lovely, illuminating every room she walked into.

Which led to my sister. Whereas I burned after thirty minutes in the sun, Bianca was born with the most perfect olive skin and long, dark hair. She often reminded me of a very young Beyonce.

I stuck out in this family. Obviously, it wasn't anyone's fault, but I still wished I fit in better.

"Excited for your party tomorrow?" I asked Bianca between bites.

She nodded, chewing, the corners of her mouth lifting upwards with enthusiasm.

It was her birthday tomorrow, and my parents were throwing her a sweet-sixteen.

I didn't get a massive party for my sweet-sixteen. I guess I hadn't asked for one like Bianca had, but still.

"Do you have a lot of friends coming?" I asked.

"Yeah," she smiled at her plate.

Oh no. I knew exactly what she was thinking.

Boys.

She was officially at that age where she was obsessed with the idea of having a boyfriend. Every time I visited home, she was talking about a different guy she liked. It was hard to keep up at this point.

"It'll be fun," my mom said. She looked up at me. "I'm glad you'll be here for it."

"Me too."

"Also," she said, "we were talking about coming to visit in the spring once the weather isn't so crappy. How's that sound?"

I froze with my mouth full. I still hadn't told them about our living arrangement. Part of me had been hoping I could just avoid this conversation until Kota and I were moved out and this was all far in the past, but if they were going to come visit, there was no hiding it.

I'm just gonna rip the bandaid off.

"Uh, yeah, that sounds good," I said, picking at my plate. "There's actually something I've gotta tell you guys."

Three pairs of eyes dashed up at me. All three of them held different expressions.

Bianca was insanely curious, eyes creasing in the corners with delight like she was about to hear something juicy.

My mother looked worried, like I was about to tell her I'd gotten kicked out of school or gotten pregnant or something.

My father— I couldn't quite read. He almost looked confused? Indifferent?

"Kota and I..." I paused, ripping my eyes away, "are unfortunately and accidentally stuck living with two boys."

Bianca choked on a piece of turkey, gasping for air as she reached for her throat, then washed it down with water.

"You okay?" my mother asked her.

She nodded rapidly, twisting back towards me.

Mom sighed. "Sweetie, what are you talking about?"

I explained the story to them, waiting for some explosion of a reaction, but all I got was continued composure from everyone. *Other than Bianca choking.*

"Well," my dad shrugged, "nothing you can do about it now, I guess."

He'd never been a super protective girl-dad. Bianca was getting older, but since I didn't live at home, I wasn't sure if he was the same way with her that he was with me. Any time I'd brought a guy home in the past, he seemingly became their best friend. There had never been that "don't screw it up with my daughter talk" that you'd get from other dads.

"Are you at least comfortable?" Mom asked.

"Yeah!" I assured her, stabbing into my turkey. "Lane and Crew are good guys. They're not too terrible to live with."

Dad's eyes shifted upwards from his plate. His voice came out with an unconventional crack. "Lane and Crew?"

"Yeah..."

"The hockey players?"

"Yes."

There was a crash as he threw his fork onto his plate. "Oh my God! Why didn't you say so? This is huge!"

I forced myself not to roll my eyes. My dad was a big hockey fan, which thinking about it now, might've been why he'd approved of all my past boyfriends. I knew he occasionally watched college hockey, but I didn't think he was familiar with it enough to know specific players.

"Dad, it's not that big of a deal."

He planted his elbows on the table, resting his chin in his hands, completely engulfed in a fangirling moment. "What are they like?"

"Oh my God. Dad, *stop*."

He turned to Mom. "We might need to visit her sooner."

I sighed under my breath. At least they approved of my living arrangement.

Chapter Forty-Four

Lane

"**Y**our mom looks tense," Cooper whispered.

"She always looks like that," Dawson said.

Hazel scoffed, thumping the back of his head. "Dawson. That's his *mom*."

He rubbed the spot, shooting her a dirty glare. "Yeah, I know who she is."

My mom was the oldest of three, so naturally, Liam and I had been the oldest out of our cousins. Cooper, Hazel, and Dawson were all siblings, belonging to my Uncle Greg. They were a bit younger than us; Cooper was nineteen, Hazel was eighteen, and Dawson was fifteen.

My other two cousins here were my Uncle Pat's. Kylee and Joshua were only seven and five, and they were currently running around the house with more energy that I'd had in probably a decade. I was getting exhausted just watching them.

I sat back against the couch, crossing my arms over my chest, counting down the time until I could leave and go to my dad's.

I hated being at my mother's house, and knowing her, she'd be happy when I left. She'd hardly said two full sentences to me since I'd gotten here, and I arrived an hour ago.

The only thing that would've been worse than being here right now would've been being here alone with my mom. At least I had my cousins, aunts, and uncles as a buffer.

I remained quiet, eyes zipping around the living room with impatience.

Every wall was filled with something of Liam. Pictures, awards, an old, framed hockey jersey.

I was basically nonexistent in this house; the only appearances I had were photos of Liam that I just happened to also be in.

My mother stood in the walkway to the living room, seeming to only acknowledge my cousins as she spoke. "Food's ready."

They flew into the dining room, ready to eat. I took my time standing, basking in the remaining few seconds I had outside of my mother's presence.

All nine of us filled the long table, leaving one empty seat at the head. Sitting adjacent to the vacant chair, I struggled not to stare, knowing Liam should've been occupying it.

I didn't like gravy, but my mashed potatoes were currently bare, and to my misfortune, the salt and pepper were in the middle of the table, far out of reach.

I almost kept my mouth shut and ate them as they were, but I decided to be brave. "Mom," I said, clearing my throat, "can you pass the salt and pepper, please?"

Pretending like she hadn't heard me, she started up a conversation with my uncle beside her.

So much for being brave.

Hazel's brows were slanted lightly, an apologetic gleam casting over her features. She grabbed the salt and pepper and sent them my way.

"Thanks," I muttered.

Part of me wanted to get up and leave. This was exactly why my mother and I rarely spoke. She was always giving me a cold shoulder, looking at me like I was a demon she was stuck with. She hated me, and she wasn't shy about showing it.

"So, Cooper," my mom said, "how's hockey going?"

My fork stopped halfway to my mouth. *Funny how she could ask him about hockey but didn't bother asking her own son.*

"It's good," he nodded. "I'm gonna finish up this year and then hopefully transfer to a bigger school."

"Where to?"

"Probably UofM. I considered Cedar, but I don't really wanna live in Lane's shadow," he smiled at me.

Grinning, I shook my head, about to reassure him that his own talent had nothing to do with me, but my mother's grimace held me back.

"Mhmm," she hummed, resent hovering over her like a storm cloud.

"You know, Joyce," Uncle Greg said, "Lane has been doing exceptionally well. There's still time for you to convince him that the NHL is a good idea."

Ire rippled through the air as she spoke, heading straight for my throat. "That's going to have to be his own decision, Greg."

And this was exactly why I was not telling her the decision had already been made.

I'd tell my father, of course. I knew he'd be happy for me, support my decision, and guarantee me that it was my own hard work and dedication that got me here.

My mother on the other hand? There was a good chance she'd never speak to me again. I wasn't as upset with the idea as I used to be. I was at the point where I'd given up on trying to get her to like me or to be an active part of my life or to simply not hate the fact that I was her kid.

"But Joyce—" he started.

"Enough about hockey," she rushed out. "Hazel," she smiled deceivingly, "how are you?"

She went from person to person, asking how everyone was, all while skipping over me completely.

The second my plate was empty, I basically ran out of the house.

Chapter Forty-Five

Bridget

Not much had changed over the past few weeks, other than Crew and Kota going back to absolutely hating each other.

Lane and I weren't sure what happened between the time we left for Thanksgiving break and the time we got back, and neither of us cared enough to ask. Assuming it was some pathetic argument, it just seemed like everything was back to normal.

The most eventful thing that happened was running into Mitch at a hockey party. Instinctively, I ran the other way and Jett let me hide in his room for a little bit until Lane barged in, worried that I was being held against my will. Once I told him why I was in there, it took a while to convince him not to say anything to Mitch or start a fight.

We settled on sending a few of the boys to kick him out instead. And whatever sophomore on the team that had been inviting him to the parties got an earful and a warning to stop.

Lane and I had spent time at the library almost every day this past week, helping each other study for finals. Since my major was English, two of my finals were essays rather than exams. Then, I had one psychology exam and two English exams, which shouldn't have been too bad. The only bad part was that they were all scheduled for the end of the week, which meant I had three days of doing next to nothing.

My first essay was due tomorrow morning, which kind of sucked, yet I was thankful to get it out of the way. But as a result, I'd have to basically pull an all-nighter tonight. The assigned essay was a ten-page paper on F. Scott Fitzgerald, author of *The Great Gatsby*.

Apparently, my professor was obsessed, considering we had one of our earlier essays on *The Great Gatsby*. Now, for this essay, I had to research Fitzgerald, and write ten pages about his early life, how he came to be a writer, his effect on the literary world, and so on.

I had five pages done already, so I was only halfway.

Kill me.

Lane had some meeting with his coach, so I went to the library alone today and knocked out two more pages of the Fitzgerald essay, plus I wrapped up the other essay I needed to do, which thankfully, was not as strenuous as this one.

I decided to stop at one of the cafes on campus before heading home. If I was going to stay awake to finish this freaking essay, I would need a coffee.

I joined the line, waiting patiently. As it dwindled down and I got closer to order, I spotted a familiar face waiting by the end of the counter for her drink.

A friendly grin encompassed me as I waved, but instead of receiving the same response, Ava shot me an ice-cold glare before giving me a perfectly good view of her back.

What the hell was that for?

When we all went out together before Thanksgiving, Ava was also at the bar that night. Her and Lane exchanged a hug and spoke briefly, but the second he was back by me, her demeanor changed.

Since we'd met in passing a few times while her and Lane had been together, I tried saying hello that same night when I bumped into her in the bathroom, but she completely ignored me. I figured maybe she just didn't hear me or something, but now I was thinking otherwise.

I was still a little put off by the time I got home, and apparently it showed on my face, because the second Lane caught sight of me, he was quick to comment.

"What's wrong?" he asked kindly, his books and papers scattered across the kitchen island.

"I have a question," I said, hanging my winter jacket in the front closet.

"What's up?"

"Does Ava... not like me or something?"

The starlight in his eyes faded, turning bleak. "Why? What do you mean?"

"Well," I sat beside him, "do you remember when we all went out a few weeks ago?" He nodded. "She was kind of giving me dirty looks all night and ignored me when I tried saying hi. Then, I just saw her at the café on campus and she pretty much did it again."

He pushed his mouth into a hard line. "Hm," was all he said.

"Hm?" My head jutted forward lightly. "Does she not like me for some reason?"

When Lane inhaled, it was long and sounded a bit shaky. He took his bottom lip between his teeth, looking deep in thought. And if I didn't know any better, I'd say I could hear the fast drumming of his heartbeat.

I was prepared to hear that she hated me for some bullshit reason or was jealous that fate chose me to be stuck as Lane's roommate instead of her, or some other dumb explanation for why she was acting the way she was.

But then Lane shook his head. "I'm not sure."

"You're not?"

"No," he said, brows furrowed as his eyes briefly dropped to his lap.

"Oh," I responded under my breath. "Okay then." I turned towards the island, expecting Lane to jump into a casual conversation like he usually did whenever we were seated here together, but instead, he was quiet.

Abnormally quiet. So quiet that it was concerning me.

I couldn't hear his deep breaths or sighs that he usually gave out while we were studying. I couldn't hear any sort of rustling beside me.

It was just silent.

And the eerie silence was making me uncomfortable.

I cleared my throat. "How was your meeting?"

"It was good."

"What was it for?"

Lane spun back and forth on his stool, a faint smile appearing. "I had some news that I wanted to tell my coach."

My brows raised with both interest and concern. "News?"

The pride radiating off him was palpable. His smug smile was stapled to his face, and I could tell that whatever he was about to say was something he'd been holding in for a while.

"I've decided to go pro," he said confidently.

I stared at him with my mouth agape for what seemed like an eternity before I finally let out a jubilant squeal. "Lane! That's amazing!" I hopped off my stool and closed the two-foot gap between us, arms folding around the back of his neck like a sloth hugging a tree. My eyes closed as I gave a meaningful squeeze. "I'm so happy for you."

When we let go, Lane's hands remained on my forearms, lightly clutching onto them to keep me in place. His grin was still there, but his eyes had turned almost serious. They were this intoxicating shade of blue and looking at them so closely was like hanging over a boat and staring into the ocean, tempting you to fall in on purpose.

With every second that went by, still standing with Lane's fingers enclosed around my skin, the harder the blood began banging through my veins with the strength of the water that entered the Titanic.

Our hasty exhales were mixing together between us, and the faster my heart began beating, the more I was worried he'd be able to feel it under my skin.

Lane's tongue darted out, touching his lips for a moment before disappearing. "I wanna tell you something."

Chapter Forty-Six

Lane

The words were on the tip of my tongue, threatening to fall out.

I like you.

I've always liked you, Bridget.

The reason why Ava hates you is because she knows how I feel about you.

But I thought better of it.

Sure, part of me was afraid of rejection. But I was more afraid of what would happen if she said it back.

For starters, I didn't think breaking our house rule would be in anyone's best interest. Crew had been very adamant on keeping the rule in place since we moved in, and I wasn't trying to start a whirlwind of chaos under our roof.

Not to mention, if things ended badly, my entire friendship with Bridget would crumble.

I didn't have this type of friendship with anyone else. Crew was my best friend— practically my brother— but we didn't have the same playful, casual friendship that Bridget and I had.

With Bridget, we never got tired of each other. We could be doing the most mundane things and it was still always fun. I couldn't think of a single time Crew and I went grocery shopping together or studied together or even walked to class together. I also felt like I was able to show a side of myself to Bridget that no one else, including my teammates, saw. Not because I was necessarily hiding those parts of myself from them, but simply because they didn't bring those parts of me out.

I wanted Bridget to stay in my life. Now and in the future. Even long after I left Cedar and ended up on whatever team I was bound to end up on.

Not to mention that if something bad did happen between us, we'd still be forced to live together.

And that would absolutely suck.

Those honey brown eyes of Bridget's hadn't left my face in what felt like a lifetime, staring at me with the patience of a saint.

My grip on Bridget's fragile wrist loosened. I sucked in a breath much sharper than necessary. "I'm really thankful for our friendship."

With no idea what she thought I was going to say, I watched her reaction closely. Her eyes twinkled with admiration. As the corners of her mouth raised, she took a small step backwards, creating some distance between us. Immediately, I felt like she was too far away.

"Me too, Lane," she softly said.

My teeth sunk into my lower lip, trying to use the physical pain to distract myself from the pain inside me.

"Are you still going home this weekend?" I asked as she sat back in her seat.

"Yeah, are you?"

"Yeah, just for a few days."

"When are you leaving?"

"Sometime on Friday," I answered. "You?"

"Same, actually."

I gave her a nod. "Just gotta get through the week."

Bridget sighed, tapping her fingers along the edge of her computer. "Just gotta get through the week."

Chapter Forty-Seven

Bridget

As finals week came to an end, I was pretty confident about all my finals except one.

The fucking ten-pager.

Usually, Lane never distracted me. He was normally what *kept* me from getting distracted, because he was always busy doing his own work and encouraging me to get mine done too.

But on Sunday, he was most definitely the cause of the poor writing quality towards the end of my essay.

It wasn't because he was talking or being loud. I just simply couldn't focus after our almost whatever-it-was.

I had quite literally no idea what he was going to do or say in that moment, but I do remember a million possibilities going through my head— none of which happened.

I have feelings for you, Bridget.
I wanna be more than friends.
I really want to fucking kiss you right now.

The last one was pathetic, I know. But every single thought I had was somewhere along those lines.

So, when all he said was that he was grateful for our friendship, it warmed my heart, but it was also a small punch in the gut. Over the past few weeks, I'd been starting to think that maybe Lane did see me as more than a friend, but every time those thoughts occurred, I had to remind myself that I shouldn't have cared anyway.

Either way, it was all solidified now.

I was friend-zoned. And I had no choice but to accept it.

Now, I was sitting criss-crossed applesauce on my bedroom floor, neatly folding my clothes and placing them into my suitcase like I was playing a game of Tetris.

My phone rang, and when my mother's name lit up the screen, I put the call on speaker and placed the phone beside me.

"Hey, Mom! I'm packing right now, so I'll probably try to head out in a few hours."

"Actually, honey, that's why I'm calling you. I don't think you should come home tonight," she said. "There's going to be a huge snowstorm and I really don't want you driving through it."

I dropped the shirt I was folding into my lap, my shoulders sinking, mouth rounding into a long frown. "A snowstorm?" I asked. "Since when?"

She sighed into the phone. "A few days ago. I've been checking every day to see if the forecast changed but it hasn't."

"Ugh, well that stinks." I tossed my shirt to the side. "Should I just leave tomorrow then?"

"I'm not sure, sweetie. Apparently, it's supposed to be really bad, so I don't know how long it'll last or how long it'll take them to clear the roads."

"How much snow are we supposed to get?"

"Almost two feet," she answered.

My brows shot up to my hairline. Leave it to Minnesota to get next to no snow all December and then get a blizzard a week before Christmas.

"Geez," I sighed, squeezing my eyes shut as I rubbed my forehead. "Alright, well I guess we'll keep each other updated."

"Okay, Bridget. Love you."

"Love you too."

I couldn't help but let out another sigh as I pushed myself to standing, ditching my suitcase.

Crew left last night— lucky bastard. He finished all his finals on Tuesday. I still wasn't sure how that was possible, but apparently his were crammed between Monday and Tuesday, so, he got to do absolutely nothing on Wednesday and Thursday before leaving in the evening.

Perks of living twenty minutes away.

Kota left on Wednesday, eager to get home and spend some more time with her mom. She took Rob K with her too.

Now, it was just Lane and me. And I had no idea if he was still planning on leaving or not today.

Lane's door was cracked open already, so I peeked my head in. I hadn't heard him rustling around the apartment since early this morning, so I partially assumed he'd fallen back asleep.

And from the looks of it, I was right.

Lane looked like he'd been wrestling with his black comforter in his sleep. Half of it was hanging off his body, exposing him.

My eyes raked over him like a fire spreading across a dry field. An outline of his dick could be made through his grey sweatpants. Three perfect pairs of abs, accompanied by a distinct V disappeared into the waistband of his sweats. His breathing was even, peaceful, as he laid there with an arm resting behind his head.

I shamelessly took in the sight, fantasizing about crawling into the bed next to him.

He looked like the type of men I read about. And goddamn, it was doing something to me.

I had no idea what sound left my mouth. A moan? A word? A sigh? No idea, but apparently something did, because Lane's eyes shot open.

My lungs tightened, holding in a bubble of air for a moment. "Hey," I said in a panic.

His voice came out gravelly. "Hey."

Awkwardly, I sunk back a little. "Were you asleep?"

"Not completely."

"Oh."

A trace of a smile touched his lips. "How long have you been standing there?"

This is fucking embarrassing.

"Not long," I said. "Just a minute."

There was a glow in his cheeks as he laid there, amused. I watched his free hand clutch the edge of the comforter for a moment, and I was ashamed to admit I was jealous of fabric.

"So," his smile flickered, "did you come in here for something or do you always sneak in while I'm sleeping?"

I crossed my arms, finding a place against the doorframe. But his smirk was so contagious that I couldn't get rid of my own. "Actually yeah," I joked. "I usually take pictures of you while you sleep and sell them to all the girls that are in love with you."

His eyes narrowed slightly, but not with resentment— with amusement yet again. "There aren't any girls that are in love with me."

I scoffed, straightening. "Have you been around this campus lately?"

He playfully rolled his eyes, his crooked smirk not budging.

"Are you still going home today?"

"Yeah."

My brows rose. "Even with the storm?"

Lines creased his forehead as he pushed himself up to sit. "What storm?"

"Apparently there's gonna be a blizzard," I said.

Lane's eyes widened. "A blizzard?" he gasped. "You're joking."

"Nope."

"Ugh," he grumbled, his head dropping for a moment. "Do you know how much we're supposed to get?"

"Almost two feet, I guess," I answered.

"Jesus," Lane muttered under his breath as he shook his head. His blue eyes zipped across the room towards his window. Without saying anything, he threw the covers off him and stood.

My gaze impulsively landed on his bare skin, taking in the other half of him that had been hiding under his comforter just minutes before. Lane glanced at me, and I stiffened, assuming I'd been caught. I could feel the heat rising in my cheeks and spreading across my face, growing so hot that I may as well have just stuck my face in fire.

Lane's mouth twitched upwards in the slightest, but he still didn't comment, trudging directly over to his window and whipping his curtain open.

White flakes were coming down at a steady pace and the road beside our apartment building already had a thin layer covering it.

I gasped. "It started already? It's not even noon yet!"

Resting his forearm on the window, Lane looked back at me, and the light piercing through the window only illuminated every feature of his. It was hard not to gasp again.

Goddamn. It wasn't fair that someone so pretty was off-limits.

He didn't look disappointed in the slightest as he spoke. "Well, Bridget, it looks like we're stuck together for the day."

Chapter Forty-Eight

Bridget

Our first day stuck together was spent in the laziest way possible— watching movies. We used the storm as an excuse to finally have the *Rocky* marathon we'd been talking about having for weeks.

The snow came down steadily throughout the day yesterday, only stopping for a maximum of twenty minutes at a time, and even then, that only happened once or twice. There had to be over a foot of snow at this point, and there was no sign of it stopping or slowing down.

Lane and I had gotten through all six *Rocky* movies and were on the first *Creed* movie now.

We were laying on opposite sides of the couch, sharing a blanket with our legs tangled beneath it.

"I'm hungry," Lane announced for the third time.

"Shh," I hushed, "you're distracting me from the movie."

"Bridgettt," he whined.

"Go make food then."

"Will you cook with me?"

"No," I said.

"Why not?"

"*Creed* is on!" I argued.

With one click of a button, Lane paused the movie and sat up, staring at me intently with a brow raised.

"Lane!" I scolded.

"Will you cook with me?" he repeated.

I let out a frustrated groan, ripping the blanket off me. My stomps were the only sound echoing through the apartment, bringing me all the way to the kitchen. Lane didn't budge, still watching me curiously as I snatched a frozen pizza out of the freezer, dropped it on the counter and preheated the oven.

When I turned, Lane's frown was curved like the surface of a balloon. "Well, I don't want that."

I shot him a look.

Sinking back a little, he said, "Alright, I'll eat it."

Letting out a huff, I reclaimed my spot on the couch. "Please hit play now."

Lane's face was lit up with amusement, eyes glowing. "You're feisty today."

My shoulders stiffened against the couch cushion. *I was feisty today.*

Why was I so feisty? I just got off my period a few days ago, so it wasn't that. The logical reason would be that being stuck inside all day and night was driving me towards insanity, but I didn't think it was necessarily that either.

I'd never spent this much time with *just* Lane. We were up so late last night that we passed out on the couch, and I basked in his warmth all night before waking up to him telling me how smooth my legs were under the blanket.

Oh no. I definitely had some sort of sexual frustration with him.

He was bothering me.

Not because he was annoying. But because the way I *felt* towards him was annoying.

I took a deep breath, keeping my eyes towards the TV. "Sorry," I muttered.

His expression turned caring as he sat up all the way, his hand casually running across my back in an attempt to comfort me, but the gesture had the opposite effect.

"Everything okay?"

"Yeah," I said softly. "Just hate being stuck inside."

"I know," he gently responded, his hand sending shivers throughout me. "It should be over by the morning hopefully."

My gaze didn't stray from the TV, afraid that if Lane was able to see my expression, that he'd be able to read it for what it truly was.

The worst part was that *I* didn't even know what it truly was.

Disappointment that I was friend-zoned? Sadness? Bitterness? Confusion? Lust?

Maybe a little of everything.

"I wish we could get drunk," I blurted out.

A gruff laugh left his mouth. "I mean, we can."

"How? We have nothing to drink, and we can't go to the store."

"Do you not know our roommates? I'm sure they have something hidden in their rooms."

I shot forward. "Oh! Kota has wine in her room that we got last week."

The oven beeped as Lane smiled. "There ya go. Why don't you go get it and I'll toss the pizza in?"

He didn't have to ask me twice. I practically leapt off the couch and poured myself a glass of wine quicker than Lane could sit back down.

I'd been hoping the alcohol would ease my racing thoughts, but by the time I got to my second glass, the thoughts were still going strong— along with the weird sexual tension that was building inside me.

God, maybe this wine was a bad idea.

After two pieces for me, the rest of the pizza had disappeared faster than anyone thought possible thanks to Lane and his enormous appetite. The movie was on but all I could hear was the sound of my own misery ringing in my ears.

"I've gotta pee," I mumbled, practically slamming my empty glass on the table as it were a gavel.

The second I sat on the toilet and started to go, everything went black.

"Um." My eyes frantically whipped around, adjusting to the darkness. "Lane!"

Heavy steps slowly made their way towards me from down the hall. "Bridget?" Lane knocked. "Are you okay in there?"

"What the hell happened?"

"I think the power went out."

Fucking great.

"Well, turn it back on!" I yelled.

"Uh, yeah, I don't think it's that type of outage, Bridget. It's definitely from the storm. Not a blown fuse or something."

"Goddammit," I cussed.

"Do you need help?"

I squinted through the darkness. "Um, I know how to wipe myself, thank you."

Lane's voice got quieter as he stepped away from the door, but I could just make out the word "feisty."

After living in the apartment for months, I knew the layout like the back of my hand, but it still felt kind of like a maze navigating my way through the dark.

"Where are you?" I asked.

A light hit my face and I let out a small shriek, holding a hand out to shield myself.

"Right here," Lane smiled behind the flashlight on his phone.

"What're we gonna do?" I sighed. "We're gonna have to light some candles or something, I guess."

"How romantic," Lane joked, fighting a smile.

I angled my body to the side to hide my reaction as my teeth gritted together. It was the shit like this that Lane said or did that made the lines blur. And Lord help me, because I was only a few glasses of wine away from making some sort of mistake.

My voice came out more passive aggressive than intended. "Do you have any candles?"

His charming smirk fell to a wary line. "I might," he murmured, turning and heading towards his room. I huffed, watching the light of his phone disappear down the hallway before feeling around for my own.

Kota: How are things at the apartment?

Me: Convenient timing. Power just went out

Kota: Uh oh

Me: Uh oh is right. You got any candles?

Kota: Check on my mini bookshelf. There should be a few

Between Lane and me, we had five candles, and I managed to find another two in Kota's room. We didn't bother checking to see if Crew had any.

One by one, we lit each candle and set them around the living room. I wasn't sure why I decided to sit in the center of the floor, but Lane followed my lead.

"Geez, this is kinda creepy," I said, pouring a third glass of wine. "Looks like a séance or something."

The candles were just bright enough to catch the flecks of blue light in his eyes. "Or that one scene from *The Notebook*," he said.

I clutched the stem of my glass, breathing heavily out my nose. Every time I tried to push my irritation away and act normal, he did or said something that brought it all right back. "I don't even know what scene you're talking about."

"Oh, you know," he spoke casually, pouring himself a glass, "when they're in that old house and they almost fuck, but don't."

And now he was talking about fucking. Great. I'm going to lose my goddamn mind by the time this night is over. Might as well just go to bed now.

"They have a bunch of candles lit in that scene, right?" he questioned, his brows nearly touching. "Or am I wrong?"

I took a decent swig of wine. "I don't remember. Since when did you watch *The Notebook* anyway?"

He shrugged. "I watched it once with Ava."

227

There was a gnawing feeling coming from within me, replacing the bitterness with a different type of fire. *Uh oh.* Was that jealousy?

It made no sense that just days ago, I was asking him if she hated me and now, I was jealous hearing the sound of her name casually roll off his lips.

I just spent two whole days with him, just the two of us alone. Did I even have the right to be jealous? What was there to be jealous of?

Distract yourself, Bridget. Change the subject.

I shot up, shielding my resentment with a cloak of excitement. "Well, since we can't watch the movie anymore, let's play a game!"

The candles were making him glow, and with his light brown hair and blue eyes to match, illustrations of Superman came to mind.

Lane chuckled. "What game?" He smiled into his glass of wine, and I swore I'd never wanted to taste a grin more in my life.

I blurted out the first thing that came to mind. "American Idol."

He laughed again. "How the hell do you play American Idol?"

"You've never played American Idol before?"
"No?"

I sat directly in front of him, much closer than I thought I had the courage *or* self-control for. "That's a sad, sad life you've had then, Lane."

His grin spread, making my heart sprint. "Are you drunk?"

"No," I denied. "Let's play American Idol."
"Alright," he playfully sighed. "How do you play?"
"One person sings and then everyone else is a judge."
"But, Bridget..." he snickered, "there's only two of us."
I crossed my arms. "So?"

Lane held his glass out defensively. "Alright, alright. I'll go first, I guess." He set his glass down and stood, clearing his throat. Suddenly, he began belting out the chorus of "With or Without You" by U2.

228

My hand shot over my mouth, silencing the gust of laughter that wanted to escape, and when Lane attempted to hit the high note, the laughter found its way out.

"Why are you laughing?" he shot at me.

"I'm sorry," I wheezed, "but I really think you should stick to hockey."

"Wow." He placed a hand over his chest as if he were wounded. "You're worse than Simon Cowell."

"Don't even!" I laughed.

"This game sucks," he smiled. "Let's play something else."

I pushed myself backwards until my back was resting against the coffee table. "Like?"

Lane sat beside me, and before I could react, he laid down, resting his head in my lap.

Inevitably, I gulped, and against my better judgement, my free hand found its way into his hair, weaving through it.

For a long moment, Lane was quiet, as if distracted. When he finally spoke, his voice had a melodic ring to it, coming out as a soft hum. "I, uh, think we have cards. We could play go-fish."

Lane's eyes scanned over my face right as I gave a light grin. "When I was little, I used to think it was called goldfish," I said.

His husky laughter made my lap vibrate beneath him. "It doesn't even sound like goldfish."

"Yes, it does."

"Not really," he subtly beamed, his eyes coming to a close.

It was strange how normal it felt to be sitting like this with him even though we'd never had such an intimate moment before.

Our light breaths were the only sound throughout the room, and if I thought I'd been having a hard time resisting him all day, the universe was seriously testing me now.

I could smell the strong scent of him, like a mixture of fresh linen and the ocean. And every time my hand found its way through his hair, I had to make sure it didn't wander elsewhere— along his jawline, the thin skin on his neck, the prominent collarbones sticking out of his t-shirt.

The closeness was tempting me like never before, not to mention that it was confusing me.

Did close friends of the opposite gender usually act like this towards each other?

All it would've taken was a split second to lean down and taste that peaceful grin that I'd been staring at all night. He was that close; I wanted him closer, but I also wanted him farther away.

It took every last bit of self-control to snap myself out of the fantasy.

I stuck a finger in my mouth, then lodged it into Lane's ear.

His Superman blue eyes shot open, and I hated to admit that I was a little relieved because I kind of missed the sight when they were closed.

"Ahh!" Lane covered his ear. "Did you just give me a wet willy?"

"Yeah," I giggled.

"What was that for?"

"I was trying to get your attention."

"Well mission accomplished. What is it?"

I glanced out the window, hardly seeing the white flecks as they tumbled down at the slowest pace I'd seen in the last day and a half.

My voice fell. "Can we go play outside?"

"What?" Lane chuckled. "Like go in the snow?"

"Yeah."

"Uh, do you have snow stuff?"

"Do you?" I asked.

He shrugged, his shoulders bumping into me. "Crew and I go snowboarding occasionally."

"Oh," I frowned. "I can just layer up."

"Layer up?" he laughed again. "I don't know how much that'll help."

I waved him off. "I'll just drink a bit more wine and then I won't feel anything."

230

"Alright," he unsurely agreed as he sat up. Instantly, I felt the ghost of his touch.

I downed the rest of my glass, then reached for the bottle again.

Chapter Forty-Nine

Bridget

Holy fucking snow.

It was hardly past Lane's shins, but it went all the way up to my knees.

I had three pairs of pants on, along with three layers on top, a hat, and gloves. I'd been right though. The wine was numbing me; I couldn't even feel the cold.

After making a deformed snowman and countless snow angels, I took a seat right in the middle of the snow, slightly out of breath.

"Tired?" Lane smiled.

"A little," I admitted, my heavy eyes shutting gradually. I was zen for a moment, feeling the cool air fall over the exposed skin on my face.

Until a cold ball of snow sent me flying over.

"Hey!" I yelled through a mouthful of snow, pushing myself up.

The mischievous grin on Lane's face was unmistakable. "Did that wake you up?"

My teeth clenched, gathering a pile of snow and constructing it into a ball between my palms. I hurdled it Lane's way, smug when it hit the corner of his jaw.

He wiped the wetness off with the back of his glove, and right as he bent over to make ammo to retaliate, I got up and ran at him full force, more than surprised with my sudden strength to knock him over.

"What the hell, Bridget?" he laughed beneath me. "Did you turn into a linebacker overnight? Holy fuck!"

I chuckled, but the second I realized how close we were now, my laughter ceased.

I was lying directly on top of him, my face inches from his. It didn't seem possible that a heart could beat as frantically as mine was right now, tapping against my chest like a jackhammer.

Lane had grown quiet too. He didn't try to push me off him. All he did was study me with those eyes, waiting to see what I would do next.

I'd had four glasses of wine, which was more than I usually drank, but the current proximity to him was by far the most intoxicating moment I'd had all night.

Our breath blended between us, and in the cold, December air, there was a visible cloud of it.

Get up, Bridget. Get up, get up, get—

I ignored the screaming conscience inside my head, letting my lips crash onto his.

Chapter Fifty

Lane

Everything about her lips on mine felt right. If I could freeze this moment in time, I would.

The delicacy in the kiss was something I'd never experienced before. It was so sensual, so personal.

Our cold lips warmed up against each other, and I almost forgot we were laying in a pile of snow.

Lips slowly memorizing one another, opening and closing in a sweet rhythm, I soaked in the moment, bringing my gloved hands to Bridget's lower back and holding her to me. She eased into me, and the more she did, the more I was convinced she could feel my drastic heartbeat banging against her own chest.

I knew your brain released chemicals when you kissed someone, *but goddamn*, I was high on this kiss right now.

I'd been wanting this for so long, and it was better than I ever could've imagined.

But when she finally pulled away, I immediately recognized the look on her face. *Regret.*

Well, fuck.

Chapter Fifty-One

Lane

I was starting to get a little pissed off.

Was she seriously going to kiss me and then ignore me for a week?

It felt like the moment I'd been waiting months for was slowly getting taken from me, because I was becoming convinced that she full-heartedly wished it never happened, and that didn't make it special at all anymore.

The second she pulled away, her demeanor changed, as if she'd suddenly gotten sober and realized she fucked up. We went back inside right afterwards, and she awkwardly retreated to her room, then left to go home the next morning before I even woke up.

I'd texted her numerous times over the past week, asking what she was up to and how her break was going, and she was being so short with me.

I was definitely overthinking at this point, but I couldn't help it. I wanted to know what was going through her head, but ever since we all got back today to go out for New Year's Eve, she hadn't given me a single opportunity to get her alone and talk to her.

First, it was showering and using cleaning as an excuse. Then, it was getting Starbucks with Kota and going God knew where else considering how long they were gone for. And now it was her getting ready.

Crew and I were already dressed and ready to go, and not going to lie, he was acting weird too. I wasn't sure why, but I didn't have the mental capacity to ask. I had too much going on in my own head.

The only person acting somewhat normal in this house was Kota, and even she seemed a little off.

When the girls finally emerged from down the hall, my body tightened, as though each step Bridget took was like a bullet to my chest.

I devoured every inch of her with my gaze, not even trying to be subtle with it. And if no one else were in this room right now, I'd be pulling her to me.

Black heels made her legs look longer, accompanied with a tight black mini dress, hardly covering her thighs. Her strawberry locks were in a tight, half up-half down hair style, loose curls waterfalling down. And to top it off, her lips were glossy, wet, begging me to taste them.

Crew cleared his throat beside me, and when I finally wrestled my gaze away from Bridget, it seemed like Crew was struggling just as hard as I was.

He was awkwardly shifting his weight around, his eyes wandering over everything in the apartment *besides* Kota.

No fucking wonder.

She looked good too.

Her dress was a similar style to Bridget's, but instead of black, she was wearing red, making her dark hair and eyes pop.

Crew's voice was rocky. "Why are you guys so dressed up?"

"Because it's fucking New Year's Eve," Kota shot at him.

"Mhm," he said, looking at me. "Alright, can we go?"

"Yes, please," Bridget murmured.

"No jacket?" I asked, trailing behind the girls.

236

"We'll just be right across the street," Kota said. "We can brace the cold for a few minutes."

She was right, but I still grabbed my jacket.

The only thing was that I wasn't even sure if I was grabbing it for myself.

***

Bridget ran to the bathroom, and I used the opportunity to practically corner Kota.

"Is Bridget alright?"

She eyed me like I was on drugs. "Yeah... why?"

"I don't know," I shrugged, hoping she couldn't see through me. "Seems a little off."

"Do you want me to talk to her?"

"No," I blurted, before trying to cover my panic. "I, uh, I'll talk to her."

"Okay..." Kota's eyes narrowed slightly, a suspicious, borderline sinister smile appearing. "You're acting weird."

"No, I'm not."

"Yeah, you are."

"*You're* acting weird," I accused.

She straightened defensively. "No, I'm not!"

Crew appeared beside me with his new beer. "Who's acting weird?"

"No one!" Kota and I exclaimed in unison.

He raised his brows. "Alright then."

"What time is it?" I nudged him.

"Almost eleven thirty."

I nodded.

"Captain, oh, Captain!" a voice rang behind me. I turned, seeing Jett's jaunty smile along with a shot glass being shoved in my face. "Team shot!" he announced, handing one to me and then one to Crew.

Crew made the mistake of smelling it before giving a look of disgust. "What the hell is it?"

"Rumple Minze!"

"Oh Jesus," I muttered under my breath. "You know this shit is like a hundred proof, right?"

Jett looked at me like I was the fucking idiot here. "Yeah," he scoffed. "That's why we fuckin' got it."

"How many shots have you had so far?" I asked.

Jett did a little dance around our circle. "This would be my first... of this kind, that is. I've already had a few others, though," he smiled. "Plus some beers."

I glanced around at the other guys, doing a wellness check.

TJ was leaning against a nearby wall with slightly droopy eyes, talking to some girl.

Cody and Matt were facing each other, both chugging beers like they were having a goddamn competition.

Crew seemed to be alright, but I knew him well enough to know that too many shots mixed with beer and he'd be out like a light.

"When did you guys start drinking?" I asked Jett.

He shrugged. "I don't know. Five? Six?" He gave Matt a tap on the shoulder, who was wiping his mouth with the back of his hand. "Hey, when'd we start drinking?"

"Around three, I think," Matt answered.

"Je-*sus!*" I spoke.

Jett waved off my concern. "We've been pacing ourselves."

"Yeah, I'm sure."

"Oh, c'mon, *Dad,*" he teased, "don't be such a fucking downer. It's New Year's Eve!"

I sighed, knowing this night probably wasn't going to end well. I took silent bets on which one of them would end up with their head in the toilet first.

Definitely Matt.

Then again, he might just end up with his hand in a Pringles can.

"Are we taking this thing or not?" Crew spurred. "I'm tired of smelling it!"

"Then stop smelling it," Jett criticized.

"Yeah, a little hard not to when it's strong as fuck and right in front of my face," Crew whirred.

238

"Alright, ladies," I said, shoving my glass in the middle of the circle.

Kota stepped into the center, looking like a munchkin compared to the rest of us. "Hey! I want one!"

Crew didn't look at her as he spoke with ice in his voice. "Yeah, this stuff's a little too strong for you."

She crossed her arms. "I can handle it."

"Here," Jett intervened, handing her a shot. "You can have my second one."

"Second one?" I questioned. "You were gonna take two?"

Another shrug.

Correction. Maybe Jett would end up with his head in the toilet first.

The other guys came in, and Kota was short enough compared to the rest of us that she stayed in the center of the circle, holding her glass straight above her head to meet ours.

"Happy New Year's Eve, fuckers," Cody grinned.

Seven shot glasses were flicked backwards, and I squeezed my eyes shut as the minty poison fell down my throat. Everyone else seemed to have the same reaction, looks of disgust lingering.

"Goddamn," TJ nearly gagged. "I forgot how strong that shit is."

"I like it!" Kota smiled wide. "Tastes like mint!"

"You want another one?" Jett asked her smugly.

Crew stepped forward in the slightest. "I think she's good for now."

Kota gave him the dirtiest side eye I'd ever seen, and I couldn't help but laugh, but to my surprise, she didn't start a fight.

One by one, heads were subtly turning, glancing towards the far corner of the bar. As the crowd of people parted like the goddamn Red Sea, revealing Bridget, I let out a cough as if I were choking on air.

A muffled whistle came from beside me, and without looking at him, I smacked Jett on the shoulder.

"Ow!" he cried, rubbing the spot with his hand.

"Keep your eyes to yourself," I warned.

Seemingly just to spite me, Jett cracked a wicked smile. "Hey, Bridget!"

"Hey," she smiled back.

"Here, B," Kota intervened, handing her a drink. Bridget accepted but looked at her silently. "Vodka sprite."

She nodded before taking the straw between those perfectly full lips and taking a long sip.

God fucking dammit.

It was becoming harder and harder not to stare at her. I bit the inside of my cheek, because fuck, ever since kissing her last week, it was all I could think about now. Those shiny lips were teasing me.

I could not be standing next to her when midnight struck. Because if I was, I would absolutely kiss her. Shamelessly, might I add.

I still needed to talk to her, though, and I needed to do it tonight for my own sanity.

Without a word, I placed my hand on the small of her back, leading her a few feet away from everyone.

"Hey," I said, "are you alright?"

Rather nervously, she rubbed her opposite arm with her free hand. "Yeah."

"You sure? I just... feel like something's off."

"I'm fine," she said, attempting to give me a reassuring grin. But to my dislike, she stepped around me, leaving it at that.

Now I was even more confused.

Did she just simply regret the kiss or was there more to it than that? Was it bad? Did she feel awkward around me now since we're such good friends? Did she think our roommates would be mad if they found out, considering our no hooking up rule?

I overanalyzed every possibility as the clock ticked closer and closer to midnight. And when the countdown began, I made sure not to be standing next to Bridget.

A few of the guys grabbed random girls to kiss while the rest of us cheered and slapped down another shot.

"You guys coming over after this?" TJ asked.

240

I glanced at my roommates, who all seemed to nod in agreement.

"Yeah," I said.

"Cool. Jett and I are heading back there now. Matt and Cody are staying for a bit. Let us know when you're on your way."

I gave him a nod before turning and lightly grabbing Bridget's wrist. "Are you planning on changing before we go to the house?"

She shifted awkwardly. "Yeah."

Leaning forward, I placed my mouth close to her ear. "Walk with me?"

With a gulp, she glanced back at Kota before nodding, and for the first time tonight, my chest lightened.

"Hey," I tapped Crew. "Bridget and I are gonna stop at our place before the party." I motioned to Kota, "You got her?"

With the quickest glance at Kota, he gave a sigh. But instead of distaste in his voice, there was a trace of defeat. "Yeah. I've got her."

I gave him a casual slap on the back. "See you at the house."

Without looking back, I covered Bridget's hand with my own, leading her out the back door. If she'd let me, I would've held her hand the entire way back, but the second we were in the cold air, she broke that cherished contact.

I shook my jacket off and draped it over her shoulders.

"Thanks," she whispered.

The anticipation was suffocating me now. I had approximately two minutes to get answers to the clusterfuck in my brain.

As we turned the corner around the building, I considered that my next move wasn't a good idea. Using alcohol and emotions as fuel never typically ended well, but I didn't seem to have time to stop myself before I was grasping onto Bridget's wrist and pushing her against the wall.

I rested an arm against the brick above her head. "Hear me out," I breathed heavily. She stared up at me with those innocent eyes, her lips pressed together as both of our hearts pounded like heavy rainfall. "I don't know what changed between last week and now, but I can feel you pulling away from me and I fucking hate it."

She seemed more and more nervous with each passing second, and for some reason, I found it attractive.

Her voice was a whisper, but it came out like a strained scream. "I shouldn't have kissed you."

I'd assumed she regretted it but thinking it and hearing it were two different things. "Why?"

"Because I know you don't feel that way about me." Every word coming out of her mouth was dripping with embarrassment and torment. I stared at her, feeling like I was burning as my brows knitted together. "You told me so," she added.

"When?" I shook my head.

"You literally made it a point to tell me how much you appreciate our friendship. That sounds like the friend-zone to me."

My eyes clenched shut and I let a deep breath out my nose. "Bridget," I spoke as my eyes opened, "I like you. I've always fucking liked you. Why I never said anything, I don't know. But I can't keep pretending like I don't have the biggest crush on you. It's too fucking hard."

I should've pulled away, knowing that I'd already just complicated things even further under our shared roof. But apparently, I was the world's biggest masochist, because instead of pulling away, I pushed forward.

Our lips meshed, and she intertwined her fingers behind my neck. After staring at her mouth all night, her lips tasted even better than I could've imagined, the strong taste of strawberry hitting my tongue.

My free hand found its way to her waist, wrapping around it and giving a light squeeze before snaking around her backside and doing the same with her ass.

I swallowed the small moan she let out, and before I knew it, I was smiling against her mouth. Now, I was losing my mind in a good way.

I pulled away just a little, before going back in for one last kiss and holding it until I ran out of breath.

242

When my eyes met her face again, I took a mental snapshot to remember later. Her cheeks were flushed, and I took pleasure in knowing that it wasn't just from the cold.

This time, her whisper didn't come out as a scream. It came out sounding like a prayer. "I like you too."

I broke into a smile, planting a soft kiss on her pink cheek before stepping away from the wall. "Let's go get you changed," I said, offering my hand.

Instead of pulling away this time, she accepted the gesture.

Chapter Fifty-Two

Bridget

Kota's mom had some sort of conference to attend in Chicago, but since it was only a day long, the three of us decided to make a trip out of it.

It was my first time in Chicago, and honestly, the experience wasn't disappointing me at all. The sights and architecture were beautiful, and I kind of loved how alive and busy the city was.

I loved the atmosphere here. If I could enjoy it this much in the winter, I wondered what it was like in the summer.

It was cold as hell, but for three people who lived in Minnesota their whole lives, it wasn't much of a temperature shock. We were already used to it.

I was a little upset that we missed seeing the Christmas decorations by just a few weeks, but it gave us an excuse to come back.

By the time we got back to our hotel room by the end of the second night, we were exhausted, climbing straight into bed.

My feet were aching, eyes struggling to stay open. We'd easily walked over six miles between yesterday and today, and I couldn't even remember the last time I walked more than one.

"So," Kota's mom asked from her bed, "what are you girls gonna do tomorrow while I'm at my conference?"

"I was thinking we could go shopping," I said.

"That's a great idea," her mom said. "Kota, what do you think?"

When there was no response, I turned on my side to see Kota snuggled in a ball, her eyes closed and mouth parted open, breathing as evenly as a metronome.

"She's passed out," I giggled.

"Of course," her mom laughed, leaning over and flicking the tableside lamp off.

My body fell limp as my eyes came to a close, but unlike Kota, I couldn't fall asleep right away. It seemed like my body was ready for it, but my mind was looming.

Lane texted me this morning that him and Crew decided to take their snowboarding trip early this year and impulsively hopped on a plane to Colorado.

He hadn't responded since this afternoon, and I couldn't help but wonder what they were up to. He didn't mention how long they were staying either, and I sort of wanted to ask, but I didn't want to seem too clingy.

It had been about a week since New Year's, and I was still thinking about it. The entire night was carved into my mind like an etch-a-sketch.

The raw confession he'd given— *"I can't keep pretending like I don't have the biggest crush on you. It's too fucking hard."*

The way he towered over me as I was trapped against the brick wall, inevitably succumbing to his charm.

The loose ends and blurred lines of our friendship finally tangling as our lips met.

It didn't stop there either.

When we got to the party that night, he didn't leave my side. And he made it incredibly obvious that he was struggling to keep his hands off me, reaching for me one second before dropping his hand the next, remembering we weren't the only ones in the room, which led to him occasionally pulling me around the nearest corner just to give me a kiss.

The thought of coming home to an apartment where he wasn't waiting there for me was more than disappointing.

There had been a few times over the past few days that I almost let it slip to Kota, but every time, I got too scared.

I didn't necessarily think she'd be angry about it, but I had no idea where things with Lane would go, and I didn't want too much of the dynamic in the apartment to change at once.

Plus, I knew Lane wasn't planning on telling Crew any time soon, and I was kind of glad about it. I couldn't imagine the absolute turmoil Crew would cause if he found out.

Overall, I knew getting into something with Lane was probably a bad idea, but I couldn't resist him anymore.

The bed gave a light buzz beside me, and I moved at a snail's pace to grab my phone.

Lane: How's Chicago?

Seeing his name pop up on my phone was exactly what I needed to end my day the best way possible. I hid under the covers to make sure the light didn't wake anyone.

Me: Good!! It's so beautiful here

Lane: It is. I haven't been there in a few years though

Me: This is my first time

Lane: Really?? That's surprising

Me: I know

Lane: Crew is trying to convince me to sign with the Blackhawks

Me: You should

Lane: I'll consider

Only because you said it though, not him

Me: *laughing emoji*
I'm glad you value my opinion

Lane: I do
I have a question

Me: Yeah?

I stared at the dots on the screen that told me he was typing, and even though there was a huge possibility that he wasn't about to ask anything serious, my heart was still beating rampantly.

Lane: When we both get back, will you go on a date with me?

My face physically hurt from how big I was smiling. Considering he was still my roommate and things could get messy, everything about this felt better than it should've.

I read the message at least five times before bringing my fingers to the keyboard.

Me: Yes (:

And suddenly, I couldn't wait to get home.

Chapter Fifty-Three

Bridget

Things were weird.

Like, really weird.

Not with Lane, but with our roommates.

We both felt awkward knowing we were about to leave to go on a date and our roommates had no idea.

It seemed like they were both lost in their own worlds though. Per usual, they hadn't really looked at each other since we all got home. I'd gotten used to the malice that drifted through the air like dust particles whenever they were in the same room, but this was different.

It didn't seem to be malice this time, but with that being said, I couldn't figure out what it was.

I had my hair straightened and only put a light amount of makeup on to make it look like I wasn't going anywhere important. With one last look at myself in the mirror, I covered myself with a jacket, zipping it as high as I could without looking suspicious.

Lane and I walked towards each other from opposite ends of the hall, and I could tell he'd been thinking the same way as me. He already had his winter jacket on, accompanied with khaki pants.

With no idea where we were going, I hoped I wasn't under or overdressed. When Kota and I were shopping in Chicago, I found a periwinkle blue sundress that was on sale since it was out of season, and after sending a picture of myself in it to Lane while I was in the dressing room and reading his overly sweet reaction, I decided it had to be worn for our date.

To hide it, I'd covered my top half with my jacket and tucked the rest into the waistline of my blue jeans.

We'd been hoping Crew and Kota would've been in their rooms or not home at all when we left, but Kota was lying on the couch, hair tied in a messy knot with air pods in, eyes closed while she bobbed her head to whatever music she was listening to.

I brought my finger up to my mouth, signaling for Lane to be quiet. He caught a quick glimpse of Kota and began tiptoeing the rest of the way to me.

"Are you ready?" he whispered.

I nodded and I was awfully surprised at how quiet we managed to be as we tiptoed towards the door.

"Where are you guys going?"

Jumping, I covered my mouth with the back of my hand as Crew stood there, watching us.

Lane cleared his throat. "Where... are we going?"

"Yeah," Crew said.

Lane smacked his lips together, looking lost. "Uh, Bridget, where are we going again?"

Way to put it on me. Thanks, Lane.

I was probably the only person in the house that was a worse liar than Lane was, so I wasn't sure why he trusted me not to blow it.

The stakes felt like they were heightening as Kota took an air pod out and sat up.

Everything could explode quickly, right here, right now.

"We're... going to the library," I spit out, gaze jumping between them.

"The library?" Kota laughed, swinging her legs over the side of the couch. "But it's still break. You don't have work to do."

"No," I said, "but there's this book I was telling Lane about that I want him to read."

Crew scoffed, walking off towards the kitchen. "Nerds," he murmured under his breath.

It pained me to lie to them, especially Kota, but I knew it had to be done. At least for now.

"We'll be back in a bit," Lane said, practically bee-lining for the door with me on his heels.

We dove into Lane's car like we were escaping from a crime scene. I'd never seen him start the car and step on the gas so fast.

Knowing how uncomfortable Lane got by driving people around, I'd offered to drive, but he refused, not wanting to give up the location of wherever we were going. He said it wasn't far anyway.

"That was harder than I thought it would be," Lane said, turning onto the main road.

"Yeah, thanks for tossing me under the bus, by the way."

His rich chuckle pierced straight through me, making it hard to be mad at him. "I'm sorry. If I had said something though, Crew would've known I was lying."

"We probably should've had an excuse set beforehand."

"Next time."

"Oh," I grinned jokingly, "there's going to be a next time?"

He kept one hand on the wheel as he reached over for my hand, bringing it up to his lips and planting the most subtle, yet powerful kiss across my knuckles. "Hopefully," he smiled against my skin before his anxiety became apparent because he was quick to let go of me and clasp his hand back on the wheel.

My skin burned slightly where he'd kissed it, as if his touch had physically branded it. I was overly focused on breathing, one of the few things we were born knowing how to do and it seemed like I completely forgot the simplicity behind it.

I readjusted in my seat, feeling my clothes start sticking to my skin beneath me. I unbuttoned my jeans and started shimmying them off as Lane pulled into the parking lot of the best sushi restaurant in town.

"Kyoto!" I hollered. "I love sushi!"

"I know," he smiled, giving me a glance before his brows scrunched together, doing a double take. "Uh, Bridget?"

"Yeah?"

He pointed a sluggish finger at my lower half. "What are you, uh... I don't know if we should really..."

I glowered at him, tugging the pants over my knees. "What did you think was happening here?"

His eyes scanned the parking lot, checking to see who might be around. "I mean... you're taking your pants off."

Kicking off my black bootie heels so that I could get the jeans the rest of the way off, I spoke through a grunt. "Lane, I'm not trying to hook up with you right now in this parking lot."

"Then..."

I kept my eyes on him, watching every split second of his reaction as I unzipped my jacket and revealed my dress.

"Oh," Lane smiled, "your new dress."

Once again, that smile nearly knocked the breath out of me. If I hadn't already been sitting, I would've been on my ass. It was almost deadly how charming he was.

"Yes. My new dress."

So subtly, his grin grew, his eyes skimming me over, soaking in every visible inch. "You look gorgeous."

It was taking all my focus not to jump over the console and kiss the shit out of him. I thanked him shyly before we headed in, and luckily, our server was awesome and super attentive, getting our orders in quickly.

"So, you haven't told me all about Colorado," I said.

"It was good," Lane nodded. "Got lots of snowboarding done. We went out one night too."

"Just one?"

"Yeah, the first night we were there. Crew brought a girl home, of course."

No surprise there. I nodded along, "Of course."

"It was weird though," he explained, "the girl he brought home kinda looked like Kota."

I let out a holler. Crew and Kota hated each other so much that the thought of Crew going for anyone that looked the slightest bit like Kota was mindboggling. It was quite honestly a little too difficult to wrap my head around. It seemed like there was a better chance of Crew giving up sex forever than there was of him sleeping with someone that looked like Kota.

"There's no way," I refuted.

"No, I'm serious. She looked pretty similar to her. He wouldn't talk about it afterward, and he didn't ask to go out again either."

I folded my arms across the tabletop. "Strange."

He shrugged, his biceps tensing beneath his white button down, and for a second, I forgot where I was. I couldn't tell if the moment was real or if I was fantasizing.

I was on a date with Lane Avery.

"How was the rest of your trip to Chi?" he asked.

"Good! I really liked shopping there. They had a lot of cool bookstores too."

A sinful, yet teasing grin crept across his face, telling me I might not like what he was about to say, but it was impossible not to like the view.

"Get any new, smutty little books?"

I dropped my head into my hands, shielding myself as his husky chuckle overcame the table.

It was crazy what the sound of someone's laughter could do to your heart. I could've sworn my heartrate doubled, pounding in my ears like rock music on full blast.

"No, Lane," I responded into my hands. "No, I did not."

"I feel like you're lying."

I peeked at him from behind my shield, and sure enough, that smirk of his was going strong, spearing me in a way I'd never experienced.

"I'll let it slide," he said. "But if you did happen to get any and want me to read to you, let me know."

Chapter Fifty-Four

Bridget

Lane and I had been sneaking around the past few weeks, going on secret dates every couple of days.

We'd created a list of excuses or safe places to tell Crew and Kota where we were off to if they were home while we were leaving. Otherwise, we tried to plan everything around their schedules to avoid running into them before or after our dates.

Second semester had kicked off in full swing. Even though we were only two weeks in, my classes were already busy, and most of my professors were dicks, assigning huge semester-long projects right at the start.

I was used to having a heavy workload, but since it was my last semester, Senioritis was already making its way into my head, wrecking my motivation. I was getting to the point where I wanted nothing more than to be done with school.

Since it was a Friday, I was committed to doing no schoolwork tonight or tomorrow, and just focusing on having fun. The boys had a game tonight, the first home game since Lane and I started sneaking around.

I was going through my Cedar clothes, trying to decide what to wear.

"I want you to wear my jersey," Lane said, spread across my bed.

"Lane," I chided, sliding my hangers across the rack in my closet, "I already told you, I can't."

He sighed. "Who cares what Crew or Kota say? They probably won't think anything of it anyway."

"Lane."

"You've already worn it once before. What's the difference of wearing it now?"

"The difference is that the first time was Kota's idea, solely to get back at Crew. It didn't have anything to do with me, really," I said.

His voice fell, immediately hurt. "You didn't wanna wear my jersey that night?"

I swung around, my throat tightening from knowing I'd hurt him. He gripped the bedsheets tight like he was physically wounded and needed the support.

I strode over. "No," I softly said, "of course, I did." I climbed onto his lap, hoping to see that long frown of his disappear. "All I'm saying is that it wasn't my idea the first time, so it might be weird if I just randomly wear it."

He sighed, relaxing against me. "I guess I see what you're saying." When I brought my cheek to his shoulder, he spoke again. "But in a few weeks, if they still don't know, then I don't care. I need to see you in my jersey as many times as possible before the season ends."

I gave a light gulp. Any time the end of the season came up in conversation, it physically made my stomach upset as if I drank too much and needed to hurl.

Between the thought of graduating and the thought of Lane leaving to go play hockey somewhere, the future felt so up in the air. We technically still weren't even a couple, yet I was already thinking of how we'd make it work after the end of the year.

Even if we didn't end up becoming a couple, it would still be hard to part with Lane. He'd become one of my best friends over the past few months and the thought of parting from him felt like some sort of irreparable heartbreak.

"Next game," I promised.

254

"Okay," he whispered with a nod, his eyes dropping to my lips for a moment before touching them with his own.

And damn, if that didn't make me want to wear the jersey more.

***

Since Kota was standing right next to me, I was trying not to make it obvious that I was staring at Lane.

Considering it was only warm-up and I'd struggled to look away from him for more than five seconds at a time, I had a feeling this was going to be a very long game.

We got seats directly in front of the glass again, and Lane seemingly kept gravitating towards us as he warmed up, at times so close that if there wasn't glass between us, I could probably reach over and touch him.

I'd never get tired of seeing him in his uniform. His skates made him two inches taller, letting him stand at six-four. He glided around so effortlessly that it was envious. I'd never seen anyone look so graceful on a slab of ice before.

He skated over, giving a quick nod in our direction before kneeling with his back towards us, separating his knees for a stretch.

I'd seen a bunch of the other guys do this same thing time and time again during warm-up but watching Lane do it was making my mind go to places it should not have been going to while standing in a public place.

I had Lane's ass to me, his knees circling, hips dipping with the motion. It was far too easy to envision myself lying beneath him.

The arena was already so loud, but I easily forgot my surroundings, feeling a small throbbing sensation in my lower core as my imagination filled itself with sinful thoughts. I'd never wanted to rip off a piece of clothing more than I wanted to rip that jersey off of him right now.

After a few torturous minutes, Lane stood. With his stick in hand, I watched him slide the puck around, back and forth so quickly that it looked like he was moving in fast forward.

"Think they'll win?" Kota asked.

"I don't wanna jinx it, but I think so."

They were playing Boston University tonight, another top ten team. Right now, Cedar was ranked third in the nation, and in order to keep that rank, they needed the win.

I knew how badly the boys wanted to go to the Frozen Four. They would've made it last year if it hadn't been for a loss during overtime against Western Michigan.

Since it was going to be Lane's final season of college hockey, I knew he felt an overwhelming sense of responsibility to get his team what they'd been working so hard for.

He was so driven, and it showed, regardless of how much or how little he spoke about hockey.

With under two minutes left of warm-up, the guys started filing off the ice and back into the locker room. But Lane didn't follow. He skated around the rink, taking shot after shot at the net and making the puck in every time.

When Lane was one of the last few on the ice, he made his way back over, stick handling the puck the entire way. He scooped the puck up so that it sat atop his stick, then tossed the puck upwards, letting it flip in the air before catching it back on the stick as it came down. He repeated the motion a few times, then with one flick of his wrist, sent the puck flying over the glass and directly into my lap.

I stared at it for a second, then covered the puck with both hands to make sure no one tried stealing it.

"Aw thanks, Lane!" Kota shouted with a smile and a wave. "That was so sweet!"

I let her snatch it from me for the time being, and as she was inspecting it, I used her distraction to give Lane a shadow of a smile.

His was on full display, bright and inviting, complimented by a wink.

I instantly missed him as he skated away, making me hope the next few minutes went by quickly so that I could see him out on the ice again.

"Gimme that," I demanded through a smile, snagging the puck from Kota.

"I was just lookin' at it," she murmured defensively.

"Well, it's mine," I grinned wider, giving it a squeeze before bringing it to my chest to keep it safe.

Chapter Fifty-Five

Bridget

I considered myself to be a pretty patient person, but being patient seemed like an impossible task at the moment.

In a high-energy, fast-paced game, the boys fought long and hard, securing the win by one goal. They'd scored one in the first period, keeping the opposing team from getting one in. But honestly, the second period was rough.

Not only did Boston score three goals, but it seemed like they had it out for Lane, ramming him into the boards and triple-teaming him every chance they got.

I didn't know hockey that well, aside from attending a few Minnesota Wild games as a kid with my family and watching it when my dad would have it on the tv. Half the time, I hardly knew what I was looking at.

I wasn't sure what Coach Palmer or Lane said to the team between periods, but whatever it was, it must've lit a fire under their asses. Because when they came back out for third period, they were playing like they were part of a damn assembly line. The puck was going from one Cedar player to another so smoothly, as if the other team wasn't even on the ice.

Within the first four minutes of the period, a sophomore that I didn't know managed to sink the puck in, and shortly after, a penalty was called on an opposing defenseman for tripping Lane badly, sending him falling shoulder first into the ice.

It had never been easy watching him get hurt during a game before, but ever since we became whatever we were now, seeing anyone lay a hand on him was agonizing. I almost found myself wanting to hop onto the ice and volunteer to take his place like Katniss at the goddamn Reaping. There were times I caught myself clinging onto Kota's long sleeve with anticipation, holding back a cringe anytime someone got too close to Lane.

But he absolutely crushed it during the power play, racking up an assist and a goal all within those two minutes, causing the entire student section to chant *"Sex-y Cap-tain!"* repeatedly.

Although Boston ended up scoring once again late in the third period, the two goals made during the power play were enough for the boys to clinch the win, and Kota and I had no doubt that they were going to celebrate after.

Kota and Crew had already left for Stallions, separately of course, but I was waiting for Lane to get home so that we could go together. Crew said he stayed longer than everyone else to speak with his coach, so they hadn't returned at the same time.

My impatience was starting to prick up my spine, poking its way under my skin like a tattoo needle.

I filled Rob K's bowls with fresh water and dry food, then found myself wiping down the kitchen counters just for the sake of keeping myself busy.

When I heard the lock of the apartment door jiggle, I carelessly tossed the rag I'd been using aside and ran over, creepily standing in front of the door like a pop-up from a horror movie.

Lane let out an expletive under his breath, followed by a deep chuckle when he saw me. "Well, hello there," he said, dropping his hockey bag on the floor.

"Hi!" I jumped into him, and when he let out a painful groan, I stepped back. "Shit, I'm sorry. Are you hurt?" I asked, analyzing him.

"Just sore," he winced.

"Already?"

It felt like my heart was trembling inside my chest as Lane sluggishly lifted one side of his shirt, revealing a baseball-sized bruise that had already formed.

"Oh my gosh," I let out, tracing my fingertips over it as gently as possible. "You need to ice that, like, immediately, before it gets worse."

"I will," he dropped his shirt. Two calloused hands gripped both sides of my face, bringing me to him for a soft kiss.

I smiled as he pulled away. "What was that for?"

"I haven't kissed you in like, four hours."

My grin felt permanent like it'd been drawn on my face in sharpie. I dropped my head, letting my hair create a curtain between us as I fished an icepack out of the freezer, wrapped it in a clean hand towel, and placed it carefully over Lane's bruise.

He let out a deep exhale, taking it from me. "Thank you."

"You're welcome. I'm assuming you need to change before we head out?"

He nodded, grabbing his bag and heading into his room. I'd already changed earlier but went to my room to get my purse and my phone that had been charging.

My door was cracked open, but Lane still knocked before walking in. "Ready?"

"Yep!"

His eyes wandered around, landing on the hockey puck sitting on my desk. "Is this the special puck?"

"Yes, sir."

Lane broke into a gorgeous smile, and my heart skipped a beat, watching him pick the puck up and flip it around in his hand, examining it as if he wasn't months away from going to the NHL and had never held a hockey puck before in his life.

With puckered lips as if he were in thought, a hand hovered over the pencil holder on my desk, plucking out a silver sharpie.

Lane brought it up to his mouth, sticking the top between his lips and pulling it open.

"Aw, are you autographing it for me?" I teased.

"Mhmm," he nodded, still holding the marker top between his perfect lips, the corners of his mouth lifted upwards as he scribbled across the top of the puck.

"Can I see?" I asked when he put the marker back.

"For you," he handed it over.

The moment my eyes met the top of the puck, I was overwhelmed with emotion. I couldn't stop reading it, as if I was waiting for the words to change in front of my eyes.

He had signed it. He had absolutely signed it. But it was what was above his signature that was causing me to feel like a child at Disneyworld for the first time.

Will you be my girlfriend?

"Lane," I blushed.

He stood there smiling, looking like a walking fantasy that had magically and coincidentally ended up in my bedroom. "Please don't say no. I'll be really embarrassed," he joked.

"Are you crazy? How could I say no?" I set the puck down and made sure to be more careful this time as I wrapped my arms around the back of his neck, standing on my tiptoes.

He buried his face in the crook of my neck. "Is that a yes then?"

"Of course, it is."

Lane's thumb and forefinger gripped my chin and pulled my mouth to his, and I could feel him smiling against me as our lips moved rhythmically together, slowly at first and then gradually quickening.

I grabbed two fistfuls of his shirt and tugged him backwards with me onto the bed.

His weight pinned me against the mattress, and as a hand raced through my hair, I found myself redirecting it to my crotch.

My legs spread to allow him access. His hand slid over my crotch atop my clothes, and I squirmed, fighting the urge to rip his shirt right off his back.

With each stroke, lust pulsed harder and harder in my veins, sending me into overdrive. His hips dipped and I gasped into his mouth, feeling his hardness bulging into me. The measly fabric of my leggings wasn't enough separation to keep my sporadic thoughts at bay, but at the same time, the barrier was somehow too thick.

I wanted the barrier gone.

The pressure in my lower belly was growing to a torturous throb, and if I didn't get any relief soon, it was possible I'd implode.

Thumb hooking into his waistband, I held it there for a second, sitting between his warm skin and the fabric. I started pulling down, maybe a little too zealous.

"Bridget," Lane stopped me.

My eyes popped open, and the first thing I saw was the depth in Lane's. It was like I had two sapphires inches from my face.

"Yeah?" I said in a small voice.

"We don't have to do anything."

I spoke firmly. "I want to."

"You're sure?"

"Yes."

His gaze searched all over my face before his lips dropped back to mine at a snail's pace. This time, he didn't prevent me from sliding his pants off, and without looking, my hand found its way around his cock.

Holy shit, I internally screamed.

I could hardly wrap my hand around him, and as I slid down his length, it seemed like it was never ending. Easily seven to eight inches.

Dear Lord, he could probably break me in half.

There was only one way to find out.

When I tried tugging my own pants off, he separated from me, resting on his knees as he gave my pants a death grip and yanked them off, my shirt following suit right after.

And just like that, I was entirely exposed.

His eyes took me in with enough heat to start a fire, the pads of his fingertips beginning at my ribs and trailing down the entire side of my body.

"You are so fucking perfect."

A shutter ran through me, and I reached for him, longing for his touch again, but he stayed back, not done memorizing the view.

With the softest graze, he guided my legs open, and I'd never felt more vulnerable, but I'd also never felt more comfortable.

I'd never been so sexually open or free, especially not ten minutes into a committed relationship, but right now, it felt more like a need than just a want.

With Mitch, I'd been hesitant to cross this line. But with Lane, it felt so natural, so unbelievably right.

Lane's eyes followed his thumb as he rubbed the top of my clit, spreading my wetness around, which made the ache worse. So much worse.

"I wanna taste you," he uttered gruffly. "Can I?"

I nodded rapidly, anticipation fueling me as Lane's arms hooked underneath my knees, hiking them upwards as he buried his face between my legs.

The sensation was overwhelmingly good. I had to grasp onto the sheets and focus too hard to keep myself from thrashing and screeching like an animal.

And when Lane moaned against me like he was enjoying himself, a vibration rushed through my body, and I nearly combusted on the spot.

Lane's shoulder was nearly the size of my thigh, and I gripped it tight, feeling it tense beneath my touch. "Lane," I cried.

His mouth stayed put but his eyes shot up to look at me. The delicate, cozy blue I was used to was gone, replaced with lust and darkness and intensity.

"Lane," I moaned.

I watched him eat me up, and if I didn't know any better, I'd say he was smiling while he did it.

When he finally pulled away, his tongue darted out, licking away all the remnants of me that were sitting on his lips.

I squeezed his dick tightly and he let out the lightest groan. "Lane... please don't make me beg," I whimpered.

His seductive smirk lit up the room. "Beautiful, you don't have to beg." Planting the lightest kiss on my collarbone, he said, "Let me go get a condom."

When he left the room, I kept asking myself if I was sure about this. And every time, the answer was *Hell yes.*

He rolled the condom on, positioning himself above me. "Are you sure about this?"

"Yes."

"Really, Bridget," he whispered, "we don't have to."

"Lane," I insisted, *"I want to."*

It was more than want at this point. It was a necessity now. I needed to know what he felt like.

"Okay," he said, the word barely audible. "I wanna know though... How do you like it?"

I gulped quietly. "I..."

Shock crept into his features. "Are you..."

"No!" I corrected him in a panic. "No, I'm not a virgin. I just... don't have much experience."

The most gentle, loving smile surfaced, and damn, I loved the view. "Okay," he nodded softly. "We'll start slow."

Running his hand over my crotch to make sure I was wet enough, he finally pushed himself inside me, and my breath hitched. He was already filling me, and I could tell he wasn't even entirely inside me.

Like promised, his pace was slow, rocking into me like I was fragile, and he was afraid to break me.

He let out a satisfied sigh as he drew deeper. "Fuck," he groaned. "I've been waiting for this for so long, Bridget."

The most dangerous flutter bounced around my stomach. "Me too, Lane," I murmured.

His eyes hadn't left my face, his large hand clutching onto my hip, fingers curling around me as his pace quickened. As he carried on, his thrusts were gradually getting stronger, easing the stabbing throb that had been making a home out of my lower core.

The concept of time completely disappeared; I had no idea how long we'd been going for. All I knew was that the sheets were soaked, my lungs were on fire, and the build in my belly had gotten so strong that my small moans were on the brink of becoming screams.

Fingernails digging into his back, my eyes clamped shut as I yelped. "Lane, Lane, Lane," I moaned, his name coming out as if on repeat. "Oh, Lane," I cried in a trance, my voice growing louder.

Thank God no one was home.

I quivered and cried and writhed beneath him, my body overwhelmed by the amount of pleasure circling around, taking over every inch of me.

Right as he hit a certain spot, I climaxed so hard that I felt like I was on drugs, lost in a completely different, euphoric world.

My screams echoed around the room, and as satisfyingly drowsy as I felt, my eyes managed to open enough to spot the vain smirk on Lane's face.

He didn't stop drilling into me, letting me ride out my orgasm until his eyes rolled into the back of his head and he let out a deep, raspy groan as his body relaxed.

With both of us gasping for air, he collapsed on the bed beside me.

We stared at the ceiling in silence. I could feel the warmth in my cheeks; my body was probably overheating, sweat trickling down my skin. But I peeked over at Lane, catching the same smirk that he'd had minutes prior.

"What're you smiling for?" I shyly asked.

"Nothing... I just like hearing you scream my name."

If my cheeks weren't already a rosy red, they sure as shit were now. I covered my face with my hands.

"Don't be embarrassed," he chuckled, tearing my hands away.

"I'll try to be more quiet next time."

"Please don't."

I let out a single laugh, acting far too shy towards someone who just had his dick inside me two minutes ago.

"Do you think they're wondering where we are?" I asked.

"Probably."

"Do you think they'll suspect what we just did?"

"Not a chance." Lane's eyes had returned to their regular softness. He was looking at me with so much affection that I was struggling to take it all in. Sparks consumed me as he said, "Thank you for trusting me."

"I'll always trust you," I whispered.

His thumb traced the corner of my jaw, his eyes glossy with post-sex satisfaction and sentiment. "It means a lot to hear you say that, Beautiful."

Chapter Fifty-Six

Lane

It was hard being two feet away from your girlfriend and not being able to touch her.

I loved Crew, and at this point in my friendship with Kota, I loved her too, but *Jesus,* sometimes I wished I could scream at them to get out so that I could touch Bridget. Even just casual touches. Brushing my fingertips along her arm. Giving her a light kiss. Wrapping my arms around her. Every time Bridget and I were alone, I couldn't get my hands off her.

Yes, we'd had sex now. Was I expecting it to happen that quickly? Definitely not. It was some of the best sex I'd ever had though. There was something about sleeping with someone you felt deeply about that made it so much better. But the bottom line was that I wasn't just in it for the sex. It was honestly one of the last things on my mind. Hated to say it and didn't want to throw shade at my surrogate brother, but I wasn't like Crew in that sense.

"B, we should get some wine tonight," Kota said.

Bridget made a face. "It's already eight, and I still need to clean my room and shower."

Kota sighed, heavily disappointed.

"Wine sucks anyway," Crew expressed, playing Grand Theft Auto on the Xbox in the living room.

Kota shot him a look. "*You* suck."

He smirked at the TV, choking back a laugh.

They were sharing the bigger couch, but Kota seemed to be hugging the armrest, sitting as far away from Crew as possible.

"Do you guys have practice in the morning?" Kota asked me.

"Yeah," I nodded.

She gave a pout, knowing we typically didn't drink on nights we had practice the following day.

"We can have a wine night tomorrow?" B proposed.

"I just said I hated wine," Crew protested.

"No one invited you," Kota jeered.

"Wow."

"I'll have a wine night," I butted in, my eyes on Bridget.

Her gaze was already on me. I could tell she was trying to hide her small smile. From me or from our roommates, I didn't know. But regardless of how hard she tried fighting that pretty smirk, it still showed through her eyes.

"Cool!" Kota shrieked.

"Oh, so Lane is invited and not me?" Crew complained with a trace of ice in his voice.

"Exactly," Kota answered.

Bridget rolled her eyes. "Would it kill you two to be nice to each other for five seconds?"

"Yes," Kota said. "Yes, it would, actually."

"I can be nice. It's her," Crew said, gesturing to Kota with his head.

"Don't even," she snapped.

"Mom," Crew called out, "she's being mean again!"

"Ew," Bridget cringed. "Don't call me that."

Crew and I both let out a laugh. I was far too entertained by the disgusted look on her face.

"On second thought," Bridget said, "I will down some wine right now. You all drove me to it."

"Yes!" Kota shot up. She ran over and grabbed her purse off the hook by the door. "Let's go grab some!"

Crew paused his game and stood. "I'll go. I'm getting myself beer."

Were we all supposed to be going? Was this a group activity? Or was there a way I could convince Bridget to stay back with me so that we could have a few minutes alone?

I just wanted to be close to her, to be able to sit next to her and breathe in her sweet scent, to be able to kiss her softly and hold her hand.

I kept my eyes on her, wishing and waiting for her to look at me in hopes that she'd be able to read my mind.

Out of the corner of her eye, she gave me a glimpse. "I, uh, I'm gonna hop in the shower actually while you guys are gone. Get that done so that I can drink, you know?"

Oddly enough, neither Crew nor Kota complained about having to sit in a car with each other for five whole minutes alone.

They both gave a nod, and the second they were no longer in the apartment, I had my arms around Bridget, hands tucked into her back pockets while I kissed her like I was running out of air and she was my only source of it.

She pulled away, tucking a tendril of hair behind her ear, her sweet breath fanning over my face. "Do you wanna shower with me?"

Abso-fucking-lutely.

"Um, *yes.*"

I let her pull me towards her bathroom but stopped just shy of the door. "Wait."

Bridget glanced back at me with ethereal eyes, and the way she always had the ability to switch back and forth between innocent and seductive never failed to amaze me.

"What if they come back while we're in there?"

She inhaled deeply with a trace of a nod before jogging over to her phone.

"What are you doing?"

"Buying us some time."

"How so?"

She smiled at her phone screen as she read off her messages. "Can you guys possibly stop and grab me some tampons? I'm almost out."

My brows came in. "Are you on your period?"

"Nope. Just ended it," she said, content with herself.

I let out a laugh. "Look at you being bad."

"Told you I can be bad," she smirked with a wink.

Obviously, they weren't back with the liquor, but I was already feeling drunk on her, wanting nothing more than to kiss her again. "Any answer yet?"

Once again, she read off her phone. "Sure thang, babe." Tossing it on the couch, she charged towards the bathroom, grabbing my hand on the way and tugging me along.

Every move she was making was like it was being done in double-time, from turning the hot water on to undressing herself.

"Lane," she chided, stepping into the shower. "Hurry up!"

I hadn't realized I'd been standing there staring at her, admiring every curve and every inch.

When she disappeared behind the shower curtain, a sense of panic overcame me as if she'd vanished into thin air. I practically tore my own clothes off and stepped in, steam already rising throughout the bathroom, and I hadn't even touched her yet.

Apparently, she was just as impatient as I was because her hands were immediately on me, running from my shoulders to my pecs to my abs and landing on my dick, grabbing it tightly like it belonged to her.

Who was I kidding? It *did* belong to her.

I stepped forward, forcing her backwards until she was pressed against the shower tile. As her hand started stroking me, I settled both palms on the sides of her head, basking in the moment.

For how hot the water already was, it sure as hell seemed hotter now.

Water dripped off her dainty chin, her eyes dancing with greed. My breaths were growing more ragged, more tense, and she sped up, looking pleased by my reaction.

270

A husky, gratified groan was threatening to fall out, and I had a feeling she wanted it to.

The sound echoed around the shower walls, and I pressed harder against the tile, loving the way she was gripping me with one hand and running her fingers over my balls with the other.

Knowing our time was limited, I let myself go much earlier than I normally would've, smashing my lips onto hers and grunting against them as I came all over her stomach.

Quickly, it rinsed away, and I raced to shove two fingers into her.

"Lane," she sighed, "it's okay. We don't have time."

I placed wild kisses along her neck, and as my fingers curled in the slightest inside her, causing her to let out a whimper, she seemingly changed her mind, welcoming my offer.

I went as hard and as fast as I could without hurting her, trying to make her finish faster, and it worked. Before I knew it, she was coming all over my fingers, a soft cry leaving her sweet mouth.

I watched her wash up swiftly and when we stepped out of the shower, I wasn't sure if I'd ever been so content.

Two months ago, I was jacking off in the shower to the thought of Bridget, and now, I was showering *with* her while *she* jacked me off.

We dried off and got dressed, positioning ourselves as inconspicuously as possible.

Numerous board games were brought out, and glass after glass of wine disappeared.

Crew and Kota were fighting over some rule in Scattegories, and of course, we just let them go at it.

Bridget had a red popsicle, creating a ring of red around her mouth. Her eyes lingered on me as she teased me with it, pumping it in and out of her mouth.

Goddammit. This was cruel.

Subtly, I picked my phone up, glancing out of the corner of my eye every few seconds to make sure their argument was still going strong.

Me: You're so fucking beautiful
I wish I could kiss you right now

"Why are you blushing?"

My eyes shot up to see Bridget holding her phone close to her chest. "Hmm?" she hummed at Kota.

Kota made a face. "You're blushing."

"No, I'm not. I'm just... on Insta."

"Don't try to change the subject," Crew intervened.

"I'm not changing the subject!" Kota spewed.

Bridget: Knock off the sweet talk. You're gonna get us in trouble

"Whatever!" Crew hissed. "I'm done with this game. What time is it?"

"Almost midnight," I yawned.

He rubbed his eyes lightly. "We've got practice early. I'm turning in."

"Same," I stood.

Kota and Crew cleaned up the game while Bridget brought two empty wine glasses to the sink. Since the girls somehow convinced Crew to try a glass of wine and he secretly liked it even though he refused to admit it, there were two other glasses waiting to be grabbed. I brought them over to the sink, leaning in as I stepped past Bridget.

"Don't fall asleep yet," I whispered.

She gave the lightest nod I'd ever seen, and I wanted nothing more than to kiss her before leaving her side, but I restrained myself, feeling my chest tighten as I forced myself to walk away.

"Night," I announced to everyone, heading into my bedroom while silently praying Bridget wouldn't pass out any time soon.

Chapter Fifty-Seven

Bridget

It was getting harder and harder to keep my eyes open. I'd been waiting nearly a half hour for Lane to do or say something, considering he told me not to fall asleep, but the entire apartment was eerily quiet.

I was lying in bed with my phone on my chest, waiting for it to vibrate. All my lights were off, including my string lights, so my room was pitch black, which only made me sleepier.

The vibration throughout my body made me jolt. Even though I'd been anticipating it, it still somehow scared the crap out of me.

Lane: Are you still awake?

Me: Yes

Lane: Come cuddle?

There was nothing on earth that sounded better.

I threw my slippers on and tiptoed out of my room. Thinking ahead, I closed my door behind me in case Kota came out of her room for some reason in the middle of the night.

It felt like I was breaking into someone's house, focusing far too much on making each individual step as silent as possible. I twisted Lane's doorknob entirely before slowly pushing it open, sneaking inside where he was waiting for me in bed with a smile.

"Hi," he whispered.

"Hi," I whispered back, shutting the door just as quietly as I'd opened it.

He held out both arms wide open, gesturing for me to fall into him. The second I felt his touch, I relaxed, melting against him. It felt like novocaine blocking any and every source of pain I'd ever had.

He was warm— practically a furnace, and with the strength of him caging me in, I felt safe.

For the first few minutes, he didn't say anything, just held my head against his bare chest, running his hand through my hair. I could hear his heartbeat drumming in my ear, a steady rhythm.

Lane's chest was so muscular that it was like a rock, but it was somehow comfier than any pillow I'd ever laid on. With each breath he took, my head deftly lifted and fell with it. I was drifting closer and closer to sleep, giving out a small yawn.

"I lied to you before," Lane sputtered in a whisper.

My eyes shot open, anxiety instinctively starting to course through my veins. It was like I hadn't almost fallen asleep thirty seconds prior.

"About?" my voice cracked.

"About Ava," he said. "You were right before."

I remained silent, staring at his wall as I tried to steady my rampaging heart. I still wasn't sure what he was referring to, but it was hard not to be anxious when your boyfriend brought up the girl he used to sleep with.

"She didn't like you," he said.

"Oh," I murmured under my breath.

"She didn't like you, because... because she knew how I felt about you."

"Why didn't you tell me before?"

"I figured it would upset you," he said, squeezing me a little tighter as he wiggled around, adjusting himself.

"No," I corrected him, "why didn't you tell me how you felt about me?"

Back to silence. For a moment too long.

I could tell the gears were turning in his head, and I wasn't sure if it was because he himself didn't know the answer or if he thought the answer would upset me.

"I don't know," he exhaled. "I guess I was just scared."

"Of what?"

His voice dropped even further, coming out as a muted croak. "Losing you."

I cocked my head back to look at him. His eyes were already on me, refusing to look elsewhere.

"Why would you think you'd lose me?" I asked quietly.

"If you hadn't felt the same... Or if you did feel the same and things ended..." he trailed off, struggling to say the words.

I gave a small sigh under my breath. "Yeah, I get what you're saying."

I wondered if Lane had been having the same worries as me about what would happen when he left. Part of me wanted to cut the conversation off, lay here and bask in his warmth and his touch and ultimately fall asleep beside him. But the leftover alcohol in my bloodstream decided to make an appearance, because before I knew it, the words were slipping out faster than I could stop them.

"What's gonna happen after this year?"

He inhaled deeply through his nose, filling his lungs to their maximum capacity. His eyes still hadn't left me, studying me with such intensity that I could feel it all over my body.

"Nothing," he softly said. "Nothing's going to change after this year."

I could feel the trace of a hopeful smile appearing across my lips. "Do you promise?"

Lane's thumb started at my hairline and fell to the corner of my jaw, tenderly framing my face with his touch. His other arm tightened around me like he was afraid I was about to slip away.

"I promise," he nodded.

Chapter Fifty-Eight

Lane

I was flying across the ice, my head in the zone during practice.

Even though my own teammates were the only ones around me, I still acted as if I was in the middle of a real game, pushing myself to my maximum until my lungs were about to concave and I was soaked in sweat.

I thought I heard someone shouting my name, but I refused to get distracted, skating around Keith and keeping my eyes ahead as I wisely passed the puck behind me to Crew, who sent it flying into the net with a wrist shot.

"Avery!" Coach screamed as the play ended. "Avery!"

Shit, I guess someone had *been calling my name.*

I skated through everyone and over to Coach.

"Your phone's been going off like crazy! I can hear it from here! Come get it, it's pissing me off!"

"Sorry, Coach," I heaved.

My phone was sitting atop my bag in the locker room, and sure enough, it was ringing on full blast. The second I saw Bridget's name, I dove for it.

I was still gasping for air as I shot it up to my ear. "Hello? Bridget?"

"Lane? Lane!"

She sounded frantic. I could feel the blood draining from my face, and instinctively, I started shoving my shit into my bag, preparing to run out of practice.

"Is everything okay? What's wrong? Are you hurt?" I rambled.

"What? No, no, no," she said, "I'm fine."

God fucking dammit.

I breathed a sigh of relief, exhaling all my anxiety. "Jesus, Bridget. Don't do that to me. You nearly gave me a heart attack."

"I'm sorry."

"It's okay," I said softly. "What is it?"

"I got my results back!" she blared happily through the phone.

"For..."

"My DNA test."

"Oh," I gave a smile. "Good results?"

"Yes! I—"

"Avery!" Coach yelled. "Get your ass back out here!"

"Hey, Beautiful?" I said. "I gotta get back to practice, but I wanna hear all about it when I get home, okay?"

"Okay," she agreed.

I hung up with a stupid grin on my face from hearing the sound of her voice, and this time when I hit the ice, I'd admit hockey wasn't the only thing on my mind.

Chapter Fifty-Nine

Bridget

"I just can't even believe it!" I smiled wide, sitting crisscrossed applesauce on Lane's bed with my phone in my hand. "I'm Irish, Scottish, and a tiny bit Swedish!" I listed off.

Lane was once again shirtless, which of course, I didn't mind. He was lying in bed beside me, one hand behind his head and the other tracing circles on my thigh.

He had a charming glimmer in his eye, keeping his gaze glued on me. The corners of his mouth were stapled upwards, making it hard to look away from him.

"Oh, guess what else!" I squealed.

"What?" he grinned wider.

"I already got a message from someone! I still need to answer her though."

"From your mom?"

"No. Some other woman."

"You can message people on there?" he asked. "How does that work?"

"It'll show you people you have a DNA match with, so you're able to message them if you've matched," I explained.

"Oh," he nodded in understanding, pushing himself upwards in the slightest while ensuring his hand didn't leave my skin. "Well, what did your message say?"

For the first time in a long time, I felt an overwhelming sense of hope. I'd been stuck at a crossroads in finding my mother for what seemed like forever, and now, it felt like I was making some progress.

I giddily scooted closer to Lane, reading off the message. "Hello, Bridget. Based on our DNA match, I believe I may be your biological aunt on your mother's side. I'd love to chat with you, so feel free to email or text me," I said. "And then she left her contact info."

"What did you respond?"

"I haven't yet."

"Well, what are you waiting for?" Lane grinned.

"I don't know," I fought a nervous smile. "Should I do it now?"

His fingertips grazed along my skin, sending shivers up my spine. "I think you should."

I exhaled deeply, calming my nerves. "You're right. I'm gonna do it right now."

"Good," he encouraged.

"Should I email or text her, do you think?"

He shrugged against the mattress. "I feel like text gives faster results."

"That's true," I agreed, typing in the phone number I was given and drafting a message.

Halfway through, Lane let out a small chuckle.

I peered up at him over my phone screen. "What?"

"You just look so focused," he said. "You look cute."

I blushed, blocking it with my phone. I continued typing away, pausing every few seconds to give myself a moment to think.

Holding a finger over the send button, I hesitated.

Lane's voice came out like a melodic lullaby. "What're you thinking, Beautiful?"

One side of my mouth twitched upwards. "Just... nervous to send it."

He tipped his head, deep blue eyes studying me. "Do you want to read it?"

I glanced him over nervously, shifting my weight on the bed. Blowing out a deep breath, I gave a faint nod.

"Hello, Hope," I spoke. "This is Bridget. Thank you for giving me your contact information. I'm very excited that I've found you. I'm interested to know more about you and I'm hoping to learn anything you know about my mother. I was given up for adoption at my birth and never met her. The only information I have is that she gave birth to me on April 5th at Jefferson Memorial Hospital in Cedar, Minnesota. I look forward to hearing back from you!"

When I looked up from my phone, Lane's grin had grown to a pleased and adoring arch. "I think it's perfect," he said.

I gave his hand a quick squeeze in appreciation. "Hit send for me?" I asked, turning the screen towards him.

With that grin still sitting untouched on his face, he tapped the screen, and the second the message was sent, I tossed the phone to the side and dove into him.

As my lips met his, he didn't hesitate in the slightest, seemingly unfazed by my sudden switch. His hands gripped my waist, fingers digging into my skin as he pulled me against him, and the second I felt his hardness beneath me, that familiar ache in my lower core was there, a tingling sensation sitting between my legs.

My hand found its way between us, slipping beneath the waistband of Lane's shorts and stroking his growing length, causing him to let out a small groan against my mouth. I shuddered at the vibration, gripping what I could of him in my hand.

The warmth of his fingertips explored me, moving from my hips to underneath my shirt to the more innocent places, like my arms and in my hair.

I loved moments like these— the moments where Lane was gentle while still arousing me more than anyone else in my life ever could. His presence alone was enough to affect me in the most forceful ways, and when his touch was added, everything intensified.

A ring went off and instinctively, I jumped up. "Oh, my phone!"

Lane chuckled loudly, covering his face with his hands as he shook his head.

"What?" I shyly asked.

"You," he smiled at me.

"Sorry," I murmured through a grin, realizing I'd stopped midway.

"Don't be," he shook his head, his hand resting along my thigh again, making itself home there. "What'd she say?"

"Hello, Bridget! Thanks for getting back to me. From what it sounds like, there's a very high possibility that my sister is your biological mother. If you'd be interested in meeting with me in person, we can talk things through and get to know each other better. Are you free this weekend?"

Lane studied me with a vibrant smile, waiting for me to reply. "Well?"

"I'm gonna say yes!"

"You should."

After I sent the message, my teeth latched onto the inside of my cheek, nerves ricocheting around my belly. "Lane?"

His head tipped. "Yes, Beautiful?"

"Will you come with me this weekend?"

He gave my thigh a loving squeeze. "Of course."

Chapter Sixty

Bridget

Guilt was slowly and utterly consuming me.

I wanted to meet my aunt. I wanted to meet my birth mother.

But there was this thought poking at me that I was betraying my mother— the woman that raised me.

It felt like I'd been going behind her back all these years. Thinking back, I wasn't sure why I never told her that I'd been looking for my birth mother. I was confident that I knew my mother well enough that she'd cheer me on in my search for my birth mother, but I guess I was afraid of hurting her feelings. I didn't want her to think she wasn't good enough, or that I didn't appreciate everything she'd done for me throughout my life.

After having a small breakdown to Lane and Kota, they both had given me the same advice— to just tell my mom.

I'd been staring at my phone for a few minutes, locked in my room.

Just do it, Bridget, I told myself.

I hit the call button, tempted to end the call before it even rang.

"Hello?"

"Hi, Mom," I panicked.

"Hey, sweetie. How's it going?"

"It's good!" I answered. "How are you and Dad and Bianca?"

"We're all good!"

"That's good..." I murmured. "Um, I actually have a question."

"Okay. What is it?"

I hated the fact that I was doing this over a call. I felt like it was so much more important than that but making the three-hour drive to Sumner wasn't very convenient at the moment.

I was wringing my fingers through my hair so aggressively that I was surprised I hadn't ripped any hair out. "So, I recently took a DNA test," I paused, stumbling, "and I... might've found my biological aunt and mother." I started off with that, waiting to see how she'd respond to that first before I dropped the real question.

"Wow, sweetie," she said. "That's wonderful."

"It is..." I agreed. "I was wondering how you'd feel if I met them in person?"

There was a snippet of silence; all I could hear was my blood hammering in my ears.

"I think it's a great idea," she finally said.

I was trying to pick out the bitterness or sarcasm hidden in her tone, but I couldn't find any.

"You do?"

"Yeah," she said. "If this is something you want to do, then you should do it."

"Are... are you sure?" I asked. "It is something that I really want to do; I just wanted to make sure you would be okay with it."

"Of course! Did you think I would be upset or something?"

"Not exactly..." I expressed. "I just wasn't entirely sure."

Her voice softened. "Oh, Bridget, no, of course I'm not upset. You're my daughter and I will support you no matter what. You have the right to learn about where you came from. I'm sure your father and sister will support you too."

I hadn't realized how heavy the weight of all this was until it fell off my shoulders just now.

"Really?" I smiled.

"Of course, sweetie. We love you!"

"Thanks, Mom. I love you guys too."

"Well, I want updates. So let me know how all this goes, okay?"

"I will!"

Hanging up, I couldn't even believe things were falling into place. Between my flourishing relationship with Lane and the close possibility of finally meeting my birth mother, things had never seemed so perfect in my life all-around.

I just hoped none of it fell through.

Chapter Sixty-One

Bridget

If Lane wasn't beside me right now, I didn't think I'd be able to do it. My nerves were threatening to make me explode.

We'd been sitting in my parked car, silent for the past five minutes.

"Hey," Lane softly said, his thumb rubbing over the top of my hand. "Beautiful?"

My deep exhale was the only sound between us for a moment. I wrestled my gaze away from my steering wheel and over to Lane.

"Are you ready?"

"No," I admitted in a small voice.

His hand found its way to the side of my face, tenderly cupping it. As if it were second nature, I leaned into him, bringing my hand up to his.

I'd been waiting my entire life for this— to get this close to meeting my birth mother. So, why did I feel like I wanted to run as far as possible?

I wasn't sure what it was. Fear of the truth, maybe? Fear of the unknown? Whatever it was, it was damn near paralyzing.

Lane's thumb gently moved across the delicate skin on my cheek. "It's okay," he promised. "You can do this. I'm right here with you."

The assurance in his eyes was what encouraged me to nod, and for a second, I wondered how the hell I used to go through life without him.

His infamous, captivating grin appeared, and I couldn't help but lean over the console to get a quick taste.

He gripped my face a bit tighter, holding my lips to his. If my apparent aunt wasn't inside the restaurant, waiting for us, I would've held his mouth on mine longer.

I pulled away but remained close enough to feel his minty breath fall over my face. Letting out another sigh, I shut my eyes.

"I'm ready," I said.

Lane stayed directly beside me as we walked in, letting me grip his hand tighter than a boa constrictor the whole way.

I had absolutely no idea what my aunt looked like, but when I spotted a woman alone at a booth with hair a few shades darker than mine, I beelined towards her.

The woman had both hands around a mug of coffee, her auburn hair forming a curtain around her face. When she glanced up, our eyes locked and she immediately stood, striding towards me with her arms open.

"Bridget," she sighed a breath of relief as she enveloped me in a tight hug.

I squeezed my eyes shut, a shitty attempt to keep my tears at bay.

Somehow, I managed, keeping my composure to introduce her to Lane.

As we slid into the booth across from her, it was hard not to notice how bright her eyes were, sparkling as she rested her chin in her hands.

"I can't believe you're here," she said, "that you've been this close this whole time."

"Well, I— I actually grew up in Sumner, which is a few hours away," I said, nervously tucking a strand of hair behind my ear.

"Came here just for college then?" she asked.

"Um," I fidgeted, "well, I was originally going to go to Minnesota Duluth, but everything I'd found about my mom said she lived around here, so... I decided on Cedar."

Hope gave a loving grin. "I figured you have a lot of questions about your mom."

"I do."

She nodded lightly, seemingly prepared.

A young waitress carefully approached, as if knowing she was walking in on something important. "So sorry to interrupt," she said. "Can I get you guys something to drink? Is anyone ready to put food in?"

I glanced at Lane, speaking quietly. "Are you hungry?"

"Not really," he answered before turning to the waitress. "I'll take a coffee though, please."

"Me as well, please," I said.

"Coming right up!" she smiled, wandering off.

"So..." I started, "my mom." Hope nodded, gesturing for me to continue. I sucked in a sharp breath. "Does she know that you're here with me? Or that you've found me?"

Her smile wavered. "No. She doesn't."

It felt like it was getting slightly harder to breathe. I had a question on my mind, but it seemed like it refused to come out, getting stuck in the back of my throat. There was a hollow feeling in my stomach, but as Lane gripped my thigh under the table, I could feel my equilibrium shifting back, allowing me to calm.

"Would she... be upset if she knew?" I finally got out.

Her eyes softened. "No, Bridget. Of course not."

"Then," my voice cracked, "why hasn't she looked for me?"

Hope reached across the table, grabbing my hand. "Oh, honey, she has." Shaking her head, I could see the glossiness of her eyes, the heaviness in her lungs. "She looked for you for years." With a sigh, she let go of me, and as her hands found their way back around her mug, her focus wandered off.

"Your mom is my little sister, Faith; she's four years younger than me. Our dad wasn't around growing up, so we were just raised by our mom, but," she paused, cringing as she did so, "she was very strict. Very traditional. Very religious.

She didn't let us do much outside of school and church. But when I was in high school, I ended up getting a job at a local diner, and I worked there until I went off to college."

I nodded along as she spoke, keeping myself from leaning over the table; I was listening that hard.

"When your mom was fifteen, she got a worker's permit and I helped her get a job at the diner. She, uh," Hope paused again, seemingly uncomfortable, "she met a man there, who she secretly started seeing, but um... he was much older than her."

I wanted to ask, but again, it seemed as though I was physically unable to, as if opening my mouth would only let out a sequence of unintelligible noises.

"How old was he?" Lane asked for the both of us.

My aunt's mouth formed a hard line before she hung her head and sighed. "Twenty-three."

Lane and I both let out small gasps.

A twenty-three-year-old going after a fifteen-year-old? That was disgusting. And knowing how this story ended, I didn't like where it was heading.

But I still encouraged her on.

"Keep going," I softly requested.

Hope nodded, taking a deep inhale. "So, nobody knew about their relationship. Growing up, your mom and I were close, but she didn't tell me about it. She didn't even tell her close friends either."

Our waitress returned with two coffees, quietly dropping them off before walking away as if she was afraid to interrupt again.

The warmth of my mug seemed to steady me slightly, but something about this story still didn't sit right with me. After hearing about the age gap of my mother and who I could only assume was my father, I was deeply disturbed. Even though I'd been focusing on finding my mother all these years, I had always wanted to meet my father too, but now, I wasn't so sure. Unless there was some crazy plot twist that was coming where this predatory twenty-three-year-old didn't end up being my father, I didn't think my feelings about meeting him would change much.

"Not too long after they started sneaking around, your mom got pregnant. Your father took off right away, because he was afraid of what the consequences would be when people found out he got a fifteen-year-old pregnant. Your mom hid her pregnancy for quite some time, up until she really couldn't anymore. And when our mother, your grandmother, found out..." Hope shook her head, seemingly disgusted. "She absolutely lost her mind. To start, she didn't approve of Faith being pregnant that young, and she also didn't approve of her getting pregnant out of wedlock, so she pretty much hid her from the world for the remainder of her pregnancy and then... forced her to give the baby up for adoption."

"After that," Hope continued, "our mother made us promise that we would never speak of anything again, but after she died, Faith started looking for you. She searched the best she could but couldn't find you. She got emotionally exhausted, heartbroken, and eventually, she got discouraged. She doesn't know it, but I've been looking for you ever since she stopped."

I gripped my mug tighter until it was burning my hands. "When did she stop?"

"A few years ago," she said. "I didn't tell her I was coming here because I wanted to meet you first and make sure you were Faith's before I got her hopes up. But one look at you," she smiled lightly, "and I knew."

"I wanna meet her," I blurted out.

Hope's lips thinned, the corners slightly lifting. "Okay, honey."

"Today," I added.

Her brows lifted as she sat back against the booth. "Um," she stuttered, "I can give her a call... see if she's busy."

"Okay," I murmured with a hopeful nod.

Hope excused herself from the table, and I dropped my head onto Lane's shoulder, grabbing a ball of his sweatshirt and clutching onto it.

His hand circled around my back. "How are you feeling?"

"A bit overwhelmed but also hopeful."

"I understand," he said. "This is a lot for one day. Are you sure you want to meet her today on top of it?"

"Yeah," I uttered into him.

Hope returned with a smile. "Okay. We can head over to her place. It's not far from here, about ten to fifteen minutes. I wanted it to be a surprise though, so she doesn't know that you're coming."

Anxiety gripped me, latching onto me like a leach. What if she didn't want me to come? What if this surprise was a letdown for her?

I asked Lane to drive since I was feeling so shaky, and I didn't think he would've done it if he hadn't heard the fear in my voice. He gave me words of encouragement along the way, all while keeping his eyes fixed on the road, of course.

Parking on the side of the street across the house, my mouth went dry, heart thrashing in my chest like a rabid animal in a cage.

"Alright," I muttered. "Here we go."

Lane squeezed my hand. "I'm right here." The small gesture gave me enough courage to open the car door.

As I rounded the front of the car, the front door swung open, revealing a petite woman around my height, her strawberry blonde hair thrown back in a loose pony. Her gaze was solely on me. She didn't hesitate, no words spoken as she rushed forward, not bothering to check for cars.

I met her halfway and we collided, a heap of tears as I squeezed the living daylights out of her, my mascara staining her shirt. All nervousness was gone. All doubts were gone. The only thing that remained was the most peaceful, gratified feeling that washed over me with the force of a tidal wave.

She pulled away, her hands cupping both sides of my face, examining every detail. Her eyes stung with tears, pink swirling around in her cheeks, filled with emotion.

With our matching tears and the light freckles beneath our eyes, the curve of our lips and our identical hair color, I felt like I was staring into a mirror.

"It's you," she wheezed. "My baby." I nodded against her hands, and the most buoyant, beautiful smile shone on her face. "I can't even believe it." She shook her head. "What's your name?"

"Bridget."

Her smile grew, two twin tears falling along her face. "Bridget," she repeated in a whisper. "I love it." Turning to her sister, who was patiently waiting with a smile, Faith swatted a hand at her, keeping her other hand glued to mine like she was afraid to let go. "You knew this and didn't say anything!"

Hope rolled her eyes. "I just met her an hour ago."

Faith shook her head, her voice dropping to a scratchy cry. "How did you find her?"

"DNA test. Remember? The one you refused to take because you claimed it wouldn't work?"

Faith sighed, her glossy eyes rolling. Finally giving Lane a glance, she said, "And who's this?"

"This is my boyfriend, Lane," I said.

She extended her free hand towards him for a shake. "Let's go inside," Faith announced. "It's chilly." She didn't let go of my hand the entire way in, seating us at the kitchen table. I could've sworn I heard her wince when she finally let go and made four cups of hot chocolate.

"Lane," Hope said, "would you like to go chat in the living room and we can give them some time to catch up?"

"Yeah, absolutely," Lane stood. He leaned down, blue irises inspecting me. "You'll be alright?" he whispered, his voice angelic. When I nodded, his expression softened further, and his lips brushed against my cheek before he followed my aunt out of the room.

Faith took her seat, her eyes still glittering with joy and disbelief as she handed a bag of tiny marshmallows to me for my hot chocolate.

"Thank you, Faith," I said.

"You know, um," she shifted. "You're welcome to call me mom if you're comfortable with it."

My first thought was that I'd be disrespecting my adoptive mom if I decided to take that offer. But the longer I looked at Faith and saw how much love sat in her eyes after just meeting me, the more the feeling seemed to become reciprocated, and I became fonder of the idea of calling her Mom.

"Okay," I smiled, "Mom."

Her smile grew further. "I wanna know everything. Your entire life. I wanna know all about it."

I started by telling her about my family, how wonderful of a childhood they'd given me, and how they were supportive of me meeting her. I talked about school and how I was hoping to work in the publishing industry after college. I even told her about my relationship with Lane and our not-so-cute meet cute.

She propped her elbows on the table, resting her chin in her hands. "It makes me so happy to hear all of that." Her infectious smile faltered, disappearing altogether as the glossiness in her eyes returned. "I only got to hold you once before they..." she wept with a struggled breath, and instinctively, I reached for her hand. "Before they took you away. And every day after that, I worried about you. I wondered where you were and if you were safe and happy and healthy. I wondered if you were searching for me like I was searching for you. I was so young, but maternal instincts truly are some of the strongest feelings on the planet, because the worrying never stopped... So, to hear that you've had a good life is so relieving."

Once again, my eyes were burning. "I have had a good life," I assured her.

"I wanted to keep you so bad," she confided.

"It's not your fault."

A deep yawn sounded from behind me, and my mom wiped at her eyes as I turned, spotting a tall man with a scruffy beard, stretching his arms to the ceiling.

"Tim," my mom said.

He squinted between us. "Do I not have my contacts in again? There are two of you."

She scurried to his side, giving him a casual touch on the arm. "Tim, this is Bridget. My daughter."

"Your..." he froze, analyzing me before a smile the size of Minnesota spread above his beard. "You found her!" he hollered. "You found her!"

My mom nodded. "Hope found her."

"I can't even believe it. She looks just like you!"

"I know," she smiled. "Bridget, honey, this is my husband, Tim."

"Hi," I grinned shyly.

As if she'd been away from me for too long, my mom rushed back, her hand once again wrapping around mine from across the table.

"How long have you been married?" I asked, watching Tim make himself a cup of coffee.

"Almost six years," he answered.

Warily, my eyes shifted between them. "Do you guys... have any kids?"

My mom's mouth drew into a line. "No. We, uh, decided not to."

"Oh."

"It just... The idea of having a kid and keeping them when I didn't keep you didn't sit right with me," she explained.

A trickle of guilt poured in. I didn't know if my mom had wanted more kids or not, and I knew it wasn't my fault, but the tiniest part of me wished she hadn't made that decision because of me.

"I'm sorry," I said quietly.

She squeezed my hand. "It's not your fault. It was our own decision."

"Also," I shifted, suddenly uncomfortable, "I've been meaning to ask..."

"Your father?"

I gave an unsure nod.

Her lips thinned, head tilting apologetically before shaking. "I'm sorry, honey, but he passed a few years back."

"Oh," I nodded. Surprisingly, I didn't feel any specific way about it. There was no regret about not meeting him prior; it was all indifference.

"I wouldn't have even known if Tim hadn't seen his obituary in the paper."

"It's okay."

The weight atop the floorboards shifted, making sound, and I turned to see Lane's dazzling smile, my aunt following close behind. She pointed at him and then gave me a thumbs up.

I giggled, hiding a blush as Lane settled behind me, resting a hand on my shoulder.

"Well," I said through disappointment, "we should probably get going."

I left my heart at the table as I stood, suppressing a wince when I caught the fear in my mother's eyes.

She didn't want me to go. And I didn't want to go either, but Lane and I each had things back home to get done, so we couldn't stay here all day.

My mom sprung up, reaching for me. I hugged her tightly. "I can come back tomorrow?"

"Yes! Yes, I would love that."

Today easily might've been the best day of my life.

Chapter Sixty-Two

Lane

"Take a left down this street." I could feel the shake in my voice as it left my mouth. "And then you'll turn right into here."

My head hung low with anxiety as Bridget obeyed, making the turn as carefully as possible. But she didn't speak. There was stark silence hammering between us, threatening to shatter the car windows like an opera singer could shatter a drinking glass. But even as Bridget stopped the car right before the road branched off into numerous paths, still, she didn't speak, waiting for me to give her directions.

Spirits had been so high when we left Bridget's mom's, but the second I asked if we could make a pit stop and I navigated Bridget to the cemetery, the vibe died, replaced with an eerie set of nerves and sadness.

"That way," I pointed towards the left. "Please," I added.

She silently drove, parking in the exact same spot I always did when I came to visit my brother.

It seemed like the temperature had somehow dropped drastically since we left her moms, and I knew we wouldn't be able to stay long, but I would've felt guilty knowing I'd driven right past my brother and didn't stop to see him.

As if in slow motion, Bridget's hand reached for the car key, and once the engine was cut, it truly became silent.

"Is it okay that we're here?" I let out.

Bridget looked at me with doe eyes. Her fingers laced between mine, giving a squeeze. She fit so perfectly in my hand, as if hers was tailor-made for mine. "Of course, it's okay," she said.

I gave a thankful nod. "Put your jacket back on," I lightly demanded. "It's cold."

Once we were both bundled up, I led her over to Liam's grave, a chill rippling through me.

Bridget stood a few feet off to my side, trying to allow me space. But honestly, I didn't want space. I wanted her comfort.

In a perfect world, we wouldn't be standing here right now. We'd be off somewhere, meeting my brother for dinner or going to watch one of the NHL games he was supposed to be playing in.

It wasn't supposed to be like this. With us standing here in the cold, our exhales visible in the air as clouds of grief. A tombstone in front of us, etched with the memory of my favorite person. Our boots atop a thin layer of snow, six feet above a casket.

She was supposed to meet the living him, not the dead one.

A delicate hand landed on my shoulder. "Lane?"

I lifted my head slightly in acknowledgement.

"Are you alright?"

I gave a trace of a nod, even though it was a lie. "I miss him."

She stepped beside me, finally close enough for me to feel the warmth of her. Her voice came out softer than velvet. "Tell me about him."

I rarely spoke of my brother aloud. Thinking back on it, I kind of felt like a disgrace for it. It was my job to keep his memory alive, and I hadn't been. Once again, I'd been failing him.

There were a thousand words I could use to describe him, a thousand stories I could tell. An entire library full of books about Liam wouldn't have sufficed.

"He was... so many things. For one," I said, "he was talented. The most talented fifteen-year-old hockey player I'd ever seen."

"Lane," Bridget gave the lightest smile, "I'm sure you were just as good."

"Nah," I denied. "He was always a bit better than me."

"I still doubt that," she said, "but go on."

"He was smart too. I always got slightly better grades, but honestly, I think it was only because of a lack of trying on his part. He was always so hockey-focused." My eyes hadn't left his gravestone, watching it intently as if doing so would bring him back to life. "But most of all, he was," I paused, giving a fragile smile, "wild."

Bridget's soft laughter filled part of the void that was currently in my chest. "Wild?" she asked.

"He was always so fun and full of life. Kind of a troublemaker, honestly, but if it weren't for him, I would've had a boring childhood."

"Were you also a troublemaker?" she jokingly accused.

"Do you know me at all?" I chuckled for the first time since stepping out of the car. "I'm like the biggest rule-follower."

Her voice dropped an octave, and I was both uncomfortable and disappointed with myself with the way it slightly turned me on, given our current location. "I can think of one rule you've broken."

She made it hard not to smile. I was fairly certain this was the first time I'd ever smiled while visiting my brother. "Don't put me in the hot seat."

"Alright, alright. Tell me more," she encouraged.

"We were always up to some sort of shenanigans. We used to sneak out and play hockey in the middle of the night. Liam's idea, of course," I grinned, my eyes back on the stone. "One time, when we were in middle school, Liam found one of our dad's Playboys, and we spent hours looking through it."

"Ew!" Bridget laughed, pushing me over as I chortled.

"After the first few flip-throughs, we drew funny faces on all the girls. Our dad was pissed, but we didn't even get in trouble because he didn't want our mom to know he had it in the first place."

It was like the treasure chest in my mind had finally been opened after all these years, allowing memories to flood out.

"When we were freshman in high school, Liam wanted to try the old switch-a-roo trick that you see twins do in the movies. I told him it'd never work since we were fraternal and didn't look enough alike, but he convinced me to try it anyway."

"Did it work?"

"Not even close," I bellowed in laughter. "We got caught after one class period."

Bridget and I laughed, and I found myself getting lost in story after story about Liam.

"Growing up, we wanted a pet really bad. Preferably a dog, since we both loved dogs and our mom was allergic to cats, but she wouldn't let us have a pet. But there was this," I spoke through small spurs of laughter, "little raccoon that ate out of our trash can every night."

"Oh no," Bridget murmured. "I don't know if I like where this is going."

"And one day, Liam came to me with this whole elaborate plan, and I told him it was a bad idea, but once that kid had his mind set on something, there was no changing it. So, we waited until our parents were asleep..."

"Don't tell me you guys went out and caught the racoon."

"No," I laughed, "worse."

"Worse?"

"Liam left the back patio door open and put some snacks out in the doorway."

"Oh, God."

I was laughing so hard that my abs were on fire. So much so, that I probably could've skipped doing abs in the gym for the next week. "The raccoon was running around our fucking house and our mom was chasing it!"

Bridget's gloved hands flew up to her mouth, silencing her laughter. "How did you guys get rid of it?"

"She eventually chased it until it ran back outside."

"Jesus," she chuckled. "You guys *were* wild."

I nodded, a small burst of satisfaction swirling around in my stomach. I hadn't thought of all those memories in so long, pushing them to the back of my mind all these years because they'd been so painful to think about.

But right now, standing here with both Bridget and my brother, the memories were comforting. Stories of love and brotherhood that didn't need to be left in the shadows for the rest of my life.

I needed to start talking about Liam more often.

There was a flicker of realization that shot through my mind with the speed of a comet. And just as quickly as I'd thought it, I was speaking it.

"I think maybe that's why I love Crew so much."

Bridget stared at me with nothing but confusion and empathy in her honey brown eyes, waiting for me to explain myself.

I was thinking out loud; I wasn't even sure if what I was saying made any sense or not.

"I guess I never realized how similar Liam and Crew are. They have a lot of the same attributes."

My frown felt heavy, but with each passing second, I could feel the comforting grin overtaking my face.

One brother was taken from me, and although no one would ever be able to replace him, I was at least grateful that I'd been gifted with another brother.

Crew wasn't even here, but I'd never felt more appreciative of him before.

The sound of an engine cutting came from close by, and I didn't think anything of it until Bridget lightly tugged on my hand. "Who's that?"

Any sort of comfort was gone, whisked away in the cold wind, unease taking its place.

I shouldn't have been so nervous at the sight of her.

"My mother," I whispered.

Her steps were wary as she approached, and when I caught her eyes shift, taking in Bridget's strawberry locks beneath her knit hat and the pink in her cheeks, my mother halted. It was only for a split second, but it was enough to notice.

Bridget knew what my relationship with my mother was like. During the late nights when we'd sneak into each other's rooms, we'd talk about anything and everything, and of course, my mother had come up in the conversation once or twice.

As my demeanor shifted, my awkwardness becoming tangible, Bridget's seemingly followed suit. Her mouth was taped shut, unsure of whether or not she should introduce herself.

The rest of the cemetery was empty; I hadn't expected there to be a damn party when we drove in, but I was suddenly wishing *someone* was around.

But instead, it was just Bridget.

My mother.

Liam.

And me.

My name sounded like a strained huff coming from her mouth, as if saying it made her unsettled. "Lane."

"Hey, Mom."

"What are you doing here?"

What did it look like I was doing?

She asked the question like I didn't have the right to be here.

"Visiting. What are you doing here?" I shot back.

"Visiting, same as you," she smiled tightly. "It's Sunday. I always try to come after church." To my surprise, her animosity seemed to dissipate as she turned to Bridget. "You are?"

"I'm Bridget."

"She's—" I started.

"I'm Lane's girlfriend," she finished for me, holding out a hand.

"Oh," Mom shook her hand and smiled lightly, although I couldn't tell if it was genuine or not. "Lane, you didn't tell me you had a girlfriend."

I shrugged. "I didn't think it was a big deal."

"Well, if I'd known, I would've asked to meet her earlier."

She stepped beside Bridget, seemingly more comfortable next to the stranger she'd just met than her own son.

Suddenly, I wanted nothing more than to leave.

But it seemed like Bridget had other things in mind.

"Lane was telling me," she spoke, giving a slight pause to read my mother's expression, "a lot of fun stories about their childhood."

"Oh," Mom grinned surprisingly, leaning forward to get a glance at me. "Were you?"

"Yeah."

Her shift in energy made me more uncomfortable, which I didn't think was even possible. "Like what?" she asked, curiosity peaking.

"I, uh," I stuttered as a guilty grin inevitably crept in.

"He was telling me about the raccoon," Bridget said.

My mother laughed. *Laughed.* She never laughed like that. Never sounded so... full of life. I was pretty sure she hadn't laughed in my presence in years. It was a sound I hadn't remembered hearing since my childhood. The knot that had settled in my core eased slightly at the sound, but I was still on edge.

"That damn thing! I still cannot believe you two did that!"

"We just wanted a pet," I chuckled, still unable to look her in the eye.

With the gentle touch of a mother, her hand rested on Bridget's wrist, which was more than weird considering she hadn't *felt* like a mother in so long and she most definitely didn't show *me* any sort of affection like that.

"Did he tell you about the time they were playing hockey in the driveway and decided it would be a good idea to use a baseball as a puck?" my mom said.

"He didn't," Bridget smiled at me with so much warmth. My God, that smile had the ability to move mountains. "But I have a feeling I know where this story is going."

"In my defense," I butted in with a grin, holding up a finger, "using the baseball was not my idea."

"No," my mother agreed, "it wasn't. But it was you who shattered my car windshield with it."

Bridget's laughter ripped through me in the best way possible, making my feet unsteady.

A shadow of a smile remained among my mother's face, her eyes glued to Bridget, same as mine. She shoved her hands into her pockets, a tendril of her hair flying as a breeze came and went. "I was going to grab lunch after this, if you guys wanted to join?"

I nearly laughed in disbelief. Overtaken by the urge to scoff and ask if she was being serious, I managed to hold back, peeking at Bridget.

There was nothing but purity and support sitting on her face, and I knew she was leaving this decision solely in my hands.

I looked at Liam as I responded. "Yeah, sure."

Chapter Sixty-Three

Bridget

I wasn't sure what I'd been expecting Lane's mom to be like, but I didn't think I'd ever been so conflicted about someone before.

Regardless of my own thoughts, I hadn't realized just how distant Lane and his mom were until she asked him what he was planning on doing after this year and he told her he didn't know yet.

I wasn't sure why he steered clear of talking about his NHL decision, but I remained quiet. If he was lying to her, there was probably a reason behind it.

With the fantastic luck that Lane and I had, my car decided it was going to get a flat tire on the way home from lunch with his mom. We were only ten minutes from home at that point, so it wasn't like we were completely stranded, but we did have to wait nearly an hour to get help. After calling Crew probably close to five-hundred times but the calls going to voicemail every time, Jett ended up saving our asses instead.

Thanks to my flat tire, my car was in the shop. In theory, it shouldn't have been taking so long to change one tire, but apparently, they didn't have the correct tire I needed on hand, so they had to order one, which meant I'd be without a car for a few days.

Luckily, my roommates hadn't been leaving me stranded. Each one, including Crew, had been giving me rides this whole week.

Every time Lane did, we used it as an opportunity to spend some alone time together, sneaking off before dropping me off or after picking me up.

Today was no different.

I hopped into the passenger seat of Lane's car, my lips headed straight for his.

"How was class?" he asked.

"Not too bad. Professor only rambled for half and then let us work on our group projects the rest."

"Doesn't sound awful," he said.

I shrugged. "So, what's on the agenda?"

"Anything you'd like."

"I was thinking Rave 'N' Roll. We haven't been there in a while," I suggested.

"Bowling, it is."

After two games of bowling and of course, me losing both rounds, we were about to head into the arcade when a familiar gruff timbre of a voice approached.

"Well, well, well," TJ smirked. "Wasn't expecting to see you here, Captain."

Lane's face broke into an array of emotions, all of which were quickly masked with a stunning smirk. "What're you doing here, TJ?"

TJ tossed a thumb over his shoulder. "Boys and I came to grab drinks and play some games."

With an arched brow, Lane clicked his tongue. "No invite for Crew and me?"

"We tried calling Crew like ten times and he didn't answer," TJ said. "Same with you."

"Did you?" Lane asked, checking his phone. "Oh, I guess you did. Shit, sorry, I didn't see."

"All good," TJ shrugged, before an insidious, entertained gleam appeared in his eye, his gaze shifting back and forth between the two of us. "If I didn't know any better, I'd say you two were on a date."

There was a troublesome flush in my face, the type that physically made your cheeks feel heavy. My head snapped down and I pretended like I was untying my bowling shoes.

"Very funny," Lane said, playing it cool, per usual.

"I'm just fucking with you guys," TJ chuckled. "But I think we're about to get our own lane and bowl if you guys wanna come join?"

"Uh, thanks, but we were about to head home actually."

So much for the arcade.

"Damn, alright. Well, give Crew some shit for us, will ya? He's hardly been answering the past few days."

"Will do," Lane said. "It's not just you guys if that makes you feel any better. He's been sucking at answering us too."

"Yeah," I finally spoke, once I was sure my face was back to a normal, peachy glow rather than a crimson one. "He left us deserted the other day."

"Oh yeah, your car! Jett came and got you, right?"

"Yes, thankfully."

"Is your car fine?"

"Yeah, it's in the shop. Just needs a new tire."

He nodded, "Gotcha. Well, I'll see you guys soon."

"Sounds good," Lane nodded, waiting until TJ was a safe distance away before he turned to me. "Let's get the hell outta here before the rest of the guys realize we're here."

We ran out so fast that I nearly forgot my purse.

It was becoming a bit tiring to hide our relationship from everyone. But the hockey boys had big mouths, and there was a ninety-nine percent chance that telling them our secret would end up with Crew finding out.

So, for now, no one was going to know.

Lane's laughter, as well as my own, drifted into the apartment as we scurried inside. Living in a college town, you always saw some weird things, but a guy riding a unicycle down the street, wearing a winter jacket, jeans, and a cowboy hat was a new one.

306

The blankets I'd folded neatly and hung over the back of the couch earlier this morning were already a mess, sitting on the floor.

My brows drew together in frustration, and in the brief moment of silence that followed our laughter, I caught muffled sounds that I couldn't decipher.

Kota should've been home already, and with Crew being so sucky lately with his answering habits, I wasn't sure if he was home or not.

All it took was a few clicks on my phone for me to check their locations and find out.

The noises grew louder, and I stood frozen in place, trying to listen.

"Are you hun—"

"Shh," I silenced Lane, raising a hand.

"Bridget—"

"Shh."

"Why are you—"

"Shh," I repeated harshly, clamping a hand over his mouth. 'Listen,' I mouthed.

The muffles grew into full-on moans, and both of our eyes widened in sync. I could feel Lane's jaw drop behind my hand.

Did we walk into the wrong apartment? What the fuck was going on here?

My first thought was that Kota had been kidnapped and was currently being taken to some torture chamber while Crew was obliviously having sex with some rando.

Lane cocked his head towards the hallway. Something heavy slammed against the wall repeatedly, sounding like the finale of a fireworks show.

Our slow steps became even warier, and the closer we got, the more unsure I was of if I actually wanted to know what was going on in Crew's bedroom.

But before I could decide for myself, it was decided for me.

The moans escalated until they were basically screams, and a voice that I knew all too well became clear as day.

"Crew," Kota wailed. For a second, I couldn't tell if she was enjoying herself too much or if she was getting hurt. But the breathy note in her voice gave her away.

"Crew!"

Enjoying herself, it was.

I stole a glance at Lane, whose expression resembled a man who'd just gotten kicked in the balls repeatedly— like he was on the brink of crying.

It felt like there was an earthquake; the apartment was entirely shaking.

We were both disgusted, and with every new sound, the disgust only grew. But for some reason, it was like we couldn't move away.

Was this why Crew had been sucking at answering lately? Because he'd been too busy fucking our roommate?

It seemed like we'd walked in close to the end, because within a few more minutes, the moans and satisfied sighs turned into deep breaths, the shaking had stopped, and I was deeply disturbed by this entire experience.

"Fuck," Crew groaned.

"Do you think we have time to go again?"

"I don't know. Depends on when they're gonna be home."

"Any idea?"

"Check their locations," Crew said.

Lane's and my head whipped towards each other in panic. He immediately patted his pockets in search of his phone.

Fuck. Where was my phone?

"Okay," Kota said. "I don't know where my phone's at though."

"I think it fell behind the bed."

As if on cue, Lane and I sprinted, and I nearly tripped on my own feet as we darted out of the apartment faster than we darted out of Rave 'N' Roll.

It was unsaid, but I knew Lane well enough to know we were thinking the same thing— the last thing we wanted was to be caught listening to our roommates having sex before we even got the chance to wrap our heads around the reality.

My lungs were aching beneath my ribs, struggling to get a full breath as I launched myself back into the passenger seat of Lane's car.

"Did you turn off your location?"

"Fuck!" I shouted. I wasn't even sure if my phone was in my purse, but I scrambled through it anyway, ripping apart the neat arrangement of belongings that I usually kept. "Shit," I panicked, "Lane it's not in here."

"Is it in the apartment?"

"No. I didn't take it out of my—" I tapped my jacket in realization, sighing in relief. "You think it's too late?"

"Hopefully not."

I turned my location off, and we sat there in silence, waiting and watching our phones for anything from our deceptive best friends.

I was tingling with unease, confusion draping over me like a cloak. I had a million and one questions for them right now.

First and foremost— how the fuck did this happen?

Also, *when* the fuck did this happen?

Had they been lying to us the entire time we'd lived together? And if so, *why?*

On one hand, I felt like Lane and I were hypocrites, considering we hadn't told them we were dating, but then again, we hadn't acted like we hated each other. Plus, we weren't the ones that came up with the entire house-wide, no hooking up rule. It was all their idea, and they completely broke it anyway.

Lane cleared his throat. "Well."

"What the fuck," I stared off.

"They're supposed to hate each other."

"I know."

"The thought of them... *touching...*" he shivered, trailing off.

"Um, yeah," I agreed. "It's gross."

"Honestly," his voice lightly shook, "I think I could throw up right now."

"You're not the only one."

Repulsion turning to ice, his voice sharpened. "How long do you think this has been going on?"

"I have no idea."

Lane shook his head fiercely. Seeing him heated over anything was a rare occurrence. But it didn't seem like he was very accepting of the fact that his best friend, his stand-in brother, had been lying to him for an unknown amount of time.

I didn't blame him though. I was feeling the same way.

"We need to go confront them," he said, swinging the car door open.

"Wait no," I reached for him, prompting him to close the door. "Let's wait and see how long it takes them to tell us."

He stared at me like I was an alien. Shifting around in his seat, he dwelled on the idea for a moment. "So, what, you're saying we should just walk inside and pretend we didn't catch them fucking?"

"I mean... I don't know, maybe." The deep, ragged exhale I let out was almost painful. "Just think of it this way— if we tell them we know about them, I feel like we have to tell them about us."

"They'll flip."

"Probably," I agreed. "*But,* if we don't tell them yet, then they don't know about us, but we know about them, but they don't know we know about them, so it might be kind of fun."

A devilish grin crept across his face, his eyes creasing with wicked delight. "That was a whole lot of confusing nonsense you just said, but I think I got it."

"And?"

"Let's do it."

Chapter Sixty-Four

Lane

I wouldn't say I was a good actor, but with how slick Crew and Kota seemed to think they were, I didn't need to be.

"Hey," I announced our arrival, taking in every little movement of theirs as we walked in.

"Hey," Kota said from the kitchen, a load of ingredients scattered across the counter as if she'd laid them all out for show.

"Sup," Crew nodded from the couch, Xbox controller in hand.

I took a seat beside him, my eyes burning a hole into the side of his head. "When'd you get home?"

"Uh," he shrugged, but refused to look at me, "I dunno. Like fifteen minutes ago."

Liar. You were balls deep in our roommate fifteen minutes ago.

The roommate you claim to hate, might I add.

I kept my features smooth, even though there was a small stabbing pain in my chest. It hurt that he was lying to my face so easily.

"What're you making?" Bridget asked, hovering over Kota's shoulder.

"Bruschetta chicken."

"Oh, yum!"

"Do you and Lane want some?" Kota asked.

"What about me?" Crew butted in.

"I'm not sharing with you."

"Why the hell not?"

"I don't share with people I don't like," she spewed.

The sounds of her moaning his name echoed in my head. *It sure as hell sounded like you liked him then.*

I struggled not to cringe at the memory that was now engrained in my mind like a stone carving. It was definitely in my top five list of most disturbing moments in my life, right up there with the time Crew got a boner while he was sitting next to me.

I wondered if he'd been thinking of Kota then.

I could put every ounce of energy I had into forgetting either of those occurrances for the rest of my life and it still wouldn't be enough.

If we hadn't walked in on them fucking, I would've thought this was just a normal interaction. Which led me to wonder— how many of these interactions had been staged?

Bridget turned towards the nearby wall, her hand shooting up to her mouth. Luckily, I was the only one looking at her right then, because her entire body was shaking with laughter.

It was taking everything in me not to do the same.

"Newsflash," Crew hissed, "I don't like you either."

Had they been having some sort of hate-sex? Getting turned on by their hatred for each other? Because they sure as hell seemed convincing right now.

I thought back over the past few months, trying to think of any moment or indication of when this could've started.

"Oh my God!" I shot up, causing everyone in the room to look at me.

Crew paused his game. "Dude, what?"

No wonder why he'd chosen to hook up with a Kota look-alike while we were on our Colorado trip. They must've been hooking up since then. At least.

For a second earlier, I considered maybe today was the first time. In all the years I'd known Crew, he had never hooked up with the same girl twice, but the aftermath of their hookup earlier sounded too comfortable, as if it were a routine.

I scanned the room, three pairs of eyes on me, waiting for some sort of answer of why I just caused a scene.

"I, uh," I stammered, eyes locking with Bridget, "forgot I have a homework assignment due tonight."

Crew gave a watchful nod, as if he wasn't sure if he believed me, but he accepted my answer anyway. Kota, on the other hand, seemed like she couldn't care less, turning her attention right back to "cooking."

"You should get that assignment done then," Bridget said, her mouth ticking upwards in a sly grin.

She knew I was bullshitting.

I excused myself, catching the subtle glance that Crew and Kota threw to each other as I disappeared down the hall, spitefully content.

Bridget was right.

This might be fun.

Chapter Sixty-Five

Lane

Bridget and I hadn't been going on our secret dates like usual. We'd purposely been staying at the apartment to fuck with Crew and Kota.

Usually, we snuck off a few times throughout the week, which wasn't hard considering we would go out and do things together while we were just friends. To them, it seemed normal for us to spend time together.

As much as I loved my alone time with Bridget, I was almost equally enjoying this shit show right now.

We were all scattered across the common area. Kota was seated on the floor, painting her nails at the coffee table. Crew was reclined in the smaller couch. And Bridget and I were sharing the bigger couch— a safe distance between each other, of course.

The only sound was the hockey game between Boston University and Colorado College on the TV that was a replay from last week.

No one had spoken in nearly twenty minutes.

Bridget and I kept trading glances, egging each other on to be the one to stir things up. She nudged me with her foot, and I cleared my throat.

"So, uh," I rambled, my eyes flicking between the two to make sure I didn't miss a single thing, "how was everyone's day?"

"Fine," Crew said.

Kota blew a heavy breath on her freshly painted, pink nails. "Yeah, fine."

"Nice," I murmured awkwardly.

With sweet bitterness, Bridget shot a glare my way. She wanted something more exciting, something that would make them both squirm. As did I, but I didn't know what to say that would get us there.

We were trying to get them to crack, to admit their sins like they were at confession at church.

Bridget and I had agreed that if they owned up to their lies first, then we would own up to ours.

Crew sucked in a sharp breath before speaking, and I couldn't help but notice how restlessly he was bobbing his foot side to side, his eyes glued to the TV. "Don't you guys usually go to the library on Thursdays?"

I fidgeted, glad that he wasn't looking and hadn't caught it. But whereas I was slightly put off by the thought of him being onto us, Bridget had a mischievous gleam in her eye as she suppressed a grin.

"Yeah," I said.

"Why didn't you guys go tonight?" Kota jumped in.

Bridget leapt at the opportunity, a playful edge in her voice. "Are you two trying to get rid of us or something?"

Kota remained as still as stone, only her eyes moving, zipping over to Bridget. "No. Why would you think that?"

Maybe because we know that you are.

"Yeah," Crew huffed, "why would you think that?"

Kota's glare shot over to him as if it were a threat. "Shut *up*, Crew," she said, her words slicing through the air like a sharp blade. She was practically screaming *You're a shitty liar. Let me handle it.*

"Don't tell me to shut up," he spat.

With the force of a cobra's strike and no concern for her drying nails, Kota snatched her phone, typing into it so quickly that she would've given the world's fastest typer a run for their money.

Bridget and I sat back, watching with far too much enjoyment. We were completely mirroring each other— feet resting on the coffee table, arms crossed over our chests, devious smirks imprinted on our faces.

I kept my focus on the TV, trying to seem inconspicuous. I obviously didn't have eyes in the back of my head like the saying went, but I did often use my peripherals in hockey, my own personal substitute. And I sure as hell was doing the same thing now.

Every few seconds, Crew would scowl at Kota from over his phone screen. I could see the daggers shooting from him, and if I had leaned forward a few feet, those daggers would've impaled me.

But Kota being Kota, seemed unscathed, invincible.

She typed away and he typed away and she typed away and he typed away, and before I knew it, my own phone was buzzing.

Bridget: Are they fucking texting each other right now?

Me: Definitely

Bridget: Ugh. I wanna know what they're saying
They're ruining our fun

Me: I know

Crew stood, his arms extending towards the ceiling in a long stretch. "I'm leaving."

"Where are you going?" I asked as he slipped his jacket and shoes on. My eyes were on him, and Bridget's were on Kota. We had both of them covered like we were covering our opponents in a hockey game.

"A girl's," he answered.

No reaction from Kota.

"What girl's?" I pried.

316

He played with the sleeve of his jacket even though there was nothing to adjust. "Ja..." he trailed off, before spitting out, "Janice."

Janice? *Yeah, I don't think so.*

"You've never mentioned a Janice before."

Crew scoffed. "I don't mention half the girls I sleep with."

Clearly.

After Crew walked out, the awkwardness in the room was tangible.

Kota had gone back to blowing on her nails as if she hadn't given less of a fuck about them minutes prior, and Bridget and I remained quiet, pretending like that entire exchange wasn't sketchy.

"I gotta grab something from my room," Bridget announced, heading down the hall.

And then there were two.

I was tempted to say something, to spit out *The jig's up,* and wait for the explosion of a reaction that was bound to happen.

But I kept quiet.

"Lane?" Bridget called. "Can you come help me with something for a sec?"

"Yeah!" The second I was in her doorway, she yanked me inside. "What do you need help with?"

"Nothing," she whispered. "I just wanna see something."

"See what?"

"Shh."

We stood there silently, waiting. Although I wasn't sure what we were waiting for.

The faint sound of a door opening and closing came, and I laughed once. "Did she just leave?"

Dark, twisted satisfaction spilled out as she spoke. "I think so."

"Is that why you dragged me in here? To see if she'd sneak out?"

"Maybe," she smirked.

I took my bottom lip between my teeth, fighting the massive grin that was threatening to appear. "You're enjoying this too much."

There was something wickedly attractive about her taking so much pleasure in all this, as if the rebellious side of her was taking over, the side that I had been convinced didn't exist.

"I'm enjoying it a decent amount," she admitted.

My smirk broke through, matching hers. Hooking my thumb in the collar of her sweater, I pulled it aside, revealing her soft and apricot skin. That fiery, sinful glow in her eyes ignited even further, a shocking comparison to the sun.

I stepped closer, towering over her. "Well," I murmured through a sharp breath, "since we have the entire apartment to ourselves..."

Bridget's tongue darted out, wetting her lips as I tenderly kissed the skin between her sweater and her collarbone. Her fingers curled around my bicep, pulling me towards the bed, but I stopped her, whispering into the crook of her neck. "Can you do me a favor?"

Her chest heaved as she nodded.

"Stay right here. I'll be right back." A minute later, I had my hockey jersey extended towards her. "Put this on."

There was so much lust in the air that we could get high off of it. With my dick pressed against the zipper of my jeans, eagerly waiting, I studied her as she slipped her pants and shirt off, replacing them with my jersey.

She looked like a goddess, and I was about to fuck her like she was one.

I admired her as she stood there, looking innocent like she didn't know what to do next. My clothes met the floor and arousal flushed her cheeks as I fished a condom out of the stack we hid in her nightstand, stepping behind her and carefully leading her over to her vanity.

Swooping her hair over one shoulder, my free hand planted in the center of her back. "Bend over," I softly demanded. "Please," I added with a smile in the mirror. "If at any point it becomes too much, you need to tell me, okay?"

Bridget rapidly nodded, and I clutched the material of my jersey over her hips as I pushed myself inside her, immediately sighing from the sensation.

Smoothly, I rocked into her, pleased as she gripped the edge of her vanity, knuckles turning white. I could see the sweet, desirous glitter in her eyes, sending me further into a frenzy.

Every few minutes, I went a little harder, a little faster, waiting for pain to flicker over her face, but all I saw was satisfaction.

Pausing inside her, my thumb and forefinger caught her chin, forcing her to look back at me. My voice became a low, respectful growl. "You're mine. You know that?"

Her cheeks were glowing a deep pink, bedroom eyes lively as she nodded.

"I need to hear you say it."

Out of breath, she replied, "I'm yours."

Lips tattooing her forehead with a kiss, I went back to fucking her, savoring every second until eventually, her legs were shaking, about to collapse, and I was groaning against her neck as the best orgasm washed over me.

Fuck. Maybe we needed to chase our roommates out more often.

Chapter Sixty-Six

Bridget

The boys won their game tonight, which meant they had only lost four games this season so far, all to top five teams.

It was very likely that their ranking would be moved up to second by next week. And if University of Michigan happened to lose their game tonight, then the boys might even be moved up to first.

I kept insisting that we went out to celebrate, but Lane was adamant that he was too tired. He took some nasty hits on the ice, so I didn't blame him, but still, everyone else was going out and I didn't want him to miss out on celebrating with his team.

Crew hadn't decided if he was going out either, but I was convinced it had to do with Kota. I'd never seen Crew sit out of a party, so it seemed a bit too convenient for him to start now.

Like Lane, Kota had reiterated that her exhaustion was too intense. *Unlike* Lane, her exhaustion was due to having had two bio exams this week and not due to getting rammed a dozen times against tempered glass.

I wasn't sure which one was worse.

"Crew," Lane groaned from the couch, five icepacks scattered across his body.

"Hmm?"

"Go clean your nasty dishes that have been sitting there since yesterday."

Crew's deep voice turned to a measly whine. "I'll do it in the morning."

"No," Lane shot. "Do it now."

The raspy, raw groan that rolled out of Crew's throat resembled the roar of a lion. He fought to push himself off the couch, heavy steps heading towards the kitchen before stopping to peer over Kota's shoulder.

She'd been drawing a lot lately, her new hobby that she took up as a stress reliever.

Except she wasn't very good at it.

"What is that?" Crew asked.

Kota grinned at her masterpiece. "A panda. Duh."

Crew's brow raised in doubt, but he didn't challenge her. "Okay then."

I couldn't see the paper from where I was sitting, but I suspected it didn't look like a panda at all.

The faucet creaked as it was turned, the sound of running water taking over the common area.

Thank God Crew was finally cleaning those dishes though. They'd only been there since yesterday, but they already smelled. He had a horrible habit of not rinsing off his shit before tossing it in the sink.

Crew spoke over his shoulder. "So did you decide if you wanna go out tonight, babe?"

Immediately, you could hear a pin drop. Every jaw was on the floor.

I wasn't sure if it was everyone's silence that caused Crew to realize his mistake or if he realized it on his own, regretting it the second it left his lips.

"I, uh," he stumbled, "I was talking to Lane."

Lane looked equal amounts amused and disgusted. "Did you just call me babe?"

The pain on Crew's face was apparent, the words sounding like they were reluctantly getting ripped out of his mouth. "Yes..."

I wasn't sure how Lane was managing to keep a straight face. "Never call me that again."

"Got it."

Lane flashed me a crooked half-smile, making my heart stutter in the walls of my chest. "Alright," he said. "Let's go."

Guess we were going out after all.

***

Since we were late to the going-out-game, the hockey team had already left the bar and were going back to their house for a celebratory afterparty.

As suspected, our roommates made excuses as to why they couldn't head to the hockey house with us, promising they'd meet us there while emphasizing a hundred times that they would be arriving "separately."

According to Crew, he had to run to the liquor store.

According to Kota, she needed to shower.

We knew that both of them were full of shit.

Two hands grabbed me by the shoulders from behind and my heartbeat spiked before dropping back to a steady rhythm at the sight of Jett's friendly face leaning over my shoulder. "Bridget! Your hands are empty. You want a vodka lemonade?"

I chuckled. "I'd love one. Thank you."

"You're welcome! I'm on it!"

He disappeared up the stairs, and I had a faint flashback of the night I came here for the first time.

"Either he's got a thing for you, or he views you as a sister."

It was funny how easily he'd picked up on that, yet how long it took me to. Even after Lane had admitted his feelings for me, part of me didn't believe it. I'd been convinced that it all had to be some elaborate joke, that any second, the ball would drop.

But it hadn't.

322

A few minutes later, a vodka lemonade was in my hand and Jett leaned close, all seriousness in his voice. "If any girls ask, you got it from me."

A wave of laughter rushed out. "Jett, I admire the hustle, but I don't think you need to bribe girls with special drinks in order to get with them."

The corners of his lips ticked upwards, icy blue eyes melting into a warm pool of water. "Wow, Bridget. I think that's the nicest thing you've ever said to me."

That earned another gush of laughter from me because I could tell he was being serious. I nudged him in the shoulder. "Of course, Jett. I'll always hype you up! Speaking of which," I leaned in, my volume dropping, "there's a really pretty girl in the corner. Dark skin, curly black hair. And she's practically eye fucking you right now."

Jett's eyes trailed to the corner, his mouth sliding upwards. "You're right."

"Are you into it?"

"I'm into it."

I offered my fist and he bumped it. "Go get her, tiger."

He stood up straight, his shoulders broadening even further. He emitted confidence as he wandered over and introduced himself.

"Look at you playing matchmaker."

I grinned at the voice coming from behind me, my chin dipping towards my chest. I turned, seeing my boyfriend smiling at me, undoubtedly my favorite view.

Stepping closer, but not close enough to make anyone suspect anything, I cranked my head back to look him in the eye. "I'm trying to teach him that he doesn't need special drinks to get a girl."

Lane glanced over my head at the new couple I'd pieced together. "It seems to be working."

"Good! Anyway, how'd your issue go? Was there actually a problem this time or did Matt get his hand stuck in something again?"

A husky chuckle left his mouth, his grin growing to a full-on smile, and I wished more than anything that I could pull him to me right now and taste that smile.

"There was actually an issue this time," Lane said. "Ironically, it still had to do with Matt."

"What happened?"

"I don't know, some freshman was flirting with him and then her boyfriend stomped in and decided he was gonna start a fight."

"Oh." My fingertips shot up to my lips. "Is Matt okay?"

Lane's laughter was even louder this time around. "Matt's one of the best defenseman in the country; he's fine. The other guy didn't look so good though. I wouldn't be surprised if he needed stitches."

"Geez, it was that bad?"

"Matt's a fucking animal," Lane nodded. "It took three of us to get him off the guy."

"Yikes," I murmured, drowning the word with a swig. "Any word from our roommates?"

"Nope. You?"

"Nope."

We stared at each other for a moment, both of our lips seemingly lifting at the same time.

"Are you thinking what I'm thinking?" Lane asked.

"You wanna fuck with them?"

There wasn't a trace of uncertainty in his voice. "Hell yeah, I do."

"Fuck with who?" Cody appeared.

"No one," we said in unison.

Wow. That was two times within the same sixty seconds that we'd read each other's minds.

What a couple we make.

Cody's brows flew up as he gulped his Coors Light. "Whatever," he muttered carelessly before walking off.

I kept my voice low, leaning in as much as one would consider it to be a friendly distance. "I'll check their locations."

Either the app wasn't loading because of the shitty service in this house, or their locations were off, because neither of them were coming up on my phone.

I'd bet money it was the latter.

"Hmm," I hummed.

"What?" Lane peeked at the screen.

"Their locations are off."

He crossed his arms, a mischievous gleam igniting in his eye. "They just think they're so fucking smart, don't they?"

"What're you suggesting we do?"

Lane puckered his lips in thought. "Let's call them."

"And say?"

He shrugged off the question, grasping my hand before remembering there were people around. The ghost of his touch lingered as he pulled away. It was the first moment since we started dating that I wished everybody knew. I was growing tired of having to play the best friend card in front of everyone, pretending like I didn't want to be all over Lane every second of every group gathering or party.

Instead of holding my hand to lead me through the sea of people surrounding us, all he did was cock his head, signaling for me to follow.

I wasn't overly pleased as I complied, but Lane's continuous glances behind him to check on me eased the frustration.

As he led me up the stairs, my eyes scanned three-sixty around me, checking to see who was around. Assumptions would definitely be made if anyone caught us sneaking upstairs together.

But to my relief *and* my disappointment, we didn't go into a room; we stood at the top of the banister. I nuzzled my shoulder against him, embracing the comfort of his warmth, a small action that meant a lot when we had to go hours at a time without touching each other at all.

The phone was placed between us on the banister, put on speakerphone. It gave a ring, then another, and another, and by the fourth ring, I assumed Crew wasn't going to answer. To be honest, I hadn't had much faith that he'd answer in the first place, considering his awful track record lately, plus knowing he was probably screwing my best friend right now.

"Hello?" Crew panted.

Lane shifted, nearly jumping. "Hey, uh, where you at?"

Crew's response was almost too quick, too confident, as if it had been rehearsed. "I'm at the liquor store with Cody."

325

"Uh, Cody's here," Lane challenged.

Even though Crew wasn't standing in front of us, we could *hear* that stone wall of confidence crumble. "Oh, did I say Cody? I meant Keith."

"Right... Well, hurry up."

"Will do."

The phone went silent. Did he just fucking hang up on us?

I mean, he hadn't known I'd been listening in, so I guess he just hung up on Lane, but still.

"Is it just me," Lane grinned deviously, "or did he sound slightly out of breath during that conversation?"

"A little," I giggled.

"Alright," he nodded once at me, "your turn."

Chapter Sixty-Seven

Lane

After we called Kota and made her sweat, Bridget and I headed back down to the party, although, I did it with an extreme amount of reluctance.

Crew and Kota weren't even here yet and I already wanted to leave so Bridget and I could spend quality time together.

We knew we couldn't keep our secret forever, and I didn't think either of us wanted to anyway, but we at least wanted to stay on the down-low until Crew and Kota fessed up.

The house was packed tonight. We didn't usually throw parties this big, but after tonight's win, it seemed like everyone was celebrating pretty hard. More and more strangers were filing in by the minute, either invited by friends that had found their way here or from seeing the fucking rager going on as they walked by.

I took it upon myself to basically stay sober for the night, only having had two beers. There had already been one fight tonight; someone had to be sober in case there were more, and of course, as captain, it had to be me.

It was insane how many more people had come in since we walked upstairs ten minutes ago. Once again, I led the way, pushing through the crowd with Bridget on my heels.

I'd been told all throughout my life that I had a calming, sensible aura to me. Right now, I was trying to make sure that wasn't the case. I was giving off the vibe that I typically saved for the ice— *deadly.*

I wanted every guy in this house that I didn't personally know to back the fuck off, doing everything in my power to make obvious what was mine without the ability to physically do so.

I towered over most of the people in the room, only getting beat out by my own teammates. Since I hadn't made a round since shortly before Matt's fight, I knew a sweep of the house was in check to make sure there weren't any more issues going on, but no way in hell was I going to leave Bridget.

"Cody!" I yelled, waving him over.

"Yes, captain?"

"I need you to do a sweep."

"Why can't you?"

My jaw tightened, frustration bleeding into my face. "Because Crew isn't here yet and I'm not leaving Bridget alone in this fucking zoo."

He shrugged too nonchalantly for my liking. "Take her with you."

"Cody," I dared.

"Or she can stay by me," he offered.

God fucking dammit. Was he really only giving me those two options?

Outside of the rink, Cody had always been one of the laziest guys, but apparently, I underestimated him. Guess you could add sloth to the running list of sins Cody had going.

Cody may have been a lazy idiot at times, but I trusted him to protect Bridget in my absence.

"Fine," I nearly growled. "Do *not* leave her side."

He brought two fingers up to his forehead in a salute. "Got it."

"I gotta do a quick sweep of the house to make sure everything's alright," I told Bridget. "I'll be back within five minutes. Are you alright staying here with Cody?"

She nodded surely, but for some reason, I wished she hadn't, wished she told me to stay with her.

Now I had to go check on my teammates while worrying about Bridget the whole time. I knew she was fully capable of handling herself, but the house was full of so many strangers that I didn't trust anyone.

I made my way through the house, mentally checking off my teammates as I accounted for them.

Most of the freshman and sophomores were in the basement, playing beer pong or dancing with girls. Keith, our talented second-string right-winger and also the one who was apparently in two places at once, considering he was "with Crew" right now, had a girl practically screaming in pleasure in what used to be Crew's room. Jonah, the sophomore who had replaced me in the house, had his head in what used to be my toilet.

Matt's door was cracked open, light fanning into the hallway. I could hear mumbling in the room as I approached, and I stopped in my tracks for a second, wary about whatever might've been going on in there.

I slowly pushed the door open with my fingertips, relieved to just see Matt icing his bloody knuckles and TJ sitting at the end of the bed, staring intently at his phone.

I sighed a breath of relief. "Thank God it's only you two. I thought I was about to walk in and see something that would make me wanna clean my eyes out with bleach."

TJ snorted, but Matt didn't seem amused. He must've still been pissed about the fight.

That was the thing about Matt. When he got really angry, it always took a while for him to come down from it.

There had been numerous times where he'd gotten into fights on the ice, all of which were broken up before they got too bloody, but a lot of the time, Matt would show up late to the afterparty because he'd still be too pissed to see anyone right after the game.

My chin raised. "Lighten the fuck up, Matt."

TJ didn't look up from his phone as he spoke. "He's just pissed because of El."

"What now?"

"Nothing," Matt huffed before locking himself in his bathroom.

My eyes darted to TJ, waiting for an explanation.

"Don't look at me. I hardly know shit."

I sighed, turning on my heels. El, short for Eleanor, was Matt's childhood best friend that every person on the planet knew he had a thing for. I didn't know all the details, and quite honestly, I wasn't interested in hearing them.

Heading down the hall, I peeked inside Jett's room.

I had a clear line of sight to him, watching him pour vodka into a solo cup, a container of lemonade sitting beside it.

"What the hell are you doing?"

He spun around so quickly that I was surprised he didn't knock it all over. "Hmm?"

"Vodka lemonade? C'mon, man."

"Well..."

I shook my head in disapproval. "Don't let Bridget see that. You'll break her heart."

He sighed, head dropping in defeat. "I'll go pour it out."

"Well, don't waste it," I judged.

Jett blew out a deep breath, acting torn. His eyes jumped between the cup and me, as if he was about to make a life-changing decision.

"Well, good luck with that," I said. "I gotta go find Bridget. I left her with Cody."

His eyes widened as he lightly scoffed. "You should *definitely* go find her then."

I checked Jett off as the last teammate I was looking for as I headed back downstairs. All teammates had been accounted for and weren't getting into any sort of trouble, and it seemed like all the patrons were behaving themselves too—outside of anything sexual, of course.

Bridget was right where I'd left her, and I thanked Cody before escorting her around the nearest corner, hiding in the dark hallway.

In a gentleman-like fashion, I carefully dug my thumbs into her hips and pushed her against the wall. One hand gripped her waist while the other cupped the back of her neck tightly, chest dragging with each breath as I leaned close. "You look so good tonight. It was getting too hard to keep my hands off you." My fingertips trailed the length of her, from her hip and up her side, all the way to the side of her face, loving the way she shivered from my touch, looking like she was about to jump out of her skin. The edge of my thumb glided across her bottom lip, feeling the stickiness of her lip gloss. "Strawberry?" I asked.

She took her lip between her teeth, giving a tight nod.

Suddenly, I didn't give a fuck about who was around.

Our mouths met with relief, hands immediately grabbing each other in all the ways they'd been dying to all night.

Gripping onto my hand like it was her lifeline, she yanked me into the nearest bathroom.

I hardly had time to lock the door before she was fighting with the button on my jeans.

This was risky. Way too risky.

But why did that turn me on more?

Bridget sank to her knees as my pants dropped, my dick flinging out in their absence.

Her small hand gripped my shaft as her mouth circled around me, working my dick in and out. My head dropped backwards, palms flattening against the countertop behind me.

Bridget's cheeks hollowed out, her mouth sucking me in like a vacuum, and when she opened her throat to allow me further access, I fought a moan.

Any noise in this bathroom was sure to echo, and that sure as hell wouldn't be good.

Inherently, my hips pushed forward in the slightest and she gagged, causing me to gulp. There was something about her struggling to take all of me that made me want to do it again.

She had a little over half of me in her mouth, my dick poking the back of her throat, making her eyes water.

Fuck.

Her mouth was always perfect, and right now, closed around me, perfect was an understatement. I was unconditionally hooked by the view.

My heart pummeled, legs locking as she continued, minutes ticking by.

"Bridget," I warned, panting, "I'm about to..."

She didn't pull away, her eyes sealed on my face, daring me. She was too irresistible to deny; I'd gladly give it to her.

I'd give her the fucking galaxy if she asked for it.

I kept my grunt as quiet as possible as my come shot into her mouth, and I zoned in on her throat, watching it bob as she swallowed every drop.

When she finally pulled back, she flashed me a sexy grin, proud of herself.

I caught my breath, almost too wounded to tug my own pants back up.

My pants were half-zipped when Bridget opened the door.

"What the fuck?"

Jett looked mortified— mouth wide open, staring at us like everything up was down and left was right. His eyes shot to my hand that was buttoning my jeans.

Bridget looked equally mortified. Bubblegum pink had flooded her face, and her chin dropped in embarrassment, hiding herself in all the ways she hadn't when that bathroom door had been closed.

His finger went between Bridget and me. "I just— you two— but—"

"Jett," I interrupted sharply.

"Does anybody know? Does Crew know?"

It was rare that I used my authority on my teammates outside of the rink, but the warning in my voice came out naturally. "No. And Crew isn't going to know because you aren't going to tell him. Right, Jett?" He didn't agree, didn't say anything. I leaned forward in the slightest, the threat clear in my voice. *"Right, Jett?"*

With a massive gulp, he nodded. "Right, captain."

"Thank you," I said. "Now let's pretend this never happened."

"Lane," Bridget uttered, "they're here."

I gave her one last look, wishing I could touch her once more. *But I was out of time.*

Turning, I could see Crew heading straight for us. He nodded once in greeting. "Hey, guys."

I plastered on a fake smile, wondering when both of these lies we'd built would finally wash to the surface. "Hey."

Chapter Sixty-Eight

Bridget

"**H**ow long is your class again?" Lane asked, his eyes trailing over the building as he adjusted the strap of his backpack on his shoulder.

"An hour and fifteen."

Reaching for the bill of my Cedar U hat, Lane wiggled it around my head.

"What are you doing?" I laughed.

"Fixing it," he smiled.

"Does it look silly on me? I never wear hats like this. I feel like it looks dumb on me."

It was a chilly day, but the warmth of Lane's smile could be felt all the way down to my toes, covering me like a heated blanket. "No," he said. "It looks good on you."

"Okay... But if someone makes fun of me, I'm blaming you."

"If someone makes fun of you, they better watch the fuck out," he grinned wider.

It was moments like these that were on a loop in my head twenty-four seven. Whether it was the affectionate comments or subtle touches, the cascades of laughter or secret dates, it was on a replay in my mind all the damn time.

The cold wind swept between us, sending a gust of Lane's scent towards me. I inhaled it, welcoming the aroma of fresh linen and the ocean.

"I'll wait for you at the library and then we can go pick up your car, okay?" Lane offered, cradling my face in his calloused hands.

I nodded with a trace of disappointment, masking it behind a graceful smile.

As thankful as I was for my car to finally be fixed, I also hated knowing this was the last day that Lane would be waiting at the door for me when I got out of class.

The entirety of class was spent mentally fighting myself on trying to focus. It was a continuous, aching cycle between listening to my professor and replaying every detail of seeing Lane right before class started.

Often, I found my chest feeling like it was constricting when I was apart from Lane, and right now was no exception. I knew I was just being dramatic every time it happened. For God's sake, I lived with the guy. Being away from him should've been a breath of fresh air rather than a punishment.

But self-talk didn't always take away the ache.

On my way out of the building, I took a mental snapshot of Lane by the front entrance, his lethally beautiful smile threatening to kill everyone in its wake.

He reached for me, and I dove at the offer, taking his hand.

We purposefully walked a certain path to the parking lot to avoid running into anyone we knew.

"Are we just going straight home after we get my car?" I asked.

"Did you want to?"

"I mean, I have a little bit of time before I need to get any homework done."

"Okay," he nodded. "I have a team meeting in a few hours, but we can do something quick if you want."

"Team meeting? What for?"

He sighed casually, but I sensed more stress behind it than what he was letting on. "We've got our conference game coming up."

I forgot about the boys' conference game. It was coming up quickly— less than two weeks now.

"Wouldn't it be easier if your coach had a meeting tomorrow before or after practice?" I asked.

"In theory, yes. But the meeting might be long and Coach hates wasting any amount of practice time."

"Ah, I see. Well, what would you like to do then?"

"Are you hungry?"

"Not really," I answered.

"Are you thirsty?"

I smirked, the bill of my hat hiding the rush of red drowning my cheeks as I dropped my chin to my chest. "Was that a legitimate question or..."

Deep, euphonious laughter echoed around the parking lot. "It was a legitimate question, yes."

"Oh," I shivered in embarrassment. "What were you thinking?"

"I was thinking along the lines of like, Starbucks, but hey, if you wanna go down that road..."

"Starbucks is good," I ducked into the passenger seat.

As usual, the line was long, and we spent the entire wait laughing about Kota's birthday dinner from the week prior.

Kota had gone to the bathroom, and *conveniently*, Crew had to go at the same time. They were gone for far too long, and *conveniently*, came back two minutes apart, both claiming that there had been a long line, even though the restaurant had only been half-full.

The post-fooling-around was evident the second they reappeared at the table.

Leave it to Kota not to fix her hair and to Crew for not zipping his pants up all the way.

They weren't good at covering their tracks. It made me wonder how oblivious they truly thought we were.

After Starbucks, Lane and I parted ways for the drive home from the car shop since I needed to drive my own car back. But the second we saw each other again, it was like the conversation had never ceased.

The second we walked through the door though, everything seemed to halt. From our conversation to our lighthearted mood to the straw that was halfway to my lips.

Kota and Crew were standing there, arms crossed, staring at us like they were both tempted to throw a punch.

"Hello?" Lane cautiously spoke, on edge. "Can we help you?"

Crew's cheekbones sharpened, his ravenous gaze swooping over us. "How was your date?"

I was gripping my plastic cup so tight that I was surprised it hadn't broken and sent my coffee splashing all over the floor.

"What?" Lane hurled.

"We know," Kota raved, voice full of venom.

I'd never been on this side of her wrath before, and I sure as hell wasn't a fan.

The earth was shifting off its axis more and more, and I was convinced that at any second, the floor was going to flip to the ceiling.

Lane gave me the quickest glance, checking me over, although, I wasn't sure what he was checking for. To make sure I was still breathing? To see if I was pissed? To see if I was about to say something?

Kota dropped her arms at her sides, giving a stiff shrug. "How long have you two been secretly dating?"

We could've lied if we really wanted, denied it like we'd been framed for a crime we didn't commit, dug ourselves deeper into the hole we were already trying to crawl out of.

But Lane hung his head low, a sigh rumbling out. "Almost two months."

Both of their mouths dropped. "Two months?" Kota roared. "You've been lying to us for two months?"

"Yeah, well..." I unsteadily said, my voice climbing to match hers. "We know that you two have been fucking!"

She gasped, sounding like she was choking on air. "We have not..."

Crew made a face, rubbing the back of his neck as Lane threw his hand through the air, waving her off. "Don't give us that shit. We've heard you guys loud and clear."

"Alright," Crew said, "so we've hooked up once or twice."

I slammed my coffee on the counter, just to have the ability to put both hands on my hips. If they wanted to point out our bullshit, I'd gladly do the same. "Once or twice, *my ass*. We know you guys have a whole routine going. You were probably going at it before we walked in."

Their guilt was showing through their moment of silence.

Crew's muscles became rigid, his jaw twitching in the slightest while he somehow managed to keep his voice somewhat calm. "This isn't about us," he grumbled.

"Then what's it about?" Lane scowled. "Us? Because that hardly seems fair."

When we first moved in, it was Kota and me against Crew and Lane. Now it seemed like there had been a switch-up of teams.

We grimaced at them, and they sneered at us, bitterness and betrayal bouncing around the room. It was tangible, circling through the air like cigarette smoke.

The silence was both refreshing yet maddening, loud yet deafening.

With a tight jaw, Lane stalked forward, his shoulder bumping into Crew as he passed him. "Let's go talk."

Crew stared at the ground for a second, a blend of agony and anger staining his face like clothing after a wine spill.

His sigh was the only sound in the room, his chin barely lifting as he followed Lane down the hall.

There was an uncomfortable, hollow feeling in my stomach as Kota silently tipped her head and shuffled towards our hall.

With each step as I followed, that sick feeling in my gut only grew, and I didn't have time to soothe it before Kota's bedroom door shut behind us.

Chapter Sixty-Nine

Lane

Crew had his back turned towards me, staring at the ceiling like the sight of me was sickening and he'd rather be looking anywhere else.

I was expecting a whirlwind of flames to shoot out of his mouth like a dragon, strained with judgement and resentment with the purpose of giving me third-degree burns.

But instead, his voice was placid— breathless even.

And that somehow hurt more.

"I really hope you're not about to blame this on that stupid rule," he said. When he finally found it in himself to look at me, I wasn't sure who I was looking at.

After all these years of friendship, I thought I had seen every side of Nicholas Crew. But it was hard to recognize the expression in front of me; it was one I'd never seen on him.

The betrayal sat clear on his face, all furrowed brows and glossy eyes. But that tick in his jaw didn't mask the ire that was swimming behind the sadness.

"I don't care about the rule, Lane," Crew said. "I care that you lied to me."

It wasn't just anger that poured out of me; it was much deeper than that. My voice came out as some sort of scratchy explosion, like a bomb that didn't quite detonate right. "And *you* didn't lie to *me*?"

His throat bobbed as he swallowed, having nothing to say.

"Sure, I left part of the truth out, but you *knew* how I felt about her! I'm not the one that's been going on for however long pretending to hate her. Putting on a show *just* to deceive you." I shook my head, stumbling backwards as if I'd been pushed. "How long has it been going on for anyway?"

His eyes faltered around the room; he was seemingly lost in a fog of denial.

"How long, Crew?"

"A few months," he finally admitted.

I scoffed, running a hand over the stubble on my chin. "You have no right to give me any shit."

"Lane—"

"No," I cut him off. "I didn't lie to your face like you lied to mine."

"That's bullshit. That's such bullshit."

"Name a lie that I told you to your face," I challenged.

"What about every time I asked what you were up to, and you always responded saying you were just hanging out with Bridget? When in reality, you were sneaking around behind my back, going on secret dates?"

I grabbed the back of my own neck, my nails digging into my skin. "Technically, I wasn't lying. I was hanging out with Bridget like I said."

"Don't try to get me on a goddamn technicality, Lane! The bottom line is that you fucking lied."

I sucked in a crisp breath, lungs begging for the oxygen. The guilt was attacking me now. It felt like a virus was swarming through the apartment, taking over our bodies and seeping into our brains. No one was going to get out unscathed.

His words were registering, slowly, yet surely, and the poisonous truth was too much to bear. I could deny it all I wanted, could try to get off loose on a technicality, but at the end of the day, I was a fucking liar.

Apparently, everyone in this house was.

Crew's voice cracked, his palms lifted and shaking towards the ceiling as he spoke. "I had to find out from fucking TJ! Fucking TJ! Instead of from you. It seems like everyone on the damn planet knew before I did. Do you know how upsetting that fucking is? We're supposed to tell each other shit! Brothers are not supposed to lie to each other!"

Brothers.

It felt like the gun was loaded that time and I could feel every bullet searing through my chest.

The pain in the room was alive, pulsing with its own heartbeat.

I blew out a strained breath, one that physically hurt as it left my lungs. "Crew..."

"I'm serious."

"I know," I croaked. "I'm sorry."

He eyed me like he wasn't sure if he'd heard me right.

"I am. I'm sorry," I said again.

A shaky exhale rolled out of his throat. "I'm sorry too... Can we please never do this shit again?"

"Yeah," I agreed quietly.

He stepped forward with his arms open, and I mirrored him. There were only a handful of times that I could recall us hugging in the past, and I'd say most, if not all, had to do with hockey.

This might've been the first that didn't.

"Alright," he pulled away after a minute, "long enough."

I rolled my eyes and he let out a chuckle, and I'd be lying if I said I wasn't thankful to hear the sound after the entire conversation we'd just had.

"You think the girls are fine?" he asked.

I shrugged, "Probably."

He scrunched his face, looking worried. "I mean... you know how Kota can be."

"I know," I said, a small smile coming, "but Bridget can hold her own."

Chapter Seventy

Bridget

I looked over the room as if I'd never been there before, unsure of what to do or where to sit.

When Kota took a seat on the bed, resting against the headboard, I sat at the opposite end, maintaining a safe, yet awkward distance.

She still seemed to have trouble looking at me, her eyes studying her purple comforter. There was woe laced into her voice, as if her vocal cords had some sort of brutal injury. "Why didn't you tell me, B?"

Her obvious pain was making me feel bad, making me feel like I'd been a shitty best friend. But at the same time, I refused to let her get off easily. She'd betrayed me just as much as I had her; this wasn't a one-way street.

"Why didn't you tell *me?*"

"Because I was embarrassed."

Well, that was not the answer I'd been expecting.

"Why would you be embarrassed?" I asked.

"Because Crew encompasses everything in a man that I hate. Everything I always promised myself I wouldn't go for." She sighed, her voice lowering to a disappointed mutter. "Yet here I am."

I scooted closer to her. "Kota, you don't need to beat yourself up over hooking up with someone."

Her mouth formed a hard line, as straight as an arrow. "Well, it's a little bit more than that."

"Oh."

"We aren't together, but we've talked about that being a future possibility."

"Oh."

Apparently, I hadn't realized how messy our living arrangement had become, especially without any of us knowing the extent of it.

Kota shrugged, but the expression on her face gave her away. Like a light switch, her defense mechanism was powered on. She was trying to act like this conversation bothered her less than it did, was trying to do that infamous thing where she pretended like nothing could touch her.

"Kota," I said gently, with just enough sternness to catch her attention. "You don't have to keep acting like you're invincible. It's okay to talk about your feelings, or to *have* feelings for that matter." I gestured around us, "I'm the only one in the room anyway."

Slowly, she nodded, and that guard of hers lowered in the slightest. "I guess I was in denial that..."

"That you have feelings for him?" I finished for her, earning a glare to be shot my way. "It's okay to admit it."

Kota gave a deep, raspy sigh. "Okay, yes. No matter how much I hate it and *loathe* myself for it, I do have feelings for him."

"It's alright that you do. There's nothing wrong with that."

"I knew you'd find out eventually," she said. "I just thought it would be from me."

I choked on a laugh. "Trust me, it *was* from you."

She playfully pushed me over. "Shut up!"

"Honestly though," I said, "I feel kinda bad."

"Why?"

"Because you just gave me a legitimate reason of why you didn't tell me, and truthfully, the only reasons I have are that we didn't want to piss you guys off about breaking the rule and we also became too stubborn to fess up first," I admitted.

She studied me for a moment, and for the first time since I sat down, I was entirely lost as to what was going through her mind. Her facial expression looked like a blank page, and I was a little on edge thinking about the possibility of her wrath coming back.

But all she did was shake her head. "You and Lane being together doesn't bother me. I always kinda knew you guys had a thing for each other, but you never mentioned it, not even once, so I figured I had to have been wrong."

I bit my lower lip. "I'm sorry."

"So am I. And I'm also sorry if I made you feel like you couldn't tell me."

"There were so many times where I wanted to tell you. Really, I did. At first, I didn't say anything because I wasn't sure where things with Lane would go, and I didn't want everything in the apartment to be thrown off if everyone knew. But as we got a bit deeper into our relationship," I shrugged, "I still couldn't do it, and I don't know why. I know for Lane, he most definitely didn't want *Crew* knowing but..." I trailed off, dropping my hands into my lap.

She scoffed lightly. "I don't blame him. Crew's the biggest hypocrite. He probably would've lit the apartment on fire."

"Exactly," I chuckled.

"And I mean, yeah, it sucks that I got to miss the beginning with all the most exciting parts of you guys getting together, but if you're happy with him, then I'm happy for you." Her hand lightly touched my forearm, eyes searching for the truth. "Are you happy with him, B?"

"I am."

Kota nodded. "That's what I care about most."

"Are you happy with Crew?" I asked.

She snorted, pulling away. "Most of the time."

I let out a laugh. "So, you forgive me?"

"Of course, I do. Can you forgive me?"

"Yes." Relaxing, I gave a trusting smile. "No more secrets?" I asked, bringing up crossed fingers.

"No more secrets," she agreed with a smile before offering her pinky for me to shake with my own.

Chapter Seventy-One

Bridget

Today was going to be interesting.

The first game of the conference tournament was today, and the boys were playing their rivals— St. Cloud State.

If they could clinch the win today and tomorrow, the conference title would remain theirs, and they'd automatically secure their spot in the NCAA tournament.

I just happened to be attending the game with the oddest group ever.

Me.

Kota.

My mom.

My other mom.

Crew's mom.

And Lane's mom.

Why were there so many fucking moms?

There would be *a lot* of introductions today, including Kota's first time meeting Crew's mom, and both of my moms meeting for the first time.

Since Crew and Kota weren't official, everything would be kept under wraps for the time being. She would just be introducing herself as his roommate for now.

346

My dad was on a business trip, so he couldn't make it to the game, and he seemed to be heartbroken about it. Even though he wouldn't be attending, my mom had been dying to meet Lane for a while, so she gave Bianca the green light to spend the weekend home alone.

I'd wanted my sister to tag along, but apparently, she didn't want to. I assumed she was up to no good in our empty house.

I sat criss-crossed applesauce on Lane's bed, leaning back into my hands as I watched him pack his hockey bag.

Let me correct myself— I watched him take everything *out* of his hockey bag, double check to make sure everything was there, and then put it all back into the bag.

He'd gotten quieter than he'd been all day, and I wondered what was swimming around in that pretty head of his. Something hockey-related, no doubt.

"You excited?" I asked.

The deep exhale that came out of his nose was audible. "Nervous."

"You're gonna do great."

"There's a lot of pressure riding on this weekend. If we fuck up, especially if *I* fuck up, no one's gonna be very happy."

I spoke softly, "You put too much pressure on yourself, Lane."

His voice fell. "Hard not to."

I couldn't even imagine how he must've been feeling. How he probably felt *every* time he got onto the ice.

Lane had been one of the top NHL prospects since high school, and after years playing at a difficult level, he'd climbed his way to the top of the list. It was probably exhausting trying to maintain his placement in the league, not to mention his reputation.

Not only was he leading a team, but he was leading a school, a community. There was an entire army of hockey fans watching.

I wasn't sure if I should say what I was about to, but before I could think, it was slipping out. "Your mom confirmed that she's coming."

Lane froze halfway to his bag for a moment before shaking it off. "Yeah, we'll see if she actually shows up."

"I'm sure she will," I said in a small voice.

He laughed once without humor. "Maybe to support Crew, not me."

Lane was convinced his mom liked Crew more than him. Frankly, he was convinced she liked *everyone* more than him.

I'd never say it aloud, but I didn't think he was that far off.

She wasn't very good at hiding her emotions. You could see it all over her face at the cemetery and at lunch— she held a grudge against Lane.

I'd never lost a child, so I could never understand her grief, but you'd think that losing one child would make you hold on closer to the other.

Apparently not.

"Lane, c'mon," I said.

The edge in his voice seemed to sharpen, and I had to remind myself that the blade was pointed at his mother, not me. "If that's not why she'd show up, then it would probably be because you're the one that invited her, not me."

"I'm sure that's not true," I said, only partially believing my own words.

"Oh, it's true," he grimaced, and I couldn't help but notice how much more violently he'd been shoving things into his bag since his mother was brought into the conversation. "Do you know how many games I've invited her to over the years? I think the most games she's shown up to in a season was three."

I kept quiet, noting the sudden darkness in his eyes.

"We play between thirty and forty games a year, Bridget. And she's shown up to a maximum of three. If she shows up today, this will be her first of the year."

I bit the inside of my cheek to keep my mouth from falling open.

The boy's season was almost *over,* and she hadn't been to a single game yet?

I tripped on my own words, practically choking on word vomit as I attempted to change the subject. "Well regardless of what happens, I know you'll play a great game."

That dark cloud that had been hovering in his eyes faded, returning to the clear blue skies that I knew and loved. "Thank you," he gently said, reaching towards me to stroke my cheek with his thumb.

"And Lane?"

"Yes, Beautiful?"

"Can I wear your jersey?"

He stepped closer, towering over me as he stood between my legs. I was completely sober, but suddenly, I felt drunk, absolutely and utterly intoxicated by every part of him. His smile, his touch, his smell.

With his hands resting on my thighs, he smiled wider. "I was waiting for you to ask."

***

"I'm nervous," Kota whispered from the passenger seat.

I gripped the steering wheel. "Don't be."

"What if she knows something's up? For God sakes, I'm wearing his freaking jersey."

"She's not going to think anything of it unless you're acting weird. Just pretend like you guys are friends. I'm wearing Lane's jersey. For all she knows, we just wanted to match or some shit."

"I guess so. How are you feeling about your moms meeting?"

A twinge of anxiety pooled in my stomach at the reminder. "A bit jittery, but I think it'll go well."

She studied campus as we drove through it, watching the buildings pass as if she'd never seen them before. "We're gonna need to find a way to differentiate between your moms."

"I know."

"How 'bout Mom One and Mom Two?"

I laughed. "Like Thing One and Thing Two? Yeah, I don't think so."

"Ugh, fine. How 'bout Mom and Bio Mom?"

I tipped my head side to side. "That's not bad, actually." She was right that a differentiation had to be made. Hell, I'd already been mixing them up in my own head by calling them both "Mom."

There didn't seem to be many good options that were both accurate and respectful, so I guess Mom and Bio Mom, it was.

Kota had met my mom plenty of times over our years of friendship, and she recently met my bio mom for the first time.

The three of us went out to dinner, which was nice. Having my bio mom in my life was starting to fill the void in my heart that I hadn't realized I'd had.

I always knew part of me was missing. I felt like it had less to do with having "birth parents" and more to do with finding out who I was and where I came from. But I guess I hadn't realized just how much of me had been missing until I found her.

Bio Mom had been putting in a lot of effort to form a relationship with me, and I was beyond grateful for that. I felt fulfilled after every time I saw her, and it meant a lot to me that she was coming to Lane's game today. I was sure it meant a lot to him too.

As for my mom, I wasn't sure how she was feeling. Every time I spoke to her about Bio Mom, she seemed to be happy for me. But I couldn't silence this nagging voice in the back of my head, poisoning me with the idea that she was mad at me for all of this.

After spending far too long trying to find parking, we headed inside. Usually, we'd stand in line at the student entrance, which always took forever since the line wrapped around the building, but since we weren't sitting in the student section today, we went through the front entrance.

Bio Mom was standing inside waiting, bobbing up and down on her toes.

"Mom!" I waved.

"Oh!" she squealed, trekking over with a hug for Kota and me.

She cupped my face in her hands for a moment, and once again, I could've sworn I was looking into a mirror. "How are you, honey?"

"I'm good," I assured her. "How are you?"

"Good," she answered. "A little nervous, if I'm being honest."

I gave a reassuring grin, doing my best to hide the nerves that were consuming my own skin.

We went in and found our seats. When I saw my mom making her way through the arena towards us, I hopped to my feet, waving to catch her attention.

My nerves ignited further, making every inhale burn slightly. I couldn't believe that two of my favorite people were about to meet.

"Hey, Mom," I smiled as she got to us. Gesturing to Bio Mom, I said, "Mom, this is—"

They had their arms wrapped around each other before I could finish.

Bio Mom's eyes were squeezed shut, once again overwhelmed with emotion as she murmured against my mom. "It's so nice to finally meet you."

"You too," Mom said.

Bio Mom pulled away, holding Mom gently by her shoulders. "I'm so grateful for everything that you've done. Thank you for taking care of our daughter."

Under the harsh arena lights, I could make out the glassiness in Mom's eyes, the moderate quiver in her lips. "And thank you for bringing her into the world."

Chest lightening as all my anxiety vanished faster than I could snap my fingers, my heart felt extraordinarily full. So full that it could've burst at the seams.

I'd thought about this moment the entire way here, a thousand possibilities, both good and bad, running through my head, and the reality ended up being better than I thought.

No one knew how much this meant to me. I wouldn't trade this moment for the world.

The four of us sat, and the next fifteen minutes were occupied with small talk, stories, and a short speech from Bio Mom about her insane appreciation and gratefulness for how I was raised.

When Lane's and Crew's moms arrived, they joined in on the conversation after being filled in on the backstory of my two moms.

Suddenly, the announcer's voice blared in the speakers, declaring the arrival of St. Cloud State's starting lineup.

I went to stand, and Kota gripped my arm, yanking me down.

"Ouch! You just pulled my shoulder out of its socket!" I screamed in a whisper.

"Sorry, but unless you want all five-hundred moms to think you're a wack-a-doodle, sit down."

My frown took up half my face. We'd never actually sat outside of the student section before. I guess all the traditions and chants were programmed in me.

I bobbed my knee up and down, gluing my mouth shut to keep from screaming along with the student section.

"At center, a six-foot senior out of Birmingham, Minnesota... Ethan Silas!"

I shivered at the name, my head whipping over to Kota as she did the same.

"Did they just say..." she trailed off.

"I think so."

"That can't be him, right?"

After spending every second of the day up until we got here with an upset stomach and nerves poking at me, I'd finally relaxed.

But now, there was a jolt in my core. It wasn't just nerves this time. It was damn near panic.

Scanning over the opposing team's jerseys, my eyes zeroed in on number fifty-nine. "That's his number," I swallowed.

"I didn't know he transferred."

"Me neither," my voice shook.

I watched as Lane took his position on the ice, standing opposite of number fifty-nine.

352

Fuck.

Lane was about to go head-to-head with my ex, and he didn't even know it.

Chapter Seventy-Two

Bridget

St. Cloud hadn't scored a single goal, putting us in a good spot for the night. The boys were up by two in the middle of the second period, but my anxiety still hadn't gone down. Kota had to grip my kneecap to stop it from bouncing.

My eyes followed the puck, watching it skid across the ice from one player to another. It was moving around so quickly that it was hard to keep track of at times; I kept losing it in the chaos.

Before I knew it, Jett was on the opposite side of the rink, the puck in his possession as he managed to maneuver his way through a sea of red, swerving through them like he was racing through traffic on the highway.

With more force than I could wrap my head around, he slammed the puck towards the goalie, who miraculously blocked it.

As if he'd teleported there and appeared out of thin air, Lane was ready for it, snagging the rebound and tapping the puck straight into the goal.

The buzzer went off, signaling another Cedar goal, and an explosion of cheers encompassed the arena.

Our entire group sprung to their feet, clapping and shouting and high fiving each other. Even Lane's mom looked happy, wearing the brightest smile I'd seen on her since we met. If I didn't know any better, I'd say she looked proud.

She should've been. After all, she had an entire arena of people cheering for her son right now.

The boys brought it together for a group hug, the only proper way that hockey players ever celebrated a goal. Stiffly skating backwards out of their way, Ethan bumped into the glass, and although we were a few rows back, my head shot down out of instinct from being too close to him.

I waited for the moment to pass, for him to skate off before he had the chance to scan his surroundings.

But that moment of safety I was waiting for didn't come.

"Uh, oh," Kota muttered.

"What?" I spoke towards the ground.

"He's looking right at you."

My chin stayed down, only my eyes carefully peering up. It was like I was too afraid to physically move, mimicking the way a small animal would play dead when it knew it was getting hunted.

There were thousands of people here, and I hoped he didn't recognize me, but unfortunately, my hair had already condemned me.

Any blonde or brunette could get away with just being another face in the crowd, but I stuck out like a sore thumb.

The squinting of Ethan's eyes was unmistakable. His spine seemed to stiffen, making him grow an extra inch. He scanned the length of me, stopping far too long on Lane's jersey. I crossed my arms over my chest, trying to hide the number, but when Ethan skated off, purposely ramming his shoulder into Lane on the way, I knew I'd failed.

Chapter Seventy-Three

Lane

I was happy but I was disgusting. I looked like a walking ball of sweat.

We won four-to-one and considering St. Cloud had been ranked fifth in the nation, it looked even better on us to win by such a gap.

As usual, Coach's happy face was no face at all. Rage was seemingly the only emotion he'd ever shown. The one time I'd ever seen him actually crack a smile was when I told him I'd decided to go pro. And even then, the smile was so small that it was questionable. I might've just been imagining it.

Nonetheless, he praised us for our patience and cleanliness on the ice tonight. We'd only gotten two minor penalties throughout the entire game, a new record for the team.

I didn't bother showering in the locker room; I was too excited to see Bridget that I decided to wait to shower until I got home.

I know. I was disgusting.

But she was always finding her way into my head, making it hard to stay away from her longer than I had to. Even when I was at my most focused on the ice, I still had her face in the back of my mind. It was like I'd be completely dialed into the game, my only worry being the puck, but once each play was over and there was a gap in my concentration, she always managed to slip through the cracks.

When the final buzzer went off, signaling the end of the game, the only thing I was looking forward to was seeing her in my jersey.

I waited outside the locker room in the exact spot I'd told Bridget to meet me in. People were still trickling out of the arena, and as St. Cloud State walked out of the guest locker room, all saggy shoulders and scowls, I choked back laughter.

We were one game away from the conference title and a spot in the NCAA tournament, and after the way we played tonight, I was more than confident that we'd have our hands on that trophy tomorrow.

"Lane!"

I turned, and even from twenty feet away, I could spot those star beams in Bridget's eyes as she hurdled her way towards me, wearing a smile so bright that it was blinding me.

Relief and pride made one hell of a mixture as they drifted down my spine, the same way my skates slid across the ice.

Just like last time, the jersey was huge on her, hovering just above her knees. But somehow, it still looked better on her than it did on me.

"Careful," I said as she got closer, "I'm all swea—"

I grunted as she jumped into me. Guess she didn't give a fuck about my sweat.

Her voice came out muffled as she spoke into the crane of my neck, causing me to shiver. "You did so good."

"Thanks, Beautiful," I smiled. It was probably the tenth time I'd heard those words since getting off the ice, but they seemed to mean more coming from her.

She pulled back to look at me, clasping her hands behind my neck. I wanted to kiss her, but with the amount of sweat that had poured out of my body over the last few hours, I thought better of it. Suddenly, I was regretting not showering yet.

"I wanna kiss you," she mumbled shyly.

"You can, but I can't guarantee I'll taste good."

With a giggle, she tapped her lips against mine quickly. "I'll give you a better one once you're clean."

"Fine by me. You're probably also gonna need to shower now, sorry. My filth has probably infected you."

"Ugh," she jokingly grumbled. "How gross."

There was someone hovering in my peripheral vision like a shadow you'd catch out of the corner of your eye. I had a feeling of who it was, but I was afraid to look.

"Lane," my mother called, causing a snarl to nearly echo out of my mouth as a response.

Reluctantly, I placed Bridget back on her feet.

Some people would've been happy that their estranged mother had shown up to their game, but I was the opposite. Being in her presence was tearing me down from my high.

I'd already spoken to my father through text after the game. Like a supportive parent, he rarely missed any home games. He didn't often stick around after the games though since it got too hectic. He usually tried leaving with a few minutes left in the third period to avoid all the traffic getting out of the parking lot.

I would've been much less on edge if my mom had done the same tonight. That way, she'd have the bragging rights of saying she came and was a "good parent," all the while I wouldn't have had to see her face.

Bridget's eyes jumped between us. She motioned behind her. "I'll wait for you."

"Okay," I said, turmoil growing as she walked off.

My mom turned to me. "You played a great game."

I eyed her, confusion at the forefront. I didn't remember the last time she'd complimented me on anything, let alone hockey. "Why are you here, Mom?" I let out.

That, she hadn't been expecting. She pushed her lips together, shoulders dropping.

"Because Bridget asked you to be?" I spoke. "After all these years of me asking you to come to my games and you rarely showed up and now you decide to show up?"

She blinked rapidly, chin dipping. "Lane..."

"No, really. Why are you here, Mom?"

Her chest struggled to lift, as if she had a pile of bricks sitting on her. "I'm here because I realized."

"Realized what?"

Her voice raised in the slightest, her words coming out strong, regardless of the pain hidden behind them. "That my son was so distant from me that he didn't tell me he had a girlfriend or that he committed to playing in the NHL."

A surge of betrayal ripped through me. "Who told you that?" I asked. "Bridget?"

"No," she said with a tremble, "your father." I knew they occasionally checked in, but I didn't think my dad would say anything, especially after the conversation we'd had about it on Thanksgiving. "I've known for months. And I was waiting for you to tell me yourself, but you didn't."

Now I was the one tripping on my words, focusing too hard on keeping my voice steady. "I didn't think you'd be very happy about it."

She studied me like I wasn't making sense. "Why wouldn't I be happy about it?"

I could feel myself starting to crumble, and I couldn't look at her while I did. Through a cracked voice, I spoke, my finger pointed to the center of my chest. "Because you don't think I deserve it... Because you wanted this to be him, and you wanted *it* to be me."

The harsh lights illuminated every feature of hers as her face fell. "What?"

"I heard you. I heard you, Mom!"

"Lane," she shook her head, "what are you talking about?"

"It was years ago," I said, feeling like I could hardly get a breath in, "before you and dad divorced. You two were fighting and I heard what you said."

She eyed me quietly, lost.

"You said that you wished it had been me."

My heart rattled inside my chest as she stuttered, eyes wide. "Lane, I—I don't... remember saying that. And if I did, I am so sorry, I didn't mean it. It was probably just the grief—"

"The grief?" I exploded, tears threatening to spill over. "*I* was there! I was fucking there, Mom. I watched everything as it happened, and I had to deal with the aftermath myself because *you* weren't there! Because you hated me."

"Lane," she wept, "you are my son. I could never hate you."

"Then why do you act like it?"

Her voice was strained, but stern. "Lane, I love you. I will always love you. But after we lost Liam... it became hard to look at you—"

"Because in your eyes, I killed him," I blurted out.

"No! *No,*" she denied through a surge of tears. "Because every time I looked at you, I saw him."

Her words cut me, and selfishly, I hoped mine were cutting her. "How do you think I feel every time I look in the mirror?!"

Both shaking hands were brought up to her mouth as a raging tropical storm poured out of her eyes.

"Do you think it was easy for me to see my other half in a casket? I dread my birthday every year! I become a shell of a person every time his death date rolls around! I can hardly get behind the wheel of a car if other people are in it because I'm so scared of fucking up again," I broke down. "You wished it was me... and most of the time, so do I."

At this point, her head was towards the ground, both hands covering her face as her shoulders violently shook.

I hadn't seen my mom sob like this in a long time, and instinctively as her son, I felt the need to wrap my arms around her and comfort her, but I didn't.

I hadn't meant to make her cry, but I'd been holding in too many things for far too long. I wasn't sure why I never stood up to her before, and even more so, I wasn't sure what gave me the strength to now.

She was crying so heavily that I had to focus to understand what she was saying. "I'm so sorry, Lane. I've been such a horrible mother. I promise to be better from now on. I'm not going to ask for your forgiveness because I know I need to earn it... Will you please give me the chance to be better?"

I could see it in every tear streaming down her face, could read it as if she had it written across her skin. She felt guilty.

360

Looking away, I nodded.

Luckily, there was nobody around to witness this mess— no one, besides one.

Crew stood at the corner, head bowed as if he was trying to pretend he hadn't been listening.

When a squeezing sensation came over me, it was as if I was brought back to my body. My mom had her face nuzzled into my chest, arms clutched around me like a rope tightening.

I had my arms lifted the way cops told you to raise them. There was a strange, awkward panic running through me for a moment before I finally brought my arms around my mom, keeping them awkwardly loose around her small frame.

I couldn't remember the last time we'd hugged.

She held onto me for what felt like a small eternity before finally pulling away with a deep breath, slightly more composed.

"I'll be here tomorrow, okay?" she said.

I nodded.

"I love you."

A twinge of pain rolled through my chest, tapping at my heart. Even though she'd said those words to me over the years, this was the first time that it felt like she meant it.

"Love you too," I muttered.

With heavy steps, she walked off, and the second she was out of sight, my eyes zipped over to Crew.

I blew out a massive breath, one so big that you'd think I'd been holding it for minutes on end. I could feel the redness lingering in my face from holding too many emotions.

That conversation was fucking hard.

With no hesitation, Crew jogged towards me, arms opened.

I met him halfway, dropping my head into his shoulder as my eyes squeezed shut, trying to keep my tears at bay.

I guess we'd officially hugged twice now over non-hockey things.

He gave my back a brotherly pat, his voice soothing. "You wanna go get a drink?"

"Yeah."

***

Two hours and a lot of instructions later, we were at Stallions, cleaning out my emotional wound with an ice-cold beer.

No one was allowed to get drunk tonight, per my strict rules. Tipsy, fine. But under no circumstances were we getting wasted.

We'd never gone out after a Friday game before because we typically always had a game the following day. Obviously, we had one tomorrow, an important one too, but a drink felt necessary.

I'd put my foot down earlier; this was not a team event. Only our line was allowed to go to the bar. We kept the plan on the down low and all other teammates were absolutely prohibited from going out or drinking at all. It seemed unfair, but until the lower classmen could figure out how to drink without going overboard, it had to be this way.

Although our line tended to get obliterated and be dumbasses when they drank, I knew the guys well enough to know they weren't messing around tonight. We all knew what was at stake tomorrow, and no one was going to sacrifice that trophy for an extra drink.

This was the most relaxed I'd felt all day, seated on a bar stool with my arm slung around Bridget's waist and "Thinkin' Bout You" by Frank Ocean playing in the background.

"Lane," Bridget whispered against my skin.

I turned, my nose touching her cheek. "Yes, Beautiful?"

She shivered against me at the term of endearment. "This is the exact spot we met."

I held her close, my eyes skimming over her fragile face, noting all my favorite features of hers from the few freckles above her cheeks to the honey in her eyes. There was an odd flutter in my chest, and in that moment, I'd never been more mesmerized by anything.

362

"You're right," I replied, then motioned to my beer. "If you want, we could reenact that moment."

Her head tipped back in laughter. "How endearing, but I think I'll pass."

Her sugary, playful tone jumpstarted my heart, as if my heart hadn't felt like it was bleeding hours prior.

Bridget, I love you.

I could feel the words lodged in my throat, aching to be let out.

And I would've said them. I swore I would've, had a sea of crimson red not walked into the bar.

Chapter Seventy-Four

Bridget

I tugged on Kota's arm.

"What?"

The ghost of Lane's touch was evident as I pulled away from him, but I had to. I spoke through gritted teeth, "Guess who just walked in."

Her face fell, eyes immediately swooping around the bar. "Where?"

With as much discreet as possible, I tipped my head. "Far right."

She did a quick glance. "Shit."

"I still haven't told Lane," I admitted.

Kota sucked in a sharp breath, her eyes flitting around in thought. "Do you think you're gonna?"

"I don't know. I want him to be able to focus normally on the ice tomorrow, to play the best he possibly can without any distractions. Plus, after what happened with his mom earlier, I don't wanna add more stress to his plate."

"Not sure if this is gonna make you feel better or worse," she mumbled, eyes darting over my shoulder, "probably worse... But it looks like all the guys are already on edge."

I swung around, a knot in my stomach. Kota wasn't wrong. Both teams had stiff jaws and tense shoulders, and I was pretty sure every Cedar player was no longer sitting—including Lane.

St. Cloud had only been in the building for two minutes and the room was already thick with tension. I could practically smell the animosity and masculinity swirling in the air.

As if trying to assert their dominance, our starting line was crowding the bar, six pairs of thick shoulders blocking everyone's way.

My anxiety seemed to double in seconds. Other than catching glimpses of Ethan at the game today, I hadn't seen him since our breakup, and I sure as hell hadn't spoken to him since then either.

Some of the last things he said to me ran through my head like a song on replay.

"You're not leaving. Sit the fuck down, Bridget. Let's talk through this."

"C'mon, I need you. Everyone makes mistakes. You're just going to have to accept mine."

"You can't break up with me. I'm the best you're ever going to get."

He was a manipulator, and I was glad I got out when I did. If I'd stayed, things surely would've gotten worse. He'd made me feel some of the most painful emotions I'd ever had, and him being here was bringing some of them back.

"I need to go to the bathroom," I wavered.

"Do you want me to come with you?"

"No, I just need a minute. I'm just feeling a little overwhelmed."

"Okay... I'll be waiting here for you."

I prayed that there wouldn't be a line. Mentally, I wasn't sure if I could wait.

As I rounded the corner and saw an empty hall, hope consumed me. My pace quickened, eager to be alone in a stall.

"Hey, Strawberry," a voice echoed behind me.

Oh, fuck no.

All my instincts were telling me to keep walking, to ignore him and pretend like I had no idea who he was. But knowing him, he'd be here waiting for me when I stepped out of the bathroom.

Anxiety was coursing through my veins, threatening to make me collapse. It felt like my throat was in my stomach and my stomach was on the floor.

But I refused to show it, masking my fear with a thick layer of confidence.

I twisted around, chin up. "What do you want, Ethan?"

He shrugged far too nonchalantly, acting innocent. "Just wanted to see how you are."

"I'm fine, thanks."

"Good." His voice seemed to darken, stretching towards me with an envious spike. "So, what's goin' on with you and Avery?"

My jaw tightened in defense, and it was taking everything in me to keep my expression calm. Afraid of what Ethan would say or do if I told the truth, I spit out, "Nothing."

"Nothing? Because I'm pretty sure I saw you wearing his jersey earlier." He came closer. *One step. Two steps. Three steps.*

I was paralyzed in place. He eyed me like a predator mocking its prey, and while I wanted to be strong and stand my ground, my better judgement was telling me to go find Lane.

I could smell the trace of alcohol on his breath as he leaned forward. "Remember when you used to wear *my* jersey, Strawberry?"

The hair on the back of my neck stood up. His closeness was pushing all my senses towards panic mode. Not to mention I hated that fucking nickname. When Ethan first started calling me it, I thought it was cute. But by the end of our relationship, I wanted to cut my ears off, just so that I wouldn't have to hear it anymore.

Ethan was unpredictable in general, and I wasn't trying to find out the lengths that jealous Ethan would go to. Although, I wasn't sure why he was jealous when he was the one that cheated on me.

"Back off, Ethan," I spewed, stepping around him and dashing out of the hall before he had the chance to stop me.

Kota was the first person I saw, and I sprinted towards her, pulling her out of her conversation and over to the bar.

"Are you okay? What's going on?"

I didn't say a word until I had us maneuvered between Jett and Cody for safety. "Ethan just stopped me in the hallway."

Kota's eyes were glowing red, a trail of smoke starting to ease out her ears. There was so much disdain dripping from her voice that you could fill a drinking glass with it. "What? Did he follow you back there?"

"I think so..." I couldn't stop looking around me, my eyes bouncing throughout the bar like I was waiting for the killer to appear in a horror movie and stab me to death.

"That's not okay," she nearly growled.

"Where are the guys?"

She let out what sounded like a mix between a sigh and a scoff. "They're getting interviewed by George."

My eyes widened. "Seriously?"

Sure enough, George had Lane and Crew in the corner, a microphone far too close to Crew's face.

"George is gonna have to do this interview another time," Kota griped. "I'm going to get them."

I screamed in a whisper. "Don't fucking leave —"

It was no use. I saved my breath as she disappeared, leaving emptiness to my right.

Where the hell did Cody go?

"Why are you avoiding me?"

I jumped as Ethan appeared beside me. "I don't wanna talk."

"Strawberry, c'mon—"

"*Stop calling me that.*" I inched closer and closer to Jett, virtually ramming into him with my small shoulder.

Jett was leaned into the bar, every muscle seemingly tensing beside me. He tipped his head, giving a listen.

The cold, jagged edge in Ethan's voice jabbed at me. "You used to love that nickname."

"No, I didn't."

"That's not what I recall when you'd respond to it in bed."

A crash hit the floor as Jett's hands, ghost white, flattened atop the bar, pushing himself backwards and knocking a barstool onto the ground.

A large forearm scooped across my front as Jett gently pushed me behind him. "What the hell's your problem, Silas?"

I recognized the tick in Ethan's jaw— he was looking for a fight. I'd seen him wear that expression countless times when we went out together while we were dating, and every time, the night ended with some random guy on the floor. He thrived off of control, and although he'd never been physical with me, physical altercations with strangers were one of his favorite ways to gain the power he craved. I was pretty sure that was why he played hockey— so that he could be violent.

"Why don't you back the fuck off, Jameson?" Ethan growled.

Both boys were around the same build, nearly identical in height. And neither one seemed to be backing down.

The bright blue in Jett's eyes completely froze over, leaving nothing but ice-cold, callous rage. "How 'bout you leave her alone and get the fuck out of our bar?"

Once again, I was getting led behind someone. This time, it was Cody, reappearing from wherever he had gone to. "Get outta the way, Bridget," he muttered. "This could get really ugly, really fast."

I watched as he positioned himself beside Jett, TJ following his lead as numerous St. Cloud players did the same for their teammate.

Ethan came forward half an inch, feeling far too powerful. His voice came out like fire, all heat and flames and smoke. "Yeah? Who's gonna make me?"

A body pushed their way through the boys, fearlessly standing inches from Ethan. "I am," Lane said.

Chapter Seventy-Five

Lane

"Ah," Ethan smiled, "the man of the hour."

My voice came out casually, but authoritative all the same. "I suggest you leave, Ethan. Unless you and your teammates want to sit out tomorrow due to injuries."

"Is that a threat?" he hissed, both a question and a warning rolled into one. Letting out a single, stiff laugh, he gestured to Bridget. "Is this about your teammates or about her?"

Both, but mostly her.

He was testing my patience, and he knew it. I'd like to say I was usually a very patient person, but right now, all bets were off. I had a long, stressful and exhausting day, and the last thing I needed was for someone to mess with what was mine.

I wasn't sure why Bridget didn't tell me about her past with him in the first place, but it didn't matter now. What mattered was that he was making her uncomfortable, disrespecting her, and I sure as hell didn't like hearing about how he'd gotten in her space earlier.

As if there was some magnetic field drawing us together, Crew was right next to me, fists clenched and ready to fucking swing if it came down to it.

"Don't make me tell you again, Silas," I said through clamped teeth.

He wasn't as tall as me, but he raised his chin as if that would make him grow a few inches. Wearing a sinister smirk, he said, "Why do you want her anyway, Avery? I feel like you could do better."

As Crew stepped forward, I brought the back of my hand up to his chest, stopping him in his tracks. He didn't fight me on it and retreated.

I could feel the anger of my teammates building behind me, rising in the air the way smoke rose in a burning building. They were ready for a fucking brawl, and I'd be lying if I said I wasn't on my way there too.

But I was trying to be smart, to think ahead. I knew we could take them. Our starters versus theirs? I didn't think they stood a chance, especially with Matt on our side.

But on the off chance that things went south, we couldn't afford for one of our starters to sit out tomorrow.

My eyes made their way to Bridget. She had her arms wrapped tightly around herself, sullen eyed with a quivering frown.

Suddenly, it felt like someone had injected ire straight into my veins.

"If you want to be half as good as you need to be tomorrow," I said, "I suggest you leave and go to bed. This is our fucking bar, Silas. And we sure as hell don't have room around here for assholes trying to start shit or pussies who mess with our girls, or any girl for that matter."

That shit-eating grin was wiped from his face, replaced with a glare full of malice. His breaths became ragged for a moment, then all at once, that malevolent grin came back, bigger than ever.

Don't get me wrong— I got *mad* on the ice. But it was very rare that I reached that same level of anger off the ice. *I think I was passed that level of anger now.*

"Just a word of advice, Avery," Ethan said.

I don't want your fucking advice.

He leaned forward in the slightest. "All you have to do is drop the L word to get her to open her legs."

All reasoning had left my body; I became nothing more than a vessel of violence, my hands planting on his chest and launching him backwards into his teammates, and one by one, they fell down like dominoes.

My teammates took it as a green light. I knew exactly what they were all thinking right now— *free for all.*

St. Cloud's players stumbled over each other to stand, but they didn't have much time before they all had a designated Stallion wailing on them.

Ethan was the last to stand, and similarly to the saying, I kicked him while he was down. "Get the fuck up," I spat.

Innocent bystanders ducked out of the chaos; a crowd had formed a crescent around us, dozens of people eagerly waiting to watch.

He swung as he stood, knocking me in the shoulder. I grunted under my breath, recovering like I hadn't felt the punch.

He swung again, and again, and each one was effortlessly dodged. For how fast he was on the ice, he sure as hell seemed to move at a sloth's pace when his skates were off.

When a moment of stillness came, I took it. With a handful of Ethan's shirt in in my left hand, holding him in place, my right fist drilled him.

One to the cheek. One to the jaw. One to the eye.

A siren wailed, growing louder by the second. Immediately, I dropped Ethan, people scattering through the bar as hectically as they would if a natural disaster was about to strike.

St. Cloud players, including Ethan, were fleeing, disappearing one by one. I didn't think it was possible for my adrenaline to soar higher than what it was already at, but it did, reaching so high that it was definitely putting too much pressure on my rampaging heart.

In a panic, I shouted towards the boys. "My place! Now!" As risky as it was, I stayed put. A good captain would sacrifice himself for his team. I needed to be the last one to make sure everyone else got out. The tall windows at the front of the bar made it far too easy to see the blue and red flashing lights approaching. Pointing to Bridget, I yelled at Crew, "Grab her!"

With a rushed nod, he grabbed both girl's wrists, one in each hand, dragging them towards the back exit. Bridget's heels dug into the ground, a crease in her forehead as she tried to undo his grasp. Her golden eyes kept finding their way back to me, somehow still captivating within all the madness.

Don't worry about me.

The police cruiser slowed up front, and once the only people in sight were strangers, I booked it.

Chapter Seventy-Six

Bridget

Standing beside the door, I stared at it, praying for it to open. The minutes were going by like hours, and as each one ticked by, I was more and more tempted to go out and find Lane myself.

I'd tried checking his location the second we got back, but since Stallions was only fifty feet away, it was hard to see where he actually was.

Kota was playing nurse, which seemed quite out of character for her, handing out ice packs like candy.

For the most part, the boys were fine, currently taking up every square inch of our two couches. They had a few cuts and bruises, but nothing major. Except Matt seemed to be untouched, not a hair out of place. Taking one look at him, I never would've guessed he'd just been in a bar fight.

Seeing the boys fight was the equivalent of watching an action movie. I wasn't going to lie though, I was a little shook up. It wasn't like they'd been fighting just anyone. They were fighting _my ex-boyfriend_. Someone I used to be convinced I was in love with.

It was almost unsettling to think about that time of my life. Back then, Ethan was so charming, so polite. It was towards the end of our relationship that he showed his true colors, but even his slimy words then weren't as bad as tonight. It must've had to do with Lane. He was trying to get into Lane's head, to taint his focus and knock him off track. And I prayed he hadn't succeeded, but I wasn't so sure. Lane was hardly bothered by anything, but tonight, he seemed like a different person. I'd never seen him lose himself so much and so quickly, not even on the ice.

I didn't want to leave him at Stallions, but I'd pretty much been dragged home against my will. I knew Crew only did what he'd been told to do, but that didn't keep me from holding a tiny grudge against him right now.

"Where the hell is Lane?" Crew stood.

The ball of anxiety in my stomach grew to a full-sized knot. If something happened to him, anything at all, I would never forgive myself.

"I don't know," Matt said, "but if he's not back soon, we need to go find him."

Cody shook his head. "I say we go find him now."

TJ was slumped against the couch, his chin dipping as a cold glare clouded his eyes. "You guys think they went back for him?"

The danger in Matt's voice seemed to bounce from wall to wall around the room. He leaned forward, "They're dead if they tried."

Crew inched closer to where I stood, still hovering in our foyer. "I'm more concerned about the cops."

"Way to bring that up," Jett grumbled, examining his bloodied knuckles.

"Just being realistic."

"Does anyone need water?" Nurse Kota asked, holding up two bottles.

As she divvied some out, the apartment door burst open, and I leapt forward. "Lane!" When he gave a light groan as I jumped into him, I eased back. He rolled his shoulder, and a new swarm of guilt hit me. I hadn't realized that he'd actually gotten hurt.

I saw the punch Ethan drilled into his shoulder, but there had been little to no reaction from Lane, so I figured he was fine.

All the guys were up and looking ready— for what, I wasn't sure. Captain's orders? Another fight?

But all of Lane's focus was on me.

"Are you okay?" I swallowed.

The tenderness in his eyes was a stark difference to what I saw twenty minutes prior. His reddened hands cupped my face. "I'm fine. Are *you* okay?"

Not exactly. "I'm fine."

I backed out of the way as the guys came over to check on Lane. Telling by the way his eyes shifted between each one, it seemed like he was inspecting them for injuries.

"Are you alright?" Kota whispered, pulling me aside.

I shrugged, my eyes remaining on Lane as if I was afraid he'd vanish in thin air if I glanced away. "Could be better, could be worse, I guess."

"Honestly... I thought the whole fight was kinda hot."

"Kota!"

"What! B, you had an entire group of hockey players fighting on your behalf." I scoffed at the menacing grin she wore. "If Crew had just pulled the same shit that Lane did, I'd be *all* over him right now."

I couldn't hold back my disgust even if I wanted to. "Ew."

"Sorry," she shrugged. "We agreed not to keep any more secrets."

"Yeah, well, I think I could've lived without hearing that one."

"It's getting late..." Matt said. "We need to go home and get to bed. We've got morning skate."

Lane replaced his feet, giving a light sway, but there was no sway in his face. He was wearing the expression of a stone sculpture. "No one's leaving," he announced. "There are cops all around us right now, and on the off chance that they see a group of slightly bruised and bloodied hockey players after getting called about a bar fight, we'd be screwed."

Without a trace of rebuttal or judgement, Cody questioned, "Are you locking us in, Captain?"

"Team sleepover!" TJ exclaimed, earning eye rolls and avoidance.

Lane's eyes trailed over the group as he spoke, ensuring he had the full attention of each teammate. "We've got plenty of room for everyone here. Crew and I will drop everyone off at the house in the morning so you guys can grab your shit before morning skate."

The boys fell silent. I couldn't tell how they were feeling or what they were thinking. Their facial expressions gave little to go off, much too stoic. They were harder to read than an instruction manual that was in a foreign language.

When there was no immediate response, Lane's tone hardened. "Got it?"

"Got it, captain!"

"Good," he nodded, dismissing them.

"Um," I spoke loudly, forcing myself not to shy away when six heads snapped over to me, "someone could take my bed tonight."

"Oh, me!" Jett called.

Matt gave him a bump in the shoulder. "I want the bed."

"Not unless you wanna share it."

"Hell no!" Matt shuddered. "You'd probably try to spoon me in the middle of the night."

Jett gave him a nasty side eye. By the way they interacted, it was almost easy to forget that they were good friends. "Oh, please."

Kota lifted her hand, unsurely stepping forward like she was about to convict herself for something. If she was trying to be subtle, she failed. Miserably. Her gaze lingered far too long on Crew before she spoke. "Someone can have my bed too."

That one earned some furrowed brows and dropped mouths.

"Mine!" Matt practically screamed before joining the rest of the guys in confusion. "Wait..." he slowly said, eyes dancing back and forth between Crew and Kota. "You two, too?"

"Sorta," Crew admitted.

"I knew it!" TJ yelled.

Crew gave him a look. "Shut up, TJ. You didn't know shit."

Jett wore the same expression he had when he caught Lane and I coming out of the bathroom. "What, so... you two have been fucking?"

Trading glances with Kota, Crew looked uncomfortable in his own skin. He shifted his weight, refusing to look at any of his teammates. "It's not just like that. We actually... sort of care about each other."

"Ew!" the guys exclaimed like a cheer.

Kota scoffed, crossing her arms. "It's not gross."

"I'm sorry," Cody said, "but Crew having feelings is a little gross."

"Welcome to my world," Lane said.

"I gotta side with them on this one," Jett agreed. Kota pierced him with a heartless glare and he retreated, sinking backwards. "It's nothing against you, I promise!"

"Mhmm," she hummed.

Jett brought his hands up. "I promise I didn't mean it like that. Please don't dye my underwear pink or hurt me in my sleep." He shifted closer to me, bringing the back of his hand up to shield his mouth. "Do you have a lock on your door?"

A gust of laughter left my mouth. "Yes, Jett."

"Okay good."

Kota and I grabbed what we needed from our rooms for the night, then helped the boys get situated. Once they were all tucked in, I headed to Lane's room.

Shutting the door behind me, I quietly said, "We better not hear them fucking tonight."

Lane snorted. "Once was enough."

He was all snuggled up in bed, and even though he was only a few feet from me, it felt like he was light years away. My skin was itching without his touch. I rushed over, sliding into bed with him. His arms were immediately around me, giving a light squeeze.

Fire burned through my chest as I urged myself to speak, fragility in my voice. "Thank you for what you did tonight."

Lane's thumb and forefinger were under my chin in a split second, lifting it towards him as his thumbprint branded my skin, minty breath fanning across my face.

Most people would say blue eyes reminded them of ice or cold water— a chilled view with a delicate touch. But right now, I'd never seen anything warmer.

There was conviction in his voice, certainty. It was a promise and a statement combined into one. "I will always defend you."

Was it possible to feel butterflies all over your body and not just in your stomach?

I had no words to give him; I was speechless. As a thank you, my lips left a light kiss on the corner of his mouth. I nuzzled my head into his chest, reaching for his right hand.

His knuckles looked to be split in some areas, skin red that would soon blossom into bruises. As if his hand was deadweight, succumbed to the small forces of my own hands, I slowly brought his knuckles up to my lips, giving another kiss of appreciation.

"Bridget," Lane said. I kept his hand against my cheek, unwilling to let go as I looked at him. "I love you."

My heart was no longer in my chest; it was no longer mine. It was fully in his possession, and there was no hope of me ever getting it back.

Awe weakened my voice. "I love you too."

The gentle, gratified grin he gave absorbed all my attention, inviting me in.

I cupped both sides of his face and brought our lips together, relaxing into him as he clutched onto me tighter. When he pulled away, he brushed my hair out of my face.

"I'm so lucky to have you," I let out.

"It's not luck, Bridget; it's love," he said. He shook his head lightly as he spoke. "Luck is being in the right place to get the puck passed to you to score the winning goal. Luck is getting stuck living with the most beautiful girl in the world. Luck is a lot of things, but it isn't this. This is all love."

I'd never experienced this type of love before. This deep, heartening, healthy kind of love.

There was a light burning in my eyes, and with a heavy breath, I blinked back tears.

"You're so amazing," I melted into him, resting my head on his chest. "I love you."

"I love you so much," he said, his thumb brushing across my forehead as we fell into silence, inhaling and exhaling in sync before we ultimately drifted to sleep.

Chapter Seventy-Seven

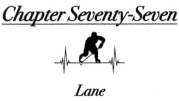

Lane

"**W**hat the hell happened to you guys?" Coach spurred as we stumbled into the locker room.

I sat quietly on a bench, eyes down. "We, uh, got into a little scuffle with St. Cloud last night." I cleared my throat. "It's my fault, Coach."

Jett stepped forward, and the rest of the guys stood, convicting themselves. I'd never been more thankful for this group of guys than right now, having my back both on and off the ice.

"We all participated, Coach," Jett said.

Coach's eyes flitted around the room, his expression emotionless. By the tick in his jaw, yet the lightness in his eyes, I couldn't tell if he was pissed or proud.

He crossed his arms over his chest. "What was the fight about?"

I couldn't say it, couldn't repeat the repugnant things Ethan had been saying about Bridget. The invisible rope around my neck tightened, making it hard to swallow.

Cody's voice was sharp while remaining respectful, a clear-cut sign that he stood behind his own actions last night.

"Silas was being extremely disrespectful to Lane's girlfriend, Coach."

I still refused to look, but I could feel Coach's gaze on me, freezing me in place. I waited for his voice to turn into the gruff yell that it did during a game, to shout, *"This was all over a girl?"*

But contrary to my belief, he said, "Did you at least beat their asses?"

A few of the guys responded, but I was not one of them. "Yes, Coach."

My chest lightened as I looked up to see him nod. "And everyone's good to play?" he asked.

"Yes, Coach."

"Alright," he said. "You all better be playing at a hundred and twenty percent then, cause from what it sounds like, they're gonna be out for blood today."

The unease in my stomach flared. I had a target on my back, and I knew it. If I went down, I refused to take everyone else down with me.

I wasn't afraid of Silas. The only thing I was afraid of right now was letting my team down.

I popped my headphones in and tried getting my head on the right track with my pre-game ritual— listening to Liam's favorite song, "Black Hole Sun" by Soundgarden. Usually, it helped me relax and recenter, but it wasn't helping as much as it normally did.

Yesterday's win was almost too easy.

But that wasn't to say today would be the same.

Chapter Seventy-Eight

Bridget

Since Lane gave me a tour of the facilities a few months back, I knew exactly where I was going. I snuck through the basement halls of the arena until I reached the guest locker room.

They really should have people monitoring down here.

I wasn't usually the confrontation type, but I was feeling extra protective of Lane. Ethan was the last person I wanted to be alone in a room with, but if there was a chance that confronting him would make him ease up towards Lane on the ice, even the tiniest bit, then I'd make that sacrifice and swallow down my own fear.

Ethan didn't like being shown up. His ego was far too big to take last night with a grain of salt; he was going to use this game as a pathway to revenge.

I remembered all the worst parts of him, but I also remembered his pre-game superstition.

He had to be the last one to leave the locker room.

With my hand hovering over the door handle, I almost listened to the frightful voice in my head telling me to run. But my anger simmered a bit too deep, and my mind went blank as I strutted into the locker room, praying not to find any surprises.

But as expected, it was just Ethan, tying his skates.

"Hey, Strawberry," he said when he saw me, as if me being in there was normal.

I cut straight to the point. "Why do you have it out for me?" The blackish purple rim around his eye caught the light, accompanied by several small bruises scattered around his face. "You look like shit, by the way."

"Thanks, Strawberry," he grimaced. "You look great too."

The stark differences between him and Lane were overwhelming. I was used to having butterflies around Lane, and right now, all I could feel were wasps stinging the inside of my stomach. "Why do you have it out for me?" I repeated.

He casually shrugged. "You broke up with me."

"You cheated on me!"

He raised a brow like I was overreacting. "I said I was sorry."

I scoffed, nearly laughing. *I said I was sorry.* What the hell was that?

Eyes browsing around the room, noting all the duffle bags and belongings with no occupants here to claim them, I realized how isolated we were. My bloodstream flushed with anxiety, but I stayed put.

Ethan sighed. "I've never had a girl break up with me before you."

"Get over it. And leave Lane out of it," I hissed.

"No can do, Strawberry."

"Why the hell not?"

He stood, having grown a few inches from his skates. Intimidation was a beast, and I could only hope it wasn't showing on my face.

He held his helmet tightly against his side. "Because he's a threat, Bridget."

It was the way he had called me "Bridget" instead of "Strawberry" that had me shaking. Because the tone of this entire room just did a twist. I welcomed my own wrath, willed it to tie him up and squeeze the life out of him. But the sudden storm cloud of ire and seriousness that loomed over him made my insides knot with fear.

He was not going to play nice today. He'd decided that last night.

"Now, if you'll excuse me," he said indifferently, slipping his helmet on, "I have a game to go win."

"Good luck," I gritted through my teeth. "We all know you'll be needing it."

I caught the malevolent grin he flashed beneath his helmet, and it made me want to hit him over the head with a hockey stick.

"And by the way," I added as he strolled passed me, "I hope you know Lane is better than you. On and off the ice."

That horrific grin was gone, replaced with an even more unsettling sight— the face of a monster before it destroyed a city.

I immediately regretted what I'd said, knowing that I just riled him up more.

This game was not going to be easy to watch.

***

I didn't think that I could be any more on edge than I was at the game yesterday, but boy, was I wrong.

With seats against the glass in the student section, Kota and I had a clear view of every detail of the game, and it was making me want to get up and leave.

It was still the first period and Ethan already had one penalty for tripping Lane, which no doubt, was on purpose. He was taking every opportunity to practically attack Lane, playing dirty enough to hurt him, but just clean enough to get away with it.

Lane wasn't engaging more than he had to, undoubtedly trying to avoid getting penalized. It was making my heart slowly shred apart, and Ethan probably found joy in knowing it.

The boys set up shop on St. Cloud's side of the rink, positioning themselves for the perfect play. Red jerseys were crowded in front of the goal, defending it like it was their newborn child.

The puck slid from Crew to Lane to Jett, back to Lane, who brought his stick back and launched the puck into the top left corner of the net, scoring the perfect slapshot.

The student section sprang up, repeatedly screaming *"Sex-y Cap-tain!"* followed by five claps.

We were up two-to-one now, and I wanted more than anything for this game to be over already.

I loved watching the boys play, truly, I did, but I couldn't help but feel like Lane was getting ambushed because of me. It wasn't just Ethan either. Every single player in red, regardless of if they were there last night or not, seemed to have a vendetta against Lane. It was like they were all out to destroy him.

That wasn't to say the other boys weren't taking some nasty hits too. There was a long list of rivalry between these two teams; any time they played against each other, tension could be cut with a knife. But this was much different.

This game was personal.

I gripped Kota's forearm as Ethan came from behind Lane, ramming him face first into the glass directly in front of us, causing the entire line of glass to shake.

"Kota," I whimpered. My body felt like it had just taken a beating, as if I'd been the one to endure the hit.

She patted my hand. "It's okay. He's a hockey player. He's used to this."

"Why didn't they call a penalty on that?" I sneered.

Just as the student section started chanting *"Bullshit! Bullshit! Bullshit!"*, the whistle blew, and Ethan was escorted into the penalty box.

My eyes darted to the scoreboard, and I sighed a small breath of relief knowing Lane had two minutes without having to worry about Ethan.

I just hoped the next two periods went by quickly.

Chapter Seventy-Nine

Lane

Maybe if my idiotic teammates weren't playing so fucking dirty and didn't get too many penalties to count, we wouldn't be tied three-to-three going into the third period.

Coach was pissed. I was pissed. I was practically letting them toss me around like a fucking ragdoll out there just for the sake of ensuring I didn't wind up in the penalty box, and here my teammates were, drawing a penalty every chance they got.

Crew, TJ, and Matt were playing dumb. Every time a St. Cloud player hit them, they hit back harder. Got cross-checked? They did it back harder. Elbowed? They elbowed back. *Harder.*

I understood the tension was heavy and stakes were high, but they were playing like fucking children.

Meanwhile, Silas was doing everything he could to get me to snap. And he was doing a damn good job.

Whether it was the repetitive hits or talking shit, he was taunting me. Torturing me. And it was taking all my strength not to do anything about it. Now that he knew my weak spot, he was using it to his advantage.

"How's my strawberry doing?"

"I saw Bridget in the stands. She's looking good as hell."

"Did you take my advice from last night?"

The last one had nearly knocked me off my skates because it disgusted me so badly.

The thought of someone lying to Bridget just to take advantage of her infuriated me more than anything else in the world.

Clearly, he never loved her if he treated her the way he had.

She deserved everything, and I wanted to be the person that gave it to her.

One more period until I can see her, I kept telling myself.

Between missing Bridget and the suffering I was enduring on the ice, I could confidently say I'd never been so excited to get to the end of a game in my whole fucking life.

With each bullshit call, Ethan's ugly, cocky ass grin was growing, and my enmity was growing with it. I'd gone forty minutes with my rage clawing at my chest, begging to be let out.

I skated behind the net at the end of the play, but my pathway was cut short as Silas bulldozed into me. I managed to stay on my feet, but instead of skating away like every other time I'd done during the game, I pushed him back.

"Hey Avery," he smirked, knowing he had my attention, "you know she came to visit me before the game, and I fucked her in the locker room?"

With blood that was already on the brink of boiling, he'd just pushed me over the line. My body reacted before my mind had the chance to process. All the anger I'd been holding in finally escaped. In a second, his back was on the ice, my gloves were off, and my already bruised knuckles weren't holding back.

Whistles were blowing in my ears, but before the refs had the chance to pull me away from Silas, another St. Cloud player was hurdling towards me, quickly knocked onto the ice by Crew before he had the chance to reach me.

Red was staining the pure white beneath us, and out of the corner of my eye, all I could see were sticks on the ground, red jerseys flailing against white ones.

Jesus, it was like last night all over again. This time, with an even bigger audience, and open for the country to see on national TV.

The refs had their hands full, separating each fight one by one. I wasn't sure how many it took to get me off Silas, but I could feel more than one pulling me away. I fought against their grip, thrashing like a wild animal.

When I was taken far enough away from Silas to see the damage I'd done, I was out of breath and overwhelmed by adrenaline.

Coach was screaming at the top of his lungs. Silas was still on the ground. Numerous players from both teams were getting piled into the penalty box. And I was getting escorted out of the rink.

I'd been ejected from the game.

Chapter Eighty

Lane

I hadn't spoken to anyone since the game ended a few hours ago.

After getting my ear screamed off by Coach and wallowing in the guilt of knowing I cost us a loss, I didn't speak to a single person when I got home, locking myself in my room.

I didn't open the door for Kota or Crew, or even Bridget.

A bunch of the guys had texted me afterwards, offering their condolences and letting me know they weren't upset with me. It should've made me feel better, but it didn't.

I'd let my emotions get the best of me. I did the one thing I told myself I'd never do— I let my team down.

I didn't regret standing up for Bridget, but I did regret the time and the place.

We were one period away, one *goal* away, from keeping our conference title, and now, a third game was set. Whoever won tomorrow would take home that trophy.

The good news was that the league was going to let me play. They'd reviewed the entire game and determined that Silas was partially the instigator, especially considering the penalties he had and the zero I had prior to the fight. Because of that, I wasn't disqualified from the game tomorrow.

I think Coach would've doused the rink in gasoline and lit a match had I been.

I had far too many missed calls and texts from my agent, Thomas, praising me for the fight. NCAA didn't allow fighting, but the NHL did. So apparently, my fuck up was appealing to some teams.

Although I didn't respond, Thomas messaged me that the list of teams wanting to talk to me had grown and that he couldn't wait to discuss everything at our meeting next week.

I wasn't looking forward to it. I needed things to slow down for a second; there was too much happening at once. I needed to focus on one thing at a time. And that started with winning this fucking game.

Chapter Eighty-One

Bridget

I'd never been so relieved to hear the obnoxious screech of a buzzer.

Every Stallions hockey player flooded the ice, tackling each other as if they played football instead.

The arena was fueled by energy and excitement, hundreds of people on their feet, jumping and shouting and smiling.

As Lane accepted the trophy on the team's behalf, the arena managed to get louder.

Pride consumed me, and truthfully, I was joyous to see Ethan and his douchebag teammates skate off the ice sulking.

Winning on our home turf must've made this extra special for the boys, and after all the hard work they put in all season, along with the hell they'd been through the past few days, I think a weight had been lifted off everyone's shoulders.

They deserved this. Lane deserved this. Especially after last night.

I knew I hadn't asked him to fight for me, to leave Ethan bleeding on the ice, but I still felt guilty anyway. Whether I wanted to admit it or not, and whether Lane did admit it or not, I was part of the equation of why he was ejected.

And that sure as hell didn't feel good.

All I wanted to do afterward was console him, to make his pain and worries go away, to cheer him on the best I could and promise him that things would work out.

But he wouldn't open the door.

Not going to lie, standing outside his bedroom door with my head down and my heart in my hands, only to get shut out, had been one of the worst feelings.

I brushed it off and pretended to let it go because I knew he hadn't meant to hurt me; he was just drowning in his own hurt.

But today was a new day, a better day, and I knew tonight would be a better night.

We had some conference champions to celebrate.

***

The entire hockey team stampeded into the bar as if they couldn't be touched. Judging by some of their wild eyes and disorderly steps, I'd say they'd already begun celebrating before they got here.

Matt had the championship trophy snug against his shoulder, trampling towards us. He was soaked in confidence, as if he'd bathed in it before walking in.

"Look at this thing!" he smiled at Kota and me.

"Why the hell is it so big?" she asked.

"Because we're champions, that's why," he answered.

The thing looked like it was half my height, maybe taller.

"That thing is obnoxiously large," Kota said.

Matt's eyes narrowed. "Or maybe you're just a hater."

"Yeah, Kota," TJ stepped in with a cocky grin. "He's a champion, you can't talk to him that way."

Her smirk matched his. "Don't try me, TJ."

He brought his hands up, surrendering.

"Well, I think you guys did great," I butted in.

"Thanks, Bridget!" Matt said.

"Yeah," TJ smiled, slinging a friendly arm around Kota's shoulder, "why can't you be nice like Bridget?"

That illicit grin of hers didn't budge, but her eyes did roll. "Because we're good cop, bad cop. And I'm the bad cop that's going to break your arm if you don't move it. *So, move it.*"

I'd never seen anyone move faster.

"Alright," Matt said, glancing around, "we gotta get this shit going. Where's Captain?"

I was wondering the same thing.

Lane and I had hardly spoken today. I was honestly a bit nervous that he was mad at me.

After the game, him and Crew went straight to the hockey house, and we hadn't seen them since.

Suddenly, the team started cheering loudly, jumping in a circle like they were creating a mosh pit. I watched a girl run out of the circle in fear.

I didn't blame her. Being caged in, surrounded by six-foot-plus men that were flinging their bodies around with no regard for their surroundings sounded like an ER trip waiting to happen, for sure.

The circle opened, the boys pushing Lane towards the bar where Matt was readily waiting, trophy extended towards him.

I'd never seen a wider smile on Lane. Every step he was making felt electric, charged by pride and relief, poise and elation. For the first time all weekend, bliss was staining the air.

Not to mention how fucking good he looked. He was like a living, walking dream, strutting up to the bar like he owned the place. And right now, he kind of did.

He was on top of the world after leading his team to this long-awaited victory. Chin upwards in the slightest, exposing his cutting jawline, he emitted a sexy amount of confidence.

I shifted in my barstool, seeking to rid the torturous tingling between my thighs.

The trophy was placed atop the bar, hovering above everyone's heads, even the tallest players.

Matt nodded to the bartender. "You know the drill. One beer please."

The bartender nodded, grabbing the nearest stool and climbing it as she popped a Coors Light open and dumped the entire thing into the cup of the trophy.

With a pompous smirk dancing across his lips, Matt summoned Crew. "You wanna do the honors with me?"

"Fuck yeah, I do."

"Take a knee, captain," Matt said.

I watched in astonishment as Lane dropped a knee on the floor, head lifted up and ready as the entire bar started chanting *"Cap-tain! Cap-tain! Cap-tain!"*

Kota and I jumped on the bandwagon even though we hardly knew what was going on.

With Matt and Crew each holding a side of the trophy, the cup was directed to Lane's mouth. Some of the liquid fell off the sides, drenching Lane's blue tee, but he didn't budge. His Adam's apple bobbed repeatedly as he chugged the liquor, entirely unaware of the fact that he himself resembled a nice alcoholic beverage right now. One I most definitely wouldn't mind tasting.

When it was empty and he stood, the bar cheered louder.

I was so fucking proud to say that that was my boyfriend. I'd never been one to gloat, but I was feeling awfully boastful right now.

Everyone dispersed, the rest of the guys fighting over who got to go next. Lane's perfect smile sat strong, but as he stepped over to me, it completely faded, and instantly, I'd gone from feeling pretentious and horny to feeling like I'd been sucker punched.

With the lightest touch, he tucked a strand of hair behind my ear. "Can I talk to you for a minute?"

"Yeah," I shook, hopping off my stool. I followed him over to the corner, blood freezing in my veins.

"Can I ask you a question?"

"Of course."

The complete change in his vibe was worrying me. First, he refused to speak to me last night. Then, he hardly said much to me today. And now, he was pulling me aside, asking to talk to me?

My mind headed to the worst places, a million negative possibilities rolling through.

He gulped. "Did you go to see him yesterday before the game?"

"I did," I admitted.

Immediately, he paled. His hands grasped his stomach as if he'd been stabbed there.

My breath caught, realizing what he must've thought. "No," I shook my head in a panic. "No, no, no. Lane, it's not what you think." He stood there silently, chest heaving, waiting for me to explain. "I went to confront him, that's all."

Lane spoke like he was choking, like the beer he'd just chugged could come up any second. "He... said something to me on the ice. I didn't believe it but... then someone told me they saw you leaving the locker room."

Tears pricked my eyes. "Lane, nothing happened. I *promise*." His face remained dismal, and I trembled. "Please believe me," I begged. "Please. I would never do anything like that to you. I love you, Lane."

He took a minute to take in my honest expression, and ultimately, his eyes softened. He blew out a steady breath, nodding slowly. "I believe you."

My heart relaxed, arms wrapping around the back of his neck, and I squeezed like it was the last hug I'd ever give.

"I love you too," he murmured against me.

***

Lane finally seemed back to normal. After our conversation, he'd been by my side most of the night, other than the few times the guys swept him away for something.

Our hands had been interlocked for at least twenty minutes. My palms were starting to sweat from the contact, but I didn't have it in me to separate myself from Lane.

He squeezed my hand tight for a moment, causing me to look at him. "Do you wanna go home soon?" he asked.

Based on the playful look in his eye, I had an idea of what he had in mind. And considering the horny thoughts I'd been having about Lane throughout the night, I was all for it.

I nodded subtly, and he gave a nod back in agreement.

Lane led me to where Kota and Crew were all over each other near the bar, and our hands finally came apart.

Lane spoke to Crew while I tapped Kota on the shoulder. "Hey, I think we're gonna go."

"What!" she whined, before her eyes shifted between Lane and me, a wicked grin slowly taking over her face. "Ah, I see," she nodded firmly. "You guys want some alone time, huh?"

"Kota," I blushed, dropping my chin.

"Have fun," she grinned wildly.

I was relieved when Lane guided me out of Stallions, sweeping me away from continued embarrassment.

As usual, the walk home lasted a mere two minutes, and the second Lane's bedroom door closed behind us, I wanted nothing more than to be close to him.

A surge of arousal rushed over me seeing his muscles flex, hardening to stone as he hooked his arms under the back of my thighs, lifting me effortlessly.

Our lips meshed with certainty and passion before separating as Lane set me down on his bed.

The heat of the moment eased into a comfortable warmth as Lane laid beside me, his thumb brushing over my jaw.

I held his hand against my cheek for a moment, then placed a kiss on his knuckles. With a deep inhale, he watched as I extended his hand for access to his fingers. Keeping my eyes locked with his, I took one in my mouth, pumping it in and out to earn a low moan from Lane.

He stared at me with too many emotions behind his eyes— admiration, pleasure, *pure hunger*.

396

Two calloused, bruised hands grabbed me at the waist, fingers digging into my skin. In seconds, I was flipped onto my back with Lane hovering above me.

He kissed me like he held no other purpose in this world, one hand still gripping my waist with enough pressure to make me combust.

His tongue tangled with mine, slow and steady, and as his hand left my waist and trailed between my legs, I let out a soft whine against his mouth, which he eagerly swallowed.

My legs wrapped around his back, and he sat up, bringing me with him. With all the patience in the world, he slowly lifted my shirt over my head, so carefully as if I were breakable.

Love and lust were saturating the air as the rest of our clothes slid off our bodies. Lane situated himself between my legs before reaching for his nightstand.

"Wait," I grabbed his wrist. "No condom."

I couldn't decode his expression. There wasn't judgement or worry, no excitement or eagerness either. It looked more like he was trying to read *me*.

My voice dropped to a breathy whisper. "I wanna know what you actually feel like."

He brought his hand back, running it over my hair. "Anything you want, Beautiful."

An explosion in a chemistry lab was nothing compared to the alchemy that occurred when he pushed himself inside me.

His head dropped. "Oh God, Bridget."

My nails scraped along his back, butterflies swirling in a frenzy in my stomach as those sapphire eyes of his locked on my face.

Lane completely filled me, barely fitting, the sensation almost being too much to bear. He pushed deeper and paused as our hips met. It felt like he was all the way in my stomach. His forehead met mine as he spoke breathlessly, his voice a raspy vow. "I'm all the way inside you right now," he said. "You feel fucking amazing."

My fingers sank into the back of his neck, driving his lips onto mine. I'd never had sex without a condom before, and although Lane always felt good, this was a whole different level.

There was something so sensual and meaningful behind every thrust, and there was nowhere else in the world that I'd rather be than right here.

He took his time, keeping a steady rhythm, feeling every part of me. As his tempo switched up, becoming faster, it was getting harder to contain the desperate moans that had been building up in the back of my throat. I glued my mouth shut, but my teeth bit down so ruthlessly on the inside of my cheek that the metallic taste of blood came about.

The bed rocked beneath us, and I turned my head against the pillow, feeling the chaste kiss Lane planted on my open check. His mouth hovered over my ear. "Come for me, Beautiful," he softly demanded.

"Lane," I let out. I could feel it building in my lower belly, and as his angle drew upwards, hitting the perfect spot, my whimpers could no longer be held back. "There," I said, clutching onto him. "There, Lane."

He groaned, watching me, waiting for me to shatter beneath him. My body shook, overwhelmed by the feeling.

"I'm gonna..." I cried, my chin tipping upwards as my head dug into the pillow.

"Look at me when you come."

Head snapping back to see the ecstasy in his eyes, I finished all over him right on the spot. The tightness in my stomach gave, my body relaxing, mind in a trance as I let out a satisfied yelp.

Lane's hand closed around my throat as I attempted to catch my breath. "You're so beautiful when you come."

I'm gonna do it again if you keep talking like that.

He buried himself deeply inside me, no hint of stopping or slowing down. "Lane," I moaned, "I love you."

He rocked into me with purpose, seemingly fueled by my reaction. "I love you too."

I had no idea how much time passed before I'd finished again, earning more praise. His breaths were becoming more ragged. "Where do you want me to finish?"

"Anywhere."

I was empty again, the filling sensation gone as Lane took himself out and showered my chest. I moaned, welcoming it. He collapsed beside me, the only sound being our lungs struggling for oxygen.

I checked the clock on the nightstand. "Oh my god," I said, "it's been almost forty-five minutes."

He chuckled. "You have no idea how hard it was to hold myself back from finishing sooner." We studied each other for a moment, fully satisfied, before Lane's eyes dropped to my chest. "Let me go get you something."

He came back minutes later with a handful of tissues held in my direction. I pushed myself onto my elbows, my middle finger dipping into the liquid and dropping it onto my tongue.

"Bridget," Lane warned.

"Yes?"

"Do *not* turn me on again," he smirked. "We need to get at least *some* sleep tonight." He took it upon himself to wipe me off. "In fact, put your clothes back on. Sleeping next to you naked is an invitation to no sleep at all."

"Fine," I sighed, getting dressed. "Lane?"

"Yeah?"

"I love you."

He smiled. "I love you too."

Chapter Eighty-Two

Bridget

Crew's jaw ticked, sharp eyes flitting over to Kota. "Quit stealing my tater tots."

She leaned towards him on their side of the booth. "I'll steal as many as I want," she challenged, plucking two more off his plate.

He let out a frustrated huff, lightly shaking his head before piling more food into his mouth.

"Wow," Lane teased, "you guys are truly such a lovely couple."

Both their eyes flicked upwards, daring Lane to say anything else.

"Did you just drop the C word?" Crew threatened.

Lane suppressed a laugh. "The C word? You mean—"

"*Don't* say it," I nearly jumped out of my seat.

Crew's brows shot up, amused. "Not a fan of the word—"

"Don't say it!" my voice grew so loud that people from other tables were looking at us.

The boys laughed, hands slapping the table. Snatching another tater tot, unbothered, Kota spoke, "She doesn't like any sort of word like that."

"Not sure what you define as *any word like that*, but may I ask why?" Crew said.

I wanted to spring out of my own skin, both embarrassed and uncomfortable and fired up all in one. I didn't even want to glance beside me to see whatever look was on Lane's face.

"Because," I explained, "it's just like... *why?* Like why can't people just say pussy?"

Lane dropped his head into his hands on the table, shoulders shaking through a wave of laughter. Shooting up, he shrugged, dumbfounded, eyes glossy and entertained. "You prefer the word pussy over anything else?"

Crew rubbed his chin, giving a shrug. "Hell, I'll say pussy all damn day."

Kota scoffed, eyes rolling like they were stuck. "Nice."

When Crew swiveled towards her, there was a quick change in his eyes; they glazed over with heat. "You like when I say it."

I'd never say it aloud because I didn't have a death wish, but I noticed a rosy swirl flourish in her cheeks as her chin dipped. "I don't like shit," she spat.

Lane cringed, covering his face. His voice came out muffled behind his hands. "Ahh, alright, we get it, you two are gonna fuck when we get home. Please just... don't start here."

This was one interesting victory lunch.

Kota and I brought the boys out as our own gift for winning conference. For me, it was also a token of appreciation for everything that happened with Ethan.

Having been out until nearly two am last night, we all woke up violently ill with a horrid hangover, in addition to being late for all our responsibilities.

Luckily for the boys, they hadn't had practice today. Coach Palmer gave them the day off after playing three days in a row and winning the title. They still ended up missing class though.

Originally, Kota and I were going to take them out this weekend, but since all four of us missed class, we figured, *fuck it, let's just go today.*

401

Kota folded her hands on the table, wavy black hair swinging over her shoulder. "We're not gonna fuck when we get home."

Crew's voice fell, "We're not?"

"No," she said. "Bridget and I have plans."

"Where are you two off to?" Lane asked.

I opened my mouth to respond but was silenced.

"Oh, let me say it!" Kota squealed. She waited until every person was looking at her before she revealed the news. "We're going to get tattoos!"

Brows skyrocketing to his hairline, Lane faltered. "Actually?"

I nodded, tight-lipped.

Disbelief swam in the oceans of his eyes as they bounced between us. "You two are seriously going to get your first tattoo today?"

"It's not *my* first," Kota said.

"You have a tattoo?"

"It's a little one," Kota and Crew said in unison.

As casually as if he were telling us how his day was, Crew dipped a tater tot in ketchup, speaking, "You can only see it if she's naked."

"Jesus Christ," Lane muttered, glancing over his shoulder and waving down our waitress. "Can we get our check please?"

Kota was spaced out like her mind was elsewhere, and I sure as hell did not want to know where. I gave her a nice kick underneath the table.

"Ouch!"

"Sorry, accident," I lied.

With a dirty look, she sank back against the booth, crossing her arms.

"Can we come?" Crew suddenly asked.

I wasn't sure if I was fond of the idea or absolutely against it. "You wanna come to our appointment?"

"Yeah," he nodded. "What if I wanna get something?"

A small flutter went through my system when I looked at Lane. He wasn't doing anything special to trigger it— nothing other than breathing.

402

"I wouldn't mind going," Lane said.

"Are you gonna get something?" I asked.

"I might."

Kota slung an arm around Crew's shoulder, and through his scowl, you could make out the tiniest trace of a smirk. "Aw, Crew," she said, "did I hear you say you wanna drive? That's so sweet of you!"

He gave a long, unprecedented sigh. "Yep, that's exactly what I said."

She kissed his cheek, causing Lane to fake gag beside me. Or maybe it was a real gag, who knows?

"I'm just gonna pretend like that wasn't disgusting," Lane joked, turning to me. "So, when's the appointment?"

***

An hour later, we were all piled into Crew's car.

He shot a murderous glare at Kota in the rear-view mirror. "You guys *had* to choose the parlor that was the farthest away?"

Kota scrolled on her phone beside me in the backseat, not even bothering to look upwards. "You offered to drive."

"Uh, I'm pretty sure I didn't, actually."

I butt in. "All the places around us had bad reviews."

"Still," Crew protested, "a forty-five-minute drive?"

"Well, I wasn't going to let someone poke me with a needle and brand my body permanently if they had shitty reviews, *Crew*."

"Fair enough," he said.

The car fell to silence with faint music playing in the background, but I couldn't even make out what it was.

My mind was running, trying to talk me out of what I was about to do. My parents disapproved of tattoos, but I'd always wanted one growing up. Luckily for me, they weren't the type of parents that would outright disown me for getting one.

I wasn't going to lie though, I was scared. I wouldn't say I had a low pain tolerance, but I also hadn't been tested enough to know how high my pain tolerance actually went.

"Turn some jams on," Kota demanded.

Suddenly, "Say It Ain't So" by Weezer was blasting through the speakers and the boys sang along to every word, getting way too into it. Their fists were pumping in the air to the beat, and when I glanced beside me, Kota looked so pissed off that I couldn't stop giggling.

The song was followed up by "Inside Out" by Eve 6, where they continued their own private concert.

It made me wonder if they were always like this when no one was around.

Kota unbuckled her seatbelt for a moment, leaning between their seats when the song came to a close. "You guys are fucking losers. Let me pick a song."

"No," Crew said.

"Oh, pretty please! Just let me pick one song!"

He sighed. "Fine."

Within the first few beats, I recognized the song, my head bobbing along with the melody.

I'd admit, Kota had good taste.

"Unwritten" by Natasha Bedingfield took over the car, along with Kota's and my voice.

"C'mon, guys!" I said to the boys. "Everyone knows this song!"

When the chorus came, Lane smiled at me in the side mirror, singing along.

Crew glanced back and forth between Lane and the road, equal amounts of disturbed and disappointed. "What the fuck?"

We all egged him on, peer pressuring him to jump in. Slowly, he started to crack, and although he didn't know the words, his smile shone through, head nodding.

Somehow, this became one of my favorite moments.

I glanced at my bare pinky finger that soon would be occupied with half a heart. The other half would be on Kota's pinky, and although I'd been having doubts when we got into the car, it seemed like it all faded away now.

Chapter Eighty-Three

Lane

"At this rate," Thomas spoke over the chatter of the restaurant, "you're pretty much going to be able to sign with any team you want."

"Blackhawks?" I questioned.

"Yep."

"Minnesota Wild?"

"Yep," he confirmed. I opened my mouth, but he cut me off. "*Any* team, Lane."

"Those are my top two," I said.

He nodded. "Well, I'm sure you have a lot to think about with your season coming to an end, so give me a call when you've decided."

I bit the inside of my cheek. "Thanks, Thomas."

With another nod, he headed out of the restaurant, leaving me with nothing but an empty seat across from me and the feeling of having a razor lodged in my stomach.

Chicago Blackhawks or Minnesota Wild.

I didn't even allow myself to think outside the scope of the two. I didn't need to confuse myself with too many options. I wanted to keep the decision as simple as possible, even though it was feeling anything besides easy.

Obviously, Crew was heading to Chicago. And Bridget told me a while back that she would most likely be staying in Minnesota after she graduated.

I kept thinking of Liam, trying to piece together what he'd do. I couldn't stop envisioning the Minnesota Wild flag he used to have hung on his side of our room.

My hand slid across my chest, feeling the shred of soreness that still lingered atop my skin.

There was never a moment in my life where Liam wasn't part of me. He was in my DNA, in my thoughts and dreams, in my heart. And now, he was in my skin.

The angel wings that cradled Liam's name were placed precisely over my heart, the only right place for them to be.

Flipping my wrist over, my thumb scraped across the number that was now permanently etched into my skin.

18.

It was small, no bigger than a quarter, but the meaning was more than significant. Not only was Liam part of me, but now Crew was forever a part of me, as was I for him.

No matter where I went in the world, he would be with me. Both of them would be.

I hadn't anticipated to get two tattoos. Hell, I hadn't even anticipated to get one when I woke up that day.

But I'd always wanted to get something in honor of my brother, and it brought me comfort knowing that I finally had.

I sat back in my seat, a hollow feeling in my chest. Not only did it feel like I was choosing between teams, but it felt like I was choosing between people.

And I fucking hated it.

Liam, Crew, Bridget.

I sat there in my lonesome, ordering one coffee after another, trying to put myself in Liam's mindset until the answer became clear.

***

Campus was crawling with people, and I dodged out of everyone's way as they exited Archway Hall.

Today was the first really nice day of spring thus far, the sun baking everyone at seventy-five degrees. Groups were tossing footballs and frisbees in the grass, people were sitting out on blankets, soaking up the warmth, and after a long and cold winter, everyone was dressed like it was the peak of summer.

It was strange to think this was one of my final weeks on campus. Within the next month, I'd be living in a different city, far away from this lifestyle.

A radiant, infectious smile lit up Bridget's face when she saw me. She trudged down the front steps of the hall faster, my teeth digging into my bottom lip as my eyes landed on her bouncing tits that were pouring out of her tank top.

Not the time, I told myself.

The small Stallions cap she wore hung over her eyes, not hiding the freckles above her cheeks that were exposed by the sun.

"Well, hello there!"

"Hi, Beautiful," I smiled, handing her the iced coffee I picked up for her on the way.

"I didn't know you were gonna be here; this is such a nice surprise. What's the occasion?"

I walked alongside her, trying not to wear my emotions all over my face. "Well," I fought back a grin, "other than the fact that I'm pretty much obsessed with you and hate being away from you for long periods of time, I also wanted to celebrate." My hand found the small of her back, guiding her around a group of people she was about to walk into. "Even if the celebration is just a coffee and a walk through campus."

"Oh yeah? Your meeting went well then?"

Minus the stress over the biggest decision of my life, yeah.

"It did," I said. "I can pretty much go with whatever team I want."

"Lane, that's amazing!" she squealed.

"There is one team I'm leaning towards." My heartbeat drummed so loudly in my ears that I thought I might go deaf from it. I guided her off the pathway and into the grass, my grip remaining light on her wrist as I faced her. "I think I'm gonna go with the Blackhawks," I said. "And I want you to come with me."

I was hyperaware of every small reaction she was giving. The small oval her mouth had formed. The rapid blinking as she stared at me. The beat of silence that was far too long.

"To... to Chicago?"

"Yeah," I nodded. "I figured since Crew and I will be there that maybe you and Kota would both come with? We could all get another apartment together or we could each get two bedrooms like we'd originally planned but..." I shrugged, eyes falling to the lush green beneath my feet. "I know you said you loved Chicago when you visited, so I figured it would be perfect for us."

Lane, I'd love to go to Chicago with you.
Lane, this is going to be perfect.
Lane, I love you. Of course I'll come with you.
"Lane..."

The crack in her voice was not very promising.

"I don't think I can move to Chicago," she said.

Disappointment clogged my throat. "Why not?"

The regret came out in waves as she spoke, crashing into me like a strong tide. "I spent my entire life searching for my mom, and now that I finally found her... it doesn't seem right to just leave."

I lowered my head, catching sight of my heart that was currently on the ground.

"What happened to Minnesota?" she asked gingerly.

"I just..." I shook my head, "Chicago felt more right."

The starlit beams in her eyes had faded to a dull ray. "Well... you have awhile still, right?"

"A few weeks, yeah."

"Then take your time," she said.

It felt like my soul was shaking. I truly thought this conversation was going to go exactly how I'd pictured it in my head, and that it'd end with us rushing home with hopeful hearts, spending the rest of the night fucking while she wore my jersey, and falling asleep talking about Chicago and our future.

Apparently, I was way off.

Chapter Eighty-Four

Lane

My mind had been in shambles since the second we got home yesterday.

"I'm going over to my bio moms for dinner," Bridget said, throwing on a cardigan. "Do you wanna join?"

It was hard to look at her right now. Because every time I did, my stomach plummeted, and I was reminded of the impending decision that was right around the corner. "Can I take a raincheck?"

"Is everything alright?"

Her normalcy was bothering me. Why wasn't she as stressed out as I was? She seemed entirely unaffected, and it was tearing me up.

"Yeah," I answered hoarsely. "Just a bit stressed."

She gave a nod, leaving a faint kiss on my cheek. "I'll be back in a few hours if you wanna talk, okay?"

I nodded, watching her slip out the door. My eyes lingered there for far too long, burning, completely stuck on the fact that she just disappeared.

"Alright," Kota leaned over the kitchen island, "that was weird."

"What was?"

"You," she said with conviction. "What's bothering you?"

"Nothing."

"Bullshit."

I stared at her blankly.

She tipped her head, leaning into her hands. "I know you better than you think, Lane. What is it?"

My raspy sigh echoed around the room. "Do you promise to keep it between us?"

With eyes narrowed to slits, she asked, "Are you cheating on Bridget?"

"What the fuck, no!"

Kota casually rounded the island, collapsing on the adjacent couch. "Then yeah, I can keep it between us."

Kota was someone I could trust to confide in. Only thing was that there was a fifty percent chance this conversation ended with her comforting me and a fifty percent chance it ended with her telling me to suck it up and make a choice.

"This decision is stressing me out," I admitted.

"What decision?"

"Which team I'm gonna end up on."

"Oh."

"Oh what?"

She shook her head lightly. "I just didn't know there was a decision to be made... I thought you were staying here with Bridget."

"Why'd you assume that?"

"Because it seemed like that's what *she* assumed."

My throat went bone-dry, thoughts going from swimming in rough waters to drowning entirely. I pushed forward to the edge of the couch. "Why would she assume that?"

She blinked at me, expression vacant before shifting to judgement. "Because you promised her nothing would change?"

I promised her nothing would change? When did—
Oh.

I did. On one of the many nights she'd snuck into my room, I'd given her a promise that was now unprotected, a promise I was no longer sure could be kept.

I didn't let it show on my face, but internally, I was screaming at myself. *Now, it felt like the stakes were heightened.*

Sitting at the restaurant, contemplating everything after my meeting, I had kicked myself after wasting so much time going back and forth between everything until I realized *Why choose one when I could choose both?*

But now that possibility had eroded to dust.

I just couldn't accept the fact that Crew and Kota were the two people I loved most in the world, and I was about to break one of them.

My head fell into my hands, head pounding from the pressure.

Kota's voice turned unusually soft. "Lane? Are you okay?"

"I'm really struggling," I said, the sound muffled.

I had never wanted anything more than I wanted Bridget. She had pulled me into her orbit, and now, instead of sitting comfortably in it, I was spinning in it— zero gravity, completely out of control.

Things were typically so easy and straightforward in my head, but this decision was poisoning me from the inside out.

"When Liam passed," my voice broke, "there was this... hole inside of me. And it wasn't just grief or guilt but... Liam was quite literally my other half and as time went on without him, that hole just fucking grew and to this day it's still there but the only person who's been able to fill it in the slightest is..."

"Bridget," Kota finished.

"No," I corrected her, "Crew."

"Did I hear my name?"

The second Crew caught sight of my glossy eyes, he stopped mid-step, his smile disappearing like a ghost. "Is everything alright? Am I interrupting something?"

"Actually, uh," Kota stood, nervous eyes ricocheting between us, "I think you guys should talk."

"Okay..." Crew said. "You wanna come talk in my room?"

I pressed my palms on either side of me, arms flexing as I pushed into the couch. "Yeah," I said so softly that I hardly recognized my own voice.

He closed the door behind us. "So, what's going on?"

I'm coming to Chicago and I'm not sure how long-distance with Bridget will work.

I'm staying in Minnesota with Bridget instead of going to Chicago with you.

I'm not going to the NHL at all.

"I wanna sign with the Blackhawks."

Crew's face lit up like the goddamn Vegas strip. "Are you serious? Holy shit! I knew you'd come around! I knew—"

"Wait," I held a hand up, gut wrenching. I'd just carried him on top of Mount Everest and now I was about to push him off of it. "Bridget wants to stay here."

I knew Vegas never shut down, but it sure as hell just looked like it did.

Disappointment immediately laced the air, straining my lungs as I breathed it in. Crew's eyes fell to the floor, and he stepped over to his desk, taking a seat in his desk chair like he would've fallen over if he hadn't. He drew in a pained, lengthy inhale. "So... you're not coming with me?"

"I don't know."

"Why can't Bridget just come with? I'm sure Kota—"

"I tried that. She wants to stay here to be closer to her mom."

He tapped his foot on the floor, soaking in every word. When he looked up at me with as much sadness in his eyes as my own, my soul split. "Lane... you know I'd follow you anywhere. I'd stay in Minnesota just to make your life easier, but," he shrugged, "I'm already signed. My hands are tied."

"I know." I caught sight of the *1* on his wrist, and my eyes shot away, unable to handle the pain.

"But I want you to know I'll understand if you choose Bridget," he said.

"If this were flipped, would you choose Kota?"

"No." His answer was immediate, and that only made me feel guiltier. "Over anyone else, I'd choose her. But not you."

I tugged at my own chest. *Jesus, it felt like my heart was underneath the floorboards.*

"You don't have to rush this, Lane," Crew said. "You still have a little bit of time."

"Barely."

"Stop looking at it like the countdown to a bomb explosion. Try not to think about it anymore tonight. Sleep on it."

I gave a reluctant nod.

"And just know that either way," he stood, "I'm on your side."

Something about that reassurance brought me a sense of strength. My arms opened, and he waved me off. "We've been hugging too much lately," he shook his head with a shit-eating grin.

"Fine," I smiled back, "didn't want to anyway."

Chapter Eighty-Five

Bridget

Other than the small whimper I'd just let out, the apartment was eerily quiet.

"I'm sorry," Lane broke.

He was shattering right in front of me, a few straggling tears, mouth quivering, hands shaking as he reached for me.

But it was I who felt like I'd just gotten a stake driven through my heart.

My options were as follows: accompany Lane to Chicago, attempt long-distance, or break up.

I wasn't a fan of any.

"But I thought..." I stuttered, "I thought you were going to stay in Minnesota with me."

Rivers had formed from my eyes, scorching my skin on their way down my face.

"I'm sorry," he repeated. "But I can't."

"But why?" I wheezed.

His throat bobbed as he gulped. "I just can't lose another brother."

I understood that Crew was like his brother, his other half. But going through most of my life feeling like I was never chosen, this was hitting me hard. My chest constricted, voice coming out as a scratchy, broken record. "But you're fine with losing me instead?"

His silence was more damaging than any answer he could've given. Lane cringed, plunging the stake deeper into me and twisting it with what felt like far too little remorse.

I shot off the couch, my hands instinctively reaching for the wound on my chest to keep me from bleeding out.

"I want you to do what you need to do, but I've lost people too, Lane. I've been hurt too. And now, *you're* the one leaving me."

"Bridget," he reached for me, a million shards of sadness in his voice.

My emotions took over, all rationality disappearing from my mind. "You promised me, Lane. You promised me that nothing would change!"

"It doesn't have to," he cried with his hands out.

I could've sworn I saw blood all over them.

"You promised." I shook my head, my voice a weak whisper. "You were so convincing too."

His voice remained soothing regardless of the shake behind it. "Bridget, let's talk about this."

"Apparently, there's nothing to talk about."

He shook his head, his voice falling. "Please reconsider your decision."

"What about yours? There's really no changing your mind?"

Lane's eyes squeezed shut, and suddenly, I didn't think I was the only one bleeding anymore.

"Beautiful, *please*," he pleaded.

That nickname slashed through me, and I let out a light sob.

"I will get on my knees and beg if I need to."

I stared at him, aching. I didn't even know what to do with myself right now. He was usually the one I went to for comfort, and now, all that comfort had been ripped from under me like a rug.

The floor rattled as Lane's knees dropped onto it. "Bridget Emily Bell, please. I will do anything. I will sit here and beg as long as it takes. I will go out right now and buy a

416

ring for you. I will pay for your mom to visit as many times as she wants or vice versa. Just *please,* please come with me."

The groveling was making me feel a whole lot worse, which I would've said was impossible two minutes ago.

"If you wanted me that badly, you'd stay," I blamed.

I buried my head into my hands, tears flying faster, burning me so deeply that I should've been a pile of ashes on the floor by now.

His voice wavered. "I hate seeing you cry."

I ducked as his hand extended towards me, dashing into my bedroom and locking the door. My wails grew, springing off the walls, sounding so distressing that our neighbors probably thought I was getting tortured.

In a way, I was.

The softest knock sounded. "Beautiful?"

"Go away," I wept, collapsing into a fortress of pillows.

Another knock. "Please open up."

"Go. Away!"

I was mourning. Mourning the ideal future I thought we'd have. Mourning the luxury of seeing Lane every day. Mourning the person I had become after he touched my heart.

I cried. And I cried. And I cried. Until there was no more water left in my body to cry.

I didn't want Lane's comfort. I didn't even want Kota's comfort. The only person's comfort that I currently wanted was my mom's.

At least an hour had passed when I cracked open my bedroom door, spotting Lane sitting beside it.

A small bit of hope lit his eyes when he noticed me there. "Are you okay?"

I didn't respond. All I did was open the door entirely, revealing the bag at my feet.

Any hope he'd had vanished. I tried to take back my heart as I drifted past him but failed miserably.

My heart was his. It always had been. And I had never been one to take things that weren't mine.

He spoke through misery. "Where are you going?"

"Home."

Following me to the front door, the begging continued. "Bridget, c'mon, please. Don't go."

I didn't have the bravery or confidence to look at him. If I did, surely, I would've caved.

"You're the one that's going," I indicted over my shoulder before shutting the door behind me.

Chapter Eighty-Six

Lane

*F*ive days.

I couldn't believe she left five days ago.

Every day, I'd been telling myself it would be the day she came back. And every day, I was wrong.

She turned her location off when she walked out the door. She hadn't answered any of my texts or calls. She hadn't even talked to Kota in days.

Kota called her shortly after she left, and I wasn't sure what was said between them, but whatever it was, Bridget apparently didn't like it.

I should've been focused, but I wasn't. At all.

Today was the start of the NCAA tournament, which meant we were only four games away from a national title. It also meant that no fuck up was acceptable. Even the smallest mistake could cost us a game and losing meant the end of the tournament for us. Every minute on the ice would count, and I needed to be dialed in, but it was like my brain refused. Each thought of mine was foggy, and it was becoming far too difficult to separate out my fantasies with reality.

I kept finding myself turning a corner in the apartment, assuming Bridget would be around the bend. Or walking in after practice, thinking her nose would be deep in a smutty book while she lounged on the couch. The other day I cooked dinner and accidentally made two plates before remembering that I was eating alone.

Morning skate was rough today. I was off, and it showed. If one more teammate asked me what was wrong, I would've slammed my head against the boards.

But every time, I put on a poker face and said everything was good. I didn't want to worry anyone with the truth.

But the truth was that if Bridget wasn't in those stands, branded with my name and number, tonight was going to be a rocky game for me.

I yawned, struggling to pull my key out and jam it into the lock. Sleep had been on the long list of difficult things lately.

I convinced myself on the ride home from morning skate that Bridget would finally be back, that she wouldn't miss my game for the world, that she'd be sitting in the living room, already wearing my jersey even though the game didn't start for eight hours.

But like last time, and the time before that, and the time before that, and so on, I was wrong.

Crew was already back in bed by the time I took three steps into the apartment, taking his traditional game-day nap.

"Still no Bridget?" I thought aloud.

"No," Kota murmured, washing the dishes.

"Have you heard from her at all?"

She sighed. "No."

"This is just..." I shook my head. "This is ridiculous. She needs to come home."

"I've tried, Lane," Kota's voice weakened in defeat. "She'll come home when she's ready."

It sounded selfish, but I needed her to be ready now.

It was fucking hard going from seeing someone every day, *living with them*, to not seeing them at all.

The keys I'd just tossed on the island were back in my hand already, shoes I'd just taken off, back on my feet.

"What are you doing?"

420

"When Crew wakes up, ask him to pack my bag for me."

"Lane... where are you going?"

"To go get her," I said.

Kota looked at me like I was speaking gibberish. "You're going to make the three-hour drive to Sumner right now?"

"Yeah."

"Um, are you forgetting you have a game tonight? A very important game, might I add? And might I also add the fact that it's nearly an hour away?"

My hand was already on the doorknob. I didn't have time to waste. "I need to do this."

"Why?"

"Because she needs to know how much I love her."

***

After getting verbally harassed by Crew over the phone and dodging numerous missed calls from Kota, I had my phone buried under a bunch of shit in the passenger seat.

The elements of spring were all here— bright green trees, blooming flowers, a sun that didn't hide behind gray clouds, and although driving through the scenery was no doubt a beautiful sight, the ride was anything but peaceful.

My thoughts were far too loud, much louder than the music I had blaring.

What was she going to say when I appeared on her doorstep? What was *I* going to say? I didn't have a plan, didn't have an impressive speech to give. All I knew right now was that I was an hour away from her house, about to show up like Romeo.

In a perfect world, she'd welcome me with open arms, tell me how much she missed me and loved me and that she changed her mind, prepared to hop on a flight to Chicago as early as tomorrow.

But I was fucking petrified that she'd tell me to screw off.

The least I was hoping was that I could convince her to come home.

My music paused, and the display in my car lit up with Kota's name. I sighed, declining the call. She hadn't called since shortly after I left; I'd been convinced that she finally gave up. *Guess not.*

Another call. And another. And another.

"Hello?" I nearly growled.

"Lane!"

"Kota, don't worry," I sighed. "I'm gonna make it back."

Her voice sharpened, and I could only imagine the ferocity on her face right now. "Lane, listen to me," she demanded. "I got a hold of Bridget."

Now she had my attention.

My spine straightened, hands clutching the wheel tighter. "And?"

"She's not in Sumner."

"What?"

"She's at her mom's," she said. "Her *bio* mom's."

Fuck.

My car screeched as I hit the brakes, illegally whipping a U-turn using the crossover that was only meant for "authorized vehicles".

"A—alright," I stuttered, my foot tapping harder against the gas. "I'm on my way."

"Home?"

"No."

"Lane," Kota warned. "Crew is about to have a literal breakdown."

"I'll be there," I promised.

Two hours north just to head two and a half hours southwest.

Poison was dripping through the phone. "You don't have as much time as you think you do, Lane."

"I'll be there."

422

Chapter Eighty-Seven

Bridget

"He's on his way to Sumner right now to see you,"
Kota had said.

It was the first time I'd spoken to her in days, the
longest we'd gone without talking since the start of our
friendship.

We'd had plenty of moments where we got fed up with
each other, but with my emotions being so high, the small
disagreement felt like a massive betrayal.

*"I just want somebody to choose me for once," I said
through the phone, wiping an angry tear off my reddened
cheek.*

"He is choosing you," Kota said.

"No. He's not. He's choosing Crew."

"Well..."

"Well, what?" I snapped.

*She spoke like she was walking on eggshells, but
regardless of the soft and wary tone, I still took it harshly. "It's
just a bit hypocritical, B."*

I scoffed. "How?"

*"Because you're not necessarily choosing him either...
You're choosing family instead of him, and he's choosing
family instead of you."*

You're wrong.

You're so wrong.

"Whatever. I'll see you guys when I see you. Bye."

But she'd been right. It took me a day or two to realize
it, but I had.

And the reality was almost more painful.

I'd been selfish. I wanted to stay here, to have both
Lane and my bio mom with me, and in a perfect world, it
would've worked out that way.

In the moment, I acted out; I let my emotions get the
best of me and I threw a tantrum like a child. I understood how
much Crew meant to Lane, and I felt like a hypocrite after it all.

"Bridget, honey," my bio mom said with an arched
brow, "you're gonna burn a hole in the floor if you keep pacing
like that."

"I don't know what to do, Mom. Tell me what to do."

"Well... considering you still haven't told me what
happened, I'm not sure what advice to give you."

I didn't want advice; I wanted her to give me
directions. Advice gave the opportunity for me to think about it
and change my mind a hundred more times.

I was pretty sure Tim could hear the huff I let out from
the next room over as I flopped down in the seat beside her.

I'd been here for five days and hadn't told her anything
other than *"I think Lane and I broke up."*

"Lane wants to move to Chicago and sign with the
Blackhawks, and he wanted me to go with."

She pressed a palm against her cheek. "So, what's
wrong with that?"

"I can't move to Chicago."

"Why not?"

Pain flooded me from top to bottom, filling every
crevice of my heart. Eyes burning, blinking back tears, I stared

at her in silence, watching her face break into a million pieces in realization.

"Oh, Bridget... Tell me this has nothing to do with me."

I can't.

Her eyes turned glassy, both hands reaching for mine. "Don't let me hold you back from anything, honey. You need to do what you need to do. Don't worry about me. I'm not going anywhere, even if you moved across the globe. I will be here rooting for you."

"But," I wept, squeezing onto her, "I just found you."

"I know," she said softly, "but that doesn't mean you shouldn't live your life."

"I'm not going," I refused. "I don't wanna be so far away from you."

She sucked in a deep breath, staring off for a moment. "Okay," she nodded. "Then how about I come with you?"

My voice came out hardly audible. "What?"

"How about I move to Chicago?"

Before I knew it, my vision had blurred. "Really?"

"Really," she grinned faintly.

"What about Tim?"

"He'll come with," she shrugged. "I've been meaning to get outta this town for a while anyway."

I wiped my running nose on my own shoulder. "For how long?"

She fought a strong smile. "Twenty-two years."

"Then why'd you stay?" I whispered through a cry.

Her hand ran through my hair. "In case you came back looking for me," she softened. "And it paid off."

I could feel my heart melting inside my chest, turning to liquid. My whole life, there was nothing I wanted more than this— my mother.

I grew up seeing the relationship between Bianca and my mom, the special bond they shared. I always knew I was loved, but I never felt like I was loved as much as my sister.

I wanted that bond they had, and no matter how hard my mom and I both tried, it just wasn't there. She had raised me and given me a loving home, and for that, I was forever grateful. But I wanted the opportunity to expand that bond with my birth mother, and I had the right to.

"I love you, Mama," I bawled, gaining a weep from her in response.

"Oh," she cried, "I love you so much, honey. You have no idea."

Arms tightening around me, I'd never felt so safe and secure, never felt like I belonged so much. It was more than just a hug; it was a transaction, a trade of love and gratitude. Her warmth shot through me, relaxing every little bit of worry that had built up over the past five days, convincing me that even if things with Lane didn't work out the way I hoped, that I would still be okay.

I had no idea where Lane was right now, but I hoped he made it to the game on time. Regardless of anything that was said or done, I still loved him, and I loved him too much to see all his hard work go to waste.

"Alright," I breathed, "I think I know what I'm gonna do."

Chapter Eighty-Eight

Lane

I spent the following two and a half hours praying not to get pulled over. I was pushing eighty-five in a seventy on the highway, keeping an eye out for any nearby cops. I didn't have time for another delay.

I was supposed to be in St. Paul in an hour and a half, gearing up to play one of our most important games, but instead, I was driving all across the state to find Bridget.

And I didn't think twice about it.

Logically speaking, there was a chance I didn't make it to St. Paul on time, and in that case, I'd be letting my teammates down.

But I also didn't think I'd be much of an asset to them right now with my current state of mind.

I was determined to make it back on time though, with Bridget accompanying me.

Crossing the threshold into Jefferson County, my adrenaline pumped higher, testing the strength of my heart.

Each minute felt like ten, and as I found myself driving through downtown Jefferson, the dropped speed limit raised my anxiety. I needed time to slow down and my tires to speed up.

I whipped into the driveway, nearly forgetting to turn my car off before running up to the front door.

With my heartbeat managing to triple as I unsteadily shifted my weight side to side on the doorstep, my palms flattened against my stomach, failing to ease the queasiness.

"Lane?"

"Hi, Miss. Bower. I—"

"What are you doing here?" she frantically asked. "Don't you have a game?"

"Yes. I just really need to see Bridget," I let out in a breathless rush.

She shook her head in awe, a hand shooting to her own chest. "She didn't specify where she was going, but she left about thirty minutes ago."

You've got to be fucking kidding me.

My eyes shot around, just now noticing that her car wasn't here.

Goddammit. I was running out of time.

There were only two places I could envision her going right now— home or St. Paul.

My gut told me she was heading to St. Paul, but there was no way to confirm that by wasting more time standing in place.

"Okay," I desperately said. "Thank you."

Getting back in the car felt like square fucking one.

East, we go.

I traveled often for hockey, but I genuinely didn't think I'd ever seen as much of the state as I had today. It really was a beautiful state, and I already had a running list of new places I wanted to take Bridget in the future.

If I ever got the chance.

I couldn't believe it had been this hard to find her. It felt like I was trying to catch a fucking butterfly, a monarch that kept landing before quickly fleeing as I reached for it.

The day had been eaten away by driving, and the sinister clock on my dashboard kept easing closer and closer to warm-up time.

I was sailing at a smooth ninety, but there was no way I'd make it. There was exactly an hour until puck drop and I

428

was an hour away. Teleportation would've come in handy right now, but the closest thing I could do was hit the gas a little harder as I raced against time.

A buzz vibrated against the passenger seat, and my knuckles whitened around the steering wheel as I accepted the call.

"Hello?" I gulped.

"Where the actual fuck are you!" Crew screamed.

"I'm almost there," I lied.

"'Almost there' isn't fucking good enough, Lane! I've got everybody asking about you, Coach is about to have a fucking aneurysm and is breathing down my neck, and—"

"Did you tell him?"

"No," he gnarled. "I've been covering for your dumbass this entire time!"

I was getting pushed closer and closer to the edge, and at this point, I might as well just jump off it.

"I'm sorry," I uttered, unsure of what else to say.

"Just get here," he hissed. "How far are you? We're forty mintues away from warmup."

An hour.

"Forty minutes," I lied again.

"Well, you better make it thirty."

"Alright, I'll see you soon... Oh, wait!"

He gave a low grumble into the phone, and I had no doubt I had some unkind words waiting for me when I got there. "What?"

"Is Bridget there?"

"Are you— How the fuck am I supposed to know?"

"Has Kota said anything to you?"

Crew's scoff came out like a growl, deep and unconfined like a rabid animal. "Lane, I've been in the locker room for God knows how long, getting ready for a *national tournament*, you fucking idiot. Do you think I've spoken to her recently?"

My brows skyrocketed to my hairline, jaw lightly ticking as I let out a sigh. "Alright. See you shortly."

"Yeah, you fucking better," he warned, hanging up.

Jesus, I was a little nervous to walk in there and feel everybody's wrath. It sounded like Crew might even lay me out a few times on the ice even though I was on his team.

Ninety turned into ninety-five, my hands so tight on the steering wheel that it could've turned to dust.

I eased into the drive, *barely,* before a set of red and blue lights were trailing behind me, a siren echoing.

Fuck. So much for not running into any more delays.

Pulling over, my license and insurance were already in my hand, window rolled down, more than prepared to accept a ticket and be on my way.

"Sir," an officer approached, "do you know why I pulled you over?"

"I was speeding," I admitted.

He stepped back, head tipped as he eyed me with interest. It seemed like he'd expected me to pretend like I had no idea, to play dumb like I was going to try to flirt my way out of a ticket.

Warily, he stepped closer. "Can I see your—"

I shoved the materials in his face before he had the chance to finish. The five seconds it took him to grab them was five seconds too long.

"Thanks," he muttered, flipping over my license to take a look. Each second he spent studying it was another second I could've been miles closer to St. Paul. "Hey, I know you," he said. "You play hockey at Cedar, don't you?"

"Yes, sir."

"Don't you have a game tonight?"

"Yes, sir."

He leaned inside the car, catching a glimpse at my clock. "It seems like you're going to be arriving awfully close. Is that why you were speeding?"

I stared out the windshield, answering again, "Yes, sir."

He tapped my license against the open window in thought. "I'll tell ya what. My son's a big fan. If I can get an autograph or something, I'll let you off."

Deal.

I fished around in the backseat, snagging a puck and the silver sharpie I kept in my extra gear bag.

We exchanged items like a drug deal, and I sped off, accelerating back to ninety like I hadn't just gotten pulled over five minutes prior.

When I finally arrived at the arena, there was no parking. I was pretty sure I parked illegally, but I didn't give a single fuck.

Tow me, I don't care.

I grabbed my shit and ran like I was running for my life. Luckily, we'd played here before, so I knew where the player's entrance was.

My frantic steps slowed before halting altogether as a flash of black and silver hit my eye, paired with strawberry blonde.

Six feet shy of the door, there she stood in the flesh, the girl I'd just driven five and a half hours searching for. We stared at each other, and I took in every inch of her like it was the first time I'd seen her.

Her hair sat in light waves past her shoulders, a small crease in her forehead. Those honey brown eyes had become my favorite color over time, and my jersey rested perfectly against her fair skin, the only place it should ever be.

It had only been days since I'd seen her, but it felt like a lifetime.

Time had passed far too quickly today as I wildly flew across the state, but now, everything slowed. With her standing in front of me, the rush to get inside was gone. I didn't care if I was missing warmup. Hell, I didn't even care if I was missing the game.

"Hi," I finally said.

She took the smallest step forward, eyes glazed and full of sentiment. "You were gonna miss your game for me?"

My head slowly bobbed, turning into a rapid nod. "I mean, I was hoping I'd make it on time, but," I paused, "I wouldn't have cared if I hadn't."

Her small sniffle tore at me like a sharp claw, my lungs sitting heavily in my chest as she closed the gap between us, diving into me.

I caught her and held her and squeezed her in all the ways I'd been envisioning the past five days.

Bridget muttered against me, but I couldn't make out what she said.

"What, Beautiful?"

Her stunning smile appeared at the sound of her nickname as she tipped her head up at me. "I'm coming with you."

"What?" I whispered.

"I'm coming to Chicago with you."

The sun was making her glow, a shimmer sitting in her eyes as she peered up at me, illuminating warmth.

I'd never seen a more breathtaking sight.

My heart took a pause, overwhelmed by the moment in the best way possible.

"Actually?"

"Yeah," she nodded through a hopeful smile. "And I'm so, so sorry for the way I acted. I know how much Crew means to you, and I never should've made you feel like you had to choose."

"And I'm sorry if I made you feel like you weren't as important. You mean everything to me."

I clutched onto her tighter, doing my best not to break her. Setting her on her feet, I cupped her fragile face in my hands, driving our lips together with the force of a rocket.

"I love you," I murmured against her.

"I love you too." She licked her lips like she was savoring my taste. "Now go," she demanded through a smile. "You have a game to go win."

"Right," I nodded. "I'll see you immediately after." I branded her cheek with a kiss as I zoomed past her, sprinting to the locker room.

There were three minutes until puck drop, and they were finishing up singing the national anthem when I appeared through the tunnel.

Coach's face was redder than fire, his jaw so unhinged that I was surprised it hadn't fallen off. "Where the flying fuck have you been?" he screamed when his eyes landed on me.

"Were you trying to put me in cardiac arrest? Get your ass on the fucking ice!"

Glares from the team were shot my way as I skated on, some filled with annoyance, others filled with relief. Denver looked like they were starting to sweat at my entrance, probably having been told I wasn't present for the game.

Crew's scowl was fixed on me, his brown eyes darkening to a sleek black. "Look who made it."

I shifted side to side, trying to warm myself up considering I didn't get a warmup of any kind. "I'm sorry," I stared at the ice.

There was a beat of silence before he sighed. "Did you at least find her?"

I nodded, "I did."

"Good," his expression slightly softened. "Now you have no excuse to suck tonight."

I shook my head through a chuckle, skating over to my starting position.

Knowing she was here, showing off her place in my life with my name and number stamped on her, I was finally able to breathe.

I focused on the puck as it fell in front of me, all my worries melting away like ice as I zoned in on my favorite game.

Chapter Eighty-Nine

Bridget

I brought my last box to the door of the apartment, and the second Lane saw me, he broke into a gorgeous smile, reaching for the box to ease me from carrying it.

"Lane," I grinned, "it's not that heavy. I'm fully capable of carrying it."

"What kind of gentleman would I be if I let you carry this big box?" he teased.

I gave an eye roll, watching him set it down by the apartment door.

He rubbed his hands together. "Did you do a final sweep?"

"Yep! Everything's gone, champ."

That grin of his was so charming I wanted to taste it, piercing eyes so blue I wanted to dive into them. "For the thousandth time," he said, "quit calling me that. It sounds like I'm a five-year-old kid."

After three incredibly high-pressured games, the boys had catapulted to the national championship, fighting their way through the final game to earn the title.

NCAA national champions.

I'd been jokingly calling Lane champ ever since.

With the small gap between the tournament and my graduation, we used the time to find a four-bedroom apartment in Chicago, right off the Magnificent Mile.

At first, Kota and I were against the choice considering how expensive it was, but with their NHL contracts in full swing and a heaping amount of money pouring into their bank accounts, the boys insisted.

I was genuinely excited though. I'd never lived outside of Minnesota, but Chicago was so amazing when we visited that I was more than ready to settle into the city lifestyle and embrace it.

I had interviews scheduled with a few publishing firms later this month for editing positions, and Kota was already set to start her new job at some biology research center. She hadn't admitted it, but I was pretty sure she took the job before I agreed to move to Chicago.

My bio mom and Tim found a place in Logan Square, right on the outskirts of the city. It was a really nice area, a perfect distance from where we'd be.

With all the excitement brewing in the air, there was also a bit of sadness.

We had to leave this place.

Our apartment, our home. The place that brought the four of us together, no matter how awful it seemed at first.

"Are we all ready?" Crew asked, appearing in the doorway with Kota at his side.

Lane arched a brow, his eyes scanning over their messy hair and rumpled clothes. "Were you two just messing around in the car?"

The back of Kota's hand trailed across her mouth, and I nearly gagged at the likely possibility of what she was wiping off.

"Well—" Crew said.

Lane's hand shot up. "We don't wanna know."

I nudged Lane with my shoulder. "Good thing we're driving separate."

"Yeah, yeah, we get it," Crew's eyes rolled, "you guys think we're disgusting. Now can we please hit the road before we're stuck in traffic all day?"

435

We nodded, the four of us pausing in the doorway.

The apartment was entirely empty, but I'd never been so fixated on blank walls and vacant space before. There was nothing to look at, yet none of us could manage to look away.

"I can't believe we're leaving this place," I said quietly.

"I know," Lane agreed. "We've had some good times here."

"And some bad times," Kota uttered.

"Hey!" Crew chimed in. "I know you're talking about me."

"Of course, I'm talking about you," she grinned, clutching onto his arm and resting her head on it.

They were so fucking ridiculous, but I loved them, shaking my head with a lighthearted grin.

Lane gave a sigh. "Are we ready?"

"Yeah," I squeezed his hand. He slowly carried my knuckles to his lips, gently connecting the two before releasing me to grab the final box. I scooped up Rob K, holding him close.

"I guess let's all go turn our keys in," he said.

"Great," Crew said, "we can give the girl at the front desk a big thank you for screwing us."

"Oh! Camila!" I squealed in remembrance.

"Orrr," Kota spurred, "we could give the credit to ourselves for not reading the contract."

With one final glance around, I shut the apartment door, locking it behind us.

My eyes found Lane's and thinking back to the day we all moved in together, I'd never been so thankful for such a mishap.

"To Chicago?" I asked.

He gave a faint nod, his smile making my heart flutter. "To Chicago."

The End.

Acknowledgements

First and foremost, I thank you for reading this book. Without my readers, I wouldn't have the same passion or motivation to write. Your support means the world! If you enjoyed this book, please consider leaving a review on Goodreads and Amazon.

To my family members, thank you for your love and support.

To my close friends— Kelsey, Kate, Lyss, Sums, Daria, Liv, Chloe, Jazzy, Sher, Clarissa, Hannah, Natalie, Josie, Jess, and Lacey, thank you for cheering me on throughout this process.

To one of my writing besties, AKA my hero for stepping in and editing this book on such short notice, thank you, Sarah! You are seriously a superhero.

To Cierra, for also saving the day. I owe you my life!

To all my Heavenly angels— my grandparents, Maggie, and Kaylee, thank you for watching over me!

Considering my hockey knowledge was limited prior to this book, I'd like to thank Trevor Bishop, Ross Hawryluk, and Kevin Uhlir for letting me ask them five thousand and one questions.

Last but not least, to my dear characters, thank you for letting me pour my heart out into you. Every one of you is special, and I'm so grateful you chose me to be the one to tell your story.

Printed in Great Britain
by Amazon

40291726R00249